THE BREAKUP ARTISTS

BOOKS BY
ADRIANA MATHER

STANDALONE NOVELS
The Breakup Artists
Mom Com

HOW TO HANG A WITCH SERIES
How to Hang a Witch
Haunting the Deep

KILLING NOVEMBER SERIES
Killing November
Hunting November

THE BREAKUP ARTISTS

ADRIANA MATHER

BLACK
STONE
PUBLISHING

Printed in the United States of America

First edition: 2024
ISBN 979-8-212-41752-5
Young Adult Fiction / Romance / Romantic Comedy

Version 1

Blackstone Publishing
31 Mistletoe Rd.
Ashland, OR 97520

www.BlackstonePublishing.com

For Candis, my first best friend. You pushed a boy off a running track at school when we were five because he was mean to me. And the next year I took a boy's chair out from under him for hitting you in the head with his notebook. Luckily, neither of us wound up in the mafia, but I do think we'd make an excellent two-woman team in an adventure novel!

And in memory of Smeagle (Swee in this book)—my soulmate cat bestie. Thank you for living a full twenty-two years and for being the strangest and most wonderful creature I've ever met. You snored, you relentlessly stuck your paw in my coffee and my water, and you slept under the blankets and would bite my legs as you pleased. There was no better snuggler and no bigger heart. I'll love you forever.

PROLOGUE

While I don't believe in soulmates and I'm not convinced true love isn't just a pretty idea used to sell movies and holiday cards, the fact that we're helping people matters.

LAST SUMMER

I get out of my Jeep Wrangler (or rather Valentine's Jeep that I'm pretending is mine) in the parking lot of the Italian restaurant where Alice, Valentine, and I hung out for the first time three weeks ago. I'm exactly on schedule—her boyfriend is always late and I'm aiming to be nothing like him. And while I'm usually on time in general, she doesn't know that, because the truth is she doesn't know anything about me, not really.

Alice spots me from across the lot and runs up as the Jeep door clicks shut, all smiles, throwing her arms around my neck for a quick hug. It's hard to believe this is the same girl I met three weeks ago. She was quiet, hiding herself behind oversized hoodies with her arms always crossed.

Now she's all big energy—shoulders back and head held high. "You're here!" she squeals.

I laugh, but before I get a word out, she's talking. Fast. "Oh my god. I did it. Don't get me wrong, I fully planned on doing it, but part of me thought I'd chicken out, ya know? But nope, I broke up with him!" She puts her hand on her forehead in disbelief, jostling her blond-tipped curls.

I lean back against the Jeep door. "How'd he take it?"

"Just like you said. First he was confused. Then upset, blaming me for everything. And then he cried and swore he'd change. How did you know he'd—"

I shrug. "He's a guy. I'm a guy. We're simple creatures."

"Well, maybe, but he's nothing like you," Alice says, and now she's leaning in, close enough that I can smell her citrus body lotion.

And before I can redirect, she wraps her arms around my neck and kisses me. Her eyes are closed. I know this because I see them, because my eyes are open. I also know how long this kiss will last. Three seconds. This is a thank-you kiss. They're never long.

Three . . . two . . . one . . .

She pulls away. "Thank you," she says.

See.

She steps back and I feel my face flush.

"I didn't do anything," I reply, some of my embarrassment leaking into my voice.

"But you did. I was in a . . . not-so-good place and . . ."

"And you pulled yourself out of it," I say, giving her full credit—not me, not Valentine, not weeks of strategizing to help—just her.

Alice nods. "I knew he was every kind of wrong for me. I just hadn't checked in with myself in so long that I didn't know who I was anymore." She spreads her arms and the corners of her mouth tilt up. "But tell me, what do you see when you look at me now?"

I smile back. "Hmmm . . ." I say, drawing out my answer, because this is my favorite part—the happy aftermath of an overdue breakup. "I see someone who's creative and funny; someone who's interesting and kind."

Now it's her turn to blush. Her gaze wanders to my lips, indicating she's definitely considering kissing me again, and so I start talking and shift my weight so there's more distance between us.

"I'm really happy for you, Alice," I say, choosing the perfect line to begin our end.

"Maybe even happy for . . . *us?*" she asks with a hopeful smile.

This isn't the first time someone wanted something more, but it's never my goal. Valentine and I try to show up as exactly the friends the person needs to see their life more clearly. Often all it takes is us believing in them and reminding them they're great. But sometimes that kindness gets confused for a more intimate connection. "The thing is . . ." I say, holding back the rest of my sentence. Only there is no rest of the sentence. But she doesn't know that.

RULE #13 – Don't linger when the job's completed. Get out before things get complicated.

With each passing second, the silence gets louder.

"Chris?" she says (my name is actually August), and when I don't immediately answer, she follows up with, "What's wrong? You can tell me."

I shake my head and say the words I've said to two other people this summer. "I wasn't supposed to leave for another two months, but . . ."

She takes a step back, hoping I don't say what she knows I'm going to.

"The truth is, when I first got here, I hated it. I couldn't wait to leave." I give her a sad smile. "Then . . . I met you. And you were such a great friend. You made me feel so welcome."

Now she sighs, a big dreamy one that lets me know I'm having the desired effect, that I can do this without hurting her feelings. "Fate," she says. "The way we'd always randomly bump into each other."

I nod.

"But now you're leaving?" she asks.

I shove my hands in my pockets, studying my Chucks. "The call my mom was waiting for came last night. She got the job. Teaching in Indonesia. I'll be doing my senior year there . . ." I break off my sentence.

"Oh no," she says and hugs me.

I nod against her hair.

"How long do you have?"

"We leave tomorrow."

"Tomorrow!?" she says and steps back.

I make eye contact, letting her see my regret.

She exhales a long audible breath. "Okay. Okay," she says, clearly trying to process it all, emotions flitting across her face. Sadness. Disappointment. Upset. Then . . . Determination. Happiness. Excitement. "That gives us tonight. We'll just have to make it the best last night possible. And besides, we'll keep in touch, right? I mean, it's Indonesia, not Mars."

The corners of my mouth pull up with her enthusiasm. "The internet is shoddy where she'll be teaching. But I'll do my best." I open my mouth but close it again, giving her a small smile.

"What?" she asks. "What were you going to say?"

"I was just thinking what an amazing girl you are," I reply, wanting to tell her all the things people often hold back from each other. There's no acting here. I mean every word. "And how lucky I am that I got to spend these past few weeks with you."

Her face lights up. She leans her head back and beams, her curls falling behind her shoulders. "Even the air smells different when you're happy."

I smile, too. A job well done. In short, Valentine and I have a system that works. Every. Single. Time. Or at least it did, before I met Ella.

1
AUGUST

(A RIDICULOUS NAME I BLAME MY MOM FOR)

Summer break—two of the best words in the English language—promising lazy days on the beach, waffle cones at Tony's Surf Shack, and burritoing myself in my blanket until noon. The welcome end of senior year also means that Valentine (I call her Tiny) and I are back in business after officially removing the "be back soon" sign from the front page of our website. It only took forty-eight hours for the whisper network (as Tiny calls it) to realize we'd returned, it took five hours of interviewing worried parents and best friends to choose our first case, and it'll take just three weeks of digging around in other people's lives to complete it.

Tiny kicks off her flip-flops on the dock that connects our backyards and sits down next to me, letting her feet dangle above the calm water. Lights appear on her porch in preparation for evening and crickets hum in the brush. Illuminated, Tiny's large house dominates our small inlet. In comparison, my family's small Victorian with the peeling paint looks like an unkempt garage.

She opens the notebook she's holding and pushes a stray piece of straight brown hair behind her ear. Her expression is smug. "Guess who just got off the phone with Katie's best friends?" She wags her eyebrows at me. "Me, that's who. They were gushing about us, August. GUSH-ING. They said she's happier than they've ever seen her, that she's excited about college again, that she actually started talking to her parents over dinner like she used to. They said they're writing us a rave review."

In our small harborside town in Massachusetts, summer jobs are easy pickings. Rich vacationers from Boston and New York flood rental properties with luggage piled high in convertibles, cash in hand, and the local businesses can't hire fast enough. But Tiny and I aren't applying at one of the waterfront restaurants. We aren't trying to be lifeguards or gathering references to work on one of the yachts in the harbor. In fact, no one in our town knows what we do. Our friends think we've had some elusive intern job with Tiny's dad's music production company in Boston for the past year and a half. And our families think we work for a catering company. But really, we break people up for a living through a business with the cheesiest name imaginable—Summer Love Inc. —a combination of our names, August and Valentine.

Tiny (the creator) loves the name, and she loves love. She believes that we're speeding people along on their path to finding their soulmates, steering relationships off a cliff so they can find better matches down the road. But me? I like the Inc.—a clinical suffix for a company that exposes relationships for what they really are so people can heal. And well, this job is personal, a service I wish had existed for my sister.

"Good," I reply. It's nice to know we helped Katie, the kind of nice that lifts your chin and bolsters your step. I smile at the water, the small ripples catching the last of the evening light and transforming it into a moving canvas. Without meaning to, I sketch a fast line drawing on it in my thoughts—a weird reflex that I thought had gone away.

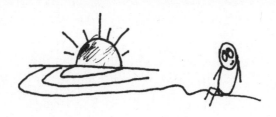

Tiny laughs. "Will you stop being emo for five minutes and focus? I have some golden info here on our new case and I need you to appreciate my genius."

I turn away from the water, my imaginary drawing dissolving into ripples, and I look at her. Her white T-shirt falls low on one shoulder, exposing the top of her bathing suit, and she wears a grin—all enthusiasm. I told her recently (in the middle of an optimistic rant about how she'd survive the zombie apocalypse *and* create a better world) that in her past life she was a Christmas tree or Fourth of July fireworks, something celebratory and neon and way over the top. To which she replied that in *my* last life I was Oscar the Grouch, only I made art out of found objects.

"Our new case," I repeat.

"Exactly. So excited to be back at it. All that time off for finals felt like a lifetime and a half," Tiny says, not needing me to say more than three words to understand me—she's been translating my nonspeak since we were toddlers. "How ready are you to swoop in, expose some crapjock boyfriend, and then cry about having to go back to Canada and return to your job shearing sheep nuts?"

I laugh. "I never cry. Their transformations just hit hard sometimes and I get a little misty."

She stares at me for a long second. "Right, because crying was the most objectionable part of what I said."

"Shearing sheep nuts is honest work."

"First of all, no. Just no." Tiny's smile is big and warm, the kind that's contagious, the kind I imitate when I do these jobs but can't seem to find in my everyday life. While I'm definitely better at pretending to be other people than I am at being August, Tiny's the opposite. She's been absolutely herself since always.

Tiny flips open her notebook. "And second of all, I'm quizzing you, so get ready." She tilts the page away from me, not that I'd be able to read her massively terrible handwriting. "Start with the basics—full name, birthday, etc."

I lean back, resting my palms against the wood of the dock, easing into our familiar routine. "Ella Becker. Born August eighteen[th] in a small town near Boston not unlike this one, where she's lived her entire life—"

"Correction: no place is as small as this town." A town that Tiny's been planning on leaving since she found out planes existed. "Now, back to Ella."

I shoot her a smile—because on this we agree: the farther we can get from here the better. "Her favorite movie is *Romeo and Juliet*, the version with Leonardo DiCaprio. She spends most afternoons at the coffee shop with friends." I picture Ella's parents, who we interviewed in a café twenty miles from here to avoid running into anyone we knew.

"She's always been independent, fiercely strong willed," Ella's mother explained as she took small sips of her mint tea. "But this past year every-thing shifted."

Tiny flipped through the folder of background information we requested from them. I could already tell she liked the case by the way she was reread-ing some of the details.

Ella's father pressed his lips together and straightened his broad shoulders. He had a precise haircut that you might expect from someone in the military, but he was really just a finance guy with an affinity for order. "It all started with her dating this boy, this absolute cocky—" he said, and Ella's mom touched his arm. He paused. "Anyway, it all started with him. *Not two weeks after she began dating him, she gave up her position on the school newspaper to join cheerleading because he's a football player. Then she started applying to schools she never cared about because that's where her friends want to go." He leaned forward. "We've been working on her college list since she was a freshman: she desperately wanted to go to Europe; she's passionate about travel journalism. Now, even though she got into her dream school in London, she's accepted a godforsaken college in Massachusetts—" Another touch from Ella's mom as his volume increased.*

Tiny and I exchanged a knowing glance.

Ella's mom sighed. "We've held off on rejecting the London school, fig-uring she'd change her mind, but the final deadline is just four weeks away and she still says she's not going. We don't know what else to do. We're des-perate for help."

I nodded and Tiny flipped to the "Information" page in her notebook. But before she could tell them about our process—how we research and execute our plan—Ella's father interrupted her.

"Whatever you're thinking of asking for this job, triple it," her father said. "I'll pay anything to get him away from her before that acceptance deadline."

"Boyfriend?" Tiny asks, looking at her notebook.

"Justin," I reply. "Friends with her friends and a central part of her social group. Popular. Football player. The kind of bro who does donuts on the front lawn of the school in his dad's Porsche and then doesn't get in trouble because his parents claim the car was stolen instead of making him own up to it. Obsessed with himself—"

"And his hair," Tiny interjects. "The time spent on that coif is a lot, and the time spent documenting that coif in selfies is even more." She looks at me with a mischievous smirk. "But alas, not everyone is blessed with a side-part, natural hair flip like you."

I shoot her a warning look that only makes her smile grow. When we were twelve, I made the mistake of telling her I thought my best feature was my hair and she's never let me forget it.

"Ella's interests?" she asks before I can dredge up an embarrassing memory of hers to counter with.

"Travel—wants to be a journalist."

Tiny waits a beat, but when I don't continue, she says, "Right. But you forgot to mention that she has a super popular horoscope blog that she's low-key obsessed with."

I cringe. "I didn't forget."

Tiny rolls her eyes. "August Mariani, you can't ignore an important part of her life just because you think it's ridiculous."

I open my mouth to argue, but I know she's right.

"Social status?" she continues.

I scratch my eyebrow. I've never liked this section of the assessment. I know it's important, key really, to getting someone out of a crappy relationship, but that's the part that bothers me. "Was a bit of a nerd growing up. And now she'd be cast in a lead role in *Mean Girls*."

"Big-time popular," Tiny agrees.

Before I can respond, a screen door snaps shut on the small house next to Tiny's and out comes a shirtless muscled dude in khaki shorts and penny loafers. Bentley Cavendish—the prep to end all preps, with a name that could make aristocrats feel common. He's also the only other person our age who lives in this inlet.

"Yo, Valentine!" he says with a grin, clunking down a cooler on his part of the dock. "Party at my house, nine o'clock." He doesn't bother to include me in the invitation. He's been mastering the art of ignoring me since ninth grade, when he asked Tiny out and she said no. He refused to believe it had anything to do with him and instead decided that I was the problem.

Tiny shrugs. "Sorry, it's movie night," she calls across the short stretch of water.

Bentley shakes his head. He knows all about movie night; he even came to a few when we were in middle school and repeatedly pointed out that we don't watch the movies so much as talk at the screen and quote our favorite lines in sync with the actors. "Tell me you're not really going to spend the *first Friday night* of summer watching old movies you've seen a million times when you could be cannonballing off the dock into a narwhal?" He motions toward a box of inflatable animal-shaped tubes.

Tiny lifts her hands as though it's an immovable fact. "Yup. But thanks for inviting us."

Us. This is what it means to have a best friend: there's no flaunting that she was invited and I wasn't—everyone knows Valentine is a hundred times cooler than me anyway—and there's no subtle regret that she's missing out.

Tiny turns from Bentley without a second thought. "Also, can we pause a second and talk about how much money her parents offered us?" she says. "This job is *the rest of what we need* for the first year of Berkeley tuition." She looks at me to join in on her enthusiasm.

Berkeley's business program is THE dream. But her comment on tuition isn't about her—her parents can and will pay—it's about me.

And right now, the last thing I want to tell her is that I used my entire savings to help my mom with bills this past year. But it's fine; I don't have to. This job should get me back on track before tuition is due.

"We've only got four short weeks to break them up, August," she continues like maybe I don't understand what a big deal this is.

While I'm with Tiny on the good-news part, to me it all sounds like pressure. Not to mention we only get paid if we complete the job. "It's nuts," I say.

"Not that we're doing this for the money, but man, is it a perk," she adds even though she doesn't need to—we would never take a case without merit.

There are rules (documented in one of Tiny's lists). Rules we argued over when we first started this business two years ago, trying to ensure that we wouldn't wind up working for friends who were doing it for selfish reasons, for parents who were trying to control their kids, or worse, for anyone who was a discriminating jerk. The idea isn't to manipulate people into breaking up but to expose what's really there, lay bare the truth and let them do the rest.

HOW TO CHOOSE A CASE:

1) Clients fill out an electronic form detailing why they need our service

2) Interview the ones whose concerns make the cut

3) Do independent research to confirm relationships are harmful

4) Choose the most urgent or time sensitive relationship

And with Ella, it's number four. The decisions Ella makes in these next few weeks will change her life.

"What do you want your name to be for this one?" Tiny asks, bringing the conversation back to strategy.

While I dislike the social-assessment part of this job, it's fun creating a new identity—and strangely liberating. "Holden," I say with a grin.

She smirks. "Pretentious much?"

"Totally. And if her town is like ours, then I'll just be another rich summer tourist with a boat and a heart of gold."

Tiny laughs. "That's actually kind of perfect. Must get your genius from me."

"What about your name?"

"Mia," she says without needing to think about it, "same as always." She pauses to read over some scribbled notes. "Well then, *Holden*, I say we try the *Pretty in Pink* strategy to start, and let you swoop in as the sweet preppy hero."

"I mean . . . that *should* work—" I start.

"Oh, it'll work," Tiny says, cutting me off.

"It's weird how you struggle with confidence. You should really work on that. Maybe commune with a narwhal while cannonballing with a shirtless dude."

She puts her notebook down on the dock and looks up at me innocently, not that I buy it. I know she's plotting. Half a second later she makes her move—a shove. But I'm ready, and the instant her hand hits my shoulder, I grab her wrist, pulling her off the dock with me.

She yelps in surprise as she hits the cool water and goes under. But the moment she resurfaces, she's laughing again.

She wipes water off her face. "You suck, August."

I push back my dripping hair. "You mean Holden?"

"I mean, *wow, Holden*, you're so dreamy. And look at those muscles, you must work out . . . on your boat, in between buying an island and drinking a martini with your pinkie in the air," she says overarticulating with gestures and facial expressions.

"Damn. That was convincing. Maybe we should switch spots on this one—you get close to Ella, and I'll do the brilliant strategizing."

"Pffft," Tiny says, disturbing the droplets of water around her mouth and enjoying that I just called her brilliant. While Tiny takes the acting lead on a case here or there, she's more than happy to hand over the majority of it to me, naming herself the mastermind; but if you ask me, it's because she gets too attached to the subjects. Even the word *subject* bothers her—*They're people, August. PEOPLE, capital* P, she says.

"Put your game face on, August." Tiny kicks her feet up, splashing me in the process. "Because tomorrow we officially start the biggest case we've ever had."

I smile and lean back in the water, letting it hold my weight. Summer. Is. The. Absolute. Best.

2
VALENTINE

(AN AWESOME NAME THAT I'M SHOCKED MY PARENTS CAME UP WITH)

Purple Post-it notes cover my puzzle mat, detailing Ella's life. I lean over them on the soft cream carpet of my bedroom floor, chewing on one of the strings of my white hoodie.

A fuzzy unicorn alarm clock blares a magical whinny at me, and I reach up to my bedside table, turning it off without looking. Since we started Summer Love a couple years ago, I've set an alarm on days we're working, not to wake up—I'm up by nine no matter what, dancing and singing to wildlife (as August puts it)—but to wake up August, who'd gladly sleep until two without noticing. It's not that he won't set his own alarm, but he'll hit snooze until the last possible second and then stumble out of his house like an unkempt swamp monster with good hair.

I take one last look at my Post-its. There's something about this case that's making me nervous, like there's something important I'm missing, and it's driving me nuts. I scour Ella's social media again and check all my notes, but whatever the thing is eludes me. So with a sigh, I roll up my puzzle mat, putting it back in its canvas bag, hidden from my parents.

I grab my shoulder bag off my vanity chair along with my fake catering outfit and leave the lavender-and-white room—a color combo I chose when I was eleven that still makes me happy. I head downstairs to our living room, which looks like it was plucked straight out of a *Hamptons* magazine with its tans and navy blues. The couches are oversized, the art is impressive (or so my parents' friends say), and my dad's music awards on the far wall always get ooohs and aaahs.

I make my way into the kitchen, where my parents sit at the breakfast table next to a large picture window facing the water. Dad's typing away on his laptop and Mom's doing a crossword puzzle in the newspaper.

"Morning, Valentine," they both say, looking up.

"Morning, parents of mine," I say, giving Dad a quick hug. He's not my biological dad, but he's the one who raised me, and the one who proposed to my mom a mere six months after she found out her IVF worked. She desperately wanted a baby but never knew if she might have a partner in it. She likes to joke that he behaved like she impregnated him. And when I was old enough to fully understand, he offered to adopt me, which I said I'd only agree to if I could have his last name. He cried. And not that it matters, but anyone who saw us together would assume we share DNA. Even though my biological dad is supposedly Italian and not Indian like my adoptive dad, I have straight, dark hair and dark eyes with long eyelashes that resemble his. I also have my mom's small nose and heart-shaped lips.

"Have some food," Dad says with a smile, gesturing at the table. "Your mom's ordered the good bagels again and those warm chocolate croissants."

I grab two of everything for me and August on my way down the table to give my mom a kiss on the cheek.

"I *always* order good bagels," my mother, a serious connoisseur, corrects him. She even wears her blond hair in what can only be described as a bagel-shaped bun on top of her head. Only in this moment, she's too smiley. Don't get me wrong. My parents are happy people, but her grin is suspiciously big.

I look from one to the other, to see if I'm missing something. "What are you working on over there?" I ask Dad.

"Actually, *we're* working," Mom corrects me with an uptick in her voice. "Planning your dad's company party."

Now I smile, too. Dad's big work party—an annual event of epicness August and I look forward to all year, also known as an upscale cook-out that we host for Dad's fellow music producers, important execs, and some of their top clients. It involves transforming our backyard into a sea of white twinkle lights and pitched tents. Some drool-worthy musicians inevitably wind up stopping at our little town country store or homemade ice cream shop in their limos, and it's the talk of the town for about a month afterward, not to mention the celebrity gossip sites.

But as I look at Mom, a half-finished crossword puzzle by her coffee cup, my thoughts flash back to our case. Ella's mother told us that she used to do the *Times* puzzle every Sunday with her daughter. Hmmm. Methinks I have an idea. I pull out my phone and grab a quick picture of the answers my mother filled in. Then I slather the two bagels with cream cheese and wrap them in paper napkins.

"I'm out," I say to my parents.

"Another catering job?" Dad asks, looking up from his computer screen. "You've been working hard this year."

"Yup." I lift my ironed white shirt and black dress pants as evidence. Truthfully, I wouldn't mind if they knew about Summer Love—well, besides the fact that they'd kill me for lying about it for two years. But August cares. A lot. He says if my parents know, then his mom will find out. But what he won't say is that his mom would immediately spot the reason we started this business in the first place—August's sister, Desiree.

Des passed away two years ago in an accident, which August analyzed front, back, and sideways for answers that don't exist. An event he felt driven to rationalize, like if he could come up with the right answer, then maybe it'd hurt less, or better yet maybe she'd come back. And his analysis always led to the same thing—Des's boyfriend, Kyle. But that was before. That was when he still talked about her.

After he stopped, I thought he'd slowly relax into being himself again, but he didn't. He got quiet. He quit theater, he quit soccer, and he quit the one thing I never thought he would—coming over. But I devised a plan to get my best friend back, a plan that focused on the thing he was obsessed with—crappy relationships. So Summer Love Inc. was born.

And August the breakup artist is similar to August when Des was still around. But August in his everyday life is still closed off, not with me of course, but with the world. He just doesn't trust it anymore.

"Have fun, Valentine. Text us what time you'll be home," Mom says.

Shoving my breakfast spoils into my shoulder bag, I stare out the window toward Bentley's yard, where he's doing push-ups, once again shirtless. As ridiculous as he is, it's hard not to admire the view. I say a quick goodbye to my parents and step out the back door onto the porch. Bentley looks up when the door closes behind me.

I head straight for him. "Yo, Bent," I say, doing my best bro voice, crossing the grass with purpose. "Wicked push-ups, man."

"Yo, Sharma," he replies, calling me by my last name like I'm one of his football buddies. "I know."

I smile even though what he said wasn't witty. He pauses his workout to drink water and wipe his forehead with what I suspect is his mother's dish towel, given that it says something about wine and chocolate being major food groups.

"Don't pretty yourself up for me," I say, weirdly amused by his towel choice. "I just wanted to ask you before I went ahead and stole your newspaper."

Bentley laughs. "Why ask if you're stealing?"

I shrug. "I'm a polite thief?" I clock his question as agreement and take a step toward August's house.

"That's it?" he says, the disappointment obvious on his well-proportioned face. "No pointless small talk while you secretly stare at my six-pack? I feel so used."

I laugh, not bothering to point out that employing small talk as a front to stare at his body would be the definition of using him. "Send me a shirtless selfie," I say as I backstep across his yard. "I'll show it to all my friends and we'll giggle behind our hands."

Bentley sighs dramatically. "If only." He gets back into push-up position and I turn.

"Will I see you at the cookout later?" he yells as I walk away.

"Maybe," I answer over my shoulder, although I doubt there will be time with this new Ella case, and even if there is, I double doubt I could convince August to go.

"Then *maybe* I'm excited," he replies. This is Bentley's thing—charm, charm, charm, date for two weeks in a showy PDA way that makes everyone uncomfortable, and then on to the next relationship. Good at the wooing, bad at the commitment. Bentley and I have been doing this dance for four years now, but only recently he's been more enthusiastic about it, like he's made a bet with himself that he can get me to kiss him before I leave for college. And honestly, I'm not against it. Guys like Bentley are basically made for summer kissing. Not that I'd ever admit that to August, because he'd probably turn purple and stop breathing.

I climb the ladder secured to the side of August's house and push open his second-story window with one hand. I step easily into his bedroom, where I find him with his head shoved under his pillow, arguing with his ancient cat, who has one gray paw on August's back, claws extended. I drop my shoulder bag on the hardwood floor, feeling the familiar sense of accomplishment of an awesome entrance.

The ladder wasn't exactly my idea, but it was a stroke of brilliance nonetheless. The summer before seventh grade we marathoned all six seasons of *Dawson's Creek*, and I was totally inspired.

"That's us," I said, sprawled across August's bed, admittedly getting popcorn on his comforter. "And if you sprinkle in some summer tourists and some Massachusetts accents, that's our town. Can you even believe how weird this is? Oh my god. What if there are lots of us, August? Lots of smart, beautiful, level-headed girls hanging out with clueless dork dudes."

And despite the fact that this is New England and the weather is wicked unpredictable, I could not be talked out of it. I even convinced August's artsy mom to build me a custom ladder that connects to the house, because while I'm not afraid of heights, I'm also not an idiot. And I've been enthusiastically using it ever since, much to August's disappointment.

August doesn't say hi. Instead, he mumbles something about the unfairness of mornings.

"Want me to feed him?" I offer, nodding at his cat, Swee, even though he can't see the gesture because he's still face down.

He groans, removing the pillow from his head. "Are you strategizing with my cat to wake me up?"

"Are *you* strategizing to win the grumpiest-sloth award? It's ten thirty."

He runs his hands over his face and glances groggily around his room. Where my bedroom is all light colors and new furniture, his is dark blues, dark wood, and antique lamps. Papers lie haphazardly across his desk, where he undoubtedly stayed up half the night researching Ella. His bookshelf is overflowing with nonfiction. And his favorite charcoal-gray grandpa sweater with the wooden buttons is draped across his desk chair.

"Exactly. And we don't need to be at the coffee shop until noon, sooo—" He stops abruptly as I head for his closet. "*Tiny*," he says like I should know better.

I look at him. He looks at me. A standoff.

He raises a warning eyebrow.

"Fine," I say with a long exhale, lifting my hands in surrender. "Pick out your own clothes. See if I care." I pause, unable to restrain myself from commenting further. "Far be it for me to stand in the way of you and your three favorite James Dean outfits, but I think you're gonna need something more Holden-ish for this one." I pull a pair of boat shoes (swiped from Dad's closet) from my bag and toss them on August's floor with a satisfying thud.

He eyes them wearily as he pops into his bathroom to open a can of cat food for Swee. He used to feed him downstairs in the kitchen, but when you have a creaky twenty-year-old cat whose life is built around lounging in bed, it's easier to have food nearby. And the sacrifice of having a stinky bathroom because it makes his cat happy is a perfect example of why we're best friends. He likes to pretend that he's so rational and unflappable, but he's actually the most sensitive and thoughtful person I know.

"I was doing some Ella research last night—" he says over his shoulder.

"Leonardo DiCaprio," I squeal, too excited to let him finish his sentence.

"I'd be weirded out that you knew where my thought was going, but then I remembered you have access to my window," he says with a sly grin.

I roll my eyes, not bothering to tell him that I don't need to spy to be three steps ahead. We both know I'm the mastermind in this friendship.

"So anyway," he continues, heading toward his closet. "I rewatched *Romeo and Juliet*."

Some part of me is secretly delighted by August studying Romeo. It's not that he doesn't love a good rom-com or a dram-rom (???) in this case, but August was once supposed to play Romeo in our town theater. And when Des died, he gave up not only on the play but on acting in general. I never thought I'd see him pursue Romeo again in a million years. I imagine now that the sheer idea you could fall in love at first sight and then be willing to die for that love makes him queasy. I, on the other hand, am all for falling head over heels.

I clasp my hands together. "Oh. My. God. Please tell me you want to ditch our *Pretty in Pink* strategy in favor of Star-Crossed Lovers!"

His widening smile confirms it. "Ella's mom told us that Ella's making decisions based on her friends and boyfriend instead of her own best interests, right?" He pauses, and I stifle the urge to interrupt. "So, I'm thinking I come in as the Star-Crossed Lover"—he grimaces at the word *lover*, and it makes me smile—"let's say Star-Crossed Friend in this case. Basically, the exact opposite of her current relationship and social group. Make her feel like everything *she's* interested in is important and doable. A painter, not a football player. Someone who has everything but couldn't care less about popularity. You get the idea."

For a moment I hesitate, shocked that he's bringing art into this job. He hasn't so much as lifted a paintbrush since his sister died. No more line drawings in the margins of his notes, not so much as a doodle. A glimmer of hope zings through me and I want to comment, but I worry that if I make a big deal out of it, he'll change his mind. So instead, I dig through my shoulder bag for my rainbow notebook that has all our Summer Love Inc. lists in it.

I land on the page I'm looking for. My feet inexplicably do a little two-step in happiness. We rarely use this move, but it's always been one of my favorites.

STAR-CROSSED LOVERS—showing up as an opposite to the subject's person's current situation, letting him or her fall for your way of thinking and enthusiasm, entranced enough to change his or her life.

August pulls a pair of plaid shorts and a Johnny Cash T-shirt out of his closet and steps into the boat shoes I brought over. Preppy enough to be convincing and Johnny Cash enough to be cool.

Victory is mine! A Holden-shaped star is born.

I turn around and pet Swee's oddly flat head while August throws on his clothes and pops the top off his deodorant. Not that he needs it. The temperature goes above eighty and I instantly smell like an onion, but he only ever gets a slight musky scent that makes him smell familiar instead of bad. It's the most unfair thing ever.

"Good?" he says and holds out his arms for my evaluation. And as it turns out, he's a thing of wonder. His shirt is faded in all the right ways, the red plaid of his shorts is showy, and his hair leans slightly to the messy side.

"You're *so* ready to spread the love," I say.

"More like ready to crush a bad relationship."

"Same same," I say. "The ending of a bad relationship creates an opportunity for a good one. For *love*. Who knows, the next person Ella meets might be her soulmate."

He snorts.

I point at him, and my neon bracelets give a satisfying jingle. "Don't snort your disbelief at me, sir. I know you don't believe in soulmates, and I'm here to tell you that you're dead wrong."

"I think what you mean to say is that you're romanticizing—" he starts like he's preparing for a dissertation.

I plug my ears in self-defense. "Nope, not letting you rain on love today. No room in my schedule." I toss him the keys to my Jeep Wrangler. "You're driving."

I pick up my shoulder bag and head out of his bedroom door before he can respond. As I reach the top of the stairs, though, his footsteps cease in the hall behind me. I don't need to look to know where—he's by Des's door.

I turn around to find his face blank, his enthusiasm from thirty seconds ago missing, replaced with a calm, unreadable force field that I call The Wall. No one gets past The Wall. Not even me on my best and brightest days. He wipes the dust off Des's doorknob with his shirt, not opening his sister's door, which (I'm guessing by the dust) hasn't been disturbed in months, her things from two years ago frozen in time behind it and poised to evoke tears from whoever encounters them.

I move to August's side, but he doesn't look at me, just stares ahead silently thinking his piece. I sigh, not for me, but to shake him out of his statuesque position. He doesn't acknowledge me, however, and the familiar ineffectual feeling of being trapped outside The Wall rises in my chest. I want to hug him and tell him that I miss Des, too. I want to yell at him for not trusting me with his hurt, cite my love for her and for him as good reasons. But instead, I stare unsure and tongue tied at the watercolor of Des's name twisted with sunflowers that's tacked to her door. August made it for her when he was eight. And I'm instantly mad at myself for not knowing how to talk to him about this and for not being better at weaving her into our everyday lives instead of un-comfortable isolated moments.

"Des, what are you going to do, I mean later, after you finish college?" I asked, gesturing at all the college brochures on her bedside table. "I feel like you're going to be in charge of stuff, or people. Or both. Mayor, maybe?" I used the same sophisticated voice my dad always used when he asked me about my goals and attempted to stand taller than my twelve years to em-phasize my maturity.

Des moved around her room, putting on a silver charm bracelet and a black choker. She paused in front of her vanity mirror, pink lipstick in hand, and turned to look at me. No matter what she was doing or how much she was hurrying, she always seemed to have time for me and August.

"Right idea about the helping-people thing, but politics aren't for me,"

she said, giving it some serious thought. "I was playing around with the idea of being a vet, but I think my heart is too breakable for that. You know what I've secretly always wanted to do, though?" *She tilted her head like she was entrusting me with a hidden treasure.* "Be a relationship detective."

August looked up, considering the fanciful idea, probably specifically so he could ask practical questions about it. "Is that a job? How would it work?"

Yup, there he goes.

"See, that's the awesome thing," *Des said.* "It's not a job. But it should be."

"Let's go," August says quietly. It's the kind of quiet that shuts you up, the kind that tells you his heart is breaking and that if you push, you'll shatter it into a million pieces.

We didn't talk about that conversation with Des when we started Summer Love, even though we both know this is about her and righting some inexplicable wrong of a boyfriend August can't make peace with. I've avoided bringing it up since, nervous that if I shine a light on it before he's ready, our company will disappear behind The Wall, too.

I follow August down the hall, looking momentarily over my shoulder. *This one's for you, Des,* I think.

3
AUGUST

Tiny has her bare feet up on the dashboard, her latest Ella list on her lap, and one neon-braceleted wrist hanging out the open window riding air waves. Even when she drives, which is rare, she tries to keep a foot awkwardly balanced on the dashboard. But I don't mind driving, especially since we usually take her Jeep, which is a heck of a lot nicer than the dented fifteen-year-old Volvo station wagon I share with my mom when she's not working, which is most of the time.

"Want to go over it one last time?" Tiny asks, turning down the music but not taking her eyes off her list.

I glance at her as we drive past a welcome sign for Ella's town. "That's the second time you've asked that in ten minutes."

Tiny looks up, like she hadn't realized she'd been repeating herself. "It's the biggest case we've ever had," she says, like I'm not thinking clearly. "And we have a nonnegotiable three-and-a-half-week deadline in which to complete it. Do you remember that disaster two Christmases ago? The *only other time* we used Star-Crossed Lovers, might I add."

I lean back in my seat; I've been waiting for her to bring this up ever since I suggested it. "That was one case. And it had nothing to do with the strategy; it had to do with our being green. We've *nailed* our cases since. All of them."

She shakes her head like I've got it all wrong. "This case has a shiny popular boyfriend, which is a challenge in and of itself, a controlling (also popular) friend group, making things doubly hard, and I keep thinking I'm missing something important." She pauses, but her mouth remains open with an unspoken thought. "Plus, it's only natural to be a little rusty, especially since you haven't really talked to anyone besides me for the past month or so." She says it like a casual observation. But Valentine doesn't do casual observing.

We stop at a red light, and I turn to look at her, about to point out how not subtle she's being, but think better of it.

"What?" she says with innocently wide eyes (also not subtle). "You haven't."

I shrug, now convinced she wants to have a conversation about my lack of socializing, one I'd rather avoid. Tiny has always been well liked. In fact, there was a moment when she was invited out so much that I worried she might cross over into the popular crowd and leave me in the dust, but she never did. And as Tiny's popularity started to increase, mine plummeted.

"All I'm saying is it wouldn't hurt to be more social," she says, like she heard my thoughts and decided to be contrary. "Even a little itty bit more, like go to the diner on a Saturday morning when everyone's there or walk along the harbor on Friday night. You never know; you might like it."

"I'm afraid I'm just not that cool."

But Tiny has pulled her head out of her notebook and is laser focused on my face. "Actually, you're not uncool."

I sigh, because I know that look and I know it means we're going to talk about it whether I want to or not. "You have to admit that no one would say I'm cool. Ever. It's not like anyone cuts my backpack straps or flips my lunch tray, but they don't acknowledge me, either. I'm that quiet kid who sits in the back of the class. But hey, that suits me."

"Yeah, but that's not *who you are*. Look at you." She gestures at my outfit. "Given half the chance, you play a character like a boss, talk to girls, and stand up to jerk-offs without blinking an eye. You know what I think, August? You're hiding."

Her cheeks are flushed and she grips her notebook. And even though her tone is calm, I can read her well enough to know that what she said made her nervous, which in turn makes me nervous. I scratch the back of my neck even though it doesn't itch, hoping that she'll drop it and we can go back to having an awesome day.

"When you stopped at Des's room before we left . . ." she says, pausing halfway through her thought.

Or not.

"Des never missed an opportunity to talk . . . to anyone, for any reason." Tiny smiles, but it's the sad kind. "Before—"

"Don't," I say quietly, cutting her off before she can tell me what I was like before Des died.

Tiny pushes her hair back from her face. "Sorry, I just thought you might like to talk about her."

"Yeah, no, I mean, I don't know," I say, stumbling over the words.

Tiny goes quiet, waiting for me to continue, but I don't. And as usual with the mention of Des, an awkward stillness descends. We both stare out the window at the beach filled with people and the ocean behind them.

After a few moments, she returns to her list. "Also," she says, like that exchange never happened, "remember when Ella's mom said that until a year ago, they always used to do the Sunday crossword puzzle together? I was thinking it might be a good way for you to connect with Ella," she says, chewing. "I copied some of my mom's answers for you." She points to the rolled-up newspaper in her shoulder bag.

"Right, because a crossword puzzle screams 'Befriend me; I'm cool.'" I turn onto Main Street in Ella's town, complete with brick storefronts and polished boutiques.

"It does," she insists, shoving the last piece of bagel in her mouth and getting crumbs all over the seat. "You just have to be creative. Maybe work your love for crossword puzzles into your love for horoscopes." Her grin turns taunting as I give her a warning glare.

I pull into a parking spot half a block down from the coffee shop.

Tiny hands me the newspaper. "How about this? If I'm wrong about the crossword puzzle, I'll buy you lunch."

I groan. She knows I can't turn down a bet. "You're on," I say and tuck the newspaper under my arm.

Tiny's phone dings and she glances at it. "Text from Ella's mom. She says Ella just left the house with the girls."

I know there's no rush, but I hop out of the Jeep anyway, ready to get started.

"Wait!" Tiny says as my feet hit the pavement, and she yanks a worn rainbow notebook out of her bag, flipping it open to the first list she made when we decided to start Summer Love Inc.

RULES OF ENGAGEMENT

1) Approach the subject person in a group, gaining interest without putting pressure on the ~~subject~~ person

2) Hook an invite to a party or something social from the ~~subject's~~ person's friend (No Flirting! It'll cause drama)

3) Build trust and create a bond with the ~~subject~~ person by talking to them about things they care about

She holds up the notebook. "Kiss it for good luck," she says, leaning over the center console.

"Definitely no."

She shrugs and kisses it herself. "Fine, but bring me an iced mocha if you want to continue this friendship!" she yells after me as I walk away.

The sidewalk is full of chatting families and people eating at outdoor brunch tables. The Saturday energy is contagious, and I feel myself standing a little taller as I breathe in the salty air.

I step around a shaggy dog on the curb and grab the door to the Beach Brew. The bells on the door chime, and I'm greeted with the scent of pastry dough, warm chocolate, and coffee. I scan the small, popular café, decked out with driftwood and a mosaic made of shells. Most of the seats are taken, except for a couple of stools by the window and a four-top.

The corners of my mouth pull up as I formulate the beginning of a plan. I plop the newspaper and my phone down on the four-top and walk to the counter, ordering from the disinterested guy behind the counter, who sports black suspenders and tight jeans. He looks markedly out of place in the nautical-themed café, like a blaring reminder that sand gets caught in unwanted places if you wear the wrong clothes to the beach.

I shift to the part of the counter where the drinks come out, keeping an eye on the window and reviewing what I know about Ella.

"Holden," the suspendered dude announces unenthusiastically and places an iced mocha and a black coffee on the counter. As I grab the drinks, three girls walk up to the café door—one with a blond bob and a strut, who I know from my research is Amber, the talkative, self-proclaimed leader of the group; a tall girl with box braids woven into a high bun named Leah, the most confident of the three; and Ella, with her wavy brown hair falling down the middle of her back and an exhausted look.

I take my drinks and slide into a seat at the four-top, pulling out my phone.

Me

They're here.

Tiny

Dun dun dun!!!

Aaalso, have you realized the genius of the newspaper yet???

Me

Shhhh

Tiny

Never

If (read when) you lose this bet, I'm making you take me to Bob's for lunch. Shush that, Holden McDreamy!

It's guaranteed that everyone from our school will be at Bob's Beachfront Diner for lunch, where they can conveniently go from eating fries and strutting to jumping in the ocean and then strutting some more.

I look up when I don't hear the door chime as expected, and find the three girls stopped on the sidewalk. But instead of coming in with Ella, Amber and Leah continue down the sidewalk.

Damn it. Engagement rule number one—approach a subject in a group.

Me

Ella is solo.

Tiny

BE CAREFUL! Remember what happened with the Brad case??? I talked to him alone, his girlfriend thought I was hitting on him, and it took me a whole week to walk that back.

I look at the four-top I snagged and frown. I was going to offer up my table to Ella and her friends, giving me a conversation starter, but now Ella will easily fit at one of the available stools by the window.

Ella orders her drink, something long and complicated that makes me wonder how there can be ten substitutions on a drink that only has three ingredients. I watch her in my peripheral vision, careful not to look up from my phone.

Me

> What I remember is that Brad tried to kiss you, missed, and wound up licking your cheek.

Tiny

> Never speak to me again.

Ella walks toward the window as I predicted, coffee in one hand and a beach bag in the other, lost in thought. She sits down, pulling out her laptop and hanging her bag over the back of her stool, and immediately starts typing. I tap my fingers on the table, brainstorming how to get her attention without something lame that might convince her I'm hitting on her.

The bell on the door chimes and a family with two children comes in, pausing to assess where to park the stroller while they order.

And I'm back in the chivalry business. "You can have my table," I say loudly enough for them to hear me and with a happy lilt to my voice that earns me approving nods from the nearby customers.

Ella, however, doesn't notice my considerate gesture. Mission not accomplished.

"That's so nice, and I'm not going to say no," one of the dads replies.

I grab my two drinks, smile at the dads trying to wrangle their children, and move toward the stool next to Ella's.

"Is this seat free?" I ask Ella, who's staring at her laptop.

"Mmm-hmm," she says but doesn't look up, doesn't smile.

Ella leans forward, her brow tensed in concentration, typing away. I know that look; it's the same expression Tiny has when she's working on her lists, and I also know that anything I say at this point will be met with dismissal.

My phone buzzes.

Tiny

> What are you doing over there? Hoping she'll slip
> off her stool and fall into your lap??? You know this
> only works if you talk to her, right?

I look out the window. Sure enough, Tiny is in the vintage music store across the street, typing into her phone and grinning at her own joke.

Me

> I was thinking about falling into hers.

I pause, my finger hovering over the send button, not because I'm rethinking my unfunny response but because Tiny's comment just convinced me something physical is exactly what I need. I look at the rolled-up newspaper and then at my coffee. I could spill a little coffee on the counter, not enough to get on Ella, just enough to start a conversation over the cleanup. But with her laptop out, it's a risk. I could also make it so she spills my coffee on me, not my favorite choice, but one that will force us into a conversation. Hmmm.

I stare at the crisp white counter like it's a daunting blank page in an exam booklet. The words *most important case ever* and *three and a half weeks* play on loop. And as I wind myself up, a line drawing forms in my mind. I press my eyes closed, but it refuses to disappear.

My phone buzzes, but I don't check it, because I'm too focused on my timing. I pop the top off my coffee cup as Ella reads from her computer. It doesn't take long before her phone buzzes, too.

I grip my coffee, putting one leg on the floor. And when she reaches back to grab her phone out of her bag, I stand. Her swinging elbow collides with my cup, but it's not the subtle motion I imagined—a splash on the floor and a spray on my shirt—it explodes coffee everywhere, drenching us both in more liquid than could possibly exist in one cup. It's on my shirt and on her dress, not to mention the counter, my face, her face, and the window.

For a moment we both freeze, stunned.

"Holy shit," she says, immediately turning toward her computer. Luckily her body shielded it and there are only a handful of droplets on the screen.

I reach for a napkin dispenser. "Wow, I'm so sorry," I say and mean it; I had absolutely no intention of getting coffee on her, much less drenching her in it. "Here, let me help." I offer her napkins, but she grabs her own instead.

"You've already done *more* than enough," she says, and for a second, I'm shocked; while I regret the way that played out, the lack of acceptance of my apology is unexpected.

I wipe a napkin down my coffee-splattered face. "I'm not saying I don't deserve that . . . but there were definitely two of us involved in that collision, one of us with very bad timing and one of us with a hammer elbow, and even though it doesn't really cover the damages, at least the badly timed one apologized."

"Apology not accepted," she says and goes directly back to cleaning coffee off her things.

And I laugh, not because it's funny but because it's so spectacularly bad—the actual worst introduction I've ever had to another person.

"Asshole," she says under her breath.

I pinch the bridge of my nose. I'm failing here, and if I don't do something fast and clever, I'll have no shot of ever talking to her again.

"Scorpio," I retort and wipe coffee off my arms.

Now she turns to me. "Excuse me?" she says, squeezing coffee out of her long wavy hair. "I'm *not a Scorpio*. I'm a Leo."

I do know her birthday after all. But as someone who knows what it's like to obsess over specifics, I knew she literally could not resist correcting me. "Then don't act like one."

Her mouth hangs open. "I'm . . ." she blusters and settles on, "Ugh."

I suppress a smile. "Nice try, but apology not accepted."

"Seriously?" she says like she can't believe I'm allowed to exist. "You're a *menace*." Her eyes narrow. "And a Gemini," she declares. "Definitely a Gemini."

For a split second I falter. She's spot on. And she knows it, because she looks pleased by my reaction.

"Are you saying that because half of me is charming?" I ask. Even though I hate astrology, I do know the basic idea that Geminis are supposed to have two distinct sides of their personalities. I can practically hear Tiny trumpeting her victory over me for utilizing astrology. A little piece of my pride just withered and died.

"Wow, just wow," she says, and even though she's not being friendly, she no longer has ice in her voice.

"And because the other half of me is funny?" I try again.

She shakes her head, unconvinced that I should be making jokes.

"Look," I say, conciliatory. "I know I'm not your favorite person in this café right now. You may have even ranked grumpy suspender dude above me." I gesture at the guy behind the counter, and despite the fact that she tries to hide it, the corners of her mouth tilt upward. "But I really do feel bad about what happened. I'd love to make it up to you by—"

She stops me. "If you've deluded yourself into thinking you could hit on me after—"

How is it possible that every single thing I don't want to happen in this conversation is happening in hyperdrive?

"Whoa," I say, holding up my hands. "I definitely don't want to date you."

Her eyes widen, and I know I've offended her even though she has no interest in dating me (funny how that works).

"I just meant that I'd love to pay for your dry cleaning," I continue quickly but reconsider after seeing how stained her dress is. "Or maybe pay for a new dress entirely?" And as much as I hate to lose a bet to Tiny, I grab the newspaper and tear the crossword puzzle out of it, reconciling myself to go to Bob's godforsaken Beachfront Diner.

I scribble my phone number on the back and then add:

Sorry again, Scorpio.

I hand her the note and she frowns, readjusting her bag on her shoulder. "I'm not going to call you."

"No worries," I say. "A text is perfectly fine."

She opens her mouth but closes it again, shaking her head. And she walks away. She doesn't say goodbye and she doesn't look back, but she does stare at my note longer than she needs to.

I look at my phone, which now has a billion texts from Tiny, the last of which reads: *What if this strategy is CURSED?!?*

4
VALENTINE

Bob's Beachfront Diner displays a *No Shirt, No Shoes, No Food* sign, but the enforcement of said sign is nonexistent. Half their summer customers are teens in their bathing suits and towels, having just been at the beach or headed to it.

"Tell me that you have this under control," I say to August as he checks his phone, which currently has no texts from Ella.

He dips his grilled cheese in ketchup. "'Control' isn't *exactly* the word I'd use," he says in a way-too-casual tone for someone who went rogue on our carefully curated rules.

I point a fry at him. "I swear, August Mariani, you better get yourself together. We have barely more than three weeks to close this case before her dream of going to school in London disappears. Not to mention that we won't get paid."

He nods, his forehead scrunched in what I hope is concern.

I consider throwing the crazy-expensive Berkeley tuition in there as well, just to drive the point home, but the words get caught in my throat, my stomach dropping a little at the thought of going to California in two short months. I pause, taken aback by my own reaction. There are a handful of things in this world that I'm certain about—that there is a bright side to every situation, that I'd fight to the death over a warm chocolate croissant, and that UC Berkeley is the start of a life-long adventure. And by some small miracle (and three years of intense strategizing), August and I both got in. We were those weird kids who've always known what we wanted to do, only instead of wanting to be doctors or actors or whatever, we obsessively collected office supplies for our future companies. We didn't have your typical lackluster lemonade stand; we made a killing with freshly squeezed lemonade and home-made cookies during the height of tourist season, and a garden-weeding business wearing matching outfits that adults thought were too cute to say no to. Berkeley business school is the dream that came true. So why, oh why, am I stumbling over something I've thought a thousand times before with enthusiasm? Please, brain, level with me.

The people in the booth behind us, which seats four but is packed with six of our classmates, whoop and laugh loud enough to make August frown.

"Well, lucky for you, I snagged us an invite to a bonfire tonight in Ella's town that is supposed to be *the* summer-kickoff party," I say, sipping my strawberry lemonade.

August smirks. "You were in that music store for what? Ten minutes? Most of which was spent spying on and texting me. And somehow you got invited to *the* summer party?"

"So you're impressed?" I quip, feeling smug.

"I mean, yeah. Like, a lot. All the time," he says. This is what makes him good at his job—he's never afraid to give a compliment, to let other people be awesome. And unlike most humans I know, he doesn't think that other people's greatness in any way detracts from his own, something he got from Des. And as I think it, I imagine how sad she'd be that he pushes everyone away now. I consider bringing her up again, but before I get the chance, Bentley slaps his hands down on the end of our table.

He's wearing a short-sleeved wet suit that's unzipped and folded down at his waist. "Wow. First you show up in my yard this morning, and now you follow me to the diner. Should I be blushing from all this attention?" he says with a grin.

"Depends," I say. "Do you feel pretty?"

Bentley stands, rubbing one hand over his abs and puffing out his chest. "Like, really pretty," he says, and I smile.

"Bent," Charlie Atkins calls from two booths down. "We're trying to order, man."

But Bentley only waves his friends off and keeps his attention on me. "What do you say to a surfing lesson today, Valentine? Onetime offer to spend your whole afternoon soaking up sun with yours truly."

I glance out the window at the warm sand and glistening water, momentarily tempted. "No can do. August and I have work."

He shrugs like he figured as much, and his friends call his name again, flapping their menus at him to show how badly he's holding up their ability to scarf greasy food. "I swear you two are obsessed with everything boring," he says like we're offending the essence of summer itself. "Just for the record, I'm not giving up. Not now, not ever." He taps our table twice for emphasis.

August rolls his eyes and Bentley walks away, neither of them directly acknowledging the other. August looks from Bentley to me, his gaze questioning.

"What?" I say.

"Nothing," he replies and breaks eye contact, deciding not to voice his opinion.

"So the party," I say, putting us back on track.

He chews. "Cousins? Normal routine?"

"Yup." I swallow a mouthful of veggie burger. "We'll say you're staying with me in our new summer place while your mom takes your yacht up the coast. I'll make it a point to spend time with the boyfriend, see what I can learn." I pause, leveling him in my gaze. "And you find a way to make nice with Ella even if you need to break out in song."

5
AUGUST

The beach parking lot is packed. The sun set hours ago and the party is in full swing. Tiny and I timed it that way. We can't do our job at the beginning of a party, when people are too self-conscious for it to be productive.

I shut the driver's side door of Tiny's Jeep. There are clusters of partygoers perched on the beds of pickup trucks and sneaking alcohol from their cars. But most people are on the beach sitting on blankets or leaned against the dunes, illuminated by the large bonfire.

Tiny slips her hoodie over her head and steps into the sand barefoot, choosing to leave her flip-flops in the Jeep as opposed to carrying them. But me, I've got on the same pair of boat shoes from this morning (the only salvageable part of my outfit), dark jeans, and a paint-splattered T-shirt.

As we approach the party, the music gets incrementally louder and I can make out the distinctions between voices and laughter, between the pop of the firewood and the pop of can lids. However, the most pervasive sound is the ocean.

"Two o'clock," Tiny whispers, nodding at Ella's boyfriend, Justin, who's entertaining his friends with exaggerated gestures.

Tiny sighs, as though handling popular dudes is a tiring sport, even though she's great at it—remarkably so. "Watch and learn, coffee fumbler," she teases. And not thirty seconds later she has all three guys paying full attention to her.

I continue through the party, searching for Ella and navigating around people sprawled in the sand with bare feet, pants rolled up, bathing suits still on from earlier in the day. I make my way around the bonfire before I spot Ella, Leah, and Amber at the base of the lifeguard tower.

I walk toward the water and right past the girls, careful not to give any indication that I notice them. Instead, I focus on the ocean, staring at the receding white foam from a crashed wave.

"No . . . not happening," I hear Ella say behind me with emphasis, probably accented by a drink or two.

I don't turn around. I just pick up a rock and toss it into the ocean.

Five . . . four . . . three . . . two . . . one . . .

A slender finger pokes the back of my shoulder. "What the hell?" Ella says with a confident uptick in her voice.

I turn and give her a puzzled look. "Do I know you?"

Her eyes widen. "Wow."

I smile, drawing out my silence. "Don't worry, Scorpio. I know exactly who you are. I may never forget."

"Likewise. But I was hoping to give it a good try by *never seeing you again*," Ella says with exaggerated frustration, even though she approached me, not the other way around.

"Then don't follow me to parties," I say. "That's one way to solve the problem."

"Follow *you* to parties?" She's really riled up—not a tactic I've ever used, and one that would have Tiny calling me every variation of idiot, but there's no smooth way to gain her trust right now. Besides, she's in her element, her friends are watching, and she's got more fire than any of our previous subjects. I suspect that if I show her I'm easy prey, she'll eat me alive. So instead, I settle for getting her attention and hopefully integrating myself into the social scene at large, which with popular groups means utilizing a bit of brazen confidence. Mainly, I just pretend I'm Tiny and play every banter card I can think of.

"This party is in *my town*," Ella continues. "These are *my friends*." She sweeps her arm behind her.

I look back at the party, then at Leah and Amber specifically, who wear knowing expressions. "Then I guess we're going to see a lot of each other this summer, because it's my town now, too."

She pauses. "*Do not* tell me you moved here."

"I didn't move here," I say, then add: "But *I am* staying for a few months with my cousin, who *did* move here."

She groans.

"So how do you want to do this, Scorpio? Divvy up the town? I'll take the coffee shop; you take the diner?"

"You're definitely not getting the coffee shop," she says. "I live here. You don't. End of story. You can have the park bench, the one covered by trees all the way in the far corner. And that's it."

"You're giving me a make-out spot?" I say with dramatic surprise. "Funny where your mind goes."

Her cheeks turn pink, but before she can unleash on me, Amber and Leah walk up.

"So this is Mr. Coffee," Amber says as a statement of fact. "I thought you said he was an überprep?" She gives me a once-over—physically evaluating people out loud is a trademark power move of the rich and popular. Her gaze settles on my feet like she found what she's looking for. "Boat shoes."

I glance at Ella. "You told your friends about me, huh?"

Ella scowls. "You dumped coffee over my head. Talking about you was unavoidable."

"Ah," I say, nodding. "Describing my outfit was essential information, I see."

Ella huffs.

Leah laughs. "Wow, you two are like . . ." She looks back and forth between us.

"A scene from *When Harry Met Sally*?" Amber offers, and I'm doubly glad Tiny isn't in hearing range. I want to be Ella's friend, nothing more. And I'm specifically not trying to set myself up as a rival to her boyfriend.

Leah nods, finding the whole thing amusing. "Actually, yeah, exactly like that."

"That is not . . . *No*," Ella says emphatically, and I want to echo her.

"I bet Justin would find this interesting," Amber adds with a mischievous smirk.

"What would I find interesting?" Justin says from behind me, indicating Amber saw him and her comment was a power play.

Justin joins the group wearing a white T-shirt, basketball shorts, and a cocky expression.

"*This*," Ella says, a little flustered, waving her hand in my direction, "is the guy who dumped his coffee all over me this morning."

"No shit," he says and laughs, but Ella gives him a look. "Oh, wait, sorry. Not funny. We hate him?"

She shrugs, soaking up the fact that he immediately took her side. "A little."

"Sorry, man, we hate you a little," Justin says in a friendly way. He's a bro's bro, but at least he doesn't try to fist-bump me. It's obvious by the way they all look at him that they adore him. Plus, there's something oddly familiar about his whole shtick.

As if Tiny could sense that I need her, she appears next to me. "I see you've met my cousin," she says to Justin.

"Your cousin?" Justin repeats with another laugh. "Man, small world. Like, crazy small." He visibly winces, shifting his attention to Ella. "Babe, I may have inadvertently invited Mia"—he gestures at Tiny—"and public enemy number one to our party tomorrow." He wraps his arm around Ella's waist and she leans into him. "Are you mad? Say the word and we'll just cancel the party straight up."

She shrugs, more for show than anything. "Nah. Not a big deal."

"That's my girl," Justin says and kisses her head.

And I have to hand it to the guy: he's annoyingly charismatic.

Ella looks at him like he's the best thing ever, and something about her expression makes my stomach drop. Suddenly I know why he seems so familiar—he reminds me of someone I once knew, someone I despise more than anyone on this whole goddamn planet—Des's last boyfriend. *Kyle.* I glance at Tiny, and by the way she searches my face, I can tell she sees it, too—that Justin appears too perfect, that Ella appears too smitten. I look away, uneasy, my heart punching my rib cage. And for the first time since we started this business, my confidence wavers, not only in this case but also in my ability to approach it objectively.

6

VALENTINE

The cool water sparkles like a blaring invitation. I wipe my fore-head with the back of my wrist, glancing momentarily up at the gorgeous blue sky from where I sit at my and August's favorite place on the dock—the one we've nicknamed our "office." We've planned all our best stuff from this location, including the not-so-inspired idea of digging an underground tunnel from his house to mine when we were nine, before we hit a pipe and nearly gave my dad a heart attack, that is. I kick at the water with bare toes and stare jealously at Bentley and his little brother and sister, who have been competing for best dive, farthest jump, and biggest splash for the past twenty minutes. But I'm already in my party-ready clothes, and I don't have time for a swim.

Also, I don't want to go back in my house. My parents are in there, cooking and dancing. While that's not super unusual, they seem to have kicked up their romance as of late. I'm happy for them, but I just don't need to witness it.

Instead, I flip through Ella's and Justin's social media profiles. Usually this is the bit I look forward to most, the angling for clues and sussing out information that the parents don't know. But right now, Justin is making my stomach drop in a bad way. I knew I was missing something important, but I didn't imagine in a million years that it'd be his eerie similarities with Kyle, who luckily has been away at college and has yet to return, even during summer breaks. It's not that Justin looks like him, 'cause he doesn't; it's the way he captivates an audience. It's the sense that he's selling you something too good to be true.

Bentley pops out of the water near my feet, and I'm so startled I nearly drop my phone on his head. He grins.

"Well played, Bentley," I say, placing my phone face down on the wood in case he splashes me.

He crosses his wet arms and leans on the dock, resting his chin on them, but he doesn't reply.

After a long second I laugh. "Are you going to say something?"

He shakes his head, sending a couple of water droplets into the air.

"So you're just going to lounge there silently?" I ask, and when he nods, I add, "Suit yourself." I pick my phone back up, but it's impossible to concentrate with him staring. "Okay. I'll bite. What's with the silent routine?"

He shrugs.

"Please tell me you didn't google reverse psychology," I say, but he only shrugs again. "Oh my god. I swear if I wasn't worried about falling in the water, I'd push you."

I place my hands on the wood on either side of my knees, and my pinkie grazes his elbow. We both notice. And for whatever reason, the silence makes it seem like a big deal. He smiles mischievously.

"Don't think . . . that wasn't me touching you," I say, which also sounds really weird and loud considering I'm the only one speaking.

His grin only grows, and he presses his palm over his heart, doing an exaggerated sigh. I try to squash my smile, but my cheeks are refusing to cooperate.

The moment is short lived, however, because August's mom's car pulls into their driveway. August is driving, which means he was probably helping her apply for jobs again, not that he really talks about it, but everyone knows. His mom's struggle with work isn't a topic that lives behind The Wall, but it's one that puts him in a bad mood, especially when someone at school brings it up.

When I look back at Bentley, he nods like he accepts that our nonconversation is over and pushes off the dock.

7
AUGUST

The screen door clicks closed behind my mom, who carries grocery bags in her hands and her portfolio under her arm. Her brown hair is in a loose bun on top of her head and her navy skirt hangs to the floor. Tiny always says my mom's style is *Titanic* artsy, but all I think when she says that is how she resembles a doomed ship headed for an iceberg.

"I have such a good feeling about that new gallery director, August," Mom says with an extra dose of enthusiasm, dropping everything on the kitchen table with a thunk. "I think it's going to be my lucky break."

Except luck and my mother don't mix. "What about the Gibbonses' porch, Mom? Do you think Mr. Gibbons will hire you to paint it?"

"I mean, you should have seen the way the gallery director pored over my work, honey. She wasn't at all like that last one, you know, the guy with the long earlobes who was always frowning? This woman had . . ." She twirls, her long skirt flaring. "Pizzazz."

I lean back against the counter. "Mom."

"This could change everything for us," she says. "You'll see."

I glance at the stack of delinquent bills wedged behind the sugar jar on the counter and rub my neck. Getting mad is pointless. About a year ago I yelled at her to grow up. But it changed exactly nothing. Des used to say that our mom was an innocent, an artist born in a time when she couldn't be herself, which was sort of okay when we were managing to scrape by, but after Des died and the funeral bills piled up, we got so far in the hole that her on-again, off-again work schedule didn't cut it.

The screen door creaks open.

"Oh, there she is," Mom says, clasping her hands together. "And pretty as a rose in that pink dress. Valentine, you could be a painting."

"Thanks, Ruth." Tiny beams. She's always loved my mom. Everyone loves my mom.

"You should paint her, August, exactly like this, something to commemorate your childhoods together before going off to college," Mom says, pulling open a grocery bag.

I internally wince.

"You're just so talented," she continues. "And it's been much too long since you've picked up a brush. Your dad said the same thing when I spoke to him last week."

My dad—the one member of this family (if you can call him that) who actually has money but is absolutely no help. When I was younger, I overheard Mom and Des stressing about bills in the kitchen, and I ran for the phone thinking he'd want to know we were struggling and that I'd ask him to pitch in, to which he told me to put my mom on and then didn't call back for four months. I haven't asked him for a single thing since. Which seems to work for him because he only calls twice a year, my birthday and Christmas, asks how I'm doing in school, and then makes some excuse to go. And since it's neither of those holidays, I can't imagine why she was talking to him. But I'm also not going to ask.

"Drop it, Mom," I say with a controlled tone.

"Even just a quick sketch. Something to get those creative juices going."

I look out the window, trying to ignore the tightness in my chest, afraid that if I show her how much her comments bother me, it'll be a backhanded admission that I need art. That she'll somehow see that it keeps cropping up in my thoughts even though I've sworn off it. That two times this week my brain betrayed me with a sketch. The realization unsettles me; it's never happened consistently like this before.

When I don't respond, my mom looks up from her groceries.

Thankfully Tiny jumps in. "You know me—I can barely sit still for five minutes. I'd never make it through a portrait."

"Mom, Tiny and I are going out. Call Mr. Gibbons," I say, leaving no space for her to continue.

"They're redoing their porch, right?" Tiny says because our town is *that* kind of small. "My mom said the Hershwicks are building a sunroom, too. They might have some painting work if you're looking."

I glance at Tiny, grateful for the tip and the change of subject.

"Sunrooms are the best rooms," Mom says. "They heal the soul. How I'd love to have a sunroom to paint in."

"*Mom*," I say again.

She smiles a tired smile. "I'll call, honey. Stop worrying." Then she sets herself to unpacking the groceries and humming, probably thinking about the sunroom we'll never have.

8
VALENTINE

Ella's house is giant. Not in the way August thinks mine is—a remodeled middle-class home with an open floor plan and updated appliances—hers is a legit mansion. The kind of place where you gulp when you see it and worry about breaking something even when you're sitting still on the couch.

We share a wide-eyed glance as we walk down the long driveway made of stone squares, outlined by a lattice of grass. I bet someone's sole employment is making sure the thin lines of driveway grass are trimmed to perfection, not to mention the potted trees that are shaped like bubbles and have more precise haircuts than I do.

August and I walk around the looped end of the driveway to the front door, which is currently cracked open. We slip inside and follow the sound of voices and music to an enormous circular living room with teens sprawled on oversized couches. The far wall is made entirely of glass, overlooking the back deck and giant pool.

"Damn," is all he says, and I couldn't agree more. Neither of us has ever been in a house like this; we don't even know anyone who knows anyone who has a house like this. It's packed with Ella's friends, all busy socializing or eating.

"Pretty nice, huh?" Justin says, walking up behind us, taking a swig out of a glass soda bottle.

"Just about the size of my family's guesthouse, maybe a *little* smaller," I say.

He laughs at my absurd joke. "In that case, remind me to hit you up for our next party."

"Done. Just call my assistant." I've always found this type of thing easy, sliding into conversations and making people feel at ease.

Justin smiles. "Come on. I'll give you guys a quick tour."

I don't need to look at August to know what he's going to say next.

"Bathroom?" August asks, and there is an almost indiscernible tightness in his voice, something no one but me would notice. Justin, Kyle. Kyle, Justin. We haven't discussed it, but we both know the other knows, the same way I imagine twins have an instinct when the other is in trouble.

Justin points to two different restroom options.

"Thanks, man," August says and he's off, shoulders back and head high with another paint-splattered T-shirt on, once again transformed into Holden.

"Good," Justin says, assessing me as August disappears around a corner. "You wore your bathing suit." He looks briefly at my chest and then smiles like he approves.

I cock an eyebrow at him. "Too bad you didn't wear your tact."

For a second his eyes widen. Then he laughs. "You're funny."

"I know." *And you're gross*, I think.

9
AUGUST

The noise of socializing boosts my confidence with its familiarity—different town, different social strata, same party. I walk through the open glass doors onto the deck, where Ella, Amber, and Leah sunbathe on lawn chairs, surrounded by their friends. I swipe a bottle of water from a cooler and pick a spot on the opposite side of the pool, slipping on my sunglasses and plopping down in a chair.

Ella notices but deliberately ignores me. Even though the summer just started, she's already tan, tanner than me, and I'm outside every day. I sip my water, taking note of the guy floating in a giant seahorse and the girl making a show of flipping off the diving board. And I wait.

It only takes a handful of minutes before Justin appears poolside and launches himself smack onto the occupied seahorse, sinking the dude floating in it. Where there's a pool and a bunch of people trying to look cool, competition is inevitable—it's basically a golden rule, and one that helps me do my job.

The seahorse guy rights himself in the water, laughing and diving onto Justin's head. And they wrestle, catching the attention of everyone nearby. But pool fights are hard to sustain, and so after a minute, they catch their breath and pick another way to spar.

"Game time!" Justin declares over the music. He climbs out of the pool, wiping his face on the towel at the end of Ella's lawn chair. "Should we bump it up a notch?"

"Bump. It. Up," Amber replies, egging him on and lifting her palms in the air.

I spot Tiny chatting up a group at the other end of the deck.

"Asshole," Justin declares, which earns him laughs. "A friendly game of Asshole, but in the water."

I glance at Ella, who used that word to describe me only yesterday, but she stares at Justin, her eyes not wandering in my direction.

"Group race. Winner gets crowned King," Justin continues. "The runner-up is Duke. And the loser is the *Asshole*. Until the next race in about . . . I don't know, an hour, the King is boss—he can demand service or dish out shots. The Duke is next in command, and so on down the line. The Asshole is everyone's bitch."

So basically, high school.

"I'm in," the seahorse guy says, pushing himself out of the water.

I toss my sunglasses onto the lawn chair, fully planning on participating. Like I said, competition is opportunity. I make eye contact with Tiny, but she shakes her head. While she loves the water, she's a self-declared floater, not a racer. Same goes for running. If she's running, I would too because something apocalyptic is happening.

"Babe?" Justin says to Ella, who's sipping lemonade and looks content where she is.

I stand, pulling off my T-shirt and kicking off my shoes. "I'm in," I reply before Ella can.

"Yeah, man," Justin laughs. "Public enemy's stepping up."

Now Ella does look at me. I join the group poolside, where there are already about ten people lining up for the swim race.

Amber throws her phone down on her chair and gives a little shrug, shaking out her bob and readjusting her red bikini. "I'm in, too." She joins the line, picking a spot between me and seahorse guy.

She eyes me with interest. "You showed," she says like she's impressed.

"Wouldn't have missed it." I gesture at Ella, who's now headed right for us. "Scorpio is basically my best friend in this town."

Amber smirks. "You know her name is—" she starts.

"My name is none of his business," Ella says, pulling her long hair into a messy bun and squeezing in on the other side of Amber.

"*None of his business* might be your birth name, Scorpio, but it doesn't roll off the tongue the same way," I reply.

Amber laughs, and Ella ignores me.

"Okay, let's do this," Justin says loudly. "We'll all swim to the far side of the pool and back. First one on the deck is the winner. Leah, can you count us off?"

Leah puts down her phone and holds three fingers in the air, her box braids loose and long down her back. "Everyone, get ready."

Ella glances my direction, and her look is a challenge, one that says she's going to eviscerate me.

But I know what she thinks I don't—that she, Amber, and Leah have been on the swim team for four years. However, I also know me, and even though I only have the murky water in the dock and not some fancy pool, I've spent all the summers of my life swimming in it.

"Three. Two. One. Go!" Leah says from her lawn chair, and I dive.

The water cancels out the music and the hooting crowd, blanketing everything in a familiar whoosh. And I'm off, shoulders pushing against the water and eyes open. I reach the other side in no time, but with my momentum, my turn is clumsy. Ella's, however, is graceful. We're neck and neck as we kick off the wall. And as we approach the finish line, I steal a look at her. She's a stroke behind, but we're ahead of the pack— first and second of the group.

I pause, slowing my pace and strategically letting her take the lead. But instead of popping out of the water as the victorious Queen ready to smite the commoners with shots of Malibu, she touches the wall and stops, staring at me underwater. For a second, I'm confused.

Take your victory.

Still underwater, I motion at the deck above us. But my friendly gesture is met with annoyance, and just like in the coffee shop my plan goes to hell. Amber smacks the wall between us and lifts herself out of the pool, leaving us both without a title, frowning at each other underwater.

Now it's Ella who points to the surface above our heads, eyes narrowed, clearly aware I was letting her win and flat-out refusing to accept the olive branch. Not that it matters at this point, considering half the group is already out of the pool. She points again more aggressively. And while I understand her, I'm not getting out now to take some middling position that no one will notice. I can't, really. So I shake my head.

She looks like she wants to scream, which is kind of adorable underwater with her cheeks puffed out. She holds up both hands as if to say, *What the hell is your problem?* And I'm wondering the same thing— how is it that every time I orchestrate a plan, she does something I don't expect? I can already hear Tiny tearing me a new one.

I push myself down to the floor of the pool and into a seated position, trying to tell her it's no use and to give up. But she pushes down with me and stamps her foot against the bottom. And next thing I know she's sitting on the floor of the pool, too, giving me the finger with both hands. We stare at each other. But our standoff is interrupted by lack of air.

She's already struggling, and I know I don't have more than five seconds left. She fights, but it's no use. We both push forcefully out of the water, gasping.

"And we have our Asshole!" Leah exclaims. "Or two Assholes?" she says when neither of us makes a move to jump onto the deck. "I feel like that fail is definitely a tie. You two were practically having a conference down there."

Everyone around us hollers and laughs. And with a withering look, Ella pushes herself out of the pool, stomping back to her chair, where Justin already sits, drinking her lemonade. He grabs her and pulls her down, giving her a big kiss.

"There she is . . . my favorite loveable Asshole," Justin says.

Amber snorts. "Now there's a Valentine's Day card."

And so, the public shaming commences. Amber (the Queen) makes me bring her and Leah fresh towels and snacks and has me reapply her suntan lotion (twice), bowing to her and giving her a compliment every time I approach. And Justin (the Duke) makes me his beer bitch and has me replenish all his games of flip cup while wearing a bra on my head. But as the hour winds down, just as I suspected, everyone knows who I am. And I'm in. An accepted part of the group. Accepted by everyone except the one person who matters, that is.

"Okay, Assholes!" Amber exclaims, looking happily at me and Ella. "Time to document your suckage!"

I glance at Ella, who sports boxer briefs around her forehead, but she doesn't meet my eyes. Tiny, however, is looking from me to Ella and back again from across the deck.

Amber waves Ella and me to her lawn chair where she's been holding court, and as I walk up, Ella turns away from me, body language that suggests I'm even worse off than I was after the coffee incident, which I honestly didn't think was possible.

"For my last decree," Amber announces, looking at us like we're her favorite snack, "I'm going to take a picture of you two beauties, and you're going to post it to your IG accounts, where you *cannot* delete it for at least twenty-four hours."

Ella looks like she's going to murder Amber or me or both of us.

"I don't have one," I say.

Tiny subtly clocks our conversation from her spot near the snack table.

"Really?" Amber says, surprised. "Okay, then post on whatever social account you have."

"I don't have any," I say and wait for her reaction. This happens on every case.

Amber's eyes nearly detach from her head. "*What?* Like, none? Nada? Nothing?"

"Nothing," I confirm.

Leah arches an eyebrow like I just became more interesting in her estimation. "I don't know if I think that's cool or seriously questionable."

"Maybe another punishment?" I suggest and Ella looks hopeful.

"Mmmm, no can do. A picture *needs* to happen," Amber says, assessing us. After a long pause, her eyes light up. "Wait . . ."

She grabs her purse and yanks out bright-red lip gloss. She motions for me to bend down. "Since you're not posting, you need something . . . extra." She doesn't get one smear in before I know exactly what's happening. Not only will I appear on Ella's IG with a bra on my head, but I'll also have a sparkly penis on my forehead.

"Now get together," Amber says, admiring her handiwork and positioning her phone.

Ella crosses her arms, and I do the only thing I can—I smile.

Leah checks her watch, just as Amber snaps her first couple of pictures, shooting Ella a sympathetic look. "Hour's up, Amber."

Amber huffs like Leah's ruining it. "Fine. But I better see that picture up pronto, El," she says and then shouts, "Rematch!"

Justin echoes Amber, and Ella looks relieved that our servitude is finally over. She doesn't make a move to reenter the competition, and neither do I.

As people line up by the pool, I pull the bra off my head and offer it to Ella. "Yours?"

She shakes her head, lips pursed, and turns away.

I swipe a napkin from Amber's snack spread and wipe my forehead. "Might as well laugh it off, Scorpio. We all fall from grace once in a while."

She doesn't look at me.

"And well, it's your own fault," I add, because I'm once again in the undesirable position of having to needle her to get a response.

Her head whips in my direction. "*My* fault? This is one thousand percent *your* fault. I certainly didn't need you to let me win."

I inadvertently smile, because as angry as she is, she also looks ridiculous.

"*What?*" she seethes.

Leah starts her countdown and fifteen people jump in the pool.

"Nothing," I say innocently and cough, pointing upward to the boxer briefs she sports like a crown.

Her eyes double in size and she yanks them off. "At least I don't look like I got into a fight with red glitter."

I wipe my hand on my head, but barely anything comes off.

"It's color stay," she says, and the corners of her mouth tilt up ever so slightly.

"Are you telling me I still have balls on my forehead?"

"Big ones," she says and suppresses a laugh.

"If I knew all it took to get you to smile was draw balls on my face, I'd have done it an hour ago."

She makes her best effort to look annoyed, but it's obvious her heart isn't in it. "I *cannot believe* you did that to us." She sighs, the fight draining out of her. "I could have been lounging with lemonade service; meanwhile I spent half an hour blowing up a giant bunny float and calling Amber 'your highness.'"

"Yeah, but just think about the possible memes they'll make of us," I say.

Her mouth opens. "I will kill you for real."

We stand there for a couple of seconds, caught in this cycle of fighting and joking, but never actually getting to friendly.

Justin emerges from the water, this time as King. He pumps his fist in the air.

"I'm surprised you didn't race again," I say, trying to keep her engaged a little longer. "That could be you right now."

"I'm pretty good with never playing that game again." She shakes her head. "Where did you learn to swim like that anyway?"

And before I can even consider it, I say, "It was the only place I could stand to be after my sister—" The instant the words leave my mouth, I look away, shocked and embarrassed. Damn Tiny and that Des talk. Damn my brain for betraying me with the truth.

"I'm sorry," she says, clearly understanding.

I wipe at my forehead again. "Bathroom?" I say even though I already know where it is.

But as I pass her, she puts out her hand and says, "Ella. My name's Ella."

I stop, taking her hand. "Holden."

"Wow . . . Holden . . . you have those parents, huh?" she says, amused.

Even though my name isn't actually Holden, I relate in every way. *August? Really?* "You have no idea."

"Actually, I do. My middle name is Gertrude."

"Oof," I say. "But at least it's your middle name."

"I mean, yeah, but still—high school doesn't care."

"Truer words were never spoken," I say, and this time when we make eye contact, the animosity between us is gone.

But so is the conversation. Because a soaking-wet Justin picks up Ella and twirls her in the air. "Babe, you're dating the Kiiiiing!" he says, and she laughs.

Kyle twirled Des in the backyard, giving her a big kiss, both of them dripping salt water after beating their friends in a race out to the buoy.

Tiny sighed. "I can't wait to be kissed like that."

"Gross," I countered.

Tiny scooped salsa onto her chip where we sat at the picnic table, both of us having lost the past three races (badly). "But look at them. They're in love."

"Awesome conversation about my sister, but—"

"Did you see us, little brother? Absolute crushing win," Des said, ruffling my wet hair with her hand before she shoved a sour-cream-and-onion chip in her mouth.

"I mean, it was hard not to see, the way you two shouted 'Champions!' and did ballet moves on the dock," I said, doing my best impression of her.

It earned me a laugh from Kyle. "This kid is cool. You never told me your little brother was so funny."

"Lies. I tell everyone," she said and gave me a big kiss on the cheek, which instantly killed any cool points I might have earned.

10
VALENTINE

The plastic supermarket basket August carries is teeming with candy and chips, but even so I cram in a box of mint cookies. My parents went to some black-tie event in Boston and left us take-out money, more than enough to get pizza and then drain our local grocer of its sweets. They'll likely gripe about it later when they come home to find us passed out on the couch in a sea of candy wrappers, but I'll have no regrets.

"Entire bag of tiny Kit Kats or two jumbo?" I ask.

August and I share a look, and in unison we both say, "Bag."

"Now all we have to do is make the momentous decision of ice cream flavor, and we should be good to go," I say, and for some reason I'm struck with a pang of nostalgia. "Man, I'm going to miss the candy shopping here."

August laughs. "How can you miss something we're currently doing?"

"I mean when we go to California," I say.

He shrugs.

"What? You're not?"

"Not really."

For some reason his reply irks me. "How, though? This town is where we grew up. Where we learned to swim and started all our businesses. Had our movie nights." Suddenly, I'm uncomfortable, not even sure where that came from or why I felt the need to say it so adamantly.

He gives me a questioning look. "I know. And you'll have summers here."

My stomach drops fast. "*Me?* As in you won't be coming home for summer?"

He shrugs. Again. "Not sure."

My eyes widen. "I'm the one who said I couldn't wait to leave." I point to my chest as though, somehow, I have dibs on the sentiment.

"Right. And I agree with you."

I look at the candy, trying to reign in the freak-out that's threatening to come. How could he just trash our entire childhoods like that? But when I turn back to August, he's not looking at me. He's staring down the aisle. And when I see who he's staring at, I freeze.

There in the chip section is Kyle, *Des's Kyle*, who has been away at college, who hasn't come home for summers, who for all we knew (and hoped) dropped off the face of the planet. And is now right here, picking out a bag of chips as though he had any right.

I touch August's arm, as if to say, *Let's just go.* He doesn't brush me off, but he also doesn't respond. Then Kyle sees us. And for what feels like the most awful eternity none of us moves. My heart thumps in my ears, and I'm consumed with the knowledge that I can't fix this.

Anger flashes across August's face, and yet we all remain in the same uncertain posture, like we're mannequins in a store window fighting to come to life.

All of a sudden Kyle snaps out of it, his look of shock transforming into the self-assured posturing we used to admire before we knew better. "If it isn't little Mariani in the flesh," he says with a tone that's way too familiar.

Hearing his voice say August's name only further solidifies the awfulness of the moment, and I consider regaling the grocery store with profanity that would make small children's ears fall off. But no insult hurts enough. Instead, I settle on a lame and vague, "How about we don't," giving Kyle a back-off glare.

For a second Kyle looks like I slapped him. But he brushes it off with a shrug and an uneasy laugh. "I see your girlfriend's still talking for you," he says, something he used to playfully tease us about years ago.

But Kyle's delivery is awkward, and August's expression edges past angry, transforming his bad joke into a perceived insult. Kyle sighs and turns, breaking eye contact and disappearing around the corner.

My breath escapes in an audible whoosh.

But August remains uncomfortably still. He's got that controlled angry look that makes me think if he moves at all he might charge after that douche like a raging bull.

"August?" I say, unsure.

His lips form a hard line, but he doesn't look at me.

"August?" I try again, and when he still doesn't respond, I begin to doubt myself. A zing of fear shoots through me that maybe he thinks I made it worse. "Wait . . . you're not mad at *me*, are you?"

"It's fine," he lies.

"You know I was only trying to protect you, right?" But my words don't sound supportive the way I intend; they sound cheap.

"I definitely don't need you to protect me."

His tone is accusatory, and I get my back up. "And what's so bad about protecting my best friend?"

"Tiny," he says, and the annoyance in his voice sends me into full-on defense mode.

"You weren't saying anything," I say quietly. "What was I supposed to do?"

He looks up at the ceiling, taking a breath. "I'm not going to fight with you in the middle of the grocery store." He holds out the basket of junk food. "Take it."

I shake my head. "Grocery store or not, you never want to talk about this. Ever. I'm your best friend and I have no idea what's going on with you."

"You're right. I don't want to talk to you about this, because you have no respect for boundaries." His frustration tumbles out fast and harsh. "Not everything is about you." He puts the basket on the floor and walks away.

I pull in my arms as though the gesture could protect me from the sting.

He keeps walking, and I don't try to stop him.

11
AUGUST

I take the long way home, walking along the beach and kicking sand as I go. I press the heels of my hands into my eyes, but it accomplishes nothing.

Kyle. Is. In. My. Effing. Town. Any moment I could turn a corner and find him wearing his cocky smirk on his stupid face—one that shows no obvious remorse.

My fists clench as the image of him standing in the supermarket aisle quickly morphs into the image of him standing next to the caution tape two years ago, cop car lights flashing across his face, my sister already dead. I glance over my shoulder, as if Kyle might have followed me to the beach. But everything is quiet. If Tiny drove past, I didn't see her. I also wasn't looking.

The calm water laps at the shore as I kick off my shoes. I pull my shirt over my head and take my wallet and phone out of my pocket, chucking them into the sand. I dive in, the cold water pricking my skin and shortening my breath. The rhythm of the ocean grabs me, pulling me along with it.

I swim. And I swim, and I swim, until my eyes burn from salt and my shoulders feel like jelly. But even here, in the one place my mind has always quieted—I spiral.

I'm not doing this with you, I think, adamant in my position, even though I'm not sure if "you" is referring to my thoughts, Kyle, or the drawing that's formed on the dark water in front of me.

12
VALENTINE

Rom-coms make everything better, I tell myself, feet up on the coffee table. But even drowning in ice cream and watching *Bridesmaids* isn't erasing the edgy feeling. This is why conflict is the worst—it nags at you until you resolve it.

My phone buzzes on the couch next to me, and I dig it out from a pile of wrappers.

Mr. Becker

> I think we need to talk about why your colleague is pictured on my daughter's social media account with genitals on his forehead. Is this the kind of thing I'm paying you for?

I sit up so fast that I have to grab the bowl of popcorn to keep it from dumping onto the floor. Crap. My instinct is to tell him that first of all he's *not* paying us, not unless we succeed, so maybe he should just chill. But I know that's my frustration talking.

Me

It was the unfortunate consequence of a game that August lost. While I understand that the picture might have been shocking, I can promise you that this is a good thing. It means he's bonding with your daughter.

Plus, wasn't he ever young? Although now that I consider it, maybe he's always been cranky and middle aged. I tap my fingers as I wait for his reply. But three minutes pass in silence. And I have no idea if I've quelled his worry or if he's still miffed.

The front door closes and my parents' hushed voices fill the hall, only it's not their usual chatter. They talk quickly and over each other, and their intense-sounding conversation stops abruptly when they enter the living room. I turn to look at them, trying to figure out if they're fighting. Mom smiles, but Dad's mouth is tight. First, they're all over each other, and now this? Their weirdness adds to my unsettled feeling.

"Valentine," Mom says, a little too chipper, confirming my fighting suspicion. "Where's August?"

"Not here." As my response leaves my mouth, I regret how testy it sounds.

Mom gives me an evaluating look. "You okay, love? Did you two have a fight?"

I shake my head.

"No, you're not okay, or no, you didn't have a fight?" she clarifies.

I stand, now agitated that my answer made no sense, but also not wanting to explain. "Don't worry about it."

"Valentine, stop snipping at your mother," Dad says, his expression serious.

"I'm not," I reply, which proves his snippy point. *Ugh. Just stop talking, Valentine.* I head for the back door. "I'm going to get some fresh air."

I grab the handle and glance at my parents to see if they're going to object. But they wear matching concerned expressions, which for some reason makes the whole thing worse. "What?" I say, physically incapable of shutting up. "You were fighting, too. You don't see me looking at you like that."

Mom frowns. "Maybe you should go get that air." Her tone is controlled and extra mom-like. "It seems you're intent on spreading your bad mood, and I, for one, am not taking the bait."

Great. Just great. I pull the door open and step onto the porch barefoot. It snaps closed behind me, not quite a slam but not not a slam, either.

I let out an exasperated groan and shake my hands in the air. Why couldn't I just say hi to them and keep shoving chocolate in my face like a normal person?

"You good?" a voice says, and I jump.

I scan the yard. And there, silhouetted against the lights from his house, is Bentley. But even in the dimness I can tell he's freshly showered and dressed to go out.

I shrug, not remotely in the mood.

He grins. "I mean, I'm flattered that you stole my silent routine, but—"

"Don't you ever get tired of the fake charm act?" I say, ready to torch everything. "'Cause for me, it's getting really old."

He holds up his hands in surrender. But instead of snapping back, he says, "Don't worry. Whatever it is, it'll pass. Always does." Then he walks toward his driveway and gets in his old pickup truck.

I stare after him, feeling worse than I did a minute ago. Not only am I a walking tornado of grump, but Bentley Cavendish of all people was more mature than me. This blows.

13

AUGUST

Water drips off my hair and rolls down my chest as I plod across the sand, breath labored and neck bent, too tired to think.

I scoop up my things, ready to plod home and collapse in my bed, before my phone lights up and I change my mind, sitting down in the sand instead. It's a text from a Massachusetts number, and there is only one person that could be.

Ella
Hey

I wipe my damp hands on my dry shirt.

Me
Hey yourself

It only takes a second for her to text back.

Ella

Not going to ask who this is? I could be some creep.

Me

Probably are. But I know who this is. You're the only person I've given my number to.

Ella

Wow. Not sure if I'm flattered or if you're a giant nerd. Didn't you meet like fifty people today?

A smile creeps onto my face.

Me

Both? But the bigger question is, why do you like nerds so much?

I mean it as banter, but as always with her, I'm not sure if it lands. With most cases, all it takes is showing a little interest in the person's life to get them to open up. People want to be noticed, as Tiny always says. But with Ella, that absolutely wouldn't work. In fact the only thing that does seem to work is when I joke and instigate her the way I do Valentine.

Ella

Haha. I wouldn't be so sure I do.

Me

Proof: you're texting me.

Ella

> Nah. That just means I've decided not to hate you. You've merely been promoted to a mild dislike.

I laugh and the sound surprises me. I didn't think I could laugh right now.

Me

> I'll take it.

I wait a beat, but she doesn't reply, and maybe it's the emotional exhaustion combined with the swim or simply the dark cover of the beach that has me type:

Me

> Random question . . . but

> Do you ever freeze? Like from shock or indecision or anything?

Ella

> Nope. I'm a Leo.

Me

> Strong logic.

Ella

> Laugh it up, but it's true. You're a Gemini and when something big or meaningful happens, the two sides of you argue about how to respond. Hence the freeze.

I pause, not because I think my reaction in the grocery store has anything to do with astrology but because it's actually not a bad explanation for what happened with Kyle. Although why I'm talking to her about my personal life instead of my made-up Holden life is a mystery. I'm just going to chalk it up to it being a strange day.

She starts typing, stops, and starts again.

Ella

Anyway I'm not texting for me. Amber wants me to invite you to her party tomorrow.

This really isn't my day.

I stare at my phone, my fingers hovering above the keys. If I respond affirmatively, she'll think I like Amber. And if I reject the idea, Amber might try to oust me from any future invite I receive.

Second rule of engagement: Don't flirt with the subject's friends.

Me

Let me get back to you.

14
VALENTINE

Pastries don't fix the world, but on the morning after a bad day, warm chocolate goes a long way toward smoothing the rough edges. I sit on the dock in my and August's "office," absent-mindedly chewing and considering how I'm going to patch this up with him, when I hear his steps on the wood behind me.

He sits down on the dock next to me with his Snoopy mug of black coffee, without saying a word. A couple seconds pass with us staring at the water. It's not that August and I have some sparkly relationship that's devoid of fighting—we've gone through years when we've bickered constantly—it's just that this feels different. Des. Kyle. All the untouchable topics and things we haven't said.

"About yesterday . . ." I start, getting myself geared up to hash this out. "I know—"

"I was an ass," he says, and I look at him. "I shouldn't have walked off on you like that." He rubs the back of his neck.

"No, you shouldn't have."

"Agreed."

"Right," I say, and my words putter to a stop, my argument whizzing out of me. "You know, this is just like you. Deflate all my carefully cultivated insults with three sentences. How am I supposed to vilify you now?"

He leans his shoulder into mine, and in an irresistibly sincere voice he says, "Think you can forgive me, Tiny?"

I exhale. "Do I have a choice?"

"Depends. How good were those insults you were working on?"

"Like, choke-on-your-coffee good."

"Well, then maybe you should let them fly."

I squint at the water, considering. "Nah. I'll save them for the next round."

He laughs. And just like that, we both let it go.

"Ella texted me," he says, sipping his coffee.

I perk up. "Wait, really? What did she say? Good? Bad? Had to be good or she wouldn't have texted, right?"

He hands me his phone, and I smile as I read through their banter. That is, until I get to August asking her if she ever freezes. My head shoots up. August is being real with a girl he doesn't know about his heavily guarded emotions? He's barely even real with me about them.

"Keep reading," he says as though he knows what I'm thinking.

I give him a questioning look but return to the phone. And then I see it—Amber.

"I swear this Star-Crossed Lovers move has some bad luck," I say and run through what I know about Amber, relaying the highlights. "Okay, Amber. Bossy, leader of Ella's friend group, vicious when she wants to be, adored, broke up with her boyfriend Derek a couple of months ago."

"He's still in her photos," August says. "And he was at Ella's party."

I nod approvingly; August doesn't make a show of it, but he notices every detail. "True. Which means they've moved on to friends, leaving her single and available. She's like a shark, that one. 'Sharky' actually wouldn't be a bad nickname for her."

August takes his phone back and types into his chat with Ella: *Cool if I bring my cousin?*

He looks at me for approval, and when I nod, he presses send. And even though it's a little gesture, it makes me feel good. He waited for me to make this decision. We're in this together.

I hand him my phone, open to Ella's dad's message. "Also, this."

He reads it and looks up. "Quick call?" he suggests, even though I know he doesn't like talking to parents or friends, hence the fact that they always communicate with me.

"Yeah, that's what I was thinking. We just reassure him and that's that."

"Agreed," he says, and I press call.

But as I do, August's phone dings and he holds it up. It's Ella telling him that the party isn't in a backyard or on some beach. It's on a boat. *In an hour.* And if we're late, it'll leave without us. In unison we jump up, August sloshing his coffee.

"Went to voicemail," I say and press end. "Meet you by the Jeep in twenty minutes?"

"Yup," he says, and we both head toward our houses. But as I step onto my porch, I spot Bentley through his kitchen window and hesitate, remembering how I bit his head off.

Quick detour, I tell myself and jog over to his house. I knock three times on the screen door.

"Come in!" he yells, and I do.

The door opens into his living room, which is scattered with toys belonging to his seven-year-old twin brother and sister. The blue couches are faded, and the carpet is a little frayed but clean. I make my way into the kitchen, only to find Bentley wearing an apron and cooking a big frying pan of cheesy eggs.

His eyes double in size when he sees me. "Valentine? What are you . . . I mean . . . hey."

"Hey," I say, now feeling flustered that he's flustered, and possibly like I've intruded. "I just—"

But before I can get a word out, the twins run in, smacking each other with long cardboard tubes.

"Huuungry," his little brother, Trevor, says.

"Double hungry," Maisie agrees.

I stare at the three of them. Bentley cooks? I know his mom works a lot, that her car is rarely in the driveway, but I just never thought of him as the apron-wearing, babysitting type. It's about as far from his cultivated cool persona as you can get.

"I came to apologize for barking at you yesterday," I say.

He shrugs. "We all have bad days. Don't worry about it."

Because he's so decent about it, and because I'm weirdly intrigued by his domesticity, I add, "Maybe I can make it up to you. Take you to lunch?"

For a long second, he just stands there, spatula in hand, looking startled. Then the corners of his mouth lift. "Like a date?"

The twins stop hitting each other to look at me.

"Well . . ." My cheeks heat. "Maybe. Yeah."

Bentley's face lights up, but before he can respond Trevor hits him with a cardboard tube.

And the twins chant, "Bentley has a *day-ate*," in unison.

"Anyway, see ya," I say, backing up toward the door. "Also, you might want to flip those eggs."

Bentley turns toward the stove, where his eggs are browning on the pan, and jumps into action. I show myself out, and as I run through my yard, it occurs to me that in some bizarre twist of fate I asked Bentley out. *Me*. And Bentley of all people. Today is all kinds of upside down.

15
AUGUST

I drive quickly down Main Street in Ella's town, which isn't quick at all considering the speed limit is twenty-five and I'm going twenty-seven. The ride has been mostly quiet since Tiny and I drove past the street where Des had her accident. I looked away, like I always do, and Tiny looked at me, an unspoken question on her lips. But (thankfully) instead of starting that conversation again, she leaned back in her seat. She's been staring at the ocean since, riding air waves out the window with her hand, and not noticing when I look at her. And considering the small smile on her face, I'm certain that whatever she's thinking about ceased to be me a good twenty minutes ago.

"You cool?" I ask.

"Huh?" she says and then distractedly, "Yeah, for sure."

Before I can comment, she sits up, her feet sliding off the dashboard.

"There," Tiny says, pointing at a sign for the harbor.

I make a fast left onto the gravel drive and loop around the small parking lot, snagging a spot in the back near a wall of cattails. We jump out—me in another paint-splattered T-shirt, shorts, boat shoes, and linen navy-blue blazer (also from Tiny's dad's wardrobe) and Tiny in a long cotton dress that hugs her middle and has a slit up one thigh. Both of our outfits are laid back but on point, carefully curated looks that seem effortless. And I'm reminded of that Shakespeare quote that basically sums up my life right now: *All the world's a stage, and all the men and women merely players.*

"Who even are these people?" Tiny says as we approach the giant yacht being loaded with teens.

"Not a clue," I reply. While we have a few solidly upper-middle-class kids in our town, they're not remotely at this level. But somehow, no matter where you are, money and popularity seem to go hand in hand. Or maybe it's just power and more power.

We step onto the dock, where a smiling Amber greets us in a sparkly gold dress.

"Impressive," I say, nodding toward the yacht.

"Isn't it?" Amber agrees. "My parents rent it every year for their anniversary. But it's an all-day rental, and they only use it during the evening. Soooo . . . waste not, want not."

We make our way onto the opulent boat, where I recognize almost everyone from the day before. Tiny and I walk around the deck, where small groups sunbathe and drink fancy lemonades.

"Interesting that he's here," Tiny whispers and I follow her gaze to Amber's ex, "or complicated. Or both?" Derek sits on a couch in a living room surrounded by windows with an Amber look-alike as they make sexy eyes at each other.

I groan. "Incestuous friend groups are like booby-trapped mazes."

"Tell me about it," Tiny says as Justin drops onto the couch next to Derek. "That situation is basically begging for me to investigate it." And she walks off, leaving me alone on the deck.

Justin looks up as Tiny approaches. And for a quick second his cocky smile is so much like Kyle's that I do a double take, anger pricking my skin and tightening my shoulders. So I look away, leaning up against the railing and staring out at the inlet. When I can't shake Kyle from my thoughts, I exhale one loud breath, like I could eject this feeling from my body and throw it into the water, leaving it there to float away.

The boat starts to move, and I figure I'll hang out here for a while, wait until people find their party stride so I can snag an opportunity to talk to Ella. But not ten seconds pass before gold fabric appears in my peripheral vision.

"I love the ocean," Amber says, leaning up against the railing, lemonade in hand. "But then again, I'm a water baby."

I turn toward her; she came right for me. "Water baby?"

She laughs. "Water sign. Water birth. Swim like a mermaid."

"Yeah, I saw that," I say, careful to keep my tone squarely in friend territory. "You crushed everyone in that race yesterday."

"Well, not *everyone*," she says, straw in mouth. "Justin beat me once. And then there was *you and Ella*."

I shrug noncommittally.

But she's got her popular-girl laser eyes homed in on my face, ready for action. "What was the deal with you two throwing the game anyway?"

I could say it was nothing, but that won't cut it. "Was just trying to be polite."

"Oh, really? *Polite*, huh?" she says. "Or maybe . . . you have a thing for her?"

A statement, not a question. I laugh even though it's not funny. "*Or I just dumped a cup of coffee on the girl and thought beating her at her own party would get me banned from every social event this summer*."

"Hmmm," she says, and my neck bristles in warning.

I give her a smile but no words.

She considers me for a moment. "See you around, Mr. Coffee," she says and saunters away. Even her exit is part of the show, another opportunity for people to watch and be impressed. And maybe I would be if I were actually Holden.

Amber joins Leah, and I do what I do best—wait and watch. The energy is high, the music loud; the party is in full swing.

Tiny chats up Derek and Justin in the windowed cabin, and I can tell by her body language that Justin annoys her—one of the many reasons she's happiest when I spearhead the acting. Not to mention the case last summer where she took the lead with a girl who had a surprise pet tarantula that kept getting loose when she would visit. Brutal.

Then there's Ella, who sits on a cushioned bench talking to seahorse guy. Their conversation doesn't last more than a handful of minutes before he points to the snack table.

And that's my cue.

I head toward them, measuring my pace so I arrive as he stands, leaving Ella solo.

"Hey," I say, taking the now-empty seat next to her.

"Enjoying Amber's party?" Ella asks, and I inwardly groan at her emphasis on *Amber*.

"Yeah, I mean, ocean and sun . . . what's not to like?"

"Well, you've been standing near the railing by yourself for like an hour."

"You've been watching me?" I ask with a winning smile.

"Why are you so impossible?"

"Why are you?" Again, I feel that strange twinge of heightened energy in our banter and chalk it up to the fact that she's just better at it than most of our cases.

She laughs. "Most people don't come to a party to stand by themselves."

"I'm not most people. And I don't mind being by myself. You'd be surprised what you learn about people from just watching."

"Not as much as you do by talking."

"Not so," I say, and she looks unconvinced. "For instance, that guy you were just talking to"—I scan the boat—"has a crush on that guy over there with the white sneakers."

She raises an eyebrow curiously. "And how do you know that?"

"Because he keeps circling him, talking to everyone in his periphery," I say.

"That's not exactly hard evidence."

"There's also his body language. No matter who he's talking to, he's always slightly turned toward the guy he's interested in. But you know him better than I do . . . am I wrong?"

She gives me a look like she's tempted to be contrary. "Not wrong."

I grin.

"Well, you don't have to look so happy about it."

"As happy as you did when you guessed my sign?" I counter.

"That's my *thing*. Signs are my thing," she says, and I feel some small amount of relief that she's finally telling me something about herself, a stage I usually get to within two minutes of an initial conversation, not two days.

"As in . . ."

"As in I write an astrology blog." Pride lifts her voice. "I wasn't guessing your sign. I was deducing it from your behavior." Then she adds with a little snark, "Not the same thing as the pensive-loner routine you have going."

I would laugh, but it's not funny—she makes me work for every inch.

"More like observing with an objective," I reply.

She glances at me, and when I don't offer any more information, she sighs and says, "Okay. I'll bite. What's the objective? *Why* do you observe?"

"I paint," I say, even though if I were telling the truth that verb would be past tense.

She looks down at my paint-splattered shirt, then back up at me. "Like paint, paint, or like you dabble so you can wear that shirt and feel cool?"

I laugh. "Been doing it since I could hold a brush. My mom's a painter." And once again I'm surprised by how I offer real information about my life. Maybe it was her dig at my shirt, a comment I, August, would have made if the situation were reversed. But whatever it is, the truth seems to land because she doesn't send another biting comment my way.

"Lucky. I've always wished I could paint. I've tried, believe me. But I'm terrible. Like, cringeworthy. Still, I used to fantasize about living in Paris and setting up an easel in the park like some old-fashioned movie." She laughs. "Silly, huh?"

I smile. "Not silly at all. It actually sounds kinda great." I pause. "You should try again. Everyone struggles in the beginning." And seeing an opportunity, I add, "I guarantee I could show you a few things that'd make you think you're not so bad."

She eyes me. "Is that an offer?"

"It is," I say, willing to risk being shot down, in favor of possibly creating an opening where we could be friends.

But in the worst possible timing Amber appears in front of us, blinding us with her reflective dress in the afternoon sun. "Ella and Holden . . . just the people I was looking for." She grabs us both by the hand.

We get to our feet and Amber pulls us toward the back of the boat, where everyone is dancing. Ella immediately veers toward Justin, who's already in the mix, leaving me with Amber. I could tell her I don't dance, but I doubt Amber would let it go. The (regrettable) path of least resistance is to comply and then slip away as soon as possible.

16
VALENTINE

Out of breath from dancing, I grab a water bottle from the refreshments table. I so badly want to laugh at August, who I know is hating being on the dance floor and is no match for Sharky's peppy twirls and seductive shimmies. It's earning him some strong side-eye from Derek, which I'm guessing is Amber's point?

Leah joins me, also grabbing water and dabbing her forehead with a cocktail napkin. She, too, notices Amber and August/Holden dancing, only she doesn't hold back her laughter.

"It's like she's trying to hypnotize him before she eats him," I say lightheartedly.

"Knowing Amber, that's probably accurate," Leah concurs and shakes her head. "Poor dude." Then she glances at Derek and the Amber look-alike, leading me to believe my earlier conclusion was correct.

She chugs her water and abandons it on the table, turning toward the dance floor.

I open my mouth to continue the conversation before she walks off. But I change course when I spot Justin and Ella making a move for the staircase leading to the lower deck—which Amber said was off limits.

I wait a beat and follow. I kick off my flip-flops at the top of the stairs to keep them from doing their telltale slapping noise. As I head down, I hear Justin's and Ella's muffled voices ahead of me, but I can't make out what they're saying. The staircase opens up into a round TV room with a huge flat screen on the wall and a bar. I walk quietly across the carpet to the far end of the room and peek around the mostly closed door into the hall beyond it.

There, about three doors down, Justin leans against a doorway to what I can only assume is a bedroom. His hands are intertwined with Ella's and he's smiling.

"No one's gonna miss us," he says.

"Amber will definitely miss us," she says with a laugh. "She practically threatened us not to mess with the bedrooms or her parents will revoke yacht privileges."

Justin rubs the back of her hand with his thumb and pulls her closer. "You really think she's going to check?"

"Um, have you met Amber?"

"So we'll remake the bed," he says and kisses her neck. "She'll never know."

"I don't know," Ella says, hesitant.

Justin stops kissing her and pulls back. "Why do I feel like I'm having to convince my girlfriend to hang out with me?"

"It's not that."

"It sounds exactly like that."

"I want to hang out with you—"

"Just not alone," he says, and his tone goes from seductive to frustrated. He lets go of her hands.

"Don't be stupid. We hang out alone all the time," Ella says, now fidgeting with her necklace.

"You mean when we're in your parents' house with their 'bedroom door open' policy?" he says backhandedly.

She touches his arm. "Justin, look—"

"Whatever. It's fine," he says dismissively like it's not fine, and pulls back. He steps past her, leaving Ella looking deflated. But I don't have time to analyze his grade-A dick behavior because if I don't move, he's going to catch me spying on them.

Running is out of the question. There's no getting back up those stairs undetected. So I do the only thing I can, which is step through the door into the hallway, almost colliding with him.

Justin startles.

I yelp, putting my hand over my heart. "You scared the crap out of me."

"Mia?" he says, confused.

"Sorry, I know we're not supposed to be down here, but I was looking for a bathroom?" I say. "Someone bombed the one upstairs."

Justin snorts. "Probably Derek. On purpose," he says in his nice-guy voice that shows no sign of the cold shoulder he was just giving Ella.

Manipulative jerk.

"Ella will show you where it is," he says, not bothering to look at her before he walks away.

I turn to Ella, whose face is crestfallen. "Everything okay?"

For a second, she doesn't answer.

"Ella?"

"Huh?" she says. "Yeah. Everything's fine."

17

AUGUST

"Saw Justin in action, and wow," Tiny says as she climbs into the passenger side of the Jeep, picking up the length of her dress and shutting the door with a thud. "Ella's parents were right."

I look at her expectantly as I start the engine and back out.

She kicks off her sandals, plunking her feet onto the dash. "Despite his charming public exterior, Justin's a manipulative twat in private—classic controlling behavior. No wonder he got Ella to change around her life for him. He's good. Like, really good."

And again, the first thing I think is *Kyle*.

I grip the steering wheel a little tighter as I turn out of the parking lot. But all I say is, "How so?"

"I watched him full-on pressure her to hook up with him, blame her when she said no, and then walk off like he was mad. And not in the clumsy pushy way that'd have her give him the finger, in the guilt-trippy 'you really hurt me' way. Then not ten minutes later in front of their friends he was pulling her onto his lap and whispering into her ear until she laughed. Basically playing the whole 'best boyfriend ever' routine while Sharky was griping about how lucky Ella is." She pauses to take a breath. "I mean, we've dealt with controlling boyfriends before.

But never this popular and not the kind that hides his behavior like a con artist."

"So we expose him."

"Right, but how?" Tiny shifts in her seat. "Let's say what I saw today was just a bitty piece of a larger problem, that he's done this to her in any number of ways. Do her friends really care if we expose the fact that he's manipulating her into giving up her dream school? Probably not. All we'd do is embarrass Ella and possibly push her farther into his arms."

I paused at Des's door on my way back from the bathroom, ready to knock. It was after eleven, but I knew she wouldn't mind. I'd been going to Des's room when I couldn't sleep for forever.

I paused, my hand gripping the handle, when I heard Kyle's voice.

"Just come for a little while. No one will miss you," Kyle said, and I could hear him smiling.

"I don't know." Des sounded hesitant.

"It'll be fun. I promise. Your mom won't even notice," he said, which was true. Since Dad left in a wake of fighting and tears, Mom disappeared into her room every night after dinner and didn't reappear until we were already at school.

"That's exactly why I have to stay," she said. "Mom's totally checked out. What if something happens and I'm not here?"

"You really think something's going to happen if you're gone for two hours?" he pressed.

"Kyle—" she started, her tone firm.

"Des," he said, cutting her off. "You're always taking care of everyone else. Let me take care of you for a change."

She didn't answer right away, and a tightness formed in my chest, my heart pressing against it in fast, anxious beats. And I panicked. I didn't want Des to leave, to be out there in the world where I couldn't get to her, and so I knocked, knowing my presence would kill the whole plan.

"Maybe we bait him?" Tiny suggests.

The Jeep rolls to a stop at a light, and I turn to her. "I'm listening."

"What do we know about selfish, controlling partners? That when they feel their control is slipping, they get agitated, breaking their calm," she says. "Exposing themselves for the jerks they really are."

"So you want to make Justin think he's losing control of Ella?" I say. "While logically I think it could work, there are a lot of uncertainties in that scenario."

"There always are," she replies confidently.

"And we'll need to be a heck of a lot closer to Ella to pull it off," I say.

"Not we . . . *you*," she says. "If I try to wiggle into that tight-knit group of girls to get Ella to trust me over them, I'm going to meet every level of best-friend territorial resistance. Amber's not the kind of queen bee who shares."

I give her a pointed look.

"Unless you can think of a better plan?"

I open and close my hands on the steering wheel, letting out a sigh. There is no better plan and she knows it. "Okay. I'm in."

"Good. Then it's time to call Ella's dad," she says and puts her phone on speaker. She presses dial and switches off the music in the Jeep.

This time Ella's dad picks up. "Hello," he says with the same commanding voice I remember from the interview.

"Mr. Becker," Tiny says in her always-upbeat cadence, one of the many reasons she takes the lead on talking to worried parents and friends. "It's Valentine and August. We've called to discuss your concern about the picture and to give you an update."

"Hold on," he says. It's not a question.

A good twenty seconds later he returns. "Go ahead."

"Well, first," Valentine says, "there's good news—we've been getting closer to your daughter. In fact, that picture you saw was a direct result of us being invited to her party."

"The invitation was never in question," he replies. "It was the method. However, my wife has directed me to let it go. So I will. With the condition that there will be absolutely no kissing."

I look at Tiny, who appears as taken aback as I am.

"Definitely no kissing from our side," Tiny confirms, making room for the small caveat that sometimes they kiss us, even though we never aim for that.

He clears his throat. "Good. I just want to be crystal clear that I'm not paying for crassness and I'm certainly not paying someone to paw my daughter."

"Of course not!" Tiny confirms. "This is about using friendship and trust to open Ella up to possibility. It's never about seduction. Ever."

"Just make sure you're on track to break them up before her college-acceptance deadline," he says like it's purely a business deal and not his daughter's future, and before Tiny can respond he adds, "Now I have to go; I have another call."

And he's gone.

Tiny presses end. "Wow. He's a charmer."

I coast down Ocean Avenue, following the slow pace of weekend traffic. "Authoritarian."

"Ya think? I wonder if he talks to everyone that way or only the people lucky enough to work for him."

I glance at Tiny. "It explains why Ella won't discuss her life with them."

"For real, though. All the better we took this case. They're never going to get through to her saying things like 'Daughter, I command you to use your sense and ignore your friends.'"

I grin at Tiny's impression of Ella's dad.

"But whatever you do, do not kiss Ella," she says.

I shake my head. "You know I'd never do that. The few times it's happened, they've kissed me. Not the other way around."

"Of course they do, you sexy beast. They get their fingers all tangled in your gorgeous locks and—"

I give her a warning look.

"Fine, spoil my fun. Just be sure not to let it happen."

"I'll pretend to faint if I have to," I say and Tiny laughs.

18
VALENTINE

My parents are at work, August is job hunting with his mom, and it's raining buckets. So I sit on my couch, flipping through magazines and periodically glancing at the water-streaked window, waiting for one of those three things to change.

My phone dings.

Bentley
You working?

Me
I wish.

Bentley
Bentley: Good. So you're free.

I hesitate.

Me
Maybe.

Bentley

As in . . . maybe we can have lunch?

I laugh.

Me

It hasn't even been 24 hrs and you're already trying to collect???

Bentley

Obviously.

I chew on my lavender fingernail, no longer caught up in the moment like I was yesterday, and slightly regretting offering lunch in the first place. But bailing now would be super crappy, and besides, this is actually decent timing. We don't have any parties or Ella events scheduled, and August isn't around to give me a hard time. He's never liked Bentley, which isn't shocking considering they're polar opposites. But I think the moment that solidified August's dislike was when he saw him talking to Kyle at Des's funeral. August hasn't so much as said hi to Bentley since.

Me

Where do you want to go?

Bentley

My house?

Me

LUNCH, Bentley. Not hooking up with you.

Bentley

Phew. I was worried you might want to bag me on our first date and I'm just not that kind of girl.

I shake my head, smiling.

Bentley
I'm on twin duty. Can't leave. But maybe I
can make you a grilled cheese?

My cheeks redden, as I realize there's a legitimate reason for him to
want to stay home.

Me
Oh. Right! Yeah.

Bentley
Yeah as in you're coming over?

Me
Yup. See you in a sec.

I make my way to the back door and look down at my white shorts
and pink tank top, surveying my options against the pounding rain. I
could take an umbrella, but they always feel difficult for short distances.
So I step onto the porch without one.

The air smells earthy and humid, a mixture of wet grass and brine
from the dock, and the rain thuds loudly against the porch roof. I inhale
deeply and make a run for it, my feet sliding in my flip-flops and my
arm up to protect my eyes.

I knock three times on Bentley's screen door, pressing myself against
his small faded blue house to stay under the overhang.

"Hey," he says, opening it and moving aside so I can rush in.

"Hey," I reply, rubbing my wet face with the backs of my wrists and
kicking off my sopping-wet flip-flops.

His smile is so big that I give him the side-eye and ask, "You cool?"

"Always," he replies, but he's still grinning like an idiot.

19
AUGUST

Mom's been in Vinnie's Pizza for a half hour, which means either Vinnie's hiring her or she'll come out jobless with a claim that they're kindred spirits or some crap.

I press my hands against the steering wheel and stare at the windshield blurred by heavy summer rain, the kind that suddenly dumps out of the clouds and then disappears just as fast. And I think about Tiny's plan, about exposing Justin by making him think he's lost control over Ella. There are a few ways it might work, but all of those involve trust—not an easily achievable milestone considering Ella only just stopped hating me.

I pick up my phone, selecting my thread with Ella.

Me

Question: have I graduated from mild dislike yet? I'm aiming for a solid neutral.

For a few seconds there's nothing. Then the chat bubble pops up.

Ella

Who aims for neutral?

Me

Neutral is best.

Ella

Loved is best. Neutral is neutral.

Me

Disagree. Neutral is the gateway to friendship.

Ella

So you're actually aiming for friendship, not neutral.

Me

Nope. Not sure you make the cut yet.

Ella

Riiiight. Which is why you offered to teach me to paint . . . because you're so undecided. Totally believe that one.

I laugh.

Me

Nah. I'd have offered that to anyone. A world full of bad painters is the stuff of nightmares.

Ella

Said no one ever.

Me

Imagine if all the sign designers, clothing designers, building designers etc were TERRIBLE artists???

Ella

Fine. You've achieved neutral.

Me

Because I made a good point?

Ella

Lack of stupidity is definitely a plus in those I consider neutral.

I stare at my phone. This girl is witty.

Me

Woohoo! See you at the coffee shop in an hour.

Ella

Wait . . . How did you know I was going to be there?

Your parents told me you work on your blog there most afternoons, and since there are no parties and the weekend is over . . .

Me

I didn't. I'm just going to be there.

Ella

Coffee shop is mine. I told you that you could have the park bench. Soooo

I consider typing a response, but my mom opens the passenger door.

"That Vinnie is such a nice man," she says as she slides into the seat, her hair curlier than usual because of the rain. "Did you know he has five kids? How wonderful it must be to have all those children running around the house."

My heart does a nosedive. "So you didn't get the job." I start the engine.

"All that laughter," she says, tracing the rain down the glass.

I squeeze the steering wheel and tighten my jaw as I pull onto the street, trying to will myself not to care that this is the fourth place we've tried with a hiring sign, easy pickings. How do you not get hired to serve pizza? Is that even possible?

"I should've had five children. Five's a good number. Don't you think?" she asks.

No. You couldn't support two, much less five. Hell, you can't even support one.

"And think about all the grandchildren," she says and sighs.

"Stop, Mom," I say, frustration seeping through my words as I turn onto our street. "Just admit you didn't get the job."

She looks at her hands folded in her lap and then out the window. With her enthusiasm zapped she looks fragile, like a china plate balancing precariously on the edge of a table. She's silent for a few seconds, her shoulders falling and her fingers worrying at her skirt. I already regret my tone.

I exhale. "Five kids, huh?" I say, giving her an apologetic look as I pull into our driveway. "Why not get wild and shoot for ten?"

Her smile reappears and for a second, she looks grateful I didn't make her admit her defeat out loud. "Ten! We could have our own baseball team!"

I laugh, not bothering to point out that we're the least likely family to have a baseball team ever. I park the car and turn off the engine. "Go ahead in without me. I'm heading over to Tiny's."

20
VALENTINE

Bentley's kitchen table is small and pockmarked, and my rain-soaked legs stick to a vinyl chair while he flips grilled cheese sandwiches at the stove. I run my finger across a table groove that's smudged with green, like it was drawn in with Magic Marker that couldn't be removed.

"Where are the twins?" I ask, not really sure what to talk about. Bentley and I haven't exchanged more than a handful of sentences at any given time since we were twelve.

"New board game. They've been playing it all morning," he says over his shoulder.

I stand, not for any reason other than it gives me something to do. I lean my hip against the counter near the stove. "Do you take care of them a lot?"

"Sometimes," he says. "Yeah."

"Where's your mom?"

"Work," he replies and breaks eye contact, not offering an explanation.

The conversation lulls and we both stare at the frying pan. It's weird—after all the effort he put into getting me over here, I thought he'd be the one driving the conversation. Maybe it's just awkward because we're in his house? Or the unthinkable . . . could Bentley actually be nervous?

"Where did you learn to cook?" I ask, trying again at the worst small talk of all time.

Bentley laughs. "If you think grilled cheese is cooking, then I totally know what I'm making you for our next date."

"Our next date, huh?"

He looks back at his spatula, his cheeks very slightly pink under his tanned skin. Only it's hard to tell if it's from standing in front of the hot stove or from embarrassment. "I learned to cook because of the twins. They were weird toddlers. You couldn't just give them apples and bananas. They only liked super flavorful stuff. Still do. They can scarf down Thai and spicy Mexican with the best of them."

He plates the grilled cheese and holds one in each hand. In an effort to help, I reach for the one in his left hand, but he offers me the one in his right, and we both apologize.

"Here." He tries again, and this time I take the correct one.

Before I can say thanks, Trevor and Maisie tear into the kitchen, yelling.

"Whoa. Whoa," Bentley says.

"Trevor took my game piece and *wiped his butt on it*," Maisie yells, giving Trevor a death glare.

"She totally cheated!" Trevor counters.

"Did not!" Maisie exclaims. "I was about to win, when he stole my horse and stuck it down his underwear right in his booty crack!"

"Okay. Got it," Bentley says. "Game over."

"What!" they both yell at once.

"Games are for fun. You two are at each other's throats like piranhas. No fun there. So, game over," Bentley says in an adult voice I've never heard him use, and just like that the steam goes out of their argument and they start promising it's not a big deal and they're definitely having fun. He makes them agree they won't fight and offers them his grilled cheese. They each grab half and disappear back into their bedroom.

"Sorry," he says.

"Don't worry about it. I like seeing you with them. You're surprisingly mature," I admit.

"Wow, really?" He chuckles. "You might be the first person to ever call me that."

I shrug, even though if someone told me I'd be in Bentley's kitchen today complimenting him, I'd have bet money against it. "Yeah, well, you cook for them and settle their arguments. And . . . you wear an apron."

His grin is so big that it takes over his face. "You like my apron?"

"I mean, a little. I'm not gonna lie."

He looks down at his chest. "Well, damn. I wish I'd known that sooner. I may never take this thing off now."

Another silence descends, and once again I feel the need to fill the space.

"Maybe, just maybe, you're not who I thought you were, Bentley," I say and then clarify with, "In a good way." My pause unintentionally makes it sounds significant, and I instantly feel blood rushing to my cheeks.

"Funny," he says. "Because you're exactly who I thought you were. In a good way." Each word carries the weight of a real compliment.

We make eye contact and my empty stomach does a small flip, nothing life altering, but also a feeling I've never had before with Bentley.

Unsure how to respond, I slide onto a vinyl chair at the table, expecting that he's going to return to the stove to cook a replacement sandwich, but then I spot the empty bread bag on the counter.

"Want half of mine?" I ask, pushing the plate forward.

He sits in the chair next to me. "You eat."

"I have bread at my house if you want," I offer.

Now his cheeks flush. "We have food."

I fidget in my seat, realizing he totally misunderstood me. "I just meant that if you want to make another grilled cheese and you're out of bread, I'd be happy to grab some from my house."

"So," he says, quickly changing the subject, "what's your thing with August?"

"My thing?"

He leans back in his chair, balancing it on two legs. "I mean, you're always with him."

I look at him sideways.

"I just mean . . . don't you get tired of only hanging out with one person?"

Whatever fuzzy feeling there was between us vanishes. "You're asking me if I get tired of my best friend?"

"You're taking it wrong," he says and attempts to clarify with, "All I'm saying is . . . think of him as a video game. You might love the game, be obsessed with it even. But there are more games out there to try. Fun games. Better games." He says this casually, like I wouldn't die defending August's honor.

"There's no better than August. Period," I correct him.

"You're not understanding me," he says.

I sit back in my chair. "Okay, then tell me, what would these better games be? Are *you* a better game?"

He sighs, like it's me who made this conversation weird. "Maybe. Maybe not. But how will you ever know if you don't try to play?" He opens his arms like an invitation.

Now I roll my eyes.

"Relax, Valentine. It was just a question. You're the one who's getting so serious."

I take a breath. "Why can't you . . . why do you have to say obnoxious things? *Always.*" But what I mean is, *Why do you have to say obnoxious things right when I was starting to like you?*

"It's called having a sense of humor," he says, like my ability to laugh is the problem. "I know August doesn't have one, but I thought you did."

I know I should leave, but I'm pissed—the sharp kind of anger that comes from disappointment and makes you want to punish the other person for getting your hopes up.

I cross my arms. "All right, Bentley, I changed my mind. Let's see this game of yours."

He scratches the back of his head. "That's how you're gonna—"

"Girls love this game, right?"

"No complaints yet," he replies, but his tone is wary.

"Then show me what you got. I want to see what everyone fawns over."

His eyes widen. "Now?"

"Right here. Right now."

He sits up and pushes back his hair. We stare at each other for a long second, and he leans forward. *Oh shit. Is he going to kiss me? He wouldn't really, would he?*

But then he stops.

"Is that it?" I laugh, mostly out of relief, but he stiffens like I slapped him.

He breaks eye contact. "Are we done here?"

"Yeah. Very done."

He tries to hide his hurt by looking down.

And in the stillness of the sticky summer kitchen, I have a flash of regret, wondering how things got so heated and why I fought so hard.

My phone dings and a message from August lights up the screen.

August

In your living room. Where are you?

My heart jump-starts and I stand. My first thought is that I don't want to have to explain to August why I'm here. My second thought is how awful that first thought was.

Bentley looks from my phone to my obvious flight response and then away.

August

I know you read that.

And so I leave. I sprint back across the grass feeling defeated and unsure, flinging open my porch door.

August smiles, which at the very least means he didn't see me leave Bentley's.

I kick off my wet flip-flops. "So what's up?"

He laughs. "Why do you look like that?"

"Like what?"

"Like your parents just caught you drinking?"

"Pshhhh," I say but my heart isn't in it. I brush back my wet hair that's currently stuck to my cheeks.

He tilts his head. "Something I should know?"

I wipe off my damp arms, avoiding his eyes. "Nope. I was just looking for one of my notebooks in the garage," I lie and instantly regret it. Covering it up only makes it seem like I was doing something wrong. And I wasn't. Plus, I never lie to August. So I divert the conversation. "How was job hunting with your mom?"

"Same as always," he says with a resigned shrug.

I open my mouth, wanting to fess up, but the words don't come. Luckily, he doesn't see the indecision on my face because he's scrolling through his phone.

"Here." He hands me the phone with his screen open to a conversation with Ella.

I abandon my thoughts of admitting my lie and dive into the welcome distraction of reading their conversation.

"Nice," I say when I finish, and grab my keys from my purse on the table. I toss them to him. "Go work your Star-Crossed Bestie magic."

August catches the keys midair, and as he heads for the door, I plop down on my couch, all the air whooshing out of me in an audible huff. I grab the fuzzy blanket and pull it over my head, where I plan on staying for the rest of the afternoon.

21

AUGUST

The rain has downgraded to a drizzle, leaving the air refreshingly cool. I open the door to the café, book in hand, and I'm greeted with the uplifting scent of coffee and flaky croissant. Ella is already here, sitting on the same stool in the window where I first dumped coffee on her. And like last time, she's immersed in her computer.

I order a black coffee, triple check the lid is on tight, and slide into the empty seat next to Ella.

This time, instead of ignoring me, she turns. "Whoa," she says, eyeing the coffee. "Ten-foot rule."

I smile. "Is that a thing?"

"Oh, it's a thing. There's a mandatory safety radius for clumsy dudes carrying hot drinks."

"And what about clumsy girls?" I ask. "Or elbows. Clumsy elbows?"

She rolls her eyes, her wavy hair falling over her bare tanned shoulder and her lips pulling up slightly at the corners. Disdain and humor, humor and disdain—a complicated marriage of emotions that I'm more familiar with than I care to admit.

She takes a sip of her drink, something frothy and sugared, and returns to typing.

"Contrary to popular belief, raindrops aren't shaped like teardrops," I say, accessing some of the random knowledge I've acquired while doing these cases. A guy last summer was meteorology obsessed.

Ella stops typing. "Cool, but I'm trying to work."

"They start out round," I say, but still she doesn't look at me.

"Fingers typing on keyboard. Very important blog deadline."

"And because of the resistance of the air, as they fall, the raindrops end up looking like jelly beans the closer they get to the ground," I continue.

"Not relevant."

"I beg to differ."

"You can't differ," she says. "You don't even know what I'm working on."

"You just said. You're writing your astrology blog," I counter. "I read it last night. There was a reader's note on the home page about how you were almost finished with the monthly horoscopes."

Now she turns to look at me. "No, I will not sign your boobs. Please move along, sir."

I laugh. "Ouch. Is that how all famous bloggers address their fans?"

She returns to her computer. "Yup."

"So the thing about these raindrops—" I continue, but she cuts me off.

"It's weird how you look like a normal person, but then you start talking and it turns out you're a pest of the worst kind."

I give her a knowing smile. "You think in your mind that you know exactly what raindrops are, that you've seen them your whole life—they're predictable. But then you find out about the jelly bean bit and it feels wrong, annoying even. Teardrops are sexy. Jelly beans are goofy. So you ignore the idea, and you go back to thinking of them as teardrops."

"So the moral of your story is to deny raindrops their shape?"

"When things or people, especially people, don't look or act the way we envision them in our head, we ignore their truth, reimagining them as something better suited to our image." I pause. "You said in your introduction on your blog that you write both the good and the bad, and that may not be for everyone. That a lot of people want the good and the sugarcoated bad. But that's not people, and you write people. Just thought you'd appreciate that the raindrops agree with you."

For a moment she just stares at me, her brown eyes taking me in. "Hmmm."

"You're welcome."

"I didn't say thank you."

"No, but it's exactly the type of thing you could use in your write-ups."

She lifts a perfectly shaped eyebrow. "So not only did you read my blog, but you spent time thinking about what might be useful to me? Why?"

"Because I'm passionate about astrology."

"Right." She laughs and tilts her head. Her hair slides across her back, and I get a whiff of her shampoo—coconut and vanilla.

"Well then, I guess my job here is done," I say in a satisfied tone.

"So that's it?" she says, amused. "You just came here to tell me about raindrops?"

"I came here to grab a coffee." I slide off my stool, lifting my cup as evidence. "See you around." I turn.

Three . . . two . . . one . . .

"Hey, Holden?" she says, and I stop. "A group of us are going to the carnival tomorrow night. You and Mia should join."

"Maybe we will, Scorpio. Maybe we will." And I leave.

22
VALENTINE

"August Anthony Mariani," I say, climbing through his window. "Put on something other than your man briefs because we have some carnival plotting to do."

August squints at me in the late-morning light. I can tell he's been awake for a bit because he's not grunting and cursing into his pillow, but not long enough for the surly to wear off completely.

"And you know what kind of underwear I wear, how exactly?" he asks, his voice rough. Swee snores peacefully by his side, his scraggly old cat body tucked carefully under August's sheet like a person.

"Because I go through your drawers. Obviously."

He cracks a smile. "Fair enough."

I laugh. "You wouldn't care?"

"If you went through my stuff?" He shrugs. "Nope. I trust you."

I'm instantly reminded of my conversation with Bentley yesterday and feel justified all over again about defending August. Now, if I could just stop thinking about that conversation altogether, that'd be awesome.

I pull my sparkly purple notebook from my shoulder bag and plop down in August's desk chair. "Ready?"

He props himself up on his elbow. "I'm not saying I don't want to plot, but I'm definitely going to need some coff—"

"I'll get it. You feed Swee. And then we'll—"

He looks at me from under his tousled morning hair. "*Tiiiny.*"

"Yeah?"

"Is there something you want to tell me?"

My heart thuds with the unexpectedness of the question. And I feel disoriented like someone just shined a light in my eyes. "Huh?"

"Either someone spiked your orange juice or you're upset about something."

"Uh—" I start, spinning my wheels to come up with an answer that isn't a lie. If I tell him the truth about Bentley in light of him thinking I'm upset—which I'm absolutely not—he'll get the wrong idea.

But before I complete my thought, there's a knock.

"Come in," August says, and I couldn't be more grateful for the interruption.

August's mom opens his door. "Don't mind me, I just heard Valentine's voice and thought I'd come in and share some good news. Hi, sweetie," she says to me.

"Hi, Ruth," I reply, and her smile brightens. Her curls are piled high on her head in an effortless bun, and she's wearing a floor-length maroon shirtdress with a brown belt. I've always envied her style.

"Good news?" August says, and the hope on his face is hard to look at. It doesn't matter how many jobs she loses or how practical he is about everything and anything; when it comes to his mom, he keeps thinking he'll wake up one day and everything will be different.

"Well," she says, her cheeks pink. "I got a job."

"Yeah?" August says with kid-like enthusiasm. "Vinnie changed his mind?"

"Better," she says. "It's a painting job. A house."

"That's great, Ruth," I say.

Relief seems to wash over August. "When do you start? Do we need to pick up supplies?"

"The Kellermans already ordered the paint. But I'll need some odds and ends. More brushes for instance and—"

"The *Kellermans*?" August says, his voice a smidge too loud, sitting up so fast that Swee startles with a snort.

Kyle Kellerman, my mind screams. The awful image of seeing Kyle in the supermarket three days ago flashes through my head, and my stomach knots itself into a tangled mess.

"See, I ran into Nancy Kellerman at the bakery this morning, and she told me they've decided to completely redo their paint colors. I offered my services, and I guess she must have liked the idea, because she just called and told me I'm hired." She holds her hands out and opens her mouth as if to say, *Ta-da!*

August looks like someone slapped him.

Ruth drops her hands, her cheerfulness turning to confusion. "August?"

He doesn't respond right away, probably torn between wanting his mom to have a job and wanting her to refuse on principle. His shoulders slump. "Yeah, no, that's good," he lies. "Just processing the big news."

A timer goes off somewhere in the distance, and his mom turns toward the door. "Banana muffins," she says over her shoulder as she enters the hall. "To celebrate!"

I wait as her footsteps fade on the steps.

August stands and closes his door, his expression shifting like a brewing storm. "You heard that, right? It wasn't just my imagination that my mother is now working for *Kyle effing Kellerman's* family?"

I sit forward, instantly feeling the responsibility of saying something that'll make this less awful.

"Maybe you should tell her how you feel," I reply, my voice gentle.

He gives me a "be serious" look. "Tell her what exactly? That Kyle practically dragged Des out of the house that night? Or that he got her drunk before putting her in his car?"

The lights on the cop cars painted the night-shadowed asphalt in a sea of flashing blue and red. It was too bright, too loud for the sleepy street at 1:00 a.m., and for a split second I thought it might not be real. August and

I got out of the back of his mom's car, still in our pajamas, the sluggishness of sleep gone and replaced with sweaty, pulsing fear.

August's mom spoke with an officer, whose face was drawn with the burden of what he was saying. I followed August into the commotion, my heart pounding in my ears, only catching pieces of the policeman's words: "Race . . . kids . . . unfortunate accident."

But my mind couldn't make sense of it because there, wrapped around a tree, was Kyle's brand-new car, the one he took us for a ride in not two days before, bragging about how fast it was . . . had been Kyle sat in the back of an ambulance, his eyes wide with shock and blood on his shirt. But there was no Des. Des wasn't there.

Then I saw what Kyle was staring at. A body bag on a stretcher. And I knew; I instantly knew, the same way you know when you drop a glass, even before it hits the ground, that it'll never be reparable. I looked around, frantic for someone to tell me it wasn't true. But August's mom was folded over herself, wailing. And August was frozen, standing at the edge of the caution tape, gripping it so tightly that his knuckles were white.

"It might be good to say those things," I reply even more gently.

He shakes his head as he paces. "Honestly, what good would it do at this point to prove to her that we all missed something about Kyle? Why subject her to the same shit guilt I live with?"

My breath catches and my heart beats faster. "August, it's not your—"

He turns so quickly that I flinch. "Do not say 'fault,' Tiny. Don't even think it," he says with finality, and I feel blood rushing to my cheeks. For months after Des died, people kept telling him that it was a senseless tragedy, that it wasn't anyone's fault. That was when he stopped talking to people in general, even me.

I glance briefly at my hands. "Well, hey, look, I'm sure there's another job out there. All we need to do is find it."

He presses the heels of his hands into his eyebrows. "We've been through three towns applying, including the places she's been fired from before. I even stopped at the Gibbonses and the Hershwicks to ask about their home repairs, and they both told me flat out that they felt more comfortable hiring a contractor. There is no other job." He tosses his phone onto the end of his bed for emphasis. "I seriously hate money, like, *a lot.*"

I'd ask if August's dad could help. But I did that when he found out Berkeley denied him financial aid because of his father's salary. I told August I was sure he'd want to contribute, to which August spent the next ten minutes cursing about how his dad's a prick who's too preoccupied with his second family to care. "Maybe I could—" I start, but he cuts me off.

His eyes darken and he looks away. "I know you're trying to help, but this isn't your problem. It's mine," he says, and I'm instantly aware that The Wall is up and the conversation is over.

23

AUGUST

Colorful lights illuminate the old horse field; music surrounds us with a steady beat, and people happy-scream as their stomachs drop suddenly on the roller coaster. An introvert's worst nightmare.

Tiny stuffs her face with cotton candy. "I *love* carnivals. And carnival food. And games. And—"

"Overpriced neon chaos?" I offer.

She shoves a giant bite of cotton candy into her mouth. "Cynic."

"Optimist."

"There." She points a sticky finger toward a stall that reads *Balloon Pop*, where Ella and Leah throw darts. Derek and the Amber look-alike shoot hoops at the next booth over.

Justin announces our arrival with, "Everyone's favorite cousins!" as we approach, giving Tiny a high five and me a fist bump. Amber's eyes brighten when she sees me.

Ella and Leah, now finished with their game, join our circle.

"You're just in time," Amber says.

She slips a flask from her purse and takes a swig, offering it to me.

I put my hands up. "Driving."

Amber rolls her eyes. "Lame."

She passes it to Tiny, who lifts the canister to her lips. Her performance is convincing, even though I know she's faking that sip—we can't do our job tipsy.

"I think I peeled off some of my throat with that stuff," Tiny says and passes it to Justin.

"Bourbon," Amber replies with a sly grin. "My dad buys it by the case. Never notices when I swipe some."

I know she meant it as a positive, but I frown. My mother wouldn't notice if I took alcohol, either, but I don't consider that a good thing. Amber, Leah, and Tiny start up a conversation, and my attention drifts to Justin and Ella.

"Yesss!" Justin says, after a swig. "Babe?" He offers the flask.

"Can't," Ella replies.

"*Can't?*" he repeats. There's a slight edge in his voice, like this isn't the first time they've had this conversation.

"I have to finish my blog in the morning," she says, and he groans in response.

"Yeah, but you're here with me now. Don't worry about your blog." He offers her the flask again, not even subtle about pitting himself against yet another thing Ella values.

"Justin, I won't be able to write if I—"

He wraps his arms around her waist and pulls her in. "Just one easy shot. No big deal. For me."

Just like Kyle. My hand clenches and unclenches involuntarily.

Ella sighs her agreement. "One shot. That's it."

He grins at her and hands her the flask, releasing her waist. Ella takes a sip and passes the flask to Leah.

"Time for me to crush you all at basketball," Justin bellows.

Amber turns her attention to me, touching my arm. "I was wondering who was going to win me that giant stuffed bear." She points to the basketball booth prizes and gives me a sultry look. "And now I know."

I give her an apologetic smile. "I think you'd have better luck with Mia. She's way better at these games than I am."

Tiny/Mia grins. She loves a compliment, even when it's over something as trivial as carnival games. "Truth. He sucks."

"Why don't we pop over to the Ferris wheel," Ella suggests to Justin. Justin hesitates.

Before Justin can answer, Tiny says, "Who's in for a friendly bet on winner of basketball toss? Five bucks maybe?"

"You're so on," Justin replies, squashing Ella's Ferris wheel offer.

"I'm in," Leah says.

Ella looks momentarily disappointed. That's two times in three minutes he's chosen himself over her. Selfish prick.

Justin picks up Ella and makes a show of twirling her in the air. "I'm winning you that bear, babe."

"Awww," Amber says.

Everyone makes their way to the basketball booth, and Justin and Tiny pull out their betting money.

"How's the blog coming?" I ask Ella, who's lingering behind.

"Better once someone wasn't talking my ear off." She smiles in a teasing way. "But I still have a full day of work tomorrow."

"Well, if you need any help, I'm offering," I say.

Now she laughs. "You think you can write my blog? Thanks, but no thanks."

"Not even remotely. But as it so happens, I'm excellent at hashing out ideas, and I'm not bad in the coffee-buying department, either."

She looks at me sideways. "And why would you give up your day to hash out blog ideas with me?"

"Because you're interesting and what you've created is interesting," I say matter-of-factly, and while I have no love for astrology specifically, I mean what I say. She's a lot like Tiny and me, the way she's driven, and her commitment is admirable.

My words must ring true for her because even though she's not obvious about it, her eyes brighten at the compliment.

Justin and Tiny hoot as they both make their first basket. Amber, however, keeps glancing our way. And I get the sense that if I don't act fast, Amber will walk over here, negating the opportunity Tiny so artfully gave me.

"Will you do me a favor?" I say, looking out at the carnival. "Tell Mia to text me when she's done being macho."

Ella follows my gaze into the crowd. "You're not staying?"

"I'm gonna check out the Ferris wheel," I say and walk away. This is how I do my job. I don't tell people what to do—I give them choices and let them decide for themselves.

I only make it three stalls down before she calls, "Wait up," falling in step with me. "Care if I join?"

"Not at all."

For a couple of seconds, we walk side by side through the noisy carnival, my hands in my jeans pockets and hers pulling her long hair into a ponytail. Her coconut shampoo once again wafts in my direction, reminding me of the beach—suntan lotion and sun-warmed skin.

"Can I ask you something?" I say.

"Depends."

"Where are you going to college?"

She half laughs. "That's your big question? What am I doing with my future?"

"I mean, yeah," I say as we join the line for the Ferris wheel. "I just noticed how serious you are about your blog and wondered."

She's close enough that I spot a handful of freckles on her upper left cheekbone—as though a star constellation embossed itself there.

"I want to be a travel journalist. Badly," she says.

"Travel journalism . . ." I consider it even though I already knew this about her. "An international school then?"

She presses her lips together, and her shoulders tug slightly inward. "Funny . . . that used to be the goal."

"Used to?"

She hesitates. "I got into London School of Economics. They have one of the best programs in the world. But I just don't want to be that far from home, ya know?" She says this like she wants my agreement, needs it maybe.

"You want to stay near your family?" I ask even though I know that's not the reason.

"Are you kidding? My parents would be overjoyed if I went to London." She pauses. "And the Shakespeare. Oh my god. I'd be at the Globe like every week."

While I'm all set to continue my college questions, she's caught my attention, and I take a quick detour. "You like theater?"

"Love," she says. "I know everyone says they love Shakespeare, that I'm not winning any originality awards, but I really do. *Romeo and Juliet* is the most perfect love story ever. In all its iterations. Even bad high school renditions where you know the actors have no idea what they're saying. My favorite, though, is that stunning Leonardo DiCaprio movie."

This subject is one I feel pretty strongly about, and I, August, can't resist telling her what I actually think. "I absolutely agree with you about Shakespeare. I mean, the guy added more than two hundred words to the English language. But I'm not totally convinced about *Romeo and Juliet*. They both die at the end."

She shakes her head like I've got it all wrong, and her ponytail swishes with the movement. "The story is about two people who love each other so much that they literally cannot exist in a world without one another. It's beautiful."

In a way I envy her and Tiny and the way they see the world with so much possible love in it. "So if London has one of the best journalism programs *and* Shakespeare, how come you're not going?"

She dips her head and rubs her arm. "It's just that Justin and I decided to go to Boston University so that he can intern with his dad's company during his junior and senior year."

I give her a questioning look.

"What?"

"Nothing."

"That look definitely wasn't nothing. You were judging me," she says.

"Not judging." I pause, but the fact that she's self-conscious about it means on some level there's doubt. I can work with doubt. "I just never took you for the type of person who'd give up on your dream school for a boyfriend."

Her eyes widen. "I'm not."

"Okay," I say, but my tone betrays my opinion.

"That's not what happened," she says, more adamant, and I can tell she's trying to convince herself as much as me.

Des was strong willed and confident like Ella, but that's the thing about larger-than-life, controlling people like Kyle and Justin: they slowly wear you down, making you change little by little. And when all your friends rally behind them proclaiming them perfect, it's easy to lose parts of yourself.

The line ahead of us starts moving.

Ella looks out into the sea of people like she's not convinced this was a good idea.

So I change tactics. "Who's your best friend?"

She gives me an "are you serious?" look. "First question's about my future, and now about my best friend? Are you sure you're not secretly forty-five?" But she's no longer staring at the crowd like she wants to walk away.

I smile. "Because I'm so mature?"

"It wasn't a compliment."

"You think I'm different. I'm good with that."

"I think you're ridiculous," she says, but the way she says it makes me like the word.

"Tickets," a scruffy man says to us without feeling, and we hand them over. In most instances, I'd offer to pay out of politeness. But Ella would look at me askance, like I just tricked her into a date. And I don't have those intentions.

We climb into the metal seat, and the ticket guy secures the bar over our laps.

"You never answered my question," I say, as we jerk a few feet into the air.

She looks at the swaying seat above us like it might give her the strength to deal with me. But her expression edges toward amusement. Humor and disdain. "You already know my best friends—Leah and Amber."

"How long have you guys known each other?"

"Since we were five," she says easily. "Who's yours?"

"What a weird question." I fake shock as we lift higher. "Are you sure you're not forty-five?"

"Ha ha . . . very funny."

"Mia," I say.

"Wait, your best friend is your cousin?"

"Yup."

"Did you two grow up together?"

"We did. Right next door," I say, telling an unplanned truth. But Tiny and I often do this, mix the truth with the story to make it flow. "I spent a lot of time at her house."

"Like you are this summer?"

"Exactly like that."

"And your parents?" she asks as we move upward again.

"Not much to tell. We're different."

"What about your sister?" she asks, and my heart nearly stops. I've never mentioned Des in a case before, much less talked about her like I did that day at the pool. Ella must be able to read the discomfort on my face because she doesn't wait for my answer. "Sorry, you don't have to answer that—"

"No, it's fine," I lie, and this time our seat moves fluidly and doesn't stop. "I'm just . . . not that good at talking about her." Another truth.

Ella watches me, and the open-air seat suddenly feels confining.

But instead of being awkward or spewing platitudes, she says, "I get it." And for a few seconds we stare out over the glowing lights of the carnival, quiet and contemplative. "I lost my grandmother a year and a half ago."

Now I look at her. How did I not know this? Her parents never said anything, and there was no hint of it on her social media.

"It's funny," she says, stretching her slender fingers around the cool metal bar. "When you asked me who my best friend was, she was the first person who popped into my head. Stupid, right? To have your best friend be your grandmother who isn't even here anymore?" She looks up at me, and her expression is one I haven't seen. She's not her showy, popular self or her combative, humorous self; she's raw and vulnerable, carefully handing me something important she hopes I won't crush.

"Not stupid at all," I say, finding my voice. "Do you still talk to her? I mean—"

"I know what you mean," she says, relief in her voice. "And yeah, I talk to her all the time. Do you? With your sister?"

"Yeah," I admit. "More than I want to, sometimes." My thoughts immediately flit to my line drawings, which were the kind of thing I used to leave for Des with a note or slipped into one of her books when she wasn't looking. She loved them and used to gush when she found one. She dubbed them our little secret and declared them her favorite gift ever. Which is why I now hate them, even the imaginary version, because every time I think one up, I'm reminded there is no one to give it to.

As if to torment me, my mind begins doing the one thing I wish it wouldn't.

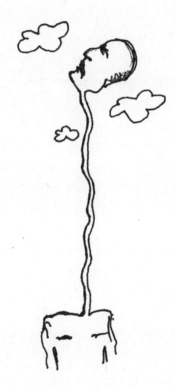

"Alone isn't a location, it's a feeling," I say to the clouds, but no one answers.

"Like something good happens and she's the first person you think of?" Ella asks, and I'm relieved to have a distraction from my own thoughts.

"Or something bad happens and you want her advice?" Her voice catches at the end of her sentence, and I feel it in my own throat.

"My sister was four years older than me," I say. "In some ways she was more a mother to me than my mom."

Again, we fall into heavy silence, wordlessly rotating.

She stares at her hands on the bar before looking up at me. "Do you think it ever gets easier?"

"No," I say, and she sighs like I gave her the answer she was looking for, like someone finally told the truth. And for a long second neither of us breaks eye contact.

"Nonna's actually the one who encouraged me to create my astrology blog," she tells me, and I know by her tone that this matters. "She drew my birth chart when I was a little girl, and she'd spend hours explaining all the bits and pieces to me."

It makes me feel oddly good that she's confiding in me. "Sounds like she was a pretty great grandmother."

"She really, really was. She made everything fun. And she always listened. My parents . . . not so much. I mean, don't get me wrong, they care, but they never had time for me the way Nonna did."

For a moment August overtakes Holden, and I hand her a piece of my world in exchange for hers. "My mom was the one who taught me how to paint. She's good. Exceptionally so. But when I'd give her a painting, she'd talk to me about technique, teach me a new skill. Des never cared about that." And while I made the conscious choice to tell her something real, the sound of Des's name on my lips startles me.

"Des . . ." she says, considering my sister's name like she recognizes it for the fragile piece of my heart that it represents. "I like that."

I can only nod.

Ella leans back, relaxing into the seat. "Sometimes you just need someone who hears you."

I press my lips together. I know I should be talking, agreeing with her, but I don't trust my own voice.

"Oh man," she says, like she realizes we crossed into heavier territory and is trying to pull us back. "Are we having a heart-to-heart on a Ferris wheel? Can you get any cheesier than that?"

"A heart-to-heart in a canoe under the stars?" I offer as a joke, happy to be on sturdier ground.

But instead of laughing, she looks at me like she's seeing me for the first time. "Holy crap, you're a hopeless romantic."

"*What?*" I choke, the August side of me taken by surprise.

She laughs. "You are. You claim not to understand *Romeo and Juliet*, but no one who wasn't a romantic would even think something like that."

"Wrong and also wrong," I say, not even sure why I decide to argue. What does it matter if she thinks Holden is a hopeless romantic?

"Then why are you blushing?"

"Heat," I say.

"Uh-huh."

I scratch my eyebrow. "So, how long do these rides usually last?"

She laughs and I laugh, too. And even though I'm making a show of wanting to escape, I genuinely wouldn't mind a couple more minutes up here.

24
VALENTINE

I spot Ella and August walking back as I collect my winnings, and they're laughing. Only it's more than that. They're not flirty, but the way they lean toward each other feels familiar. And even though that's exactly what we do, create trust so our case can see a new perspective, this strikes me as different somehow.

"So you're a basketball shark," Justin says, handing me another five bucks.

"I mean, I did warn you I'd take your money," I reply. "Less shark, more truth."

"They're back," Leah announces of August and Ella's return. "Time to conquer the Zipper!"

There are a few hoots of agreement, and like a human amoeba, we all move toward the ride that Charlie Atkins once fear-peed on in the fourth grade, soaking not only himself but also Bentley in the process.

My phone buzzes again, and I frown at the text conversation that has been slowly accumulating all day.

Bentley

Sorry

Valentine? Can we talk?

I'm shit at apologizing over text. But I really
am sorry.

The truth is . . . you make me nervous.

Good nervous.

Not that that's an excuse.

See what I mean about sucking at text
apologies?

My thumb lingers over the keys, but no response comes, none that sounds right anyway. My heart rate elevates, and I shove the phone back in my pocket. This whole thing is absurd. I don't like Bentley like that. So why do I even care? I should just accept his apology and move on.

Ella moves to Justin's side while August and I fall behind the group, close enough to eavesdrop, but not close enough to crowd them.

"Where'd you run off to?" Justin asks Ella.

She shrugs. "Went on the Ferris wheel."

"Alone?" Justin asks.

And suddenly August is searching my face like I pulled one over on him. I eye him right back, now completely convinced that something atypical happened on that Ferris wheel.

25
AUGUST

I knew Tiny was creating an opportunity for me to speak to Ella alone—
we've used similar strategies before—but I hadn't considered it from the
angle that she wants to shake up Justin's control over Ella. Did Tiny just use
me as bait? One look at her, and I know I'm right. I don't know whether
to be impressed or mad, given I didn't figure it out, nor did she warn me.

"I was with Holden," Ella tells Justin as we navigate through the
carnival.

"Yeah, I saw you run after him," he says with a barbed tone.

Ella's cheeks flush as she realizes the same thing I did—Justin's jealous. She covers her embarrassment with a laugh. "If you knew where I
went, then why'd you ask?"

"I'm not allowed to ask my girlfriend questions?" he says like she's
the one who's making this weird.

"Of course you are. It's just not a big deal."

"I guess so," he says in a way that clearly communicates it is.

Tiny gives me a satisfied look, and I frown.

Ella touches Justin's arm, but he shrugs her off. "You're mad?" she asks.
"Should I be?"

"No, you shouldn't," she says definitively.

"Fine, then I'm not," Justin replies in a tone that says the opposite. "Let's just forget about it." He reaches forward and taps Sharky's elbow. "You got that bourbon?"

Amber obligingly pulls the flask from her purse, and Justin moves up beside her, leaving Ella alone.

And the hurt look on Ella's face irks me. Not only do I have a bone-deep dislike of Justin, I'm not sure I love Tiny's tactic, either.

I slow my pace and we fall a couple more feet behind the group. "You could have warned me," I breathe at my best friend, but she only shrugs.

"I told you what we needed to do, and this set up the first domino," she says, her voice low and mostly masked by the crowd. "I know what you're worrying about, and I'm not trying to set you up as a rival and get us ousted from this group. We won't put you in that position again. This just had the beauty of a dual purpose, giving you time to bond and also showing his true colors." Then she gives me a quasi-suspicious look. "Unless you went rogue and flirted with her, which would obviously be a prob—"

"Of *course* I didn't," I say, cutting her off, frustrated that she'd even suggest it. "You know me better than that."

"Then we have nothing to worry about," she replies, but my discomfort remains like a tiny barb in a sweater that scratches me when I move but disappears every time I look for it.

26

VALENTINE

I lie in bed under my fluffy white comforter, rereading Bentley's texts for the five hundredth time. Once again, my fingers pluck at the keys. I type out *Don't worry about it* and erase it. Then I type *It was bound to happen* and erase that, too. I toss my phone onto my bed with an exasperated huff.

"What do I care?" I say and place my hands over my eyes. August is the overthinker; *I'm* the go-with-the-flow girl. And this is all really simple—I thought I might kiss Bentley, but it turns out he's unworthy. *No biggie.*

I pull my hands away from my face and look at my vanity, where my latest notebook lies. Work. That's exactly what I need to distract myself. I get up and cross the room, taking a good look at myself in the vanity mirror.

"Stop obsessing," I say to my reflection. "Just be cool."

The Berkeley sticker in the corner of my mirror snags in my view. *California*, I think, and once again, my stomach drops at the thought. I stand there for a long moment feeling uncertain and disliking my reaction a disproportionate amount. So I yank the sticker off my mirror and shove it in my drawer, not for good, just until this weird feeling passes. But my stewing is cut short by a loud ping on my window.

I turn so fast that the room spins. My alarm clock reads 11:47 p.m. For a second, I think I must have imagined it. But then, *ping*. I speed toward my window, conjuring images of things that go bump in the night.

Just as I pull back the curtain, a pebble hits the glass, startling me for a third time. But there's no monster, only Bentley on the lawn between our houses. And when I see his messy hair and pajamas, I'm instantly furious. I yank open the window and stick my head out.

"What the hell, Bentley? It's the middle of the night," I whisper yell.

"Can we talk?" he says, full volume.

I aggressively put my finger to my mouth.

"Can we talk?" he asks again, quieter, but not nearly quiet enough.

I want to refuse, but another couple of exchanges like this and my parents will wake up. I hold out my hand, instructing him to wait, and close the window. I grab my short lilac robe off the back of my door and throw it over my pajamas.

I quietly pick my way down the carpeted steps and follow the runner in the hallway to the front door like a cartoon burglar. No way I'm going out back—my parents' bedroom faces that direction and so does August's. I slide into my flip-flops and slip outside, moving from cool air-conditioning to warm humidity that smells like salt water and dewy grass.

My sandals flop on the stone path, and even though the crickets chirp and the water laps in rhythm, my sandals sound like they're on loudspeaker in our sleepy inlet.

I lean around the side of the house where Bentley's waiting on the lawn. I motion for him to follow me, and then speed walk until I reach the hedges that separate my front yard from the road.

I turn to face him, the cool grass tickling my feet. "You can't just throw pebbles at my window. This isn't a nineties movie."

He grins like a little boy. "But you came down."

"Yeah, I did. That's not the point." I'm still annoyed for a reason I can't define.

He stares at me.

"You said you wanted to talk?" Frustration affects my intonation. "So talk."

"I wanted to apologize."

"At midnight?"

"Yeah."

"My lights were off."

"You were typing in our text," he says. "I kept seeing the message bubble pop up, but you never sent anything. So I thought I'd try talking to you in person."

I tuck my hair behind my ears and break eye contact, hoping he can't see my embarrassment in the dim light. I realize his observation means he was also staring at our text thread, but the whole thing is far too romantic a notion for me and Bentley.

"I got nervous the other day," he says.

"Yeah, you said that. Don't worry about it. That fight was bound to happen anyway," I say, trying out both my rejected texts.

He looks like he disagrees.

"I mean . . . we're different," I clarify.

"But that's not a bad thing. That's why I like you." His voice is sincere.

I nervous-laugh. "Bentley, let's be real, you say that to everyone."

"I really don't."

"You do. And I get it. You're a flirt."

"I am a flirt. But that doesn't change the fact that I like you." There goes that sincerity again. And for unknown reasons it fuels my frustration.

I put my hands on my hips. "Great. We done here?"

"You're mad."

"I'm not mad."

"Your eyebrows are pushed together."

"They're not."

"Tell me what to do to fix it."

I suppress the urge to push him with both hands. "What am I sup-posed to say to that?"

"Tell me that I have to hand wash your Jeep or something, and then you'll forgive me."

I huff, not ready to give up my exasperated tone. "Let's just forget the penance part and skip forward. I forgive you."

"Then you'll go on another date with me?"

I stare at Bentley, his faded Superman shirt and plaid pants making him look way too innocent. I stand there for a good five seconds, but he doesn't back down and he doesn't say he's kidding. "Don't you think we should call it quits while we're ahead?"

"We're not ahead."

I rub my eye, thinking of a million reasons why this is a bad idea. But instead, I say, "Do you promise not to insult my best friend?"

"I do."

"And do you promise not to BS me with one-liners?"

"Cross my heart." He makes the motion on his chest.

"Fine. I'll go on another date with you."

A grin lights up his face so completely that I have to tighten my jaw to keep from smiling back.

"Tomorrow?" he asks. "For the date, I mean."

My eyes widen; he's totally incorrigible. "You're serious?"

"Valentine, I've been waiting for three and a half years for you to say yes to me. I'm not missing a day."

And suddenly my frustration is replaced with a fuzzy feeling that I also can't define. I pull my bathrobe tighter even though I'm not cold. "Oh," I stumble. "Okay."

"Okay," he repeats, once again grinning.

I shake my head. "Now go to bed, Bentley Cavendish," I say, but we both linger a second before we walk our separate ways.

27
VALENTINE

August and I sit at the picnic table in his backyard, surrounded by a giant spread of breakfast food courtesy of my mom, who has been weirdly hovering since we had that spat the other day.

I sip my fresh-squeezed orange juice, and it makes my mouth tingle from the sour-sweet. "Have you noticed anything strange about my parents lately?"

August looks up from his breakfast sandwich. "Strange how?"

"I don't know, like too lovey?" I say, hoping he'll just know what I mean.

"You're worried your parents are too much in love?"

I roll my eyes and place my elbows on the picnic table. "They're just . . . off. And the other day they were fighting. But they didn't want me to know."

"I'm not following," he says in his stupidly practical voice. "Are they too happy or not enough?"

"Both?" I say, knowing it sounds silly, but it's true.

"I haven't noticed anything."

"Yeah, maybe it's nothing," I agree, redirecting my attention to my notebook. "*Anyway* . . . Justin, eh? A rare douche if I ever saw one. And Sharky is like his main cheerleader. She practically farts Justin glitter."

He chuckles at my joke, wiping egg yolk off the corner of his mouth from an overly big bite. Mom claims she loves to feed August because he eats so enthusiastically. She chalks it up to him being an eighteen-year-old boy, but I know that it was Des who mostly did the cooking when his mother forgot or was too immersed in a painting.

"As long as you don't get us kicked out of this group because Justin thinks I'm flirting with his girlfriend," August says, clearly holding a mini grudge over yesterday.

"Cross my heart," I reply, cringing internally as I copy the motion Bentley made last night. "I'd never compromise us like that. Besides, Ella's father would have us beheaded."

He nods, like he's glad we're in agreement.

"Which is why"—I push him my notebook, open to a list entitled *Tiny's Brilliant Breakup Plan*—"we're going to do *this*."

He puts his half-finished breakfast sandwich down and dusts the crumbs off his hands into the grass, reading my numbered and subnumbered steps. "When did you write this?"

I grin, super satisfied by his surprised tone. "Late last night. Came to me in a flash of inspiration after seeing Justin in action yesterday." I kiss my fingers and hold my hand in the air like a chef.

August stares at the list. "It's . . . effective."

"Damn right," I say and bite my bagel piled with cream cheese.

His finger lingers on the page next to *STEP THREE: Call Justin the eff out on pressuring Ella.*

"But it's also risky." He sounds unsure, not looking nearly as jazzed as I expected.

"August, we have barely more than two weeks to complete this. We need bold; we need different. *This*"—I point to my plan—"is different."

"Very."

"No 'Tiny, I worship you' or 'Wow, that's the best idea you've ever had'?" I take my notebook back. "Your enthusiasm is overwhelming."

"It's a good idea," he says like he's making a concession. "A great one even. It's just . . . if this goes wrong, you know they're gonna hate us, right?"

I laugh. "Then let's get it right."

He breaks eye contact with me, pressing his lips together.

And suddenly, it clicks. "Oh. My. God." I elongate each word.

"What?"

I place my hand over my heart like I'm emotional. "This is epic."

He gives me side-eye.

"I saw you getting all squirrely last night." I point at his face. "That look in your eye, the way you were getting so frustrated with Justin. I just never thought . . ."

He shifts his weight on the bench across from me. "I have no idea what you're trying to say."

I grin at him, hard. "You, my friend, have a *crush*."

August chokes on his coffee. "Not even close—"

"You totally do. You *like Ella*. You're not worried that people will hate us—you've never cared before—you're worried that *Ella* will hate *you*."

He reverts to his poker face. "You're obviously hallucinating due to sugar overload."

But I only stare at him, amazed. "Is it possible? Are pigs flying? Is hell a fancy new ski resort?"

"*Tiny*," he objects with a glare, returning to eating his sandwich as though it were suddenly the most important thing ever.

I let out a big, dreamy sigh, resting my cheek on my hand. "Crushes aside, what do you think, Holden McLover—can you get Ella to hang out with you today so we can get this ball rolling?"

He looks like someone pinched him. "There's no planet on which I'd respond to that name."

"I'll take that as a yes," I say, still staring at him like I've never seen him before. I honestly never thought I'd see the day he had a crush. Even the word *crush* is too ridiculous a notion for him.

As if on cue his phone buzzes. Ella's name flashes across his screen, and we both reach for it at the same time. He gets to it first and gives me a warning look.

This may never get old.

He unlocks his screen.

Ella

What else you got?

I look at him for explanation.

"She means for her blog," he says. "Like a cool metaphor or a meaningful anecdote. I told her I'd help."

I pause, giving it a think. "Oooh, what about a fun fact? You could tell her that the entire human population would fit inside Los Angeles, shoulder to shoulder, or so *National Geographic* says."

August looks at me quizzically.

"Astrology advice is all about perspective, right?" I put on my public speaking voice. "Compacting the human race shows us how small we actually are, how limited our view is."

"I like it," he says and types it out to her.

Ella

Totally stealing this.

Me for the win.

Ella

And just in case . . . got anything on the unknown?

August

The unknown?

Ella

Yeah, like the way we fear the things we don't know or outcomes we can't control type of thing?

This time August doesn't look at me. He just starts typing.

August

There's a quote you might like. Give me a sec.

He does a fast Google search and returns to the thread.

August

Where can one find enough leather

With which to cover the entire earth?

Yet leather enough to cover the soles of the shoes

Is equivalent to covering the entire earth with leather.

Likewise is the case with external objects

That I cannot find ways to fully restrain;

Restraining this mind of mine is restraining all others

What else is required to be restrained?—Shantideva

The idea is that all worries and anxiety come from the combination of two things—external circumstances and internal thoughts.

> We obviously can't control the
> external world, but if we
> can control our own minds, we don't
> need to.

Ella

> Seriously?

August

> You don't like it?

Ella

> No. I love the shit out of it. I just want to
> know how you knew that.

August

> I read a lot.

The message bubble pops up, indicating she's typing. But then it disappears and reappears a few seconds later.

Ella

> Wish I knew you after my gma . . .
> I could have used a reading buddy.

He hesitates.

August

> Same.

I look up at August, my eyes wide, caught somewhere between shock and disbelief. I know it's one simple word, but that's the most open thing I've heard him say about Des's passing in years, and he said it by text to a girl he barely knows. Part of me is relieved, thinking maybe he's finally ready, that the magic amount of time has passed to break down The Wall. But the other part of me is bummed that it wasn't me he decided to talk to, even though I know it doesn't matter in the big picture.

August must read something in my expression because he says, "What?"

I cover with humor. "Nice dissertation, Professor."

He shrugs. "It's from my Berkeley essay, remember?"

"Oh. Right," I say too fast, then compensate for the weird feeling it evokes by adding, "It's a good one," which only makes my reaction more awkward, not less.

He gives me a knowing look. "You're lying."

"Not even a little," I say. "I just didn't expect you to bring it up."

"You didn't expect me to bring up my essay?" he says like he can't even begin to understand what I'm babbling about.

"No, I mean, I just forgot about those essays."

His eyes search mine. "Tiny, you read them more than a hundred times. You didn't forget about them."

Mother effer. "Who are you, the memory police?"

He doesn't laugh. "Something I should know?"

But I can't tell him because what would I even say? That I'm having doubts about the school we've worked tirelessly to get in to for years and then celebrated for a month when we did, because it suddenly feels too far away? The school I chose and championed?

"Tiny?"

"Nope. Nothing to know. I've just been stressing a little more than I should over getting ready to move."

For a moment he looks like he wants to argue, but then he decides against it and looks down at his phone, where he has a text waiting from Ella.

Ella

I owe you. That was super helpful

August
No owing necessary.

Ella
No really. I've been spinning my wheels over here. #bourbonbitesback

"Or maybe get rid of your boyfriend who pressures you to drink when you're not in the mood?" I comment, happy to change the topic.

Ella
Swinging by my fav crêpe place when I finish up here. Buy you one as thanks?

August's head whips up and we share a look. I raise my fist in the air. She's asking him to hang out alone—major step forward, and one we desperately need in order to keep this case moving.

August
You're on.

As I watch August, my phone buzzes with a text from Bentley. I glance at it below the table and out of his line of sight.

Bentley
Whatcha thinkin?

Me
Beach later? Not sure what time, but I'll keep you posted.

Bentley
Yeeeees!

When I look up, August is watching me. "Something interesting?"

For a split second, it annoys me. He shares his personal business with Ella; why shouldn't I share something with Bentley that doesn't involve him?

"Not really."

"'Cause you've been low-key obsessed with your phone lately," he says and sips his coffee. "You looked at it every five minutes while we were at the carnival."

A nervous tingle forms in my chest, and I attempt to shrug it away. "I guess we both have our secrets." The instant the words leave my mouth, I regret them. Bentley isn't a secret. Des isn't a secret. The Wall is supposed to come down, not be reinforced. But he only raises an eyebrow, not asking me to elaborate.

28

AUGUST

The crêpe place in Ella's town has a beachy, country-store vibe, complete with a porch that has beach chairs on it for people who are too sandy to sit inside. I walk up the steps to the screen door in the fading light and pull it open. Ella waits near the front window, rapidly typing into her phone.

I clear my throat.

She looks up, and when she sees me, she smiles. For some reason it catches me off guard. She's never smiled at my arrival before, and it's nice, enough so that I break eye contact and put my hands in my pockets. And as I do I hear Tiny's voice taunting me about having a crush, which I do not. I do like her, but as a person, not a romantic interest; we just understand each other in a way I didn't expect.

Ella slips her phone into her shoulder bag and chuckles. "Don't look so nervous; it's not like this is a date or anything."

And great. My cheeks are reddening, and there's absolutely nothing I can do about it. "Obviously," I say, trying to cover my absurd blush. "I never thought otherwise."

She exhales. "Exactly. Good. I told Leah you'd never think I was asking you out-out." Suddenly her intent phone typing makes sense.

I scratch a nonexistent itch on my eyebrow. "Sooo, you like crêpes, huh?"

She laughs. "Don't you dare act like I just made this awkward."

"You didn't?"

"Not even a little. We're friends. Friends eat crêpes together. End of story."

I smile inadvertently at the admission that we're friends.

But Ella must take my smile as something else because she says, "And don't grin at me like that, either. Just look at the menu. Nutella and strawberries. Bananas and honey. Smile at those."

I obediently direct my attention to the handwritten chalkboard menu on the wall and follow her to the counter. Despite my awkwardness, it occurs to me there is an opening here to discuss her relationship. "Speaking of Justin," I start.

She gives me the side-eye. "Not even remotely smooth."

"Ouch. I'd call Justin at least quasi-smooth."

She half laughs. "Not Justin. You."

"I mean, he's pretty popular," I continue.

She looks at me suspiciously. "So?"

"So are you."

She turns to face me, no longer making a show of reading the chalkboard. "And?"

I shrug. "And nothing," I say casually, knowing there's no chance she'll let my comment slide. "It just makes sense."

She studies my face, or what she can see of it in profile. "Because I'm shallow?"

"Not at all." I meet her eyes. "The exact opposite, really."

She lifts an eyebrow, unsure if she should be offended.

"But popular people always date each other. It's just an accepted fact," I say.

"I'm not dating him because he's popular," she insists like she needs me to know that. But I can also see her trying to nail down her motives, which is the whole point—self-evaluation. Tiny often says we don't really do anything in these cases but hold up a mirror, and that it's what people see in the reflection that has them choose differently.

"I didn't say you were," I agree.

"You implied it."

"All I'm saying is that people have a different level of attractiveness when they're popular, and I'm not talking about the physical. Popular people don't get scrutinized the same way, their bullying gets celebrated as humor, and so on."

"I'd say the opposite," she replies, pushing back. "I'd say their lives are under a microscope and they get scrutinized more."

I shake my head. "In the spotlight more, observed more, yes. But their flaws get overlooked. I'm not saying it's always bad. It just skews perspective."

A girl with purple hair behind the counter asks us if we're ready to order. Ella immediately shifts her attention, and I let the conversation go. I'm not trying to convince her of something, just plant a seed that Justin might not be as shiny and perfect as he seems.

We tell the girl behind the counter what we want, and she hands us a number.

Ella chooses a small table by the window overlooking the porch. "This place has been here forever," she says, changing the subject. "I used to come here with my mom before I could even walk."

I sit across from Ella at a rustic wooden table.

"Hasn't changed a bit," she says.

"Nostalgia is a funny thing."

She tilts her head as she pulls her chair in. "How do you mean?"

"I read once that nostalgia makes people feel like life has more meaning, something about increased connection and value," I explain. But what I don't say is that Tiny and I often use nostalgia as a tool in our cases. In fact, I'd have chosen to meet her here if I'd known it existed.

"That makes sense," she says. "Maybe that's why I like it so much."

"Are you close with your mom?" I ask.

She sighs, twisting a gold ring on her pointer finger. "I used to be. Well, I don't know. I guess I still am? I just . . . recently things have been different."

"Different how?"

"Do you really want to know?"

"Wouldn't have asked the question otherwise."

She shakes her head like she's not sure what to make of me. "You know, you're definitely not what I expected, Holden. You're smart. And actually kind of nice."

I laugh. "You're surprised I'm nice?"

She laughs, too. "I take it back—you're not nice. But you *are* genuine, which is rare."

For a second, I feel guilty. If she knew that I was asking about her mom because Tiny and I discussed it this afternoon, she wouldn't praise me. But just as quickly, I push the doubt away. If someone had done this for Des, she'd still be here.

She rolls her eyes when I don't immediately answer. "You basically suck at small talk, though."

I (the real August) smile at this. "That might be the truest thing you've ever said."

"I've watched you with Amber. I'm not gonna lie: it's painful."

I rest my elbows on the table. "Well, if we're going this whole truth route . . . When you told me Amber wanted me to come to her party, I was hesitant. But when I got there and she kept touching my arm, I thought she might devour me like a praying mantis."

She laughs a full-bodied laugh, and it lights up her face in a way I haven't seen before. "Amber's the queen of the arm touch, and it gets exponentially worse when she's flirting and/or drinking. Drives Leah nuts."

"I'm with Leah."

The purple-haired girl shows up at our table, giving us our crêpes and lemonades and taking the number in exchange.

"Amber thinks you like her, you know," Ella says, amused. "Thinks you're just too shy to admit it."

"Damn. I mean, I'm flattered. But Amber's not my type by a long shot."

"You're not into blond femme fatales? Are you sure you have a pulse?"

"Stupid, right?"

"Very," she agrees. "But now I'm curious. If you don't like Amber, what kind of girl do you like?"

"Uh," I say, rubbing the back of my neck. "I guess I like people who surprise me."

"You're gonna have to elaborate on that one."

"Well," I say, pausing for a beat, trying to actually answer. No one's asked me this question since I was a preteen, when Tiny said she liked blonds, and that even though she'd give anyone a chance because personality was far more important, she just couldn't help but love all that shiny hair; all I said in response was that I liked smart girls. "I've known lots of Ambers. I can pretty much tell you what she's going to do and when. But I prefer not knowing. I like when someone throws me for a loop."

Ella doesn't immediately respond with a question or banter. Instead, she raises her eyebrows. "You better not be referring to when I said you weren't what I expected. I was *not* flirting with you," she says, giving me a stern look and pointing her fork at me.

My eyes widen and I scramble to fix it. "Not what I was getting at. I didn't say you liked surprising guys; I said I like surprising girls."

Now she looks embarrassed, and I feel like this whole meeting is somehow cursed to be awkward, and that it might be Tiny's fault because of her taunting.

"Well, right, good," she replies, spearing her crêpe. "Because I don't. I like guys predictable and boring."

I laugh. "Fair enough."

"Now, what were we talking about before this?" she continues. "Oh, right, you asked about my mom," Ella says, changing not only the subject but also the tone.

I nod, readjusting. "You don't have to—"

"Obviously," she says. "But I want to." She takes a small bite and swallows. "It's just, well, my mom and I don't talk that much anymore. I mean, we talk, but not about real things. Every time we get on a heavy topic, we argue. So we both just started avoiding them." She shakes her head. "It's funny because I give people advice all day long on my astrology blog about deeply personal issues, and yet I . . ." She pauses like she's searching for the right words.

"Don't think about your own problems?" I offer.

"Never," she agrees. "Although I'm not sure you can relate. You always bring the conversation to something personal and real."

"Me?" I say, a little surprised. "Not even close."

She gives me a demanding stare.

"No, seriously." Once again I've slipped into August's truth. "I'm way better at talking about other people's problems than my own."

She leans her elbows on the table. "Okay, Holden, shoot. Tell me something you avoid dealing with."

I don't answer right away, but Ella doesn't waver. And I realize why I've never let my personality seep into cases before, because throwing out fake problems is easy and non–anxiety inducing.

"How about this: I'll go first." She wipes her mouth with her napkin.

Shit. We're actually doing this.

"So remember how I told you I think of my grandmother as my best friend? Well, I haven't been able to get that out of my head. I keep wondering what it means about my relationship with Amber and Leah that I'd choose Nonna over them even though she's gone." She fidgets with her fork. "The three of us have been friends since elementary school. But we had a falling-out shortly before my grandmother passed. And truthfully, I don't think we've ever gotten back to where we were. Something is just different, and I don't know what, and I don't know how to fix it."

I'm once again taken aback. Why didn't her parents tell us about her grandmother or this social situation? Losing first your friend group and then your closest relative is devastating and something I imagine changed her entire psychology, how she sees the world and herself in it. "Honestly, I don't know how you did it. I'm not sure I'd recover from a falling-out with Mia alongside losing Des." I mean this. I'd have been utterly lost.

She presses her lips together and nods, dipping her head with the motion and once again revealing the star constellation of freckles on her cheekbone. "Your turn," she says instead of elaborating about how hard it was. And once again I realize how similar we are.

She waits.

But I don't immediately speak. Because I feel I owe her a real answer.

Ella will never know this since I'll only be in her life for another couple of weeks, but she's doing for me what I usually do for others, providing a space to dig through all the layers and access what's underneath. I take a breath. "You know how I offered to teach you to paint?" My voice is quiet.

"I do."

I study my hands, my heart beating too fast. "I haven't painted since my sister passed."

She stops her cup halfway to her mouth. "Not at all?"

"Not at—" I say, halting as I consider my imaginary drawings.

"What?"

"No. Nothing." I shift in my chair, not willing to admit those even to myself.

She watches me for a long moment, then nods to herself like she sees more than I'm saying. And maybe she does because she says, "I hated astrology for a whole year after my grandmother died. Couldn't even look at it without bawling."

I look up at her. "I get that."

"I know you do. I think you get a lot of things about me," she says, and we hold eye contact for a long second, so long that I feel my heart-beat in my temples.

She takes a sip of lemonade.

I'm still recalibrating when she asks, "So then that painting offer wasn't real?"

"Honestly . . ." I pause to consider it. "I meant it when I said it, but that was before you knew what it meant to me. I feel . . . I don't know. A little . . ."

"Vulnerable?" she offers.

"I was gonna say embarrassed, but yeah," I admit with an audible exhale.

She eyes me, like she's trying to decide something. "Well, you know what? I had no intention of taking you up on that offer. But I just changed my mind."

I hesitate, caught squarely between a definitive no as August and an obligatory yes as Holden. Shit.

"Tomorrow. My house." She takes a bite of her crêpe like everything is settled.

And for the first time since we started Summer Love, I'm nervous. I was supposed to be providing Ella with a friendly ear, someone to hash things out with and challenge her norm to see what shakes out. How is it that she's challenging my norm? I don't know how to feel about it, and I certainly don't want to go through with it. But what choice do I have? Tell Tiny I'm sorry, but I'm giving up the much-needed tuition money this job is providing and sabotaging this case? And even if I were okay with ruining our dream-school plans, which I'm not, I'd never abandon Ella knowing what I know. Even if this case goes wrong, even if she winds up hating me, I want her to see Justin for who he really is and make a choice for herself. We all need someone to lean on once in a while, someone who'll be honest and tell us when we've behaved poorly or overreacted or in Ella's case when she's making decisions for her future based on other people's needs and not her own. I get paid to do this job, but I don't do it for the money. I do it because Des would have, and because I wish someone did it for her.

29
VALENTINE

The sun is low in the sky as I walk toward the beach, and big fluffy clouds float in the distance, promising a gorgeous romantic sunset during my date with Bentley. Damn it, August, you couldn't have made plans with Ella one hour earlier?

I kick off my sandals at the edge of the beach and retie my white hoodie around the waist of my long maxi dress. I head for the sandy path and follow it past the dunes, onto a mostly empty expanse of beach. There are a few dog owners playing catch with their pets, a few families packing up their gear, and Bentley. He's down by the break, jeans rolled up under his knees and his ankles in the water.

Bentley turns as I approach, and the glowy light illuminates his sun-bleached hair.

"Hey," he says, all nerves.

"Hey yourself," I reply, not exempt from nerves, either.

He steps out of the water and joins me on the warm sand. "You came."

I laugh, dropping my sandals. "You thought I wouldn't?"

"Maybe?"

"And risk you throwing pebbles at my window in the middle of the night again? Nope."

"No regrets." He holds eye contact and gives me a small hopeful smile. "It got you here."

No wonder girls fall over themselves to get his attention. That look is nice. Really nice.

"Should we walk?" I ask, changing my mind about the sunset being a problem.

"Yeah, sure," he says, and we turn, making our way through the sand at a slow pace.

"What'd you do today?" I ask.

"Surfed before the twins woke up, then took care of them, and now I'm here."

"Are you thinking of getting a summer job?" I'm not sure how to get away from these generic questions. We've known each other most of our lives; we live only a couple hundred feet apart. And yet, I don't know much about Bentley other than a handful of childhood memories and surface details.

"I'd kill to work at the Surf Shack," he says.

"So why don't you?"

He shrugs.

"No response?"

"I can't work there is all."

"Did you apply?" I ask. "Everyone knows you're a good surfer, I bet they'd hire you in a second."

He shakes his head but again offers no explanation.

"So that's it?"

"I guess."

I sigh, and because I'm me I call the situation out for what it is. "You know we suck at this conversation thing, right—you more than me with your nonanswers, but we're both crap. How do we fix that?"

"Sorry," he says, not joining in the humor. "Is it cool if we just don't talk about my family?"

This catches me off guard. "We weren't talking about your family, were we?"

"No, I mean . . ." He pushes his hair back from his forehead. "So what did you do today?"

I stare at him, not sure where to go from here. This is one of the most awkward conversations I've ever had, which is shocking considering I'm best friends with August.

"Okay, wait," I say, stopping in the sand.

He stops with me. "Val—"

"Hang on." I lift my hand. "Let me get this out, 'cause otherwise I think we're about to have the worst sunset walk of all time, which is basically a travesty."

He looks out at the water and then back at me.

"How come we always go from happy and easy to . . . this?" I gesture to the space between us. "I'm just confused."

He rubs the back of his tan neck. "It's not you."

"It kinda feels like it *is* me. Like at any moment I might say the wrong thing and we'll be right back to our fight in the kitchen."

"I just . . ." He drops his arm. "I didn't want to tell you that I can't get a regular job because my mom can't afford childcare, okay?"

And now I'm way more confused than I was a minute ago.

He lifts his hands. "I didn't want you to think I was a giant loser."

"Wait, what?" I choke. "That *does not* make you a loser. It makes you a great older brother."

"Your family lives in that big house. Your parents are so nice. You're just . . . perfect. I didn't want to blow it."

If I thought I was at a loss a second ago, he just upped it. "Wow, Bentley. I don't know if I think you're sweet or if I'm really insulted. You said I'm perfect, which isn't true, but okay. Let's go with it. If I were perfect, would I ever judge you like that?"

"Probably not," he admits.

"No probably about it. I'd never think less of you for that, and if I did, you shouldn't like me at all. So don't ever underestimate me like that again."

But instead of apologizing, he smiles.

"What?"

"I just didn't think you could get any prettier," he says, and I don't know if I want to accept his compliment or scowl to get my point across.

"You better be saying that because I'm honest and not because you want to bone me."

His grin grows. "I'm saying it because you're confident."

"Right, well, yeah," I say. "Thanks."

Now he laughs. "Do you remember that time when we were seven and Charlie Atkins pinned me to the baseball field and shoved muddy grass down my pants?"

I smile. I had actually forgotten about that. "I kicked him in the balls."

"You totally did. You told him that if he did it again you were going to drag him by his Batman underwear through the playground."

I laugh. "I did say that, didn't I?"

"I think half the class had a crush on you that day."

"Because I swooped in and saved you?" I say, adding humor to his admiration because now it feels more real and I'm not sure what to do with that.

"Exactly."

"It's funny, 'cause now Charlie's three times my size and you guys are best friends," I say as we start walking down the beach again, this time without the stilted conversation.

"I bet you could still take him, though." He reaches out and touches my upper arm.

I flex my nonexistent muscles in his grip. "I mean, obviously. You should bench with me." I look at his perfectly cut arm. "I could teach you a thing or two."

"Done," he says, and before I even realize what's happening, he circles one hand behind my back and one below my knees and picks me up. "You're lighter than my normal weights, but much prettier."

I laugh. "You know that isn't what I meant."

But he makes no effort to put me down.

"Bentley."

"Valentine?"

His arm is warm against my back, and I can smell the remnants of his sunscreen and the salt water in his hair. And while I've never really thought of myself as someone who was into the whole broad-shoulder thing, Bentley up close is kind of beautiful with his tanned skin and sun-chapped lips.

"Are you planning on just carrying me for the rest of the walk?" I say, secretly enjoying it.

"Nah. I'll totally put you down," he says and takes a step into the water.

Without thinking I wrap my arms around his neck. "You wouldn't dare."

"Wouldn't I?" He takes another step, so that the water hits him midcalf.

"Bentley Cavendish, I swear I will kill you."

"What was that? Couldn't hear you over the sound of that wave."

I whip my head toward the ocean only to discover he's right: a big wave is headed our way, and while it probably won't knock us over, it'll do a hell of a job getting us wet.

He stands his ground and I squeeze my eyes shut, bracing for impact. But at the last second, he takes three steps backward, and while the wave misses us, the spray mists my feet.

Bentley chuckles and puts me down in dry sand.

I unwrap my arms from his neck and hit him right in the chest. "You are such an idiot."

"Maybe . . . but I did get you to smile."

"I definitely wasn't smiling," I reply, even though I suspect I was.

Amusement teases up the corners of his mouth. "Says the girl who just called herself honest two minutes ago."

My eyes widen. "Wow. Now I want to hit you again."

He steps closer and takes my hand in his, placing it on his chest. "Here, I'll help you."

I shake my head, but logic has become an ephemeral thing, no easier to grasp than a cloud. His heart beats a mile a minute under my fingertips, and mine speeds up to match it.

His clear blue eyes soften in a way I didn't know they could. "You challenged me to kiss you the other day in my kitchen."

"Correction: I challenged you to show me your game."

"But I didn't. You know why?"

I want to respond, but my thoughts are convoluted nonsense. I'm currently touching Bentley Cavendish's *very* beautiful chest, I've recently discovered he's not the shallow idiot I thought he was, and my stomach is dipping in a way that makes my skin tingle.

"Because I've liked you since forever." His voice is uncharacteristically quiet. "And I wanted our first kiss to be better than that."

"Better?" I swallow, not moving an inch, not telling him to stop leaning closer. In fact, I think I'm the one who's gravitating toward him.

"Better," he repeats, tentatively reaching his hand out to rest on my hip. "I wanted you to know that when I kissed you, it mattered."

I feel the heat of his palm through my dress, and his fingertips press lightly into my skin. "Prove it," I say in almost a whisper, and the corners of his mouth pull up mischievously.

He glides his hand from my hip to the small of my back, gently pulling me into him, and when our bodies touch, I feel brighter, like I swallowed the fading sun and it filled me with its warmth. He pauses, our chests rising to meet one another with each breath and our lips slightly parted. His expression shifts ever so slightly to a question, as though he's checking if this is okay. I nod almost imperceptibly, not only wanting him to kiss me but needing him to.

Some part of him must understand because he lets out a breath that feels like relief and his other hand moves to the base of my neck, gliding into my hair. His stomach tightens as he tips his head down, and when his lips angle toward mine, I press against them. He's gentle with me, but as he teases my mouth open, my whole body goes pleasantly taut. I wind my hands into his hair and push up onto my tippy-toes, pressing closer even though there's no space left between us. My enthusiasm pulls a sound from him, small and quiet, but the feeling of which rumbles through my body like the base of a stereo. And suddenly, I want this. I want the taste of his sun-drenched kisses and the strength of his hands on my back.

We stay like that a long time, learning each other and finding our rhythm. And when the sun disappears and we know it's time to leave, I brush the tips of my fingers against his lips like I could take the essence of them home with me.

30
AUGUST

After Des passed, I camped out in her room for weeks with my sketch pad and paints. Her pillow smelled like her; there was a pile of clothes on her vanity chair from choosing an outfit the night before; and her journal lay closed on her bedside table like she had no concern whatsoever that her younger brother might read it. So I never did. It felt invasive, like at any moment she might walk through the door and be disappointed.

Those weeks I was quiet. I sketched and painted her over and over, went through her photo albums a thousand times, and cried until my face hurt. And when I felt that the weight of losing her might actually crush me, I closed the door, leaving behind my art supplies and some piece of my heart I knew I'd never recover.

"What are you two party animals up to tonight?" Des asked, popping into my bedroom and leaning on the door.

Tiny and I lounged on my bed in our pajamas, rationing out the last of our stash of Halloween candy.

Tiny held up a stack of DVDs. "Movie night."

"Well then, I guess it's a good thing I made this popcorn," she said, pulling not one but two bags of movie theater extra butter from behind her back and tossing them to us. They were warm to the touch and smelled like salty goodness.

"Thanks, Des," I said and meant it in a larger sense than just popcorn. It mattered that she went out of her way to pay attention to my life, to care about the little things like movie night. I knew I could always count on her.

"You got it," she said, pleased that we were pleased. "Try not to eat your-selves into a sugar coma."

"Mmmm," Tiny said, already tearing into her popcorn, even though we hadn't decided the movie yet. Des laughed.

Since then, Des's door has become a barrier that I don't know how to pass, a reminder of those weeks when I lost control. I clean the door-knob with the hem of my shirt, even though it doesn't need it.

Now that I'm not caught up in the moment with Ella, I can't believe I agreed to teach her how to paint. And as if scenting my anxiety over it like a shark smells blood, my mind mocks my promise to give up art and begins to sketch. It happens so fast that I have no chance of stopping it.

The downstairs screen door snaps shut and I turn, relieved to look away from Des's door. "Mom?" I call and check my phone. It's 11:47 a.m. and way too early for her to be back from work at the Kellermans'.

I head downstairs, part of me hoping she quit and part of me worried she got fired.

"August?" she says in her painter's overalls as I emerge from the staircase. "Can't stay. Just popping in for supplies."

"Oh," I reply, both parts of me disappointed.

She opens the closet door and leans in. I move around her, heading into the kitchen. I grab an old diner-style mug from the cupboard and pour the last of the lukewarm coffee.

Mom pulls out a tarp. "Did you know that Kyle's home for the summer?" She looks at me with uncertainty.

I freeze, midway to my first sip of coffee. "Uh, yeah."

"You didn't say anything when I told you about the job."

I put my coffee mug down on the counter, regretting coming in here.

"Do you want to talk about it?" she adds, her forehead scrunching with doubt.

We never talk about Kyle; it's one of the many unspoken agreements we've made in the past two years. I don't bring up the year she spent closed up in her room after my dad left, and she doesn't bring up Kyle or anything related to the accident.

She stands there with arms full of tarp, waiting for me to say something, and closes the closet door with a backward shove of her foot.

"No," I say, my voice definitive where hers is indecisive.

"August," she says, gently.

"No time, Mom." I abandon my coffee and head for the screen door. "Tiny and I have work."

I leave before she can respond.

31
VALENTINE

I lie on my couch, one leg tucked under a throw blanket and a half-read book open on my chest, staring out the window at Bentley's house. It's not like I haven't had my fair share of good kisses. We've gone to an absurd number of parties since we've started Summer Love, and as August puts it, I'm a magnet for a particular type of sensitive bro. Not long-term-boyfriend material, just the type to have fun with. But I rarely get involved with anyone in our town. It's too small and incestuous. No matter who you choose, you're bound to know someone they dated. And Bentley? I'd argue he's dated most of our school. And it shows in his kissing—it was so good that I'm still thinking about it, haven't stopped really. I mean, it's not a big deal. He's hot. He's charming. He's the perfect candidate for a summer fling. *Simple. Meaningless. Fun . . .* I touch my lips. *Sweet. Knee weakening. Stomach dropping. Everything that I want to do again. Ahhhh! No! Damn it, brain, get ahold of yourself.*

August opens my door, and I sit up so fast you'd think he caught me half-naked. But he's too preoccupied to notice my reaction; he looks like he's seriously miffed.

"Can I borrow your keys?" he asks, his eyes far away, thinking about some other conversation. And considering he just came from his house and I'm his only friend, I'm guessing it was with his mom.

I sit up on the couch. "Well, hello to you, too."

"Sorry," he says, his head momentarily dipping toward his shoes. He doesn't offer an explanation, and I don't ask for one.

He sighs, shrugging off whatever was on his mind.

"So your crêpe date with Ella . . . fill me in." Even though we talked about it by text, we didn't hash it out in person because after my sunset walk with Bentley, Mom and I ordered Thai and watched cheesy romance movies while Dad worked at the kitchen table finalizing details for his big summer work party.

August joins me on the couch. "Not much I didn't tell you. Things are good in the friend department—"

"Trust?"

"Yeah, I'd definitely say we're getting there," he replies.

"Great. Keep planting those seeds about Justin trying to influence her decisions. And maybe it's time to work on inspiring her a bit—you know, get her feeling like there's more out there than Justin and his controlling crap? Get her excited about her dreams again?"

"Already on it," he says, looking a little glum. "I'm teaching her to paint today."

My brain short-circuits. "Wait, *what?*"

He attempts a shrug but winds up looking uncomfortable. "Made sense with the whole paint-splattered-shirt thing," he says like my shock was even remotely about his strategy and not about the idea of painting itself.

"Wow." For a split second I get inexplicably annoyed. He doesn't paint for two whole years and suddenly he's teaching Ella? I know we built it into his character, but I never thought in a million years he'd do anything other than wield it as a cool personality trait.

"It's not a big deal," he says, which we both know is absolutely false.

"Au contraire," I reply, trying to push past my reaction and embrace the fact that he's taking a huge step forward. "I'm excited for you. What made you decide to take the plunge?"

"I don't know."

"Ella?" I offer.

He pauses. "I don't know," he says again and scratches his shoulder under his T-shirt sleeve. "I guess she does have this weird way of challenging me."

And suddenly I don't like Ella at all. *She* challenges him? What have I been doing these past couple years? Oh, right, building *an entire business* to give him resolution. Besides, the last time I *challenged* August to paint, he didn't talk to me for two days.

"You okay?" he says, and I realize I'm scowling.

I unclench my jaw. *Stop being a crap friend, Tiny. This isn't about you.* "Just got lost in thought a second. How can I help? What do you need?" I say, but he's looking out the window like he might jump in the water and hide under the dock. And in that moment my whole perspective shifts. This isn't about Ella or me or any of the rest of it.

"Just need to borrow the Jeep."

"Are you sure? Should you bring something with you?" I say, wanting to erase that worried look from his brows. "I mean, if she thinks you're a painter, don't you think she'd expect you to show up with a favorite brush or something?"

"I told her I haven't painted since Des."

But with that one sentence I'm right back to being the jealous friend. And because I know I can't let it show on my face, I scream in my head, *Ahhh! I will Hulk smash you, August Mariani!* Then I take a breath and recenter. "You're really honest with this girl."

"A little," he concedes.

"Do you think it'll interfere with the case?" I reply, which I recognize is both a real concern and maybe not the most supportive thing I could say.

His eyebrows push farther together. "I mean, I don't think so. I hope not."

"Look, don't worry about it. We're good at this, right?" I say, pulling it back.

"Yeah, right, definitely," he says and looks away. "I should probably get going."

I pull my keys from my purse and he takes them, wasting no time in heading for the door.

The instant he's gone, I lie back down on the couch with a plop. We're on the same team; we're working toward the same result, I remind myself. Being annoyed is dumb. But why does being the bigger person always feel like a kick to the nuts?

I pick up my phone and open my texts with Bentley, looking for a distraction.

Me

Want to come over after you're done with the twins?

Not two seconds later, his reply flashes on my screen.

Bentley
YES.

A warm tingle vibrates through my chest. I'm considering what to type back when my front door opens.

This time I don't get up. "Back already? Decided I was right about bringing your favorite paint color: smitten-faced red?" I say, attempting to make light of the whole thing.

"Smitten for whom?" my mom asks, and once again I jump like someone threw ice down my shirt.

"Oh, nothing. Thought you were August," I say quickly.

Mom places a shopping bag on the mail table. "Is August dating someone?" she asks over her shoulder like it's a happy surprise.

"Uh . . ." I scramble for a believable response, one that has nothing to do with the job I've been lying about for two years. But when she turns to face me, I forget all about Summer Love because her cheeks and nose are splotchy. "Have you been *crying*?"

"Crying?" she repeats back and touches her face as if to check. "Oh, that. Just some old pictures got me weepy. Nothing to be alarmed about."

I stand, glancing at her bag suspiciously. Mom isn't a sentimental crier—not at movies, not at baby showers, not at freaking weddings. In fact, the only time I've ever seen her cry is when her father passed. "What old pictures?"

"Some shots I just picked up from Sal's Photolab. I was going through them in the car before I came in," she replies, breaking eye contact with me and kicking off her ballet flats. "So tell me about this person August's dating."

"You never cry."

She laughs. "Everyone cries, Valentine, even me." And she looks at me expectantly to tell her about August, making me doubly nervous.

"It's new," I say, trying to sound casual. "He won't even admit that he likes her."

She leans in, like this is very important gossip. "Is that why he borrowed your Jeep? Does he have a date?"

My stomach wobbles in an unpleasant way. Lying for the greater good in our case adventures is one thing, but lying to my parents is different. I've gotten really good at never mentioning anything in front of them that would inspire questioning exactly so I wouldn't have to lie. When they ask about catering, I shrug and say, "Just work. Nothing special. Money is good." They think I work for one of the huge Boston companies that service both the North and South Shore. It's a prominent enough company that they feel satisfied, but just boring enough that they don't pry.

"That big a deal, huh?" she says when I don't respond.

"I, um. You know how private he is. I think he'd be embarrassed if I told you."

She considers it and nods. "Okay, well, if and when it does become a thing, I'd love to meet . . ." She holds her hand out.

"Ella," I say and suddenly feel extra weird that I told the truth.

"Ella," she repeats, and I drop back onto the couch, guilt nipping at my insides.

32

AUGUST

Ella's house is oddly imposing without all the party guests and cars. I pull to a stop in the circle at the end of her long driveway, half expecting a butler with coattails to pop out and offer assistance.

I step out of Tiny's Jeep and follow the path to Ella's front door, staring warily at the endless white stone. Super rich people make me nervous. Super rich houses make me feel like my shoes are made of banana peels.

The doorbell mimics the sound of church bells, and it only takes a second before a woman in a maid's uniform answers. She shows me inside, leading me through the round living room and out to the pool deck, where Ella is sunbathing in a lawn chair.

"Oh, hey," Ella says, sitting up and lifting her sunglasses to the top of her damp hair like she's the lead in an eighties movie.

She's wearing a simple black one-piece, the type of bathing suit you might do laps in, but the smooth skin of her bare legs and arms makes it hard to look away.

Women are beautiful, sometimes in a way that steals your breath and makes your heart stutter. The way their necks curve into their collarbones and their hands are so much softer than mine. The way their hair smells good and their bodies curve. But even though I can appreciate their beauty, I never seem to connect in a way that makes me reach out, fumble to hold their hands, or ask if I can kiss them. Not the way Tiny does where she'll date someone and lose herself in the person for a while. It's not that I don't want to lose myself; it's that I don't know how. Or maybe I don't want to let go. Either way, I've never been good at romance. The truth of it just doesn't reach me somehow.

"Hey," I say, stumbling over the word and blushing at my thoughts.

She stands with a smile, pulling a flowy black dress over her head, and smirks. "Not this again."

"What?" I say innocently, and I know she probably thinks I'm embarrassed because she's beautiful, which I am. But I can also recognize how stupid that is. I live in a beach town. I've seen attractive girls in far less bathing suit my entire life.

"That look," she says.

I clear my throat. "Your house is intimidating."

She lets out an unexpected laugh. "Isn't your mom on a yacht trip right now? I'm sure yours isn't too shabby, either."

I shrug. "Not like yours."

She watches me for a second. "You know what, Holden? You're definitely your own cat."

"My own cat?"

"Yeah, like you march to the beat of your own drum," she explains, handing me a glass bottle of water. "Cats just make more sense to me because they're so nuanced."

I smile. "I have a twenty-year-old cat, and I could not agree more."

"Totally pegged you as a cat guy."

"It's my best feature."

She smiles, too, and once again we hold eye contact.

"So painting," she says, clearing her throat and gesturing to the far corner of the deck, where an easel is already set up in the shade of the trees. "Should we do this thing?"

"Yeah," I say, trying to cover the hesitancy in my voice.

"Don't worry," she replies like she can hear it despite my efforts. "I'm way more nervous than you are."

"Nothing to be nervous about," I say to both of us as we cross the pale wood.

She sits down in a chair in front of the easel. "That's because you haven't seen me in action yet. I suck. And I'm about to show you how much and forever be embarrassed."

I nod, and in a way her worry eases my own. You can't talk someone down when you're anxious yourself. I set my feelings aside for a moment and focus on her. "When I was a kid, my mom always said that there was no such thing as a bad painter, only unexpressed artists."

She grins. "And you believe that?"

"Actually . . . yeah, I do," I say, imagining Tiny's shock that I agreed with something so optimistic. "I don't think there's any right or wrong to art. It's one of the things I like best about it." It doesn't occur to me until I've already said the sentence that I've put it in present tense. I decide not to think about it.

Instead, I busy myself with looking over the wicker table piled with the supplies she gathered. I grab a simple set of watercolors and pour some water into an empty plastic cup. It's disorienting handling paints again, almost like touching a piece of my own body that I haven't seen in years.

"So first"—I place the watercolors on a small table near Ella—"you need to choose what you're going to paint. It should be something you relate to, but not something overly complex or exacting."

She scratches her elbow. "Okay . . ." She glances around her deck and backyard. "Maybe the pool? I've always loved being in the water."

"Perfect," I agree.

"That's it? I should just paint the water?"

"You should just paint it."

She gives me a look that suggests I'm breaking my end of the bargain by not walking her through it, but she also doesn't ask for help. She chooses a brush, dips it in water, and then in blue paint. Ella turns to the canvas, staring at it like it might bite her. She lifts her brush but after a long second puts it back down.

As the time stretches, she exhales. "You think my house is intimidating. I'd argue this canvas is much worse."

"Good."

She shoots me an accusatory look. "Good?"

"You're being honest." I gesture at the canvas. "That's all you need to do."

"How's this for honesty? I'm fairly certain I want to hit you with this brush."

I laugh. "Okay, tell me . . . what's intimidating about the canvas?"

"I don't know; it's blank?" She gestures at it.

"And that's scary?"

"It's not *scary*. It's . . ." She huffs. "It's all on me. It feels like performance pressure."

"So you'd rather I told you what to do?" I say, making a veiled point about her boyfriend, her friends, and even her parents that I hope might spark something.

"Wow. Dick move. I'd rather you *taught* me, which is what you said you were going to do in the beginning."

"Right. But I can't teach you until you've at least tried to do it yourself. And anyone who claims they can wants you to do their version of art, not yours."

We stare at each other, the silence between us thick with her frustration.

"Fine. Whatever." She drags her paintbrush across the canvas in a few fast strokes. "There, a pool. Happy?"

"Are you?"

"Oh my god. Is this your talent? Driving people crazy?"

I smile. "Maybe. But that's definitely not what I'm trying to do here."

She rolls her eyes and looks at the canvas. After a minute of brooding, her shoulders drop. She glances at the pool and back again, dipping her paintbrush in some green. And this time when she places it on the canvas, she appears to actually be trying. She could have gotten up and walked away, but she didn't, and I admire her for that.

We're like this for a while, Ella needing to look at the pool less and less, until she forgets about the visual and is fully immersed in her colors. She abandons the idea of painting a rectangle with blue squiggles in it and instead brushes blues, greens, and whites over the entire canvas, creating a lighter patch of water through the center that gets darker toward the sides. Suddenly I realize what it is she's doing.

"You're painting what water looks like when you're submerged in it, aren't you?" I ask, and now I'm looking at her differently.

"Yes, yes, I am." Her frustration is gone and there's an uptick in tone like she feels seen. "And what it feels like."

"Wow. I'm . . . well, I'm impressed."

She laughs. "I mean, it's obviously not very good but—"

"I disagree. I think the perspective is actually great."

She lifts an eyebrow. "And here I thought you weren't the type to blow smoke."

"I'm not," I say and look at her so she can see I mean it. "It's not the technicality of it. You're a beginner. It's the feeling. You captured something of the peace of being submerged, and you did it on your first try."

She looks momentarily downward, then back up at me like she's hesitant to believe it. "Yeah?"

"Yeah. And if this is what you do with a blank canvas . . . damn, you might change the world." I can almost hear Tiny clapping and saying, *Take a bow, Holden.* Only I'm not using a line; I (August) actually mean what I'm saying.

Ella tries to contain a smile but fails. "God, you're the worst. Why do you always have to say the right thing?"

Now I'm smiling, too. "You might be the first person to ever say that to me." I lift my water bottle to my lips.

"Unlikely. I bet girls tell you that all the time. Speaking of which, why don't you have a girlfriend?"

I choke on my water. She didn't subtly mention a girlfriend wondering if I'd refute it; she just outright asked. "Uh . . . hmmm," I say, wiping water from my mouth with the back of my hand.

One corner of her sun-pink lips quirks up. "Well, this is entertaining."

"Glad you're enjoying yourself."

"You didn't answer the question."

I sigh. There's no saying no to this girl. "Truth be told . . . I'm not that good at connecting with people, friends or otherwise." It doesn't escape me that I was just thinking about this, that she somehow plucked my worry from my psyche the same way I often do on cases. Only she did it without trying.

She lifts an eyebrow like she doesn't believe it.

"Attraction is easy," I say with a sigh. "Actually connecting? Not so much."

For a second, she's still. "Wow, you're admitting that?"

I scratch my shoulder, more surprised than she is. "Yeah, I guess I am."

"Huh," she says and leans back in her chair. "And what are you doing here? Connection or attraction?"

If I were drinking water, I'd choke again. It's not that these conversations never come up when Tiny and I are doing these cases, but they're never this direct. So I do what I normally do and steer away from the topic, saying, "You have a boyfriend," but the words feel stilted and I think she can tell.

She leans back in her chair, one strap from her black sundress sliding down her shoulder. "That's not in debate."

Despite my best effort I look at the strap. And swallow. Like a complete effing chump. "You really like to put people on the spot."

She shrugs. "Future journalist."

I lean forward, resting my elbows on my knees and breaking eye contact so I can think.

She laughs lightly. "How about this, tell me about painting instead."

"What do you want to know?" I ask, looking back up. It feels strange that I'm relieved to be talking about painting of all things.

"What you almost told me in the crêpe place but didn't," she says, and my relief vanishes.

I pause, scraping my teeth along my bottom lip.

And to my shock she sighs and says, "Sorry."

My eyes flit up to meet hers. "Wait, why?"

"I just . . ." She shakes her head, her long wavy hair sliding across her tanned arm. "I was doing that thing I do when I'm nervous. I start asking pointed questions and putting the other person on the spot. I shouldn't have done that."

"Why are you nervous?" I ask before I can decide if I should. Because I no longer know where August ends and Holden begins; the line is all but gone.

She lifts her shoulders and drops them, twisting a simple gold ring with slender fingers. It occurs to me I never realized how delicate her hands were before, that if I held them to my own, I'd dwarf them.

"I honestly don't know," she replies. "Maybe it's the painting? Or the things we talk about? But there's something about the way our conversations always seem to strike at the heart of things, and it makes me wonder if I've . . ." She looks out past her yard to the trees swaying in the warm summer breeze. "Never mind."

Only now I want to know. "Does it make you wonder if you've been . . . numb for a while?" I ask, not because I know I'm right, because it's how I feel.

"Yes," she says with relief. "Numb. So numb."

This time when silence descends neither of us looks away. We just stare at each other for a long moment like the other might be a mirror, one we desperately needed but didn't know to look for. I think I forget to breathe.

Then I hear myself talking, telling her things I haven't said aloud, and what really shocks me is, I want to. "I didn't just paint. I also sketched," I say, just to see how it feels. "And I gave that up, too, when Des died."

She waits, not pressuring me this time.

"But"—I study my hands—"what no one knows is that . . . I still draw in my thoughts."

"In your thoughts?" She leans forward in her chair like she's genuinely interested.

I look up. "It's like this . . . I'll be concentrating, trying to figure something out, and just start sketching on the surface in front of me— the sky, the ocean, whatever. I think it's a way of processing, like having a conversation with myself. But honestly, I hate it."

"Why would you hate it?" Her voice upticks in surprise.

"Because I gave it up, you know? Because it feels like failure. Because I can't stop. Even if I close my eyes, the sketch keeps going."

"That's not failure," she says so adamantly that I almost believe her.

"And because . . ." I say, with a big exhale, "I used to leave sketches for my sister. I'd hide them in her things, like in her journal or under her pillow. And she . . ." I shake my head. "This probably sounds ridiculous."

Suddenly Ella reaches across the short distance between our chairs, made smaller by the fact that we're both leaning forward. Her soft fingers lightly touch my bare knee. "Not even a little," she says reassuringly.

And so I go on, unsure, but somehow bolstered by her touch. "Des used to celebrate every time she found one. Make a big deal about how much she loved them. Drawing them now, with no one to give them to, just makes me angry."

She doesn't say anything for a moment, but she doesn't take her hand back, either. And I'm not sure what it says about me, but I'm glad she doesn't. That spark of warmth against my skin feels like an embrace, one I didn't know I needed. I have the urge to place my fingers over hers and to rub the tips of them on the underside of her silky palm, but I know I shouldn't, so I just sit there, feeling simultaneously raw from what I shared and anchored by her presence.

She gives me a small smile and pulls her hand back. It's for the best, I tell myself.

"It's okay to be angry," she says. "No one really says that. They say it's okay to be sad or quiet or worried, but no one wants to deal with anger. It's too heavy and unpredictable. But how can it be wrong to be mad that someone you love is gone? How can you not blame the world?"

I nod while she speaks the words I've so often thought.

Ella pushes back wisps of hair from her forehead. "Remember how I told you I hated astrology after Nonna died? Most nights I used to climb out my bedroom window because I felt like there wasn't enough air. And I'd lie on my balcony, gasping and crying. I'd have screamed at the stars, if I thought it'd have made a difference."

A moment of sadness flashes across her face, and I wait for her to go on.

She lifts her hands. "Believe me, I absolutely understand why you'd want to give up your art. I, too, thought that if I could just forget astrology that the whole thing would hurt less. And for a while that worked, until it didn't. Until I started doodling star constellations in the margins of my notebooks without meaning to and guessing people's signs in my head. The worst part was when I'd realize what I'd done; it felt like getting hit by a grief truck."

"I can relate," I say with weight, agreeing with everything she said, especially the truck part.

Ella twists her ring again before continuing. "And then one night, when I thought I was finally moving on, I felt like there was no air in my room. Again. I went out on my balcony and still, nothing. I thought I was going to suffocate." She drops her hands in her lap. "I don't know why, but I started reciting the signs over and over. Saying my grandmother's chart. Saying my own. And I know this sounds crazy, but I heard her reciting with me." She hesitates. "I can't believe I'm telling you this."

"I'm glad you're telling me this," I say, and I mean it beyond just this case.

"Now every time I work on astrology, I hear her telling me to look deeper, or to stop being so judgmental, to trust myself." She sighs. "So maybe, and I'm not saying I'm right, your sketching is similar, like a love letter to your sister. Maybe it's not a failure but an opportunity to reconnect with her?"

The words *love letter to my sister* hit me hard. My heart speeds up and I look away, not wanting her to see how much they affect me.

"I've never actually told anyone about the balcony," she says in a quieter voice.

I look back at her. "And I've never told anyone about the drawings."

"Not even Mia?"

I shake my head. "Like I said, I'm not good at this kind of thing."

"I always thought I was. But the more we talk about it, I'm not so sure."

I don't know why, but this admission gets me and I feel it in my bones, that you can be in your own head every moment of every day, witness to every thought, and yet not know yourself.

"What you said about popularity the other day . . ." she starts and glances at the pool. "It bothered me."

"You know I—"

"It bothered me because it's true," she says, steamrolling over my objection. "And not just about Justin, about me, too."

I open my mouth to protest.

"Shush, or I might lose my nerve."

I watch her attentively, struck by her bravery, even as she's telling me to shut up.

"What I just told you about feeling lost? Well, being popular was kind of a Band-Aid for that. You're one hundred percent right that when you're popular, people don't scrutinize you the same way. And I didn't want people scrutinizing me or seeing me at all actually. I told you my friends and I had a falling-out? What I didn't say was that dating Justin fixed that, sealed the deal on our collective popularity. When he showed interest in me, my status rose fast. I guess it was my version of hiding in plain sight?"

For a brief moment, I'm dumbfounded by her courage. I know how hard it is to really look inside at the things that aren't pretty and shiny, but admitting those things to another person is damn near impossible. "Wow . . . I . . ."

She flinches, and I realize in one horrible flash of a second that she thinks I'm stumbling because I'm judging her.

I self-correct. "You might be the most incredible girl I've ever met." Fantastic. Now I've swung the pendulum a little too far and I feel like an idiot.

She looks as surprised as I am.

"Sorry, I just meant . . ." I try to shake my thoughts clear. This part of the job is usually so easy for me—right ideas at the right time and people make better choices. But the connection that Ella and I share over our grief is real, and I have no rulebook for that, no helpful one-liner to speed her along to reevaluate her relationship. So, at a loss, I once again tell the truth. "What I mean is . . . I wish I was as brave as you."

Her expression relaxes and with it her eyes, a small smile pulling at her bowed lips. "Well, I think you're pretty brave. You're teaching me to paint. You're talking about things that make you uncomfortable. Those are big steps."

Her words hit me hard, some part of me really wanting her approval. For the first time in a case, I experience regret that I can't talk to Ella simply as myself, and guilt that if I told her the truth, I might hurt her. "Ella . . ." I rub my forehead.

"Connecting," she says, and I meet her eyes. "I asked you what you were doing here, connection or attraction . . . a totally unfair question. And now I'm answering. I'm connecting with you. And if I'm being honest, you're the most surprising guy I've ever met."

I'm instantly reminded of what I told her in the crêperie, that my type is surprising girls. Heat rises in my cheeks so fast that I have no way to stop it. And in what can only be described as the worst timing ever, a man clears his throat. I launch out of my chair.

"Dad?" Ella says, standing, too, both of us horribly aware that her father likely heard the last things she said. "What are you doing home?"

"Forgot some paperwork," he says and looks from Ella to me. "And you are?"

"Holden, this is my dad. Dad, Holden," Ella says, gesturing in the space between us, but never looking directly at me.

I've done this plenty of times; I know how to remeet parents, I remind myself, but it does nothing to stop the feeling that I'm free-falling.

"Hi, Mr. Becker," I say, extending my hand. "Nice to meet you, sir."

He shakes it. "I take it you two are friends?" he asks his daughter.

Ella laughs. "Dad, you're being awkward." Parents are never good at this part, and that's when they're not already annoyed over forehead profanity and possible discussions about connection or attraction.

He assesses me. "Holden, is it?"

"Yes it is, sir."

He gives me a hard stare.

Ella pulls her hair over her shoulder and twists it. "Well, he's not going to be my friend for long if you keep looking at him like that."

But Ella's dad makes no effort to adjust. "I'm perfectly okay with that."

I swallow.

Ella frowns. "There was a message for you earlier. A call from London? Sounded kind of urgent."

Whatever this means, it has the desired effect of grabbing his attention. And they exchange a few quick sentences that I can't focus on because I'm stress-texting Tiny.

He walks away with no goodbye.

Ella looks embarrassed. "Sorry," she says, but it's obvious that our time is up. Neither of us knows what to say about our talk, her father, or the strange feeling of having shared too much. So I excuse myself politely and then play back our conversation a thousand times in my head on the way home.

33
VALENTINE

Me

Update??? I'm dying to hash out
next steps.

August

Still out with Mom. Errands. Come over when
I get back?

I glance at my clock from my lounging position on my bed. 7:05
p.m. Bentley is on his way over. I'll just make it a short visit.

Me

Yup. Text me and I'll climb through your
window like a boss with my power notebook.

But before he can respond, there's a knock on my door and I put
down my phone. "Valentine?" Mom says through the wood.

"Come in!"

She opens the door, revealing a freshly showered Bentley in a white

T-shirt and distressed jean shorts. "You have a visitor," she says, and one of her eyebrows goes up as though it were observing the situation and declaring it interesting.

I slide off my fluffy white comforter onto the carpet. "Hey," is all I say to Bentley, yet my mom's other eyebrow appears to join in on the amusement. So I add, "Mom, we're good."

"Kicking me out, huh?"

"Mom."

She puts her hands up and heads into the hallway.

The smell of woodsy soap and minty toothpaste drifts toward me as Bentley moves into my room and sits on the end of my bed.

He smiles up at me. "Is it weird that I missed you?"

I laugh, sitting down next to him with one ankle tucked under my knee. "You didn't miss me."

"I mean, I did, though," he replies, and I'm not sure I like the way my stomach drops. He's like that dessert you cannot resist no matter how full you are.

I bump him with my shoulder. "You just can't help but say things like that."

"True things?" he asks, practically batting his long eyelashes at me like a Disney princess.

"Line things," I correct him.

"What if I told you that I thought about our kiss about every other minute today?" Only this time when he says it his voice has a note of weight to it, and it rings true.

I decide either he's an expert at this kind of thing, or he really does fall this hard and fast, which would explain why he's had so many relationships. Unfortunately, there's no correlation between falling quickly and lasting. Not that I want a relationship from him. "I'd say that's a great line."

He stares at me like he's trying to work some meaning out of my expression. "Then tell me . . . did you?"

"Did I what?" I say innocently even though I know what he's asking.

"Think about our kiss?"

"I mean"—I pause like I need to consider—"I'd be lying if I said no."
Now he's grinning. "So you missed me, too."

"I swear," I reply with a laugh, "you're basically impossible."

He lightly touches my hand on my thigh, running his fingers along the curve of my palm, and just that feather of a touch sends heat coursing through my body. "What can I say? I know what I want."

And great, I'm flustered. "Right . . . but that changes every two weeks. Sooo." I don't even know why I'm fighting him on this. But something about his closeness and the way his damp, sun-bleached hair falls on his forehead scrambles my thoughts. It's taking all my restraint not to tackle him into my bed.

"Does that bother you?" he asks like it's a concern.

But I don't know the answer. *Does* it bother me? It's the summer before college. If we were anything, it wouldn't be serious. Besides, I've been known to fall hard and fast, too. Can I really fault him without it being a double standard? I shrug.

"What if I told you, hand to heart, that this isn't a two-week thing for me?" he says, and the overindulgent, romantic part of my brain leaps on the sentiment, even though I know it's neither true nor realistic.

I smile. "I'd say that you're wicked good at this. Talented."

"How about this," he replies, lifting my palm to his mouth and kissing it. A small gasp escapes my lips before I can pull it back, and he looks far too pleased by my reaction. "We make a deal right now that we'll be one hundred percent honest with each other."

I lean back on my bed, propping myself up on my elbows. "No one is ever one hundred percent honest. What happens if I ask you something you don't want to answer or something that makes you super uncomfortable?"

He follows my lead and lies on his side next to me, his head supported by his hand. "I'll get over it and tell you anyway."

I eye him, hooked by curiosity. "I'm weirdly tempted to take you up on this, even just as a social experiment."

"Then do it . . . unless you're scared?"

I lift a challenging eyebrow. "Never. I'm in."

"Good," he says, brushing back the hair that once again fell onto his forehead, and I have a compulsion to reach over and help him with it. "Ask me a question."

I turn on my side to face him. "Hmmm. Let's see," I say, going straight for a question he won't want to answer. "What's the most embarrassing thing that's ever happened to you?"

He grunts. "Oh man. Seriously?"

I smile, feeling a little gloaty. "Hey, this was your idea."

He laughs. "Yeah, but if I tell you, you'll never want to kiss me again."

"If you're *scared*," I say, more than a little pleased that I managed to prove my point on the first question, "we can call off the deal now, no hard feelings."

He puts his hand out. "Hang on now, I didn't say no."

But he doesn't respond right away. It takes him a couple of beats and a disbelieving headshake before he says, "Well, here goes nothing." He rubs his hand over his face, clearly trying to psych himself up. "I shit my pants."

I half laugh, half choke. "You did not."

"I did. Bad food combo before football practice. Rookie mistake. I felt the rumble and I ran for the locker room, but just as I was pulling my pants down . . . bam. I took a shower and split. Coach was pissed I disappeared, but it's basically a universal rule that if you shit your pants in public, you just go home and hide."

I'm having a hard time controlling my laughter; it's spilling out of me in a goofy way. "Wow. That's a reputation killer right there."

"You're telling me. This is serious trust, Valentine. Serious. Trust."

In a way I'm actually impressed he put himself on the line like that. His dude friends would never let him live that down if they knew.

"Okay, my turn," he says, and my stomach drops in a bright pang of anticipation. He searches my eyes with his gaze. "Did you feel something when we kissed yesterday?"

And that's all it takes for my heart to start hammering. "Feel something like what?" I stall.

"You know what," he says, more sure of himself than anyone who just told a pants-shitting story has any right to be.

My phone buzzes on the bed next to me, but I'm too consumed with his question to look at it. "Well . . . I mean, yeah. It was nice."

He raises an eyebrow. "Nice? Is that the whole truth?"

I press my lips together and then resign myself to answering. "Fine. More than nice. Like stomach-dropping, knee-weakening perfection. The kind of kiss that I'm thinking about even right now. You happy?"

The surprise on his face is gratifying. "Very," he replies. "But I'm also relieved. I don't know what I'd do if the best kiss of my life was no more than okay for you." The way his eyes flit from my eyes to my mouth makes my lips part like betrayers.

"You might be the worst," I say in almost a whisper.

But he only smiles. "I think we just established that I'm not." He gently touches my cheek, his warm and calloused fingers tracing a line to my mouth.

"My turn," I say, having a hard time focusing on anything other than his touch. "What's your favorite thing about yourself?"

He drops his hand. "Besides the fact that I just made you blush?"

"Yes, very much besides that."

"Okay, let's see," he says, thinking. "Probably that I'm a bedtime whisperer."

I tilt my head to the side. "Huh?"

"Basically that I can get the twins to sleep in under ten minutes. Always."

I stare at him. His favorite thing about himself is a parenting ability he shouldn't have for another fifteen years. "Really?"

"Yup," he confirms. "When my mom started leaving them with me, I couldn't handle bedtime. An hour of fighting and crying. I used to dread it. Now I love it."

"How come I've never heard you talk about these things before?" I ask, curious about this version of Bentley who's so different from the one I thought I knew.

He smirks. "Before a few days ago, you barely talked to me at all."

I tuck my hair behind my ear. "Fair. But do you talk about this stuff with Charlie or Cassie or whoever?" I say, referencing his ex-girlfriend who is kind of awful but an essential part of his friend group.

"Nah," is all he says.

I wonder how I never noticed that Bentley compartmentalized his life like that. I guess I just wasn't paying attention.

"Tell me something people don't know about you," he says when I don't respond, lacing his fingers through mine.

The first thing that comes to mind is Summer Love, but that's a shared secret and not mine to tell. The second is something I don't want to be true.

"I told you I shit my pants," he reminds me. "Whatever it is, it can't be that bad."

I look at him, desperately trying to think of something that fulfills his ask, but the same thought loops on repeat, one that I've been in denial about. I squeeze my eyes shut for a second, and it spills out of me. "I'm not sure I want to go to Berkeley in two months."

When I open my eyes, he's looking at me like he doesn't understand. "You're thinking of deferring?"

"No. I don't want to go, full stop," I say and feel the air whoosh out of me, shocked by how strangely liberating it felt. "The thing is, August and I have been planning on going to business school there since *forever*. We've worked all of high school to have the grades and extracurriculars to make it happen. It's *the* plan, like, our collective dream for the future."

"Why did you change your mind?"

"I don't know. I . . ." My voice trails off, embarrassment flaming my cheeks. "I kinda hate the idea of being that far from home?" I feel silly saying it, like it's a failing of some kind.

He nods. "That makes a lot of sense to me."

"It does?" I say, unsure, but also desperately wanting the agreement.

"Sounds cheesy, but I love this town."

But his answer isn't so much comfort as a reaffirmation of what I'm struggling with. Guys like Bentley stay put. They're hot and popular in high school, don't give a lot of thought to college, and wind up marrying the head cheerleader at nineteen. And when you run into them in the supermarket ten years later, you thank your lucky stars you got out. I look away, immediately feeling guilty about my unkind prediction of his future.

My phone buzzes again, only this time I break my hand hold with Bentley and reach behind me to grab it off my comforter.

August

Headed over.

A jolt of adrenaline catapults me into a sitting position. I was supposed to go to *August's house*, not have him come to mine. Did I lose track of time? Did he misinterpret my message? Out of the corner of my eye, I see Bentley sit up, too, registering my discomfort.

"What is it?" he asks.

My heart sinks. Why, oh why, did I make that honesty deal? Idiot with a capital *I*. I say the only true thing I can. "I'm super sorry to do this, but August and I actually have to work."

"So you're kicking me out?"

I exhale. "Can we reschedule?"

But before Bentley responds, my door opens, and I stand so fast you'd think I'd been goosed.

August stops dead in his tracks, clearly picking up on the tension, not that it's some feat of perception.

Bentley hesitates, like he's debating how to navigate this. But all he says is, "See you tomorrow, Valentine," and he heads for my door. And while I feel massive relief that he's leaving and I don't need to try to navigate a conversation with them both, he also said the one thing that will raise alarm bells for August.

"Yeah, okay," I say, pushing back my hair and lifting my hand in an awkward goodbye.

The door clicks shut behind Bentley, and August and I are silent for a beat.

"What was that about?" he asks, rightfully suspicious.

"Bentley? It's no big deal." Which is exactly what people say when something *is* a big deal.

"Want me to tell him to back off?" he asks, and now I'm the one who's shocked. August isn't one for confrontation.

I scratch my forehead. "Like I said, it's not a big deal."

He assesses me, and it's hard not to squirm. "Did I miss something? Are you guys . . . *hanging out?*"

"What would make you think that?" I say too quickly. I might as well just tattoo *I have a secret* on my forehead.

He looks at me like I have two heads. "'Cause he hasn't been in your room since we were twelve, and he just said he's seeing you tomorrow."

The room spins. "Truth is, um, he needs help with his brother and sister. His mom's gone a lot. You know what that's like." I instantly hate myself for saying it—for the lie and for playing on his sympathy.

"Oh," he says and considers it. "Sorry." He plops down on my bed. "Wasn't trying to go all protective on you."

I shrug, both relieved that he's letting it go and kind of wishing he'd call me out. I'm not sure I'm brave enough to flat-out tell him, especially since I've made such a big awkward deal of it, and part of me wishes he'd notice and we could clear this up. "I kind of like you protective. Brotherly love and all that."

"Bentley's just such a player. And the thought of him playing you made me see red for a second." He lies back, folding his hands behind his head.

"Totally," I agree and join him on the bed. And now my denial is complete and I feel like the biggest jerk in New England. But before I can agonize over it, my phone buzzes.

Leah

Party tomorrow night. Justin's house. Parents are out of town. #getwild

I instantly perk up, turning my phone screen toward August. "This is perfect for our strategy."

"It is," August chimes in, but his enthusiasm is lacking.

"What's crazy is that just earlier this week I'd have said we were in real danger of not completing this case in time." I snatch my notebook from my bedside table. "But these last few days have been a game changer. You really rallied."

August looks like he's deep in thought.

"August?" I say when he doesn't respond.

"Yeah?"

"You're a million miles away."

"Nah. I'm good," he says and points to my notebook. "Let's just work out our plan for tomorrow night."

I can't help but frown. August's Wall is something I've gotten used to the last couple years, but this past week it's felt like something entirely new is wedging between us. And I have no idea what it is or what to do about it.

34
AUGUST

The morning and afternoon pass quietly, with Tiny and me swimming by the dock and ordering a massive food delivery from Bob's. Ella has been texting me on and off all day, which has had me buzzing for hours. But then I'll remember that this is a case and that Ella doesn't even know my real name, and I trade my high for grim dissonance.

Now sprawled on the wicker furniture on Tiny's deck, we wind down our strategy discussion, each of us offering thoughts sporadically. Silence with Tiny is easy; we're more family than friends.

A screen door snaps shut and we both turn our heads. Bentley enters his yard, picking up weights. He keeps looking over at Tiny's porch. Not the way he usually does where he tries to get Tiny's attention by peacocking, but more like he's frustrated. And then there's Tiny, who's looking anywhere but at him.

"Weren't you supposed to help Bentley with the twins today?" I ask, trying to suss out what I'm missing.

"Trying to get rid of me?" she says cheerfully. But by the way she pulls at the hem of her tank top, I know she's antsy.

"Never."

"Well, good," she says.

We fall into another silence.

"You really think this is going to work?" I ask.

"My plan? Yeah, I do." She pulls her legs up onto the chair cushion. "Justin will undoubtedly pressure her into something tonight." Tiny examines a mosquito bite on her knee. "Then all I have to do is be there at the right moment when Justin acts like a schmuck, so I can call him out."

"Yeah," I say, unsure.

Tiny looks up. "If you have a concern, now is the time to voice it."

I hesitate. "If Ella takes his side, you know we're screwed, right?"

"Which is exactly why I'm calling him out and not you. Even if it pisses them both off, friendly concern is easy to recover from. New guy friend trash-talking her popular boyfriend, on the other hand? We'd get ourselves shunned by the entire group."

I nod, trying not to think about the many ways this could end with Ella hating me, and also hating that I care about that.

"I know Ella's talking to you more openly, and that's amazing," Tiny says. "But honestly that's all the more reason we should kick up some dust, put up a few neon arrows pointing toward Justin's douchiness, and hopefully seal the deal."

I stretch my arms above my head, leaning back in my wicker chair.

"What's with the sudden cold feet anyway?" she asks. "Two days ago, you thought it was brilliant."

"It is," I say and squint at the water beyond the dock.

"Good. It's settled," she says and sits up, giving Bentley a glance. "In which case . . . I guess now is as good a time as ever to help him."

"I should probably go shower anyway," I say, getting up and heading down her porch stairs onto the lawn. I frown at Bentley before I turn. Even though Tiny says it's just a favor, I don't love her hanging out with him—I wouldn't put it past him to try something, and I'd really rather not go to prison for killing my next-door neighbor.

"I'll help you pick out your outfit later!" Tiny calls after me.

I shake my head as I cross my lawn.

As I enter my kitchen, I feel a compulsion to glance back through the window at Tiny, who's now talking to Bentley in his yard. While I can't hear what they're saying, Tiny's arms are crossed and she's wicked uncomfortable. Bentley hardly looks at her.

Something about it makes me uneasy. It's not that I care if they're awkward, but what would they even have to be awkward about?

35
VALENTINE

Bentley doesn't look at me as I enter his yard. He just lifts weights and stares at the water.

"Hey, you," I say, an unsettled feeling disturbing the fries I scarfed earlier.

"I don't need help with the twins," he says, matter-of-factly. "So you can go back to hanging out with August."

Gut punch. "You heard that?"

"Yup."

Guilt grips my already uneasy stomach. Every explanation I can think of is lame. So I just stand there, arms crossed, like they might somehow shield me from my own carelessness.

"I do want to hang out with you, you know," I say.

"It's cool. I have to work out anyway."

"So you're mad?" I say even though he's acting calmer than I've ever seen him.

"Not mad."

"You won't even look at me." I push the flyaways from my pony-tail off my forehead.

Now he does make eye contact, and his hurt-puppy-dog look makes things so much worse. "Look, Valentine. I like you. You know that. And I want to spend time with you. God, you can't even imagine how much. But not when you're lying because you're embarrassed to hang out with me. We literally made that honesty pact yesterday."

"With you, yeah . . . but not with August," I say, and as that crap rationalization leaves my mouth, I realize how awful it sounds. "Not that I think it's okay to lie to August. It's just . . . complicated."

He puts his weights down, rubbing a towel over his face. "It's your decision."

"What's my decision?"

"All of it." He throws the towel over his shoulder.

When I don't respond, he sighs and heads for his door.

I want to run after him and apologize, tell him I was a total inconsiderate jerk, but instead I just stare as he walks away, conflicted. I could take the easy out, let him walk away and be done with it. Right? Right. So then why am I standing in his lawn stressing?

I turn around and head back to my house, trying to push our conversation from my mind. But my brain flat-out refuses.

Now inside where no one can see me, I press my fingers into my temples and fall back against the closed door. It's a grade-A awful situation, of which I can only see one way out—one very annoying way that requires admitting to August that I lied.

36
VALENTINE

Fancy cars are parked on both sides of the prim and proper street. And while Justin's house isn't as giant as Ella's, it's still obscene compared to what normal people live in—one of those three-story brick federal numbers with black shutters you imagine some important senator living in and drinking brandy with his pinkie in the air.

"This case is wild," I whisper to August as we walk toward Justin's front door. "I knew this town was posh, but it's like they exclusively live in party scenes plucked from eighties movies. All crazy, no consequence. I'm thinking of it as a staycation from our normal lives."

August shrugs. "Not my thing."

I laugh at his predictability. "I mean, debauchery isn't anyone's *thing*. It's just a way to let loose. And however much you protest, we both know you're *enjoying* this case." I wag my eyebrows at him, on the off chance he missed my insinuation.

But he gives nothing away in his expression. I could be wrong that he has feelings for Ella, but my gut is telling me otherwise.

And since we're on the topic of epically bad romantic choices, I decide to test the waters with the Bentley conversation. "Speaking of secret crushes, there's—"

But I'm cut off by Derek and his Amber-look-alike date.

"Duuuudes." Derek claps August on the shoulder. "Get ready because Justin's ragers are a thing of *legend*."

I make a mental note to pick up this conversation later after a (hopefully) successful night of Justin foiling.

Derek opens the large front door, and music that was undetectable from the driveway blasts out. Unlike Amber's swanky boat party or Ella's pool party, this one is massive. The living room is brimming with people dancing, and the back deck and never-ending lawn are the same.

I beam. It's basically every element of chaos we could ask for in order to carry out my plan.

"Kitchen!" Derek declares over the music, and we weave through the crowd to follow.

Derek grabs plastic cups and a bottle of tequila from the shiny marble island counter, pouring heavy-handed shots. He attempts to give one to each of us, but August and I grab beers instead—much easier to drink slowly or not at all.

"To dancing naked on the coffee table later," Derek declares.

I laugh, although knowing him it's probably not a joke. "Legendary parties are legendary, right?"

He and the Amber look-alike raise their shots, and we all cheers as Amber, Ella, and Leah walk in.

"The cousins," Leah exclaims. "*Now* it's a party."

Sharky, of course, gives August a kiss on the cheek, one that's so close to his mouth that it actually catches the corner of it. She glances at Derek to make sure he saw. But I glance at Ella, who looks uncomfortable.

Derek grunts. "I feel it's my duty as a fellow dude to tell you to be careful," he says to August, obviously taking a dig at Amber. "She's got claws."

Amber drags her teeth across her bottom lip and flicks her bob. "Jealousy is a bad look on you, D."

Derek pulls his date closer. "Do what and who you want, Amber. I'm over it."

Amber opens her mouth to respond, but Justin cuts her off with his entrance. "Yeah, bro!" Justin says and fist-bumps Derek. "I had a sixth sense I'd find you knee deep in booze." He slings his arm around Ella, and it's clear he's already buzzed.

"Time for a drinking game," Amber declares.

"You know I'm always down," Justin says eagerly.

"Quarters?" Leah suggests.

"If we were boring, then sure," Sharky replies with an evil glimmer in her eyes. "I'm thinking a game with more spice. Truth or Dare."

August and I exchange a look—an amazing game for kicking up dirt, but also an uncontrollable one.

"Here are the rules—" Amber says and pauses while Justin hands out beers.

Derek's date lodges an objection in his ear, but he shakes his head and says, "It's just a game; what's the big deal?" She takes her drink and exits the room, leaving him behind.

"As I was saying," Amber continues. "Everyone drinks when a truth or dare is chosen, and everyone drinks when it's completed. Leah, you're up first."

"My choice, huh?" Leah says, looking at each of us. "Justin, truth or dare?"

He grins. "Truth."

"Drink," Amber reminds us.

Leah considers her question. "Most embarrassing thing that's happened during a hookup," she says, and Amber and Derek chuckle.

"Oh man, Leah, go right for the jugular, why don'tcha." Justin sips his beer. "Most embarrassing? Easy. My mom walked in without knocking while I had someone in my bed."

Derek snort-laughs his beer.

"It was like a scene out of a movie, I swear," Justin continues. "Hair in rollers, screaming bloody murder. I got up so fast that I got my leg caught in the blanket and I fell right the hell off my bed. There I was, naked, scrambling to get back up and hide my willy while she's covering her face and wailing. She wouldn't look at me for two days."

But even telling an embarrassing story, he's practically oozing charisma—big smile and blue eyes that can do no wrong. And they all stare at him like he's a god. One look at August's hardened expression, and I know what he's thinking—just like Kyle.

"How do I not know that story?" Ella asks when the laughter dies down.

Justin shrugs. "Never asked."

"Who was the girl?" Amber says before Ella can respond.

"Nice try, but that wasn't the question."

"The answer's that interesting, huh?" Amber starts.

"Okay, Amber, truth or dare?" Justin says, cutting her off from prying further.

"Mmmm, truth," she says, and everyone takes a drink.

"Best and worst kisser you've ever had."

She immediately starts laughing. "Wow, tough one." She holds Justin's eye contact in a way that makes me slightly uncomfortable. "But I'd have to say the best was . . ."

I look from Amber to Justin. There's something flirty about their interaction, something more than Amber's usual; it's the way she draws out her words and the way his eyes periodically flit to her lips. Not that it's a huge shocker that they'd flirt; they're both the type. It's just a crappy thing to do in front of Ella, however subtle. And I think Ella notices, because her shoulders tug inward.

At the last second, Amber readjusts her gaze to August and says, "Holden is definitely a contender."

My eyes whip to August with an accusatory look, but he looks just as shocked.

"Except we've never kissed," he says.

"Happy to correct that," Amber purrs, and we both instantly realize that she just played him. "And the worst? No contest. Derek."

Derek grunts. "And you wonder why I dumped you."

Amber retorts, but I'm not listening because I'm still thinking about Amber and Justin. Did I really see flirting, or was it all just run-of-the-mill eyelash batting?

"My turn," Amber declares. "Ella, truth or dare?"

"Dare," Ella replies.

"How about . . ." Amber taps her manicured fingertip against her lips. "You French-kiss one of the guys in this circle."

Ella immediately turns toward Justin.

"Besides your boyfriend," Amber adds with a mischievous smirk.

"Oh shit," Derek says.

Ella gives Amber a death stare. "Seriously?"

"Don't be a prude, El," Amber says. "It's a kiss. If it doesn't mean anything, what do you care?"

Cheap shot.

Ella looks immediately at August and then away like she's embarrassed he was her first thought. She redirects her attention to Derek and even takes a step toward him. "God, Amber, I can't kiss Justin's best friend and your ex. It's too weird."

"Aw, come on, El, I need to redeem my *skills* after Amber's lies about my kissing," Derek says.

"Yeah, no. The way you just said 'skills' is a hard pass," Ella says, and she turns once again to August.

As she walks up to him, I can tell she's nervous. And so can everyone else. Justin is hard-core frowning. To make matters worse, Ella's delaying. She just stares at August like she doesn't know what to do, her hands fidgeting with her beer. And each second that ticks by, Justin looks more pissed.

"This is painful. Just kiss him already," Amber says.

My stomach sinks in a bad way.

Ella gives August a fast peck on the lips. Completely harmless, except for the fact that she starts blushing. My eyes flit to Justin, who's tense. It's okay, I tell myself, we can still blow past this. Ella just needs to call truth or dare and distract everyone. Now.

"I definitely didn't see any tongue," Amber says, and my hope withers and dies.

"*Moving on*," Justin says.

But Sharky's on the hunt. "I mean, personally I'd love to, Justin, but she just didn't complete the dare. Rules are rules."

August and I exchange another look, this one an acknowledgment of danger.

"It's just a game," Leah says in an attempt to derail the tension.

"Drop it, Amber," Ella says brusquely.

One of Amber's eyebrows shoots up like it's ready for battle. "Wow. Overreaction?" Amber replies with a sly smile. "I didn't know kissing Holden was such a big deal."

Justin shoots Ella an accusatory look.

"It's *not* a big deal," Ella replies.

Amber shrugs. "I don't know. I heard you were *hanging out* at the crêpe place."

For a second, we're all still. The tension rises about a thousand degrees, and everyone but Amber looks like they'd rather be anywhere but here.

"That's not what I—" Leah starts but is cut off by Ella.

"Seriously, Amber? Are you just *trying* to cause a fight? Justin knows I hung out with Holden."

"Then why don't *I* know?" Amber says like she's the innocent party. "Personally, I thought it had to be wrong because you'd never hang out with a guy I'm into without telling me. Unless you felt *guilty* about it."

All eyes are on Ella, Amber's twisted version of the truth hanging over her like a storm cloud. Justin looks like he's gearing up to be mad.

"First of all, you don't care about Holden," Ella says, pissed. "You're just playing a game with him because you still have a thing for Derek. Second, I didn't tell you because you love to cause drama." She gestures at the group. "Case in point."

Amber's eyes narrow. "Triggered much? Why go defensive over the suggestion that you like Holden . . . unless you actually do."

"Eff this. I'm not doing this with you," Ella says, turning from the group and storming off.

But she only makes it outside the kitchen doorway before Justin grabs her arm and she stops.

Justin's eyebrows are pushed forcefully together. "What am I missing?"

"You're not missing anything," Ella says. "And I don't want to talk about this here."

"Well, this is exactly where I want to talk about it," Justin snaps.

"Amber is just—"

"Amber is Amber. So what. But do you know how it makes me look that you're getting all hot and bothered about kissing another guy?" Justin fumes.

"Hot and—" Ella starts, looking like she might explode. "It was *a peck*."

"Yet I didn't hear you arguing that you *don't* like Holden."

For a second, Ella looks stunned.

Justin shakes his head. "You know what? Screw it. Kiss who you want. I really don't care." And he walks off. Derek grabs a few beers and follows.

Ella walks in the opposite direction, her expression hinged between fury and embarrassment.

"Happy now?" Leah says to Amber in disgust and walks out of the kitchen after Ella.

Amber touches her chest like she's wounded, and she, too, exits, leaving August and me in stunned silence.

By the mystified expression on August's face, I know he's as floored as I am. "What the hell just happened?"

"Amber happened," I say, annoyed that I didn't see this coming. "We need to do damage control and we need to do it fast. We *cannot* have everyone thinking Ella likes you or worse, that you return that feeling. We're about an inch from being expelled from this group and pushing Ella farther into Justin's arms."

August's brow furrows, but he doesn't respond.

So I take control of the situation. "Look, I know it sucks, but you need to steer clear of her tonight. Maybe for longer. Don't so much as look at her sideways if Justin is around, or this whole thing will implode. We need to right things with the friend group stat." I give him a hard stare to make sure he understands how sensitive this all is, but he still looks lost in thought. "Are you listening? This is a code red."

All he says is a distant, "Yeah."

37
AUGUST

The next hour is spent mediating the fallout from Amber's manipulative game. Me making peace with Justin over beer pong, and unfortunately drinking in the process. Tiny convincing Ella she did nothing wrong while Amber is neither apologizing nor speaking to any of us. Ella avoiding any and all eye contact with me. It's not handled by a long shot and our plan is wounded, but at least the fighting has died down and everyone seems to have fallen back into the rhythm of the party.

I stand with Tiny in the hallway on the endless bathroom line, eyeing the ten girls in front of us and wishing I didn't drink that beer. "I'm considering peeing in the bushes."

"Holden McLover, if you pull your peen out at this party for any reason, I will personally kick your butt," Tiny says.

I laugh despite this crappy night. "I'll just go upstairs. You coming?"

She hesitates, her eyes following Leah toward the dining room, where all the snacks are. "Bathroom will have to wait." Without looking at me she adds, "Give me a few minutes after your pee before you join me and Leah, 'kay?"

"Text me," I say, and we move in opposite directions.

I head up the stairs and around the partiers perched on them. The music is still audible up here, but less intense, and even though there are a handful of people in the hall, it's lower key. The first room I come to has four girls hanging out on the bed and no bathroom. And the second is locked.

I make my way to the third door, but before I can grab the knob, it opens.

"Oh," Ella says like she's both surprised and unsure.

"Sorry," I apologize reflexively, for more than just startling her. "I was just looking for the bathroom."

"All yours," she replies, pushing the door open behind her but not stepping out of the doorway.

I immediately feel uneasy. I'm not supposed to be talking to her, especially alone, not if we want to maintain peace here. But I'm not going to push past her or make her feel like she's done something wrong. She hasn't. And neither have I. Ella could have easily followed Amber's directive on that dare and gone in for a French kiss, but she didn't because she's not that person. Sure, I enjoy talking to her, but that's hardly a crime.

"I'm sorry, too . . ." Ella says, looking unsure. "About all that drama before."

"You don't need to apologize." I hate the idea of behaving as though we were guilty just because Amber declared we should be.

"Amber just . . . Never mind, it's not a big deal." She's not really looking at me but also not walking away.

Once again I feel the dissonance between knowing I should find a way to end this conversation and wanting to comfort her.

"You deserve better than Amber and—" I cut myself off before I say Justin's name, shocked by my own directness and attributing it to the beer I drank. This definitely isn't Tiny's strategy or any strategy we've ever used; this is August and it's not appropriate. "Sorry, Scorpio, I overstepped. I'll just be using that bathroom now," I say, my heart beating like a beast.

For a quick second she searches my face, but then just as fast her gaze moves past me and she says, "All yours," again, gesturing toward the bathroom.

Before I can turn around, Justin starts speaking with an alcohol-affected slur. "Baaabe, there you are."

I make my way into the bathroom, imagining Tiny reaming me out for almost screwing that up. And the truth is, I don't know why I did it other than maybe I care too much, which I'm definitely never admitting. Because Justin reminds me too much of Kyle, because it's possible Ella has helped me more than I've helped her, and I want to repay her kindness. Because maybe on some level I understand why Tiny always wants me to take the central role on cases—it's hard when you get attached.

I quickly use the toilet, wash my hands, and splash water on my face, taking a long look at myself in the mirror. But just as I'm about to walk back into the hallway, I hear Ella's and Justin's voices through the door, and I pause.

"You taste like tequila," Ella says.

"Derek," Justin replies by way of explanation. "Want some?"

She laughs. "Not tonight. I *do* have to go home at some point. And my parents will be pissed if I come in stumbling."

"Tell them you're staying at Leah's. And then just stay here. My parents are gone."

There's a pause.

"I have to write in the morning," she says hesitantly, and it almost sounds like she knows it's not going to land.

"You can skip a day."

"I can't, though. I have a deadline."

"It's a stupid blog."

Another pause.

Justin grunts. "What's that look for? Lighten up. You write an *astrology* blog. It's not like you save lives."

And I'm instantly pissed. Despite the fact that a couple weeks ago I thought astrology was ridiculous, it's important to Ella; it's the thing she shared with her grandmother; it should be important to anyone who cares about her.

"That's a crappy thing to say and you know it," she says.

"You know what else is crappy? That you never put me first," he retorts.

I stood in front of Des's cracked door, my hand raised to knock. After

Dad left, I only occasionally said good night to Mom, but I never once missed saying it to Des. And it had become important in a way I didn't expect, like Des was my touchstone to knowing the world was still an okay place to be. But before I knocked, she started talking.

"Can't," she said. "Maybe this weekend."

"You can't take care of everyone all the time, Des," Kyle said.

I rolled my eyes. It was always Kyle these days. He was starting to annoy me.

"Says you," she replied, and I could hear her smile.

"Have another sip of beer." There was a beat, and he continued, "How about this . . . You come out for one hour. Just one teeny-tiny hour. No big deal."

"I have work tomorrow," Des told him.

"I'll help you wake up," Kyle countered.

Des laughed. "Like I believe that one."

Another pause.

"What?" she said after a few seconds of silence.

"Nothing. I've said it before—I'm always last. You choose me last."

"Kyle," she said in a way that I knew meant he was successfully playing on her sympathy. "I don't choose you last. It's just that August—"

"Has his friend sleeping over. He's fine."

"Yeah, but—"

"But nothing. You're not his mom, Des. He's a full-grown teenager, not a baby. You need to stop treating him like one."

His words instantly pissed me off, mostly because they were true. I knew I relied on Des too much, that she had taken more than her fair share of responsibility these past few years with me, the bills, our mom, all the while juggling her college classes. But who was he to comment on it? I dropped my hand, though, not wanting to prove him right that I was a drain on my sister. For the first time since I could remember, I walked to my room without saying good night.

And what I didn't know then was that I'd never get the chance to say good night to her again.

"Are you kidding? I always put you first," Ella says, and the memory of the night I lost my sister spears me right through the heart. I type a fast and furious text to Tiny telling her to get up here because she needs to call Justin out. *Now.*

"I gave up the school newspaper for cheerleading so we could spend more time together—" Ella continues, but Justin cuts her off.

"Are you serious right now?" Justin says like she's barely making sense. "Am I supposed to feel guilty for wanting to see my girlfriend? You know football took a ton of my time."

"Right, and when it's football, it's fine. But when it's my blog or my college—"

For a second, I have a glimmer of hope that she'll tell him she's choosing herself.

"Then break up with me," Justin says like a challenge, and the anger that wells up in me is irrational. That is the lowest way to manipulate someone. I text Tiny again, my fingers pressing hard on the keys.

"If I'm standing in the way of you and some crap school in London," Justin says, "then let's call it quits, because I'm not falling in love with someone I'm just going to lose."

And now he throws in love? What an absolute chump. I can hear Tiny in my head railing about how love means wanting what's best for someone even when it's not best for you. I check my texts with Tiny, but there's no response.

"Don't be ridiculous. You know I want to be with you." There's guilt in Ella's tone.

"Then prove it," Justin challenges. "Prove it by staying the night."

"Justin . . ." she says, and her voice gets a little farther away, like they've moved down the hall, probably toward his room. I have to crack the bathroom door to still hear them. "I want to, just . . . not tonight."

"Well, I guess I have my answer then."

"Hang on," she says, and I can hear how uncomfortable she is.

"I'm starting to think you're not who I thought you were," he says like she's so disappointing.

I groan. What a line.

"How can you—"

"Choose, Ella. Are you staying here with me or are you walking away?"

For a second, they're both quiet.

Then he softens his tone and adds, "Look, El, I just want to make this work. Make this work with me?"

My heart sinks, frustration swirling through me like a storm. We agreed that Tiny would intervene between Ella and Justin, but once again I feel like that kid on the other side of the door, stuck in an impossible situation. And I'm not making the same mistake twice.

I check my phone one last time, but there's nothing from Tiny, and so I open the bathroom door and step into the hallway.

Before I can stop myself, my mouth opens. "Dude, lay off her."

Ella's eyes flit to me, widening in surprise.

Justin turns. "What did you just say?"

38
VALENTINE

Leah leans against the large dining room table and surveys the snacks. The back of her shirt is sprayed with water.

"Water fight?" I ask.

She laughs. "Just some idiots who turned on the sprinklers and are using lawn chair cushions as a Slip 'N Slide."

I smile. "Sounds about right."

Leah plops down in a high-backed wooden chair and pulls over a veggie spread.

I grab a bottle of sparkling water and open it. "Weird night, huh?"

She shrugs. "Kinda. Although, not super surprised."

"About which part?"

"All of it," she says as she chews a carrot stick with ranch dressing.

"Amber and Ella?"

"They've been taking digs at each other like that for months. This time it just happened in front of everyone."

I grab a handful of chips, considering my next move. "Must be hard for you, being stuck in the middle."

"Dude, you have no idea," Leah says. "Amber can be a lot. I mean *a lot*. But everyone knows that. It's really not as shocking as Ella made it out to be."

"Maybe because Amber went after Justin and Ella's relationship?"

Leah considers it. "Yeah, maybe she wanted to save face in front of Justin; that's possible."

I chew my chip, strategizing how to pry a little further. "I probably shouldn't say this . . . I feel like it's not my place, but . . . Nah, you know what, never mind."

Leah twists off the cap of a water bottle and laughs. "You know you can't lead with that and then leave me hanging, right? It's basically cruel."

Universal rule: gossip is irresistible.

I laugh, too. "I just . . . well, I noticed a look between Amber and Justin earlier. Like sexy eyes?"

Leah hesitates. She looks around the dining room, like she's debating telling me something, but all she says is, "Yeah, I saw that."

My phone buzzes, but I'm too focused on Leah to check it.

"You don't sound surprised," I press.

"I don't know," Leah replies, even though I can tell by her expression that she has an opinion.

"Is Amber usually a flirt?" I ask, casually.

Leah thinks about it. "Selectively."

"As in selectively with Justin?"

"I . . . You know what?" She laughs. "I'm way too tipsy to be having this conversation." And her nonanswer tells me everything I need to know.

My phone buzzes again, and this time I do look. A text from August, actually three texts from August, but not the simple *Should I join you guys?* I thought he'd send. I make a fast excuse and bound up the stairs full speed.

And there in the hall, Justin and August face each other.

"I said lay off her," August says, and my stomach drops directly out of my butt.

"Get the hell outta here, man," Justin snaps, and I know that if August pushes, it's going to get heated; maybe it already is. How much of this did I miss?

"If it'd make you stop manipulating your girlfriend, I'd be game," August says, and if I thought I was shocked a second ago, I just reached a whole new level of heart attack.

He's serious in a way that conveys strength. August is tall, and he has muscle tone from swimming, but he's not a bench presser like Bentley or a football player like Justin. Yet in this moment, I'd bet on him without hesitation. The only thing is, I don't want to bet on him. What the absolute hell is he doing?

Justin's face goes red, but before he can respond, I swiftly step between them.

"There you guys are," I say loud and cheery, like I missed the aggressive posturing. "Justin, not sure if it's a big deal, but someone turned on your sprinklers, and people are surfing your backyard with chair cushions?"

Justin looks from me to August and back again, like he's not sure he's going to take the bait.

"Nowhere near the garden, though, right?" Ella says with a little too much emphasis, and I realize she's throwing me a bone. "Justin, your mom will murder you."

I pile on her concern. "I thought I saw someone tossing a piece of a rosebush, but not sure," I reply, liberally making things up.

"You kidding me right now?" Justin says, aggravation dripping off his words, and I shake my head. He makes a move for the stairs, brushing past August and knocking him back with his shoulder. But when Ella follows him, August looks gutted.

I stare at August, conflicted over wanting to hit him myself and wanting to console him. I knew this case was complicated for him, but August has exceptional impulse control. If he jumped in, it means Justin was so bad he couldn't brush it off. But that also means his emotions are wrapped up in this case way more than I previously thought. What exactly is going on with my best friend?

"How bad?" I ask when they're well out of earshot.

"How bad what?" he says, certifiably miffed.

"You and Justin," I try again, unable to erase the frustration that he seriously compromised our case.

"He was acting like a manipulative dick," he says, and I know by his tone that he's collapsing Justin with Kyle.

"So you went on the attack? You couldn't find a way to distract Justin or defuse the situation? Because interfering with their relationship looks like you're making a play for Ella. And after the night we've had, that's basically the worst strategy you could employ."

"It needed to be said," he counters. "You didn't see him."

"I did see him on the boat, remember? You should have waited for me."

"You didn't respond to my text."

I hesitate. "So what, you're saying this is my fault?"

"No," he says, but the tension is thick. "Are you saying it's mine?"

We look at each other and the mutual blame is clear. August is too close to this one; he likes Ella too much. And if he doesn't watch what he's doing, this thing is going to blow up in our faces. Maybe it already has.

39
AUGUST

I messed up. Enormously. I don't even have a good excuse for it besides the fact that my emotions got the better of me. And I don't know what to make of that—caring about this case is making me bad at my job, making me less likely to help Ella, not more.

I push my hair back and rest my hand behind my head on my pillow.

No matter how I rationalize it, this case feels personal. And yes, part of that is because of Des, but part of it isn't. I know Tiny thinks I have a crush. I don't. A crush is a fluttery thing rife with quickening heartbeats and stolen glances. It's something to celebrate when you accidentally brush kneecaps under a table and does no more damage to your heart when it fizzles out than a dramatic groan.

But what does it mean when you want to be better for someone? When you want to share your thoughts and trudge through difficult conversations. What does it mean when you share her hurts and want her to share your joys?

Shit.

I once again look at my text conversation with Ella that has abruptly stopped, feeling the tightness in my chest increase. I might have broken this. For good. And I know that texting her now is the worst of moves.

One hand overplayed is all it takes to destroy something as fragile as a new friendship.

Friendship. Is that what Ella and I have? Is she my friend? I rub my hands over my face, knowing I have a problem here and not wanting to look at it.

I sigh at the stack of books on my bedside table and my old-man cat tucked into my arm. I have everything I need to be happy. And yet . . . today blows.

Fine with all the things I can't control . . . just trying to stuff them in a box and shove them to the back of my mind because I think I'll be more fine with them there.

40
VALENTINE

August brooding over a girl is super weird, but August brooding over a girl who's the subject of the biggest case we've ever had makes me nervous. I just don't know what he thinks is going to happen. He can't actually be with Ella. She believes he's a preppy painter named Holden whose mom is currently on a yacht. And there's no way for him to backstep from that without telling her about our job—which is guaranteed to make her never talk to him again.

And speaking of brooding people, I look at my text chain with Bentley, which is currently barren. I sent him a message during the party last night and got exactly nothing in response. I tap my purple gel pen against my mouth and then shove it in the spiral notebook binding. I slide off my bed, heading for the window, but think better of it and go downstairs instead.

I make my way into the kitchen, where the big picture window provides the perfect view of his house. The twins are swimming and his mom's watching them, but Bentley's nowhere in sight. In fact, his truck isn't in the driveway. And then I remember it's Sunday.

I startle. *"Again?* I don't stare at Bentley's house."

"Oh, I see, you're just doing your part as the friendly neighborhood watch," she says with a grin. "My mistake."

I give her a look from under my eyebrows. "You definitely don't know what you're talking about." But she doesn't stop grinning.

"What doesn't your mother know?" Dad asks, joining us in the kitchen.

"Nothing," I say.

He looks from me to Mom and back again. "Ah, the whole neighbor crush issue I'm not supposed to bring up."

"Prem," Mom says at the same time I say, "Dad!"

He lifts his hands in the air, like he's an innocent bystander. "Just trying to access the refrigerator. Iced tea, anyone?"

I throw an accusatory glance at Mom.

She pulls two glasses down from the cupboard and places them on the counter for my dad to fill, giving him a kiss on the cheek. "We're your parents, sweetie. We do talk about you from time to time."

Dad grabs the glass pitcher from the refrigerator and goofy-grins at Mom. Gross. What the heck is going on with these two? Hot, cold, hot again.

"But as long as we're on the subject, I'm not sure that Bentley guy isn't a bit of a . . . what do you kids call it, a ladies' man?" Dad says, using the most cringeworthy terminology possible.

"Okay, no. We're not doing this," I reply, wondering if the embarrassment from your dad commenting on your love life can actually kill a person. "We can talk about anything else. Literally anything."

Mom looks amused, but Dad looks like he's not sure he doesn't want to continue and thoroughly scar me for life.

"You can invite him to Dad's party on Sunday," Mom suggests. "I bet he'd look good all spiffed up."

For a split second I get excited by the idea, but my next thought goes to August, who I've yet to confess to. I missed my chance last night with the blowup.

"Actually, yeah, maybe that'd be nice," I say.

My parents retreat into the living room with their iced teas, and

I run upstairs to change, energized by the idea of using the party as a peace offering. I don't bother to text Bentley, because on a beautiful day like this, I know exactly where he'll be.

ееее

I kick my flip-flops off at the edge of the warm sand, noticing I already have tan lines from their straps—one of those comforting standards of summer that make me feel like I own a piece of the sun. I straighten my bikini under my cotton dress and stride confidently onto the beach, aware that I couldn't have picked a more public place on a Sunday afternoon.

I zigzag around blankets and families with coolers, heading just left of the lifeguard stand, where three surfboards are leaning. Most of my classmates are here, dozing in the sun or diving into waves, and as some of them say lazy hellos from under their sunglasses, I have a quick flash of worry about Bentley reverting to his showy persona—that maybe he'll act like I'm some nut who's following him around and brush me off in front of his friends.

I spot him getting out of the ocean, board tucked under his arm, six-pack gleaming, and I steel myself, heading straight for him, my stomach doing small flips.

"Hey there," I say, approaching the wet sand near the edge of the water.

Charlie sees me first. "Yo, Valentine, long time no party."

Bentley looks confused. "Valentine? What are you doing here?"

"She's looking for you, dumbass," Charlie offers.

I feel my cheeks warm.

"Look, she's even blushing," Charlie says and chuckles. "What's that I smell? Is it love? Is love in the air?"

"Shut up, dude," Bentley says without taking his eyes off me, and I'm grateful. I don't need Charlie Atkins to make me feel any dumber than I already do.

"Just look at that eye contact. I mean, talk about smolder," Charlie continues, wagging his eyebrows at us.

"Dude, seriously, piss off," Bentley says, shoving his friend, who thankfully leaves but continues to laugh and make kissing noises as he walks away. And once again I wonder why I ever thought it was a good idea to try to reconcile on the town beach.

Bentley props his surfboard in the sand, and I smell the coconut wax on it. But he doesn't say anything. And unfortunately, after all the noise Charlie made, half the beach is watching us.

"Can we, uh, go somewhere?" I ask.

"I'm surfing," he says, his voice distanced.

I dig my toes into the sand, purposefully looking anywhere but at all the prying eyes, two of which belong to Cassie, his ex-girlfriend, who is both a popular mean girl and a prolific gossip.

"Right," I say, feeling conflicted. There's part of me that doesn't want to admit I like him more than I thought, and most certainly not in front of our entire school.

Bentley waits for me to find my nerve, but when I don't start speaking, he reaches for his board.

"Wait," I say.

"For what?"

"I came here to apologize," I start.

He just looks at me.

"I know I've been, well, not the easiest." I'm aware that doesn't cover the half of it. It's like I caught a case of the August Mariani Awkward Silence Syndrome.

"You mean you've been embarrassed to hang out with me," he corrects me.

I wince. Because he's right. Because I never thought I'd like a football-playing surfer who brags about how many crunches he can do and coasts with a C+ average. He's basically the antithesis of my type. "I'm not—"

"At least don't lie about it," he says, and I curse that pact we made. Honesty blows. Whoever decided it was a virtue must have been a hermit.

"Look, okay, you're right that I didn't want August to find out," I admit. "But it's complicated."

"It's not just August," he says. "I saw your face when you realized everyone was watching us." He nods toward our classmates in the sand.

I stare at Bentley—who's obviously way more perceptive than I gave him credit for. "It's a personal conversation." *Wow, I'm lame.*

"Saying you're sorry because *you haven't been the easiest* classifies as a personal conversation?" he asks, repeating back my lackluster apology.

A breeze comes off the water, blowing some of my hair into my face, and I quickly tuck it behind my ear. "You're not . . ." But when I realize I'm about to end that sentence with *being fair*, I cut myself off.

His jaw tightens. "If anything, I should be the one trying to hide that you're embarrassed of me. Not the other way around. I think maybe it's time for me to get the hint."

I fidget with the strap of my bikini, twisting and untwisting it, and feeling like a grade-A jerk-off. "So that's it? You're just going to stop talking to me?"

"Let's be real. If you weren't you and I wasn't me, would you tell me to keep pursuing a girl who acts like it's a chore to hang out with me?"

Ouch. Big fat ouch.

This is what he was afraid of when he admitted he was the resident babysitter for his siblings, that I'd judge him and decide he was less than. And of course, I made a big deal about how I wasn't that kind of person, yet here I am hiding him from August and cringing in front of my classmates.

He reaches for his board once more, and I know that if he walks away now, this won't be reparable.

"Honesty, right?" I say as he tucks his board under his arm and looks toward the water. "You're not my type. I don't want to like you."

He presses his lips together. "Great, now that we cleared that up—"

"Wait, I'm not done," I say, but he's already turning. "Don't you dare walk off with that surfboard, Bentley Cavendish. This is hard for me, and I don't want to speed through it afraid you're going to leave, because I won't get it right. And I want to. I really want to get it right."

He lifts an eyebrow, but he faces me again.

"Like I was saying, I don't want to like you. You complicate my life in every way. But for some unexplainable reason, I can't stop thinking about you. I scroll through your messages like a thousand times a day. I think you're thoughtful and caring in a way I never imagined. And when you kissed me. Ugh. I swear, my knees almost gave out."

For the first time since we started speaking, some of the disappointment leaves his expression. "Yeah?"

"Yes. And the worst part about it is that it's not just because you're stupidly good looking"—I gesture at his chest—"but because you're also a weirdly good person. I keep trying to tell myself that I just want to make out with you and leave it at that, but I'm not sure that's true. You might claim you've liked me for a long time. But even though I'm slow to catch up, I like you *a lot*. Part of me wants to hide, sure. But not for the reasons you think. Because by admitting I like you, I'm totally and annoyingly vulnerable in a way I'm not used to. And I kind of hate you for it."

His amusement grows.

"Glad one of us thinks this is funny," I say.

"One of us doesn't think this is funny. One of us is very, very happy right now."

I try to look mad, but it's impossible when he's smiling like that. "But I'm warning you, Bentley, if this is a game and you screw with my emotions, I will sucker punch you."

"Is that your way of telling me I should start kissing you?"

I level him in my gaze. "That's my way of telling you that I'm a brute who's not to be toyed with."

But before I can get another word out, he's scooping me up over his shoulder and running down the beach, jumping over people's legs and coolers, yelling, "Victory!"

As much as this type of ridiculousness is exactly what I was afraid of, it's also what makes Bentley so Bentley. I laugh until my face hurts.

When he finally puts me down, we're both out of breath. And when he leans forward to kiss me, I lean with him, pressing my body into his sun-warmed skin. There on the sand in front of everyone, we share a stomach-fluttering, pulse-quickening kiss, followed by cheers.

That's how we spend the rest of the afternoon—laughing, kissing, and swimming. He even gives me a surfing lesson, which winds up being way more fun than I thought, especially the part where he keeps touching my waist to show me how to balance.

We get a lot of curious glances and some gossipy whispers. But he doesn't care and neither do I. The only person I can't really ignore is Cassie, who shoots a death glare in my direction every twenty minutes.

"What's the deal there?" I ask Bentley, nodding at his ex, after yet another eye roll and scowl.

Bentley shakes out his navy-and-white striped blanket and straightens it on the sand. "Cassie? Nothing really."

"Her face says otherwise," I say, lifting an eyebrow. I lie down on my back on the blanket, hair salty with ocean water and skin still tingling from the chill of the waves.

He lies next to me on his stomach, propping himself up on his elbows. "We're just friends. Believe me, you have nothing to worry about."

"So," I say, accepting his answer, "what would you think about coming to my house for my dad's annual party this Sunday?" I don't need to specify that it's the one where famous people invade my backyard and eat miniature foods while wearing pristinely white sneakers. Between the magazine and gossip-site coverage the party has gotten in the past few years, there isn't anyone who doesn't know, especially not anyone in our town.

"Are you asking me to be your date?" he says, the corners of his mouth curving.

"I absolutely am," I say, surprised by how refreshingly simple this is. I don't know why, but I thought hanging out with Bentley for more than ten minutes would involve stilted conversation and personality clashes, but there's been none of that. It's easy. Nice easy.

"Good, because I'm definitely accepting."

Charlie laughs raucously a few blankets over, claiming he just shot a jelly bean out of his nose into an open soda can. "But Charlie's *not* invited," I clarify.

"Are you kidding? I don't even let him come to the twins' birthday parties. Not mature enough."

I laugh.

"So your parents are gonna be there," Bentley says.

"I mean, yeah. Is that a problem?"

"Not a problem. Just a big deal."

I look at him sideways. "You're my next-door neighbor; you've seen my parents like a thousand times."

"I know," he says, and the look on his face is so cutely nervous that I smile. "Just never as your date. It's different."

"If I were you, I'd be more worried about August." I try to make light of it, but he doesn't laugh.

"Right," he says. "Because you guys both work for your dad."

And suddenly I don't think it's funny, either. Bentley doesn't know about Summer Love. No one does. While it wouldn't be the worst thing in the world if he found out, I'd be violating August's trust if I told him. However, if I don't tell Bentley and he asks my dad about my made-up music internship, Dad will be not only confused but furious I lied. How did I not think of this possible disaster earlier?

41
AUGUST

Swee's nails are poking my side, but he looks so comfy I hate to disturb him.

"Today sucks," I tell Swee, who snores in response.

My phone buzzes, and I grab it off the bedside table so fast that I drop my book and lose my page. Swee stares at me, bleary eyed and indignant. But it's just a text from Mom.

Mom

> Hey honey, could I ask you to do me a big favor and bring my set of detailing brushes to the Kellermans'? They're on the kitchen table.

I stare at the screen, a queasy feeling rising in my throat at the thought of going to the Kellermans'. While I'm grateful Mom has work this summer and I don't mind supporting her doing it, she's also an adult—if she forgot her brushes, she should just come home and get them.

Instead of texting Mom back, I open the thread with Tiny.

You around? Need help with something.

I figure I'll drive and Tiny can run the brushes onto the porch. Two minutes and done. When Tiny doesn't respond, I look out the window to discover her Jeep isn't in her driveway. But our station wagon is in ours, which means Mom walked to work this morning.

"Damn," I say to no one and get up. Because as much as I'd like to tell Mom no, I know I won't.

⟨eeee⟩

The Kellermans' white colonial house looks just as buttoned up and snobby as it always did with its wraparound porch and manicured garden. And while Mom's obviously made progress with repainting, I can't help but wonder if it was actually necessary or if it was just a pity hire.

I sit in our old Volvo calling her cell for the third time, but she's not answering. I push against the steering wheel. "Come on, Mom."

I stare at the Kellermans' front door and weigh my options. There's no way of knowing if Kyle's home, if he has some dumb sports car in an obnoxious color parked in the bay of their garage. A car like the one he took Tiny and me for a drive in on my fifteenth birthday, doing donuts in the supermarket parking lot while we laughed in the back seat and clung to the upholstery. A car like the one he used to race on the dead-end street by the town soccer fields. A car like the one that killed my sister.

I hit the steering wheel as a punctuation of frustration and make the flash decision to get out. I walk brusquely up the too-long brick walkway, my heart pounding so hard that I pull at my shirt. Three steps up the porch and I place the brushes on a small table with a clunk. I specifically don't look in the windows.

But just as I turn around, a car pulls in the driveway right near where I'm parked. And as a pile-on to my already crap day, Kyle gets out of the passenger door.

Panic and anger surge so violently inside my chest that I almost miss the bottom porch step, my footing momentarily faltering.

Don't look at him, I command myself.

I pick up my pace, but it's not fast enough. Kyle's already said good-bye to his friend and is stepping onto the same brick pathway I'm on.

I look past him at my dinged-up station wagon, with every intention of ignoring the fact that he exists. But he stops in his tracks, right in front of my car.

"August?" he says, my name sounding foreign and uncomfortable in his mouth.

I held on to the caution tape so hard that my nonexistent fingernails cut straight into the palms of my hands. I stared unmoving at the bright-yellow car, whose hood was crushed against a tree in front of the town soccer field, the mangled doors flung open and the windows shattered. I didn't know how long I'd been here. Hours? Minutes?

"August," Kyle said, using my actual name, something I couldn't ever remember him doing—he always called me "Little Mariani." His voice was drained and heavy. "August, I'm sorry," he said. And I instantly hated him for it. For using my name. For owning that car. For existing.

He touched my shoulder, and then I did move. What gave him the right?

"Listen," he tried again, and I could hear the admission of guilt in his tone. "I just wanted to say—"

"No." My voice was quiet but weighted, stopping him midsentence before he could give me an apology I wouldn't accept. "I heard you. Earlier. In Des's room. I know this is your fault."

He swallowed and looked away, but before he could get the nerve to speak again, Tiny was there, grabbing me in a forceful hug.

"I'm sorry. I'm sorry, August. I'm so sorry," she said on repeat between sobs, pressing her wet cheek against my shirt.

But I didn't cry. I didn't speak. And I definitely didn't accept. I was frozen in place, all the warmth of Des sucked out of the world. The wrong-ness of it pulsing through me and upending the idea that things would ever be okay.

Suddenly I'm sweating and angry, like a hose-drenched yellow jacket.

Everything I've ever wanted to say to him explodes in my thoughts. My eyes flit up, but I force them down again, my hands clenching.

I walk around Kyle, but as I do, he does the unthinkable. He says my name and grabs my arm. My anger buzzes so loudly that I see spots.

Before I can make a decision, before I can tell him that he's not worth it, I find myself turning to face him, my shoulders tense, my already fisted hand moving through the air. And I deck him. Right in the face. Hard.

He stumbles backward, his hand moving to his cheek. "What the shit, dude?" he says, staring at me from his unpunched eye.

For a split second, I feel better. Good. He deserves it and so much more. But the moment that follows isn't good. I feel dumb and vulnerable, like I'm standing at that caution tape all over again, watching them wheel away my sister in a body bag, helpless as the most important person in my world disappears.

I look away from Kyle, my cheeks hot and my eyes stinging, and I get in my car. I drive all the way home with my hands strangling the steering wheel, my breath caught high in my throat.

"Stop," I command my brain. "Leave me the hell alone!"

But it's no use. A sketch appears and with it comes memories—not anger and destruction, something I could vent over, but gentle things: the rosebush Des planted with Mom when I was born, the sound of her laugh, the salt water dripping off her hair on a hot summer evening by the dock. My chest aches, and my lips part with words I don't know how to speak. *I need you, Des. How could you leave me?*

42
VALENTINE

I shake out my hair, wet and smelling of yummy jasmine shampoo from my shower, as I walk across my lawn in the dimming light. I've left August alone for long enough to vent over what happened last night. It's time to get back to work. And well, it's time to tell him about Bentley before I lose my nerve. I'm still riding high on the feeling of Bentley's arm wrapped around my stomach on the beach blanket, and I'm hoping that it'll inspire bravery.

August's window is open and I slide through. He's hunched over his desk, buried in a pile of books, and when I say "Hey," he says it back without pulling his face from his reading.

I stare at him for a moment, considering my approach. August reading books isn't unusual, but August surrounded by so many books that he could build a fort? Definitely disagreeable. Part of me wonders if I should wait, but I'll be running the risk of August finding out on his own, making the whole thing exponentially worse and convincing Bentley that I actually am embarrassed of him.

Eff it. "I like Bentley."

For a second the room goes eerily still.

I fill the silence, figuring I should get in as much as possible before we start arguing. "I spent the day at the beach with him, and I know what you're going to say, I know you think he's a dumb jock and a player, but he's really different from what you'd expect. He takes care of his siblings, and he's thoughtful and emotional. Believe it or not, he can be mature. And all I ask is that you give him a chance. I know it's complicated. I know you have your own reasons for disliking him—"

But I stop abruptly as he turns in his chair. The look on his face, a painful combination of hurt and frustration, makes me instantly regret not waiting until he was in a better mood.

"What do you mean, you like him?" he asks, and while his voice is controlled, his expression is hard to look at.

"I mean I'm interested in him," I say, losing steam.

"From one day at the beach?"

I wince. "No. We've been texting. And I've hung out with him more than once. I didn't tell you because I didn't think it mattered."

His eyebrows push together, but otherwise he doesn't move. "If it didn't matter, then why did you lie?"

"More like omit?" I don't know why I say it other than his stillness is making me super nervous. "Fine. Shit. I lied. I'm sorry. I just didn't want you to be mad at me."

"So when I saw him in your house the other day?"

"We were hanging out."

"And when you said you had to help him with his brother and sister?"

"Lie," I say with my tail now firmly between my legs.

He leans back in his chair and once again the silence descends.

I clear my throat. "Aren't you going to say something?"

But he doesn't move. He's like an intimidating statue of forlorn dis-approval. "What do you want me to say?"

I lift my hands. "I don't know. That you're mad at me for lying or that you think Bentley sucks? Something. And then we can argue about it and get over it."

"I'm mad at you for lying. Bentley sucks."

I huff. "Good. Fine. Look, I know it's utter crap that I lied to you. I should have trusted you. I should have told you that I was confused and—"

"Tiny," he says, his tone biting.

I stop midsentence. "Yeah?"

"Go home."

"Wait, what?" I stare at him in disbelief. "You've never kicked me out."

"I don't want to do this."

Nonresolution is one of the worst things there is, and in this moment my brain has trouble accepting it. "Have an argument? Me either, but I do want to get to the other side of it. We have a case to fix and—"

"Seriously, *I don't want you here.*"

Death blow. I actually press my hand to my heart. He's been mad at me before. We've had lots of fights. But he's never told me he didn't want me around.

"You really don't want me here?" I say, my voice small.

But he's already turned back to his desk. He doesn't look up from his book. "No."

And so I reluctantly climb out his window and back down the ladder, my eyes watering and my heart heavy. I don't even really understand what happened, how it all went so very wrong.

43

AUGUST

The door clicks downstairs a second before my mom calls my name, and my stomach seizes so hard that I feel ill. I look at my window, considering climbing down the ladder after Tiny as the lesser of two crappy conversations, but before I can make a decision, Mom's standing in my doorway.

"August?" There's disappointment in her eyes, which only makes everything worse. Her expression moves from a frown to concern and back again.

"Did you need something?" I ask. Either she'll bring up the punch or she won't. And truthfully, I'm not convinced she will. The deepest talk we've had these past couple years was when she told me I should return my dad's phone call and I said I didn't see the point.

"What I need is to understand." When I don't respond, she continues, "What happened today at the Kellermans'?"

"Nothing," I say dismissively.

"Then why did Kyle come home holding a bruised face that he instructed me to ask you about," she says in a mom tone I haven't heard in a long time.

But instead of answering her I say, "Did you get fired?" because it's the only thing I want to know, the consequence that I've been dreading for the past two hours.

Her eyebrows push together. "No. Kyle didn't mention you to his parents."

So what, am I supposed to be grateful to him? 'Cause that's never happening.

"Am I right to assume you actually hit him, August?" She looks so disappointed that I almost snap, asking her what she thought was going to happen when she told me to go there today.

Blood rushes to my cheeks. "He's alive. He'll get over it." Only it doesn't sound confident the way I intend.

Her deepening concern makes her hard to look at. "That's not who you are. You're not the type to punch someone. Help me understand what's going on with you because I'm at a loss. Did he say something? Do something?"

I shake my head, glancing at my cat's weirdly hairless belly to find an anchor.

"So you just hit him for no reason? I don't believe that."

I keep my eyes down.

"Talk to me, August."

"I don't know what you want me to say."

"Anything. Say what you feel." But when I don't, she sighs. "*Help* me understand."

You can't.

I shake my head again.

Her shoulders drop. "Then I guess I have no choice but to ground you."

My head whips up. "You can't ground me. I have work."

"Work and home and that's it. And I want to see a schedule from your boss."

I stand up, feeling trapped and backed into an impossible corner. "A schedule from my boss? You don't even know what I do." And I don't want her to, but that's not the point. If I really were a caterer, she still wouldn't know anything other than I work a lot. "All that matters to you is that when things get hard, I'm the one who keeps our electric from being shut off. I'm the reason we haven't lost this house. You can't suddenly decide to be a concerned parent. It's not a job you can pop in and out of. And no one grounds their kid who's about to go to college. That might have worked two years ago, but it's an empty threat now."

The pained look on her face makes me regret my words, however true they might be. And all of a sudden, I need out. Away from Kyle and Tiny and my mom. Anywhere but here.

I pick up my phone and walk past her. All her talk about understanding and grounding halts to silence, and she doesn't try to stop me.

44
VALENTINE

Four whole days and nothing from August. This is the longest we've gone without speaking since Des passed. And it hurts. My mom says he'll come around, and Bentley says dudes need space sometimes. But I can't get over how wrong I feel—like I'm missing my heart or my lungs, something so vital to my being that I can't survive without it.

I glance out the living room window at the ladder leading to August's room. But I'm not going over there, not after he kicked me out. So I pick up my phone and scroll through my texts with Leah, Amber, and Ella, looking for a distraction. But they all say some version of the same thing—everyone is lying low. It turns out those lawn surfers were actually rowdier than my story made them out to be and Justin's mom's garden was demolished (loudly), causing the police to be called and Justin's parents to have to return from their weekend trip. Which in turn caused some of the group to have their parents suspend credit cards or driving privileges, Ella being one of them.

I sent a screenshot of the news to August, with an added *Good thing we left when we did or my parents would have killed me. And also thank god Leah's still talking to me*, but he didn't reply.

I give August's house a pointed look in the glowing evening light and walk across my front yard toward Bentley's driveway, where he leans against his old pickup truck, waiting. Bentley smiles, and my frustration with August breaks apart and scatters like a group of startled birds. I smile back.

"Man, you're gorgeous," Bentley says and opens his passenger door.

He offers me his hand and I accept it, getting a whiff of his yummy woodsy soap. I grab the skirt of my long dress—the cotton one that is arguably casual but also fits me like a glove—and slide into the passenger seat.

He goes around to his side, his smile graduating to a grin.

"What?" I say as he starts the engine.

"Nothing, I'm just . . . This is nice."

I kick off my sandals and put my feet up on his dash. "Going for ice cream is always nice. It's like the nicest of the activities." I don't know why I say it; I know he wasn't talking about the ice cream.

He turns onto our sleepy street and heads for town, a five-minute drive past beach cottages to brick storefronts and the harbor. The wind blows my hair around my face, and I don't try to pull it back. It's one of those warm evenings where the humidity is low and the salt water permeates the air. I hang my arm out the window, my neon bracelets catching the remaining light.

"I love this town," Bentley says as we pass the Surf Shack, and it affects me.

I've been hearing people say that phrase my entire life. The townies who have minimal ambition for college and even less for travel, who do their best to never leave. The tourists who loudly praise this place for all of forty-eight hours before they move on to their next romantic docking destination without looking back. I've always known I'm neither of those. Which is why my sudden problem with California is so confusing.

"Yeah," is all I say.

Bentley pulls into a parking spot on Main Street in front of the art gallery. I take my feet down from the dash and slip them back into my sandals.

"You know, I've been thinking about what you said about Berkeley," he says like he can hear my thoughts. "And I kinda looked it up? It seems like a really great school."

"You did what?" I turn toward him, annoyed for a reason I can't pinpoint.

"I just thought I could help you make a pros and cons list or something."

"Maybe," I say, cutting him off in the hopes that he'll drop it. Talking about it makes it feel like a real problem, which I've been doing my best to pretend it isn't. I open my door and slide out, closing it again before he can continue.

He joins me on the sidewalk. "You know, just to help you sort out how you feel about it," he continues, like maybe I didn't understand what he was getting at.

"What kind of ice cream are you going to get?" I attempt to step away from his truck.

But he doesn't take the bait, and he doesn't move.

"Okay," he says. "Or not. Just thought I could help with the indecision."

I tense. I don't want him to see me as indecisive, and more than that, I'm afraid he's right. "You wouldn't understand."

He freezes and I freeze, too. "What wouldn't I understand?"

"You've never wanted to leave this place. You're not . . ." I instantly know I shouldn't have started that sentence, that the only way it could end is with something unkind. I study my sandals for a beat too long. "Honestly, it's not a big deal."

"But it is a big deal. To you," he says so supportively that I almost believe we're more than a summer fling.

"By that logic, wouldn't it benefit you if I stayed here? You'd get to see more of me."

He shakes his head, like I've completely missed the point. "I'd never want you to give up important opportunities because of me."

Momentarily, I'm taken aback. And I make light of it again. "So I guess this is a bad time to tell you I'm just in it for the hookup?"

But he doesn't laugh. He looks away.

"It was a joke." I suddenly feel like we've switched places and I'm him in his kitchen on our first date, advocating a sense of humor in the most obtuse way.

"And just to clarify, I do have ambition. There's a lot you don't know about me."

I wince. Hearing him respond to the insulting sentence I never finished makes me feel sick. "I didn't mean that."

He studies me.

"Seriously, I didn't. You're lots of things, Bentley Cavendish, and I have no doubt that ambitious is one of them. Would you accept an ice cream apology, maybe a little groveling?" I say, feeling lousy and leaning back against his truck door.

"Now you're trying to hijack my date idea? No way."

"I really am sorry," I say, taking his warm palm in mine.

"No worries," he replies, rubbing his thumb along the back of my hand.

"You should at least be a little mad."

He cracks a smile. "You'll just have to live with the guilt."

I take a good look at Bentley, who not only went out of his way to look up my school but is also being way more gracious than I would if the situation were reversed. "You know what. I think you might be more than a good person; you might even be a great one."

He places his hand on his heart. "You had doubts?"

"I mean, I'm starting to think that too-cool shtick you have going is just a big fat lie." I tug on his hand a little, pulling him toward me, and he puts up no resistance.

"How dare you attack my reputation like that," he replies with a small smile, so close that my body tingles with anticipation.

"I'm serious," I reply. "You should let this Bentley out more. I really like him."

"*Really* . . . as in totally infatuated?" he says, moving his hands to my waist. His woodsy scent fills my nose.

"Truth? Kinda, yeah."

He breaks into a grin that makes my insides warm.

I lift my hands around his neck, tugging him toward me until his body is flush with mine. He bends to kiss me, and I feel his smile against my lips and the cool metal of his truck against my back. He gently bites my bottom lip, goose bumps forming on my arms and my breath short-ening. And when he lifts his mouth from mine, I pull him back.

"Damn," he says like he can't believe I'm real.

I laugh, opening the passenger door behind me. He hoists me onto the seat, and I pull him in after me, because as much as I want ice cream, I want to kiss him more.

45
VALENTINE

Five days. Screw this. I'm not doing this anymore. I place my glass of orange juice on the kitchen counter with a clang and march over to August's house. A travel mug of coffee in hand and my chin held high. I climb right through his window.

He's sleeping and I unapologetically shake the shit out of him.

"Wake up, August Mariani. You wake up and talk to me."

For a few seconds, he looks at me like he has no idea who I am or where we are. Swee blinks, too, the hair disheveled on the top of his flat head. I shove the travel mug at August, and even though he lifts a wary eyebrow, he accepts it.

"You and me," I say, pointing at him. "We're not fighting any more. We are *done*."

"If we're not fighting, then why are you yelling at me?" he asks in a gravelly morning voice and sits up.

"Look, I'm sorry. I was a total and complete jerk. I betrayed your trust. But I'm not going one more day without my best friend. So whatever you need me to do, say it now or forever hold your peace."

For a second, he doesn't reply. He just pats down his bedhead, which matches Swee's, and puts on his pensive August expression. Then quietly, thoughtfully, he says, "You lied to me, Tiny."

And the hurt in his eyes splits my heart right down the middle.

I sit on his bed, the fight draining out of me. "You have no idea how much I regret it."

He nods. "You're just . . ." He pauses, looking at Swee for answers. "You're the only person I can trust. And when you lie to me, I have no one."

Shattered. Heart obliterated.

"I'll earn back your trust. I promise you that." My voice is heavy.

"Tiny," he sighs, "it's fine." Which is about as mushy as August gets.

"It's not, though. I hurt you."

He rubs the back of his neck. "It wasn't just you. It was a bad day. Terrible."

Part of me already knew that my timing was off that afternoon; I just assumed he had a fight with his mom. "Tell me about this terrible day."

"I kinda punched Kyle?"

My eyebrows launch up my forehead. "You did *what*?"

He glances at me but doesn't maintain eye contact. "Mom needed me to drop some brushes off at the Kellermans'."

"*What?*" I say again because August's mom can be so clueless sometimes. "You should have called me."

"I did."

Once more I have that sinking feeling. He called me and I didn't answer because I was at the beach with Bentley, which was the first thing I told him when I came over that day. Double fail. "Sorry again," I say sheepishly.

He shrugs, not like he doesn't care but like he's over that realization already.

"So Kyle was there?"

He nods and takes a sip of coffee. "Pulled up just as I was leaving. Honestly, I don't know what happened. He seemed bent on talking to me, tried to stop me. Grabbed my arm."

I can actually see this play out in my head. All that tension bound up inside August bursting out when Kyle touched him.

"So yeah," he says. "It was a bad day. Then my mom came home and tried to ground me like I'm ten."

My eyes widen. This is *not* good news. We barely have a week left to save this case.

He must see the worry in my expression because he adds, "I doubt she's actually going to enforce it. I kind of laid into her."

The guilt that appears on his face makes me sad. He always beats himself up after they fight, even if what he said was true. No wonder he went silent. He took a hit from all directions, probably worst of all from himself.

"Did she lose her job?"

He shakes his head.

"Well, that's good at least." But it feels like too small of a win in comparison to everything else. I consider poking further into the Kyle thing, but the unsure look on his face tells me that it's not the time. So instead, I say, "My dad's party is in two days."

"You have no idea how much I need that right now," he says, releasing his breath.

I press my lips together. "About that," I start and stop, once again with the worst timing ever, but given our fight over my lack of communication, there's also no prolonging it. "It's not just us this year."

There is recognition in his eyes and he groans. "Seriously?"

I lift my hands. "I know what you're thinking. But I swear, Bentley's not who he appears to be."

"And what if he's exactly who he appears to be?"

I nod. This is the objection I was expecting when I first told him. "Look, give him a chance, that's all I ask. I don't expect you two to be besties. But if you spend a little time with him, I think you'll be surprised."

August stares at me dubiously. "So what are you saying? You guys are dating?"

My heart picks up its pace. "Kinda. Yeah." I fidget with the edge of his rumpled comforter. "But Bentley coming to the party isn't the thing you're going to find most problematic."

He looks at me sideways, like he's not sure he even wants to know.

I have trouble holding eye contact. "It didn't occur to me when I invited him that he didn't know what we actually do for work."

August looks up at the ceiling and shakes his head. "Damn it, Tiny."

"Sorry again . . . again."

His shoulders drop in defeat. "Have you told him?"

I shake my head. "I was waiting to talk to you first."

And even though he doesn't look happy about it, it seems like what I said matters.

Before he can answer, though, his phone buzzes on his nightstand. We both turn, and when Ella's name flashes across his screen, my heart leaps in utter joy. Maybe things aren't as broken as they seemed a minute ago. Maybe we can rectify this still.

August looks up at me, and it feels like he's experiencing some sliver of the same emotion I am. His face seems to physically loosen. "Okay . . . as much as I really don't like it, Bentley knowing is a million times better than him mentioning our fake internship in front of your parents," he concedes. "We should have corrected that a year ago and just told everyone the same caterer story."

I feel this in my bones. What were we ever thinking, trying to maintain not one but *two* false jobs. Ridiculous. August turns his attention to his phone, opening the message. I lean forward to read it.

Ella

What did you used to paint, when you painted?

August and I make eye contact.

"Ella reached out to *you*," I say. "And it's not to curse you out. This is best-case scenario. Best best case."

His fingers hover over his keys, and he takes a big inhale, like it's the first time he's been able to breathe in days.

August

Mostly portraits.

I sad-smile at his answer. Capturing people in everyday moments was always the thing he enjoyed most. He was never much for landscapes like his mom or the modern styles that employ straight lines and splattered paint you see in galleries. His art was simpler, emotional.

Ella
Do you miss it?

August
Yes and no.

Ella
But more yes?

August
. . . maybe

Ella
Do you ever think you'll give it another try?

August
I used to think never.

Ella
Are you saying something changed your mind?

He momentarily hesitates.

August
Not sure I should answer that one truthfully.

For a second, I'm stunned. Because he's telling the truth; I know by the uncertainty in his eyes. He's actually considered painting again. And he's considered it because of Ella. She's helping him take a step toward resolving one of his biggest hang-ups. But how? She didn't sit with him through his dark periods or buy him tickets to art museums that he refused to accept. She wasn't there when he'd perch on the dock for hours staring at the water. She didn't think up elaborate schemes to slowly pull him out from behind The Wall, create an entire business to help bring him closure. She just . . . exists, and while that appears to be enough, it's also enormously unfair.

But instead of texting back, she calls him.

And when he sees her name flash across his screen, he gets out of bed so fast that you'd think he'd overslept for finals. "Uh, hey," he says. "Hang on, Ella." He turns to me, pressing the phone against his chest. "Mia, can you give me a sec?"

My shock doubles. He's asking me to leave the room? For a *case* phone call? But given the fact that I've only just exited the doghouse, I'm not going to make a thing out of it.

46
AUGUST

"So," Ella says, her voice overly pleased. "Are you saying that *I* somehow changed your mind about painting?"

For a flash of a second my heartbeat stutters. I pace the faded edges of the oriental area rug in my bedroom. Holden or August? August or Holden? If I answer as Holden, I'd use distancing language and send us squarely back into friend territory in a way that would imply I never heard the hope in her tone. I want to answer as Holden, I should answer as Holden, but for reasons untold I just can't. "I think you know the answer."

"Don't try to sweet-talk me, Gemini," she says with a laugh.

"Is it considered sweet-talking if it's true, Scorpio?" I ask back, which is the most honest answer I can think of.

"To use your favorite word . . . maybe."

I can tell she's enjoying herself, and inspiring her enjoyment is now a new kind of pleasure, a better one.

"But before you think of a witty response," she continues, "I just wanted to . . . check in with you about the other night."

I freeze, suddenly nervous. "Check in with me how?"

"About that stupid male standoff you instigated."

I let out my breath. While her phrasing is accusatory, it's not

"I'm never talking to you again" pissed, and the relief I feel is so intense that I actually sit down on my bed. "I'm assuming by 'stupid' you actually meant to say 'well meaning'?" I ask, employing as much lightness as I can and hoping for the best.

"Stupid, as in I don't need you to stand up for me. Stupid, as in you royally pissed off my boyfriend. And stupid, as in you threatened our friendship."

She's annoyed, but she's bringing it to me to discuss, not writing me off. Is it strange that I want to hug her for it? "First," I say, keeping my explanation as true as I can—I feel I owe her that. I've oddly always felt I owed her that. "No one needs someone else to stand up for them. People do it because they care, even when they get it wrong the way I did. Second, Justin deserved to be pissed off; I don't feel bad about that for a second. And third, you're right. That definitely wasn't my intention. I apologize."

For a long moment she's just quiet. "You're apologizing?"

"Yeah. I was wrong. And to tell you the truth, I've been low-key agonizing over it for days."

She makes a hmmmph sound that feels like she accepts my answer. "You said threatening our friendship wasn't your intention, so then what exactly was?"

I exhale. "Nothing I feel like admitting," I say as August. Again. "But I will say that I don't think Justin deserves you." As the words leave my mouth, my heart starts hammering. This isn't an approach we've ever taken before on a case. I've never been this direct. And I don't know what Tiny would say if she heard it.

For a second Ella's silent. She doesn't say she knows, or even that I've got it all wrong and he's better than what I saw. What she says is, "That's not for you to decide."

"You're right," I say. "But what have you decided?"

Again silence. And I start to sweat. I hate how much her answer matters to me.

Finally, she says, "I don't know." Her tone isn't frustrated; it's unsure. And for the first time since we started this case, I see a crack that tells me she's not as confident about Justin as she once appeared.

"Maybe I can help you sort it out?" I offer, belatedly realizing how awkward that sounds. I thud my palm into my forehead with a silent groan.

"God, no," she says, and thankfully she laughs.

So I roll with it. "I hear I'm a good listener," I say, extending the humor. And maybe I feel a little lighter knowing she isn't confident about Justin. But whether it's August or Holden that's rejoicing over that fact, I'm not sure.

"I bet you are," she says sarcastically.

I smile. "And what's that supposed to mean?"

"You know what it means."

And now I'm full-on grinning at my phone like a doof. "Are you trying to sweet-talk me, Scorpio?"

"Only a little," she says, and my stomach free-falls into oblivion.

Oh man. What am I doing? And while I know the answer lies in the "I should knock it off" territory, I just can't seem to help myself. I, August Mariani, desperately want to make this girl smile. I want to make her laugh and bring a blush to that star constellation on her cheekbone. I barely recognize myself.

When I don't reply right away, she says, "Anyway, new topic."

And I oblige. "Mia tells me your driving privileges have been revoked? Does that still stand?"

"Why?"

"Because I want to see you," I say, leaning against my window and looking out into my backyard, the hope in my chest almost too much to bear.

"Tomorrow," she replies, and the way that word lights me up is a little astounding.

"Tomorrow works," I say.

She laughs. "Works for what?"

"Well, there's this art store I really like in Fairfield. I thought maybe you'd want to go with me?"

She hesitates. "Art store, huh? Are you buying paints?"

"Maybe," I say.

"Then *maybe* I'll come," she says, and I can hear her smiling. "Anyway, I gotta run. Very busy nondriving life over here."

"Hey, at least being home is good for writing," I offer.

"It really is."

"Text me if you need any ideas," I say.

And while she doesn't say she's going to, she doesn't say she's not. We say a fast goodbye, and I fall down on my bed next to Swee, grinning like an absolute fool.

47
VALENTINE

Whether it irks me or not, speaking to Ella did the trick—August is out of bed and acting not only like himself but kinda like the August from before Des passed. He's going to an art store tomorrow, and not just any art store: the special one he used to go to with Des on his birthday. I swing my legs in small circles above the water at the edge of the dock, the hem of my flowered dress fluttering on my thighs in the salty breeze. August leans back, his hands on the sun-warmed wood, squinting toward the horizon in the bright afternoon sun.

"Interesting," he says after I fully brief him on the conversation I had at the party with Leah about Amber and Justin's flirting.

"I had a lot of time to think while we weren't talking," I say. "And well, I came up with a plan B, one I thought might work even with our case in ruins."

August rubs the back of his neck. "Sorry 'bout that, Tiny. I really never meant to put our case in jeopardy. It's actually the last thing I'd want to do."

I swish the water with one of my feet, sending glimmering droplets into the air like daytime fireflies. "Oh, I know, Holden McLover. I'm not saying it to make you feel guilty. I'm saying it because I'm a phoenix who rises from the ashes and saves us even when it looks like all hope is lost."

August chuckles. "If the world had your confidence, Tiny, it'd be a better place."

I grin at him and flick my hair over my shoulder dramatically. "Wouldn't it, though?"

"So what's this earth-shattering plan B? Does it have something to do with outing Amber and Justin?"

"Abso-friggin-lutely," I reply, energized by his belief in me. "Look, we know Ella's having doubts about her relationship. We get this right and we have a shot at a fast breakup, which we desperately need at this point. We're running out of time."

"What do you need me to do?" he says before he's even heard the plan.

I put my notebook down in my lap and look at him. "Actually, it's what I need to do. I thought about sending you in as lead, but if it doesn't land for some reason, it'll be right on the heels of your altercation with Justin."

"True," he says. "Tell me the plan."

So I do, and we spend the next few hours tweaking the strategy, arguing over details, and then eating way too much Indian food at my house. My parents are a little short with each other during dinner, almost like they're in a fight and trying hard not to give it away. I nudge August under the table to see if he's noticing that they're being weird, but he doesn't seem to understand. Maybe it's just stress over Dad's company party? They have been working extra hard lately.

When August returns to his house, I text Bentley.

Me

Up for coming over?

He replies immediately, saying, *Always*, which is one of the things I really enjoy about Bentley. He doesn't try to be cool by making me wait; he's enthusiastic.

My parents are already in their room having movie night in bed, and so I send them a quick text telling them Bentley's on his way. Then I grab my favorite pair of cutoff jean shorts and my comfy white sweatshirt and change out of my swimming clothes. And even though I'm fast, Bentley taps on my bedroom door as I pull my sweatshirt down over my stomach.

"Hey there," he says, and the hello kiss he gives me zings all the way to my toes.

I move toward my open bedroom door. That's another thing I really like about Bentley. When I asked him why he never closes it, he laughed and said he always wants that to be my choice, that he never wants me to feel pressured.

"How were the twins today?" I ask as the door shuts with a satisfying click. It's the first day this week I haven't played with them. In a weird way they remind me of August and me; they're annoyingly in sync most of the time but also fight like it's an Olympic sport.

"Same. Hilarious. Beast-like. You know," he says and sits down on the end of my bed. "How was August?"

"Actually surprisingly good," I say, standing in front of his knees. "But then again, he got a text from a girl he likes, so."

Bentley reaches out and interlaces his fingers with mine, pulling me a couple of inches closer. He raises an eyebrow. "August *likes* someone? How'd that happen? I don't think I've even seen him talk to anyone besides you in years."

"So . . . how are you with secrets?" I start, figuring now is as good a time as any.

"Excellent," he says, eyeing me curiously. "Whatcha got?"

I brush back his silky hair from his forehead, enjoying the way it slides through my fingers. "*Wellll*, you know how everyone thinks August and I work for my dad?"

Bentley leans into my touch. "Seriously? You don't?"

I shake my head. "It's kinda tangled. See, while everyone at school thinks we work for my dad, my parents actually think we're caterers? And I need them to keep thinking that. I'd be in serious shit if they found out I've been lying."

"Okay, now I need to know what's so crazy secretive that you made up not one but two fake professions." He eyes me. "You're not drug dealers, are you?"

I can't help but laugh. "We would literally be the worst drug dealers of all time."

"So then?"

It's weird talking about Summer Love. It's been just mine and August's for so long. "We have a company . . ." I pause. "Where we break people up."

He takes a second, like maybe he didn't hear me correctly. "Hang on . . . You do what now?"

"We break people up—"

"For money?"

"Yeah."

His expression shifts from disbelief to confusion and back again. "No way."

"I swear. Parents and friends hire us to break up their loved ones' bad relationships. We create whole other personas and make complicated strategies, and then August does most of the maneuvering."

He eyes me like I'm pranking him. "You're telling me that August has a secret life where he actually socializes?"

"Way more than that. He ousts jerk-off boyfriends, and some of the cases even wind up falling for him in the process . . . not that that is ever a goal," I say. "He's basically a modern-day Romeo."

For a second Bentley's silent, like he's trying to process what I'm saying.

I examine his face. "I know you guys aren't exactly the biggest fans of each other. But I need you to promise me that you'll try to get along with him at my dad's party. He's really a wonderful guy. Like, the best. And also, my parents would kill me if I created a scene there."

"Not a problem," Bentley says, and I want to believe him that we can all hang out without it being uncomfortable.

I spot my opportunity, a way to make August more relatable and for Bentley to understand the awesome August I know. So I tell him a little bit about Des, about why we started the company in the first place, and why this case in particular is so important.

But when I'm done, all he says is, "Okay."

"That's it?" I say, looking down at him. "After all that, you say one word?"

"What do you want me to say?" he replies, but he looks a little glum.

It takes me a beat to sort out why. "Hang on . . . You're not jealous of August, are you?"

"It's just nice," he says, "the way you talk about him. He's a lucky dude."

And I realize that maybe there is a little jealousy, but not the kind I imagined. Maybe Bentley doesn't actually have anyone in his life who praises him. I know that besides me, August doesn't. Maybe they have more in common than they know.

Bentley looks away, recognizing that I see more than he wants me to.

I give him a mischievous smile, pushing my fingers back through his hair, the thrill never ceasing that it's mine to touch. "So basically what you're saying is that you want me to admire you?" I inch forward until there's no space between us, and he wraps his arms around my back. "I feel like *maybe* I could do that."

That's all the encouragement he needs to lift me up and roll me onto the bed.

I squeal as my back hits the comforter. "Wow, Bentley Caven-Hunk. Look at those muscles," I say in an overly affected voice. "You must lift weights shirtless in your backyard . . . like, a lot."

He leans over me, propped up on one elbow. "I do it for the view," he says with a grin. "Turns out I've got this really beautiful neighbor, whose attention I've been trying to get for a long time."

I laugh. "Don't be ridiculous. You've been lifting weights outside forever."

"Exactly," he says, so close now that his warm breath tickles my face.

My heart thuds at the word. "Line," I say with a grin.

He runs his thumb over my bottom lip. "Truth," he counters, his eyes so intent that my breath catches.

He closes the distance between us, his weight pressing pleasantly into me and his mouth teasing my neck with kisses. I wrap my legs around his back, and his hand finds my knee, pulling it tighter and running a warm palm up the outside of my thigh.

He trails kisses from my neck to my cheeks. He even kisses my eyelids. But when his mouth finds mine, loud voices spill into the hallway. Bentley and I jump apart, my heart pounding against my breastbone.

"That's not what happened and you know it," my mom says in an angry tone.

A door slams, and just as quickly the loud voices stop.

I sit up, taken aback. My parents never fight in front of me. Ever. "What did that sound like to you?" I ask, my tone indicating this question matters.

Bentley sits up, too. "Argument?"

"Exactly. *Finally*," I say forcefully and slide off my bed.

Bentley looks confused. "Finally?"

"I've been telling August that something's up with my parents, and he kept saying he didn't see it. But you heard that, right? *That* was a fight." I point at my closed door.

"Yeah," he agrees, searching my face. Then after a beat, "You wanna talk about it?"

The offer takes me by surprise. Despite all the new things I've learned about Bentley, pausing a make-out to talk about my family problems still isn't what I'd expect. I nod, this time not shying away from a personal conversation with him.

"Here's the thing. My parents rarely fight, and if they do, they're careful not to do it in front of me. Then all of a sudden, I catch my mom crying over old pictures, snippy comments between them followed by overly affectionate cuddling. And this." I wave my hand toward the hallway. "Now they're openly and loudly having a fight and slamming doors when *they know you're here*?"

"Maybe they're trying to fix something?" he offers.

"Like what?"

He scratches the back of his head. "Not sure if it's the same, but I have a friend whose dad had an affair, and her parents are in couples therapy. She says they go hot and cold a lot. Fighting and then making up."

"Huh," I say, not sure what to do with that information. My first thought is, *There's no way my parents are in couples therapy, and there is definitely no way one of them had an affair.* And my second thought is, *Oh crap, but what if they are?*

48

AUGUST

I pull Tiny's Jeep to a stop in front of Ella's house and quickly glance at the Holden version of myself in the rearview mirror. But before I can turn off the engine, Ella comes out of her house, saying something over her shoulder as she leaves.

I lean across the passenger seat and open the Jeep door for her, which earns me a smile as she gets in.

"Quick, let's get outta here before my parents try to suffocate me with another family discussion about actions and consequences," she says, and the air fills with her coconut scent.

"So being home all the time has been fun, huh?" I say, glancing at her as I head out of her driveway.

Her hair is in a loose braid down her back, and she's wearing a strapless dress, highlighting the smooth skin of her shoulders. There are tan lines from her bathing suit running along the curve of her neck and over her collarbones. I swallow, shocked by how beautiful she is, and decide that I just won't look for the rest of the afternoon. Or ever if need be.

"You have no idea," she says and pauses. "I mean, don't get me wrong, it's nice that my parents care. Amber's parents didn't punish her, but they didn't bother to pick her up from the police station, either.

They sent her awful older brother, who made her wait two hours because he was out with his friends."

"Sounds like my mom," I say, once again responding as August, and for a split second I feel odd that I can relate to Amber in that way.

"Yeah?" Ella says and turns to me. "What about your dad?"

I internally wince. I've written my dad off in such a way that it never occurred to me that anyone else might reference him.

"Left my mom when I was eleven," I say simply.

She stares at me for a long moment. "Do you see him?"

"Nope. Never. He left us in a crap situation. Didn't even come to see us for the first year." I lean back in my seat.

Dad gave me a kiss on the forehead, his coat draped over his arm. "See you soon," was all he said. Not I love you; this isn't about you. Not Don't worry, everything will be fine. No explanation. Nothing to hold on to.

Des wrapped her arm around my shoulders and pulled me into her side. Dad looked back once, lingering in the doorway, but when he saw me and Des huddled together, he lowered his eyes and left.

I ran for the window, yanking back the curtains, positive he wasn't really going. I knew he and Mom fought. They'd always fought, but he wouldn't leave us. Not really.

As his engine started in the driveway, Mom began to cry.

"Mom," Des said, only she didn't sound sad; she sounded annoyed.

Mom shook her head. "I'm sorry," she managed and headed up the stairs.

As Dad's car pulled out onto the street, his trunk and back seat packed with luggage, my chest tightened so fast that I gasped for breath.

I flung the front door open and chased his car. "Dad!" I yelled. "Dad, wait!"

He heard me. His window was open. But he didn't stop. So I yelled louder. I ran faster. "Daaaad!"

Des grabbed my arm. "He's gone, little brother. I'm sorry."

I yanked my arm from her grip. "No, he's not!" I yelled. But as I looked down our quiet street, his car was nowhere in sight. "He's coming back. You heard him."

"Yeah," was all she said.

I turned away from her, from the doubt I heard in her voice, and walked back to the house, my shoulders sagging.

But I heard her footsteps behind me, and soon she was standing by my side. She didn't say anything. Didn't try to make me talk about it. She just walked with me.

And when the door closed behind us, she said, "I'm going to make some hot cocoa. Want some?"

I shook my head, glancing at the stairs and then down at my feet. I couldn't go to my room without passing Mom's, where I knew she'd be crying. Des followed my gaze.

"With marshmallows," she said. "And pancakes. Chocolate-chip-banana pancakes."

I looked up at her, my eyebrows pushed together. "I know what you're trying to do."

"You mean make breakfast? Totally. Oh my god. I forgot. We have heavy cream—I'm also making whipped cream. We can make faces on them with chocolate chip eyes."

"That's what seven-year-olds do. You're fifteen."

"Don't even care. I'm making faces on my pancakes," she said and started pulling ingredients from the cupboards.

She grabbed the bag of chocolate chips and opened it, offering me a handful.

My eyes flitted to the stairs, then back to Des. But when I didn't take the chocolate chips, Des shoved the whole handful in her mouth.

"Mmmmm!" she said and rolled her eyes back. "I guess this bag is all for me."

My eyes widened. "Hang on," I said, stepping forward.

"Yes?" she replied with a mouth full of chocolate.

"I guess I'm a little hungry," I admitted.

"Oh?"

"Maybe I could help you make them?"

She grinned at me so big and bright that some of the tightness in my chest released. She poured some chocolate chips into my hand. "Grab the mixing bowl, little brother. We're making a chocolate feast!"

And even though everything was wrong, really wrong, I realized it might be okay anyway because I still had Des.

Ella doesn't respond right away, so I sneak a peek at her. "I'm sorry. That must have been incredibly hard," she says, a small worry line in her forehead.

I open my mouth and close it. The last thing I want to talk about on this very anticipated hangout is my dad. The only thing worse would be if we started talking about Kyle.

I brush it off with a shrug.

She looks at me like she's trying to decide whether she should ask another question. She sighs. "Enough about parents. Parents suck," she says, and I couldn't agree more. "Let's talk about something more interesting. Like . . . have you ever been in love?"

My laugh takes me by surprise.

She smiles. "That's funny?"

"Unexpected."

"Good," she says, and I can't help but wonder if she's thinking about our conversation when I told her I like girls who surprise me. "If you don't anticipate a question, your answer is more truthful."

"You want the truth?" I start. "It's actually kind of embarrassing."

"All the better," she says with a satisfied smile.

I laugh, mostly at myself because I can't believe I'm about to admit this. "The last girlfriend I had was in seventh grade, and I gave her a friendship bracelet and held her hand twice."

"There's no way that's true," she objects. "You're attractive and charming. I don't believe for a second you've never been in a relationship. Amber wanted to jump you on day one."

Her words make me blush. And my stomach dips pleasantly at her compliment. "I think you have a different impression of me than most people do," I say, once again as August. "In my everyday life, I'm usually really quiet."

She looks at me sideways, like she just doesn't buy it. "I'm trying to believe you, but no, I just can't. I mean, you're pensive, sure. But it just adds to your artsy vibe."

I can't help but smile, and she grins back. "How about this," I say, trying again. "I'm not good at casual. I'm not one of those people who have quasi friends or can date for two weeks and then shrug it off. It's true that I haven't had a committed relationship, but I think it's just because what I want is something real." I get the irony that I'm currently talking about how much realness means to me, when she doesn't even know my name.

"Hmmm," she says, considering it. "I can accept that. Actually, in some ways we're similar. I'm not a casual dater, either. Justin's the only boyfriend I've had in high school." The mention of Justin tightens her expression. She doesn't elaborate on her thought, though. Instead, she switches off the AC and rolls down her window. "Fresh air is so much better."

She pulls up a playlist on her phone and sets it to play through Tiny's speakers. And we ride like that for a while—wind blowing, music playing, and Ella singing. When we pull into a parking spot in the art store lot, I'm bummed it's over, making a mental note to take the long way home.

Ella hops out of the Jeep onto the warm pavement, and I join her. I'm overly aware of walking next to her. It's almost uncomfortable, the sensation of being with her, of noticing the way her mouth bows when she's holding back her amusement or the way she twists her hair over her shoulder when she's unsure. And when I open the art store door for her, she rewards me with a smile that makes me want to earn another.

The store smells exactly the way I remember—new canvas mixed with pungent alcohol brush cleaner. The shelves are stocked in a colorful Willy Wonka–inspired layout of paper, paints, and fabric.

I can practically feel Des pulling me by the hand through the aisles, oohing and aahing over craft supplies—something to decorate her backpack or make a patch for her jeans. Des never painted. She wasn't drawn to art the way Mom and I are—in fact she used to joke that she wasn't even good at doodling. But she was a self-proclaimed bedazzler—if it was possible to make it shiny, she was on it.

Nostalgia swirls around me like fog. And a sketch forms in my mind, beckoning me to follow it.

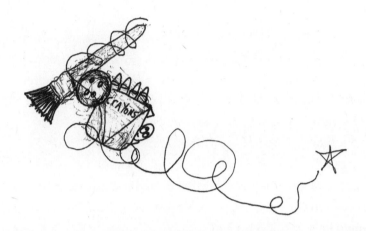

I turn to find Ella studying my face as though she's been watching me for a while, a curiosity line between her eyebrows.

"You were sketching, weren't you?" she asks, and I'm reminded of what she said about my drawings being a connection to my sister. While that idea is still far from comfortable, it's also not unthinkable like it was a few days ago.

I rub the back of my neck. "A little," I admit. "This place . . ."

"Is special?" she offers, and I'm surprised by how easily she read me.

"My sister used to bring me here on birthdays. We had this game we played." I feel a little shy telling her this, but I also can't seem to stop myself, like the sketch . . . a little piece of my sister that wants to be known. "We'd each pick two things. And then we'd make something out of all four. Worst design had to do the dishes for a week or—"

"Buy dinner?" she suggests.

I shake my head. "I was too young, but—"

"No," she says. "I mean when *we* play, loser pays for dinner."

For a moment I stand there, trying to recalibrate up from down. Ella wants to play my sister's game with me? The thought fills me with warmth I wasn't anticipating, and I raise an eyebrow at her. "Is this a ploy to get me to go to dinner with you, Scorpio?"

She laughs, but her eyes scream challenge. "If you don't think you're creative enough . . ."

"Creativity isn't my problem," I reply, and somehow it feels like we've moved closer, like the space between us is alive with current.

She shrugs mischievously, raising and dropping her perfect shoulders. "Or if you're scared of losing. No shame."

I laugh. "You're on, Scorpio."

She looks all too pleased with herself. "I'll choose first," she says and saunters off, with her blue dress swishing around her tanned legs, like she owns the place. I practically fall over myself to follow.

The moment Ella spots the display of embroidery materials, she beelines for a rainbow pack of embroidery thread. She holds it up with a smug look. "Suck it, Holden."

"Did you know that in elementary school they dubbed me king of the friendship bracelet? True story."

"You're so full of it," she says, laughing as I lead her toward the back of the store to the sewing section.

I lift a bag of safety pins.

She stares at it, like I just drew a line in the sand with my randomness. "Oh yeah? Well, let's just hope you can sew," she says and grabs a bag of fabric scraps.

"I can't," I say. "Which is why I got the safety pins. You're making it too easy on me." I flash her a victorious smile and walk to the jewelry-making section, where I pick up a bag of mismatched vintage junk jewelry (Des's favorite).

She looks from me to the bag and back again. And as much as she fights it, she grins. "I think I hate you."

"That's okay, Scorpio, because I like you. And I'm not opposed to working for your admiration." The moment I hear myself say it, I know it's true. But I also know I shouldn't have said it. I can hear Tiny chewing me out in my mind.

Thankfully she looks like she took it as nothing more than our usual banter. "So now it's admiration, huh? I thought you were just going for neutral?"

"The goalposts have moved."

Ella opens her mouth to respond, but before she does, someone says, "Jonah?" and my heart jumps so violently into my throat that I cough. "What are you doing here?" the familiar voice continues, confusion lacing its tone.

I panic—hot lava courses through my insides, and spots form in my vision.

But before the girl can get another word out, I start speaking. "Hey, Daisy," I say, finally catching up to the situation. This has never happened before. Tiny and I spread out the locations of cases specifically to avoid this type of thing. "Wow, it's been a minute."

"A year," she says, looking at me like she's not sure I'm real. "Aren't you supposed to be in India?"

I rub my temple, my pulse beating like a jackhammer. "Mom's organization lost funding. Real bummer. We just got back a month ago."

Ella looks back and forth from me to Daisy. "Jonah?" Ella says, suspicion making her eyebrow lift.

The panic lava surges, threatening to melt my brain.

"Middle name," I say and turn to Daisy. "Hey, can we—"

"Wait, Jonah is your *middle* name?" Daisy says over me.

"Daisy, can we talk a minute?" I gesture down the aisle and away from Ella.

Daisy thankfully follows my lead, although she still appears unsure. And even though Ella gives us space to talk, there is now doubt between us where there wasn't any before.

FML.

49
VALENTINE

Following Justin's SUV through town in my mom's sleek black Jaguar makes me simultaneously feel like a brilliant detective and a giant creeper. He's already stopped once at the dry cleaner, an errand exclusively reserved for private school kids and middle-aged office workers. And now he's pulling over on the side of Main Street near Ella's favorite café.

I snag a parking spot a few cars back and let my engine run, figuring he's just grabbing coffee. But instead of going to the café, he heads for a restaurant with an outdoor patio that's packed with brunchers. He takes a menu and says something to the hostess, but she doesn't seat him.

And that's it—exactly the type of opportunity I was waiting for. I pull out my phone and click on my text chain with Amber.

Me

You busy? Wanna grab lunch?

There's no hesitation, no nervous rumblings in my stomach. This is the part I'm good at. And as luck would have it, she replies right away.

Amber

> In car. Beach bound. Where were you
> thinking?

I look up at the restaurant and type out the name.

Me

> Le Petite Chat?

Amber

> Done. See you in five.

I turn off my engine and scoop some quarters from the console for the parking meter. I take my pay-as-you-go work phone from the cup holder, something August and I rarely use but has been clutch in the past, shove it in my purse, and head straight for Justin.

I let him see me first. He waves.

"Oh, hey," I say, lifting my sunglasses and giving him a "nice to run into you like this" smile.

"Getting lunch?" he asks and offers me his menu.

"Actually, yeah," I say and accept it. But before I open it, I pause, like I just got an idea. "Wanna join me?" I don't give him the polite out that most people would by adding *if you have time*. I just smile at him and wait.

He smiles back. "I was gonna order to go, but . . . yeah, why not."

Hole in one.

He turns back to the hostess and tells her we want a table for two.

"Three," I correct him. "Amber's coming."

He hesitates, like he's reconsidering, and I wonder if I read this all wrong. Maybe the flirting I saw between Amber and Justin was just a product of too many beers or a mutual frustration with Ella. Maybe it meant nothing at all.

But I'm in this now, and I'm going to make the most of it. "Where's Ella today?" I ask, even though I know, taking my seat at the table the hostess indicates.

He scoots in his chair. "With your cousin." He doesn't try to cover his annoyance.

But what's interesting is that Ella didn't hide hanging out with August like some people would. She was honest. "Oh yeah, forgot about that."

"I didn't," he says. "But hey, I'm here with you, so I guess it's all fair." Then he attempts a charming smile and lets his eyes drift down to my bikini strap.

Eyes on your menu, dickface.

And lucky for me, Amber's five-minute estimate was spot on.

"So, what'd I miss?" Amber asks, sliding into the seat next to me.

The whole lunch conversation is weirdly hard to read. Amber and Justin clearly get along. They have the same sense of humor and the same self-obsessed stupidity, but after some banter we keep hitting awkward ruts in the conversation where it looks like one or the both of them wish they weren't here. Like right now.

Justin pushes his chair back and drops his cloth napkin on the table. "Bathroom," he says like it's a decree and walks off.

When he's out of earshot, I turn to Amber. "Sorry, I guess this was a bad idea."

She spears a bite of her salad. "You mean lunch?"

I sip my mocha. "I mean inviting Justin to join us."

"Oh," she says, a little surprised.

"Not trying to pry, but it seems like you guys are a little uncomfortable," I say, most assuredly trying to pry.

She laughs. "Definitely not uncomfortable. He's just not civilized enough to make adult conversation for more than fifteen minutes."

I smile. "Okay, if you're sure."

"Positive," she says, but since I've already done the work of getting us here, I'm going to make absolutely certain. So I reach into my purse and find the pay-as-you-go cell, discreetly punching in my own phone number.

It only takes a second before my real phone, sitting on the table next to my drink, starts ringing. I snatch it up, telling Amber I'll be back, and leave my purse on the table, where my extra phone will be able to hear whatever Amber and Justin talk about.

I make my way off the restaurant patio and step onto the sidewalk, well out of earshot, just as Justin returns to the table. I press mute on my phone and then record, pretending to say hello to my imaginary caller, and keeping my back to the table so they have no reason to think I'm observing.

"You headed to Derek's later?" Amber asks.

"Yeah, definitely," Justin replies. "If I didn't, he'd probably hunt me down and drag me there caveman-style. You?"

"Maybe," Amber says, and I can hear her shrug. "I'm always up for some Derek sparring. Or maybe just outshining my look-alike he insists on toting around like a handbag?"

Justin laughs. "Now that's funny."

"For you maybe. For Derek it's just embarrassing."

I pace on the sidewalk, wondering if I should press end and return to the table. Maybe I was wrong about the flirting.

Then their conversation lulls.

"Anyway, it's nice . . . having lunch together, I mean," Amber tells him, but his reply sounds a bit like a humph or a grunt.

"Awesome response," Amber says after a beat.

"What do you want me to say?"

"I don't know. Anything," Amber says, and her casual tone wavers.

"Just trying to eat my lunch, Amber."

"Then stop making things awkward," she says. "Mia's noticing."

"So let Mia notice," he replies dismissively.

"Well, I don't need her telling Ella."

"Telling Ella what? That we're bad lunch conversationalists? Who cares?" he says, and now I've changed my mind—something is up and it's not flirting. She's too pushy and he's too glib.

I pace on the sidewalk.

"I care," Amber says.

"Then stop. 'Cause I don't."

"Real nice," Amber says, and I can hear in her tone that it's more than just pride; she's actually bothered.

Justin doesn't reply, dropping once again into uncomfortable silence.

I steal a glance at the table. Amber is pushing her food around, getting progressively more pissed while Justin is just as indifferent.

"You can save the rude silences for your therapist, Justin, because I'm not having this conversation with myself. If I get one more inkling that Mia's sensing something's off, I swear I'll tell Ella myself," Amber says, and the challenge is clear.

My stomach does a somersault, and I press the phone harder to my ear like it might help me hear better.

"Don't be an idiot," Justin snaps.

"Well, look who finally joined the conversation."

"There is no conversation," Justin says, now full-on pissed. "We were wasted. End of story."

Jack-effing-pot! I steal another glance at them, just in time to see the pinched expression on Amber's face.

"I guarantee Ella would disagree," Amber fires back.

"Damn it, Amber. Why do you have to be such a bitch?" His voice trails off, and he throws some cash onto the table. "You know what? I'm out of here."

"Charming," Amber says, but as much as she's trying to brush off his spite, I can hear the undertone of hurt in her voice. "And I don't need your money."

He half laughs. "Let's just call it a thank-you for services rendered."

Oh no. I look at Amber, whose face has gone stone cold, like she might murder him and stuff his body in her tennis bag.

"Run away and play pretend with your perfect suburban good girl," she says, her tone dangerous. "Maybe she'll never find out you're a cheating asshole, or *maybe she will*. Who can say?"

"You wanna know why Derek broke up with you?" Justin says, matching her cool aggression. "Because you're someone to screw, not someone to date. No one likes you. Not even Ella. So go ahead and tell her whatever you want. It won't stick."

Then he walks away, leaving Amber staring daggers into his back.

"Whoa," I say under my breath and press end on my pretend call, typing a text to August.

As I press send on my message, Justin breezes past me. "Sorry, gotta bail," he says, the nastiness gone from his tone and replaced with a calculated smile that makes my skin crawl. He walks backward toward his SUV. "Lunch is on me, though."

He opens his driver's side door and hops in. When I turn back to the table, Amber's asking our server for the check. Her shoulders are tense and her eyes are misty.

"Everything okay?" I ask as I approach her.

"Perfect," she says, trying to cover the upset in her voice with a sip of her iced tea. "Always."

50
AUGUST

After a short conversation with Daisy, we leave things on a friendly note. Turns out that she's in a committed relationship—a good one. She's going to open mic nights for her singing, which is shocking considering how reserved she was when I met her. And she's actually getting along with her parents. Even though this is the worst possible timing, part of me is happy I ran into her, a reminder why we started Summer Love. Sometimes it's hard to see your own life clearly—I should know; I hide better than anyone. And having a friend, even temporary ones like me and Tiny, can give you the push that makes all the difference.

I return to the aisle where I left Ella, but she's gone. In fact, she's not in the store at all. I do two laps to make sure, nervous energy buzzing under my ribs. I pull out my phone to call her. She wouldn't leave, would she? But before I press send, I spot her through the window, leaning against the Jeep with a plastic bag hanging from her wrist.

I step out of the air-conditioning into the hot afternoon sun, my stomach twisting mercilessly. But I don't immediately try to explain the name issue, knowing that if I compensate too hard, I'll look guilty.

"Well, *Holden Jonah*, I got the stuff. You're welcome," she says, not attempting to hide the "I'm calling BS" tone in her voice.

Breathe, August. One flinch and you're sunk. "Sorry, I didn't mean to interrupt our game."

"Game," she says, looking askance. "That's one word for it."

I tilt my head as though I'm asking a question, not because I'm trying to be obtuse but because my heart is beating a mile a minute and I'm trying to gain control of myself.

She huffs. "I mean, in a way I should thank her. She just outed you as a player who gives girls fake names and then leaves them for some made-up trip to India."

And that's all it takes for my inner freak-out to shift into high gear. I take a deep breath, employing the only tactic I know to lower adrenaline. "I never dated Daisy," I say without hesitation.

She raises a challenging eyebrow at me.

And so I explain, giving her as close to the truth as I dare. "Mia and I hung out with Daisy last summer. She was having a rough time, and we seemed to show up right when she really needed friends. And because of that we all got close kinda fast. But nothing more happened. I never so much as held her hand."

I don't know why, but her cheeks blush and she breaks eye contact with me. "I'm not worried about whether you dated her," she says, and I suddenly understand her embarrassment, because I suspect she was worried about it and doesn't want me to know that. "I was simply calling you out on the name discrepancy."

For a flash of a moment, I consider telling her my name is August. But convincing her I'm a giant liar won't allow me to be the friend she needs right now. So I sigh reluctantly, at both of us. "Think about it. If you had a name like Holden, wouldn't you sometimes use your middle?"

She eyes me.

"And well, my mom has been on this spiritual self-help kick since my dad left. It's exhausting. India to join an ashram, Africa to build schools, a yacht trip." I hold my hands up like I understand it even less than she does. "All I know is that we never stay anywhere long and it sucks." And even though I've done this many times, created a fake life to explain away the details, I feel uncomfortable doing it now. I don't want to be Holden. In truth, I haven't really been him. I've been August with a fake name and a few useless details. And everything in me is screaming to tell her that.

"Hmmm," she says, backing off a little.

I nod at the bag on her wrist. "Thanks for getting the stuff, by the way."

She stares like she's looking for a crack in my confidence.

"What?"

"Nothing," she says and drops the analyzing stare. "I guess that all makes sense."

But I don't feel relief. Because if everything goes to plan, in a week I'll be telling Ella that I'm going to live in a yurt in Mongolia; meanwhile I'll be half an hour away moping with my cat.

I reach past Ella to open the passenger door for her, but she reaches for it, too, and her fingers brush mine. She looks at me and then immediately away, saying a quick thanks and climbing into the Jeep.

As I close the door behind her, warmth spreading along my skin from her accidental touch, I look up at the sky in silent protest. What is wrong with me?

I walk around the Jeep and get in, starting the engine and desperately trying not to think about the star constellation on her cheek or the pink of her lips. Or the way her fingers are balanced on her thigh—

"Are you checking out my legs?" she says with an eyebrow raised and a lilt to her voice.

I clear my throat. "Just checking to make sure you were wearing your seat belt."

"Ah, yes, Holden Jonah. Safety first." She laughs at my lame excuse.

I press my palms against the steering wheel, turning out of the parking lot like the back road requires all my attention to navigate it. Are my hands sweating?

Ella puts on her playlist, only this time three songs pass and she doesn't sing a word. She just stares out her window like there is a problem floating on the wind that she can't quite grasp.

"Can I help?" I offer, which seems to startle her.

"Help?"

"With whatever's making your eyebrows furrow like that?" I say.

But still she looks out the window. "You can't fix it. You're the problem."

"Ouch. Way harsh, Tai."

She turns toward me, a laugh bubbling out of her. "Did you just . . . quote *Clueless*?"

For a split second, I internally groan. That was August again, and not the cool broody August, the nerdy holiday-pajama-wearing version. "Would you think less of me if you knew I watched eighties and nineties rom-coms? 'Cause if so, then I definitely don't."

A slow smile forms on her face just as I pull to a stop at an intersection.

We make eye contact, and something passes between us, something intangible and delicate, but I can feel it and I know she can, too, because she suddenly looks sad.

"I'm sorry," I say reflexively.

"For what?"

"I just . . ." I push my hair back. What am I doing? Why can't I keep to the script and keep my feelings for this girl in check? I'm supposed to be her friend, nothing more.

"I know," she says, almost quietly. "That's the problem."

And even though she doesn't name it, everything in me knows what she means.

I exhale, frustrated. Because it doesn't matter what I feel; I need to be what she needs. And what she needs right now is a friend. So I don't respond to the thing I know she implied.

She turns toward the open window, but unlike me, she doesn't drop it. "Hanging out with you has been . . . confusing."

And now I can feel my heartbeat throughout my entire body.

"You and I talk . . . about everything," she continues. "Something I didn't realize I was missing."

I open my mouth and close it again, conflict coursing through me. Which is when my phone buzzes with a text from Tiny, and I catch the preview before I shove it in my pocket.

Tiny

Insanity. Justin and Amber totally slept
together. Call me!!!

My already convoluted thoughts tumble over one another. Indigna-
tion for Ella. Lack of surprise. Annoyance that Justin doesn't appreciate
the amazing relationship he has. But in the midst of all this, the desperate tether I had on my self-restraint snaps, and I find myself talking
when I promised myself I wouldn't.

"Tell me what you want me to do, and I'll do it. I want you to be
happy," I say.

She looks at me, her forehead scrunched in confusion. "See, that's
the thing," she continues. "I hate saying this out loud, because I really
don't want to admit it. But talking to you has made me realize Justin
kinda doesn't give a crap about the things I care about? He likes me,
don't get me wrong, but . . ."

"But he likes himself more?" I suggest, turning into her driveway,
wishing the drive were longer.

"Exactly. It's always about him."

You have no idea, I think, my frustration once again flaring that her
best friend and her boyfriend betrayed her.

I pull to a stop in front of her house, putting the Jeep in park, my
whole body buzzing. "If you're asking me what I think . . ." I say, unlatching my seat belt, which suddenly feels too confining.

"I am."

"You deserve to be loved."

She nods, giving it some thought and unlatching her seat belt, as
well. For a second, I think maybe she's going to leave without responding,
that maybe I said too much. "Loved as a jelly bean. Not a sexy teardrop."

This statement shouldn't make my stomach drop. But it does. And
when she makes eye contact and doesn't look away, that feeling increases
tenfold. God, she's beautiful, and so smart. For a second, I imagine what
it'd be like to hold her hand, her slender fingers laced through mine. I
picture trailing kisses down her neck, running my fingers lightly across

the smooth skin of her arm, raising goose bumps and then kissing them away. And she's looking at me the same way, her lips parted and her eyes lingering on my mouth.

And somehow we've moved closer, both of us leaning toward one another like we're sharing a secret.

"You asked me what I wanted you to do . . . what would make me happy," she says, and it's barely a whisper. "I want you to keep spending time with me."

And with that simple sentence I forget about the case, about Holden, about everything, and like she's an undeniable force stronger than gravity, I reach out for her, lightly brushing the star constellation on her cheek with my thumb. She leans into my hand, her eyes momentarily closing. And we're close, so close that I can feel her breath and smell her peach lip gloss.

Suddenly, a door slams and we both launch apart. And there, standing next to his Porsche, is Ella's father.

"Shit," she says and jumps out of the Jeep.

Shit doesn't even begin to describe it.

"You should probably go," she says, not able to meet my eyes as she closes the door. And to make matters worse, her dad is staring at me like he might order a hit man. I put the Jeep in reverse, reluctant to drive away from her, but knowing I have no choice.

51
VALENTINE

August lies on my bed, surrounded by my discarded dress options.

"What about this one?" I ask.

He props himself up on one elbow. "Great."

"That's what you said about the last three."

"They're all great."

"Ugh. I swear, August, that's not helpful. I don't need great; I need wow. Like, a whole lotta wow. People are going to start showing up soon."

"By 'people,' you mean Bentley."

I give him an "I mean business" glare. "Don't even think about starting in on him. I have way too many jitters as it is. So if you insist on going down this road, I will sucker punch you into submission."

The corners of his mouth tilt up. For a second, he's silent, and then he sighs out his resignation. "The white one with the low back."

"Yeah?"

"Definitely."

"I was secretly hoping you'd pick that one." I beam, snatching it off my vanity chair.

I step into my bathroom to get changed, and when I come out, he's lying with his hands folded behind his head, dreamily staring at nothing.

"Thinking about the case?" I ask, even though I know without a doubt that he's thinking about Ella. August doesn't dreamily stare. Ever.

"I just can't believe you got Amber and Justin on tape," he says.

I plop down at my vanity and unzip my makeup bag. "I know. Craziest thing ever. I found the pot of gold; I'm basically a leprechaun. Too bad we can't use it without blowing our cover and the case with it. There's no way to explain why I recorded it."

August sighs. "Do you think Amber will follow through on her threat to tell Ella?"

I lean close to the mirror as I put on eyeliner. "I don't know. I mean, maybe? I'd say most people wouldn't throw themselves under the bus like that. But if she's angry enough with Justin, it's possible she'd do it just to get back at him."

August stares at my ceiling like he's doing mental calculus.

"Of course, with a little prodding and planning on our part," I continue, "I think we can get Amber to admit it. It'll wrap up this case in a neat little bow."

"Yeah," he agrees, but his heart isn't in it.

"You're saying yes, but I'm hearing no," I say, shooting him a questioning glance through the mirror.

He brushes off my objection. "Have you heard from Leah or Amber?"

I shake my head. "Have you heard from Ella?"

"Not really," he says.

"Anything I should know?"

He shrugs, but his cheeks flush.

And for a split second, I feel sidelined. "You know that you've literally never done this on a case before."

"Done what?"

"Not tell me every detail. You hung out with her all afternoon. It's weird how little you said. This is a job . . . one we're both doing."

He sits up, considering it. But all he offers is, "I don't know."

"You could talk to me about it, you know. Tell me how you feel about Ella," I say, trying to push my grievance aside in favor of support.

"Tiny," he says like I just embarrassed him.

"I'm serious."

But he doesn't respond.

"What's your deal? Why don't you tell me things anymore?"

"I talk to you constantly," he says like I'm making something out of nothing.

Why are guys so impossible? "Let me ask you this then—does it bother you that Ella's a case? Do you wish she wasn't?"

August winces. "Kinda." And then with a sigh he says, "Yes." After a long beat he adds, "Would it be crazy if we—" He stops abruptly, like he can't bring himself to say the words.

"Crazy if we what?"

He looks so vulnerable that for a second, I don't recognize him. "If we . . . tell Ella?" he says, his voice quieter.

"Tell Ella what? About Justin? You know that'd only put us in the hot seat. Way better if Amber does it." But by the look on his face, that's not what he meant at all. And suddenly it clicks. "Holy shit. Do you mean tell her *the truth*?"

Suddenly, he's off my bed and standing. "Never mind. It was stupid."

"You actually want to tank this case?" I ask in a shocked tone. I knew he had a crush on her, but I never imagined in a million years that he'd feel strongly enough to suggest something so reckless.

His face turns bright red. "I'm going to see if your mom needs any help," he says and exits my room before I can say another word, leaving me speechless.

My first thought is hopeful—that my best friend is having real feelings and that maybe this means he's finally peeking out from behind The Wall. But my second thought is pure anxiety. Not for the loss of the case—that I can get over—but for the risk it poses to August. I can't imagine in a million years that if he tells Ella the truth she won't hate him. Not to mention that Ella's father told him in no uncertain terms not to kiss his daughter—falling in love with her is totally out of the question. And what happens if he opens up for the first time in forever and gets brutally shut down? One step forward and thirty-five steps back, that's what.

52

AUGUST

I sit on the dock with my cup of lemonade perched beside me. My back is to the tents of socializing guests, and for the first time ever I wish this party were over. Tiny has been so busy these past twenty-four hours helping her family that I couldn't find the right moment to tell her that not only did I almost screw everything up and kiss Ella, but I'm certain her father witnessed it. I had every intention of going straight home to confess. But Tiny was gone when I got there and didn't return until late evening, by which point I'd convinced myself that maybe Ella's father didn't see us because he hadn't called to chew me out. And then this morning, I just didn't know how to say it, how to admit something out loud that I haven't come to terms with myself—that I'd burn this case to the ground for the chance to kiss her. But if I told Tiny that, I'd also have to tell her that my savings are gone and that without this job, I have no idea how I'm going to pay for Berkeley. So I decided it was better to wait until after the party, giving myself time to figure out a workable solution.

"You're missing the fun," Tiny says, her heels clicking on the dock behind me and yanking me out of my thoughts.

"Just getting some air," I say, pushing myself into a standing position.

She tilts her head. "The party's outside. Lack of air isn't a problem." Tiny gives me a knowing look. "You're brooding."

I lighten my expression, hoping to move past this with humor. "I believe the word you're looking for is 'philosophizing.'"

She smirks. "As in intellectual brooding? Nice try. It was average brooding—furrowed-brow-boy-with-gorgeous-hair-stares-at-placid-water-with-a-sigh."

I smile. "Don't knock my brand."

But her focused gaze suggests she's not going to let it go. "You know," Tiny starts, "maybe we should talk this Ella thing through? There are a lot of potential fallouts with—" Only before she can continue, Bentley joins us, wearing a khaki linen blazer and an equally stupid smile.

But I've heard enough to know Tiny's not okay with telling Ella the truth. And I get it. It'd mean the destruction of our business, gossip running wild. I break eye contact, my stomach knotting with worry.

"This party is straight-up amazing," Bentley says. "Have you tried these?" He holds up a mini filo dough cup filled with goat cheese and caramelized onions.

"They're Tiny's mom's favorite," I say, and while I mean it to simply be an answer, it comes out as dismissive and territorial, my bad mood making it hard to cover the way I feel about him.

"She serves them every holiday," Tiny adds in a chipper tone. "August and I accidentally used all her goat cheese one Christmas to concoct a magic potion, and I think we might have ruined the holiday for her. She's bought eight extra logs every year since in fear of a repeat."

Bentley puts his arm around Tiny's waist and pulls her close. "Is it too soon to invite myself to Christmas?"

"Yes," I say reflexively.

Tiny jumps in again, giving me a look that suggests we need to talk, but I look away. She smiles at Bentley. "Nope. You're officially on the list."

He leans down and gives her a kiss. If there were a path forward that didn't involve knocking them off the dock, I'd take it, not that I'd mind sending Bentley into the water.

Bentley looks up with an "if you want to be a jerk, I can just keep kissing her like this all night" expression. He leaves his hand around her waist and I clench my jaw. He doesn't deserve to be in the same universe as her, much less date her.

"I'm gonna—" I start, looking for an escape route that'll allow me to remain civil, but Tiny cuts me off.

"August, did you know Bentley is actually a really good cook?" she says, and I wish I could tell her not to do this, to just let us dislike each other for what is bound to be a short relationship.

"Yeah, actually, I did," I say, and they both look at me.

She tilts her head.

"He talks about it in the locker room," I say as explanation.

She laughs. "You brag about *your cooking* in the locker room?"

Don't say it, August. Leave it alone.

Bentley looks unsure. "Maybe a little?"

Just walk away. Walk. A-way. "Apparently it works every time. Right, Bentley?"

Damn.

Bentley's hesitation morphs into a warning glare directed at me.

Tiny stares at him, embarrassment seeping pink into her cheeks. "Oh my god, that's your thing? You used *your signature move* on me?" But her embarrassment has turned to something worse—she looks genuinely hurt. "And here I am bragging about it like an idiot?"

For a moment I feel terrible. In no way did I want to hurt Tiny, but isn't it better for her to know the truth now, before she gets attached? I lift my empty cup as an explanation for my exit, even though neither of them is paying attention, and walk off.

"You know what he's doing, right?" Bentley says behind me. "You know he's just trying to make us fight."

"I'll admit that August is a little overprotective. But he's basically my brother, and it doesn't get you out of answering the question. Honesty pact," she says, and I wonder how she could ever believe he'd be honest with her.

"Okay," Bentley says. "So sometimes I cook meals for girls."

"Before you bang them?"

I slow my pace.

"You're way oversimplifying it."

"Okay, well, what would Cassie say if I asked her?" she says, referencing his last girlfriend.

"Cassie's not you," he replies, and the music drowns out Tiny's response.

I weave my way into the party, which is now in full swing. A-list musicians are in attendance, and everyone is drinking champagne. I head for a table, taking a seat in the chair next to the one that holds Tiny's shawl, and continue to feel crappy about upsetting her. I just wanted to let Bentley know that I know—that even though we don't talk, I still hear things and that those things lead me to one conclusion only: he's a dick.

I pull out my phone and scroll through my text messages with Ella. I clock Tiny's frown from across the lawn, and their fight only reinforces the idea that I need to tell Ella the truth, that when people hide parts of themselves from each other, nothing good comes of it. I push my hair back and lean my elbows on my knees. I just need to make it a few more hours until this party is over so that I can hopefully convince Tiny and devise a plan to cause the least amount of harm.

I look at my phone, my fingers typing out a message to Ella.

Me

Busy?

The response bubble pops up right away, and I smile.

Ella

Kinda. I have a thing. Text you when
I get home?

Me

For sure.

I sigh, hoping that thing isn't a Justin thing, but judging by her vagueness I'm guessing it is. *Later*, I tell myself. I put my phone on the table and roll up the sleeves of my button-down, eyeing the water and wondering if Tiny would kill me if I bailed to go swimming. I really need to think.

But then I hear my name. And for a second, I'm positive I've imagined it, that my desire to see Ella made me hallucinate. Only it's not my name—it's *Holden*.

I swipe my phone off the table and stand up so fast that I'm lucky I don't take the chair with me. And there she is, wavy hair down her back, a blue strapless dress that hugs her body, and a huge smile—one thousand percent stunning.

"Ella?" I stammer. There is no way she could be here, no way Tiny wouldn't know if she were invited. The guest list has been set for months. This makes no sense.

Shock.

Dry throat.

White-hot terror.

"You're *here*?" I continue, finding it hard to form even the simplest of words. Which is when I discover the reason for her sudden appearance—Ella's parents are also here, standing at the edge of the crowd, grabbing two glasses of champagne from a tray.

I look from them to Ella, feeling like a train headed for a collision.

"You jerk," Ella says, her big smile unwavering, and she pushes my arm, her simple gesture sending my stomach into a somersault. "You totally saw me come in when you texted me."

Who am I? What's happening right now? Is this real? *Get your effing shit together before your world falls apart.*

I put on a smile. "Maybe."

She scrunches up her face in a way that'd be adorable if I weren't in meltdown. "I can't believe you're here!" She scans the crowd. "I mean, wow. It's awesome, isn't it? Amber was *pissed* my parents wouldn't let me add her as a plus-one. Kind of satisfying."

I hammer at my phone keys in my pocket, trying to text Tiny, but the stupid thing won't unlock. "Yeah, I mean, I come to it every year,"

I say, not actually trying to impress her, just not being able to think past the truth.

"You're kidding, right? I tried everything I could to get in last year. Lame that I had to come with my parents, but whatever," she says with a laugh, and the mention of her dad creates a fresh surge of vision-blurring anxiety.

I'm about to tell her Mia is down by the water, hopeful I can buy myself a few minutes to reason out a plan, when she says, "About earlier . . ."

My whole being snags on her words, my curiosity keeping me from moving.

She gives me a confident nod. "I'm going to talk to Justin. Tell him the truth."

"The truth?" I breathe, not knowing exactly what that is but desperate to find out.

She tucks a loose wave behind her ear and looks up at me. "I'm going to tell him what we talked about today. Because how can I make big life decisions based on a guy that I'm not sure about? I never thought I was that girl. I mean, I'm not that girl. And I'm not convinced Justin is what I want anymore."

My breath no longer flows easily, my heart trying to leap out of my body and click its heels together in glee. She's breaking up with Justin. SHE'S BREAKING UP WITH JUSTIN. It takes every ounce of my self-control not to run through the party hollering it at the top of my lungs. And suddenly I know things will be okay. She'll tell him the truth, and then I'll tell her the truth. No more hesitation. No more lies.

"I've been thinking about it all day," she continues, and every part of me pays full attention to her. "And when you touched my cheek, I felt—"

But she doesn't finish her sentence because her gaze drifts over my shoulder. And when I turn, I nearly collide with Tiny, who looks like someone just lit her dress on fire. Bentley is a hundred feet back but headed this way, which means she must have sprinted.

"Ella? No way!" Tiny says, and her voice is too happy, like she ate a bag of sugar and chased it with an energy drink.

Ella smiles. "And to think my astrology reading sucked today. I don't usually get things like full moons wrong."

Which is when my anxiety comes back threefold. This situation is delicate. Nothing can go wrong before she talks to Justin. Not one single thing, or it might crumble. Which means we need to get Ella the heck out of Tiny's backyard.

"Holden tells me you guys come every year?" Ella continues. "Lucky. I've been reading about this party since I was like thirteen in gossip blogs."

"Uh, yeah," Tiny says. "But don't let Holden convince you that he gets in on his cool points. The people who throw it are our aunt and uncle."

Which is the perfect explanation for the framed pictures Ella might see of the two of us in the house. *Tiny, you're a genius.*

"They don't have any kids," Tiny continues. "So Holden and I reap all the good invites."

Ella tilts her head like she has a follow-up question or seven, but before she can reply, Bentley joins us.

"V—" Bentley starts.

"Ella, this is Bentley," I say, cutting him off before Bentley can get Valentine's name out of his stupid mouth. "He's *Mia's* date."

Bentley looks from me (and my newfound friendly tone) to Tiny, who smiles at him like nothing is amiss.

I, however, give him a demanding glare. *I will drown you in the ocean, Bentley, if you blow this.*

"Nice to meet you," Bentley says, and I release my breath.

"Bentley, would you mind grabbing me a snack?" Tiny asks. "I'm starved."

"Sure, *Mia*," he replies, a little unsure, and he looks at each of us before he leaves.

Ella mouths "he's hot" to Tiny as Bentley walks away, and I hope that he trips over a chair and falls off the face of the planet.

"I know!" Tiny mouths back and links her arm through Ella's. "How about I show you around? Introduce you to a few people?"

"Um, that's a yes," Ella says, and Tiny shoots me a look that clearly translates to *If you don't find Ella's parents and fix this, Bentley isn't the only one who'll be drowned in the ocean.*

Except I don't need to look for Ella's parents, because they're here. *Right* here, walking up to us with the worst possible escorts—Tiny's parents. *Turn around,* I yell at Ella's parents in my head. *Get out of here before it's too late!* But it's already too late. If I were a fainter, this would be my moment.

"Our daughter . . . Ella," Ella's mom says by way of introduction to Tiny's parents, sweeping her hand forward. But her voice and smile fade as she recognizes me and Tiny.

Ella's parents look like a camera flash momentarily blinded them.

Tiny's dad doesn't miss a beat, though. "Ella, was it?" he says. "Welcome to our home. I'm Prem, and this is my wife, Piper."

"Pleased to meet you both," Ella replies politely.

Judging by Ella's parents' tight expressions, we're all experiencing the same lack of air.

"We were just about to show Ella around," I chime in, attempting to control the uncontrollable.

Tiny takes a step toward the dock to show her eagerness, hoping that Ella follows. But no such luck.

Tiny's dad continues. "I see you've already met—"

"Totally met me. We're all good here," Tiny says, cutting them off before they can say her name or specify that she's their daughter.

Tiny's mom frowns, like she knows something's up but isn't sure what.

I shoot Ella's parents a "help" look.

And thankfully, Ella's dad starts speaking. "Prem, I was hoping you could make a few introductions for me while I'm here." He turns his back toward us like we've all agreed the conversation is over.

"Come on," Tiny says, and when Ella decides to follow her, I audibly exhale.

I don't walk with them toward the dock, though. I grab my phone off the table and follow Ella's and Tiny's parents at a safe distance.

I'll explain and they'll get her out of here, I tell myself. It'll be okay. It has to be.

53

VALENTINE

My blood is pumping through my veins at record speed, and the complication of August actually liking this girl makes me feel like there's an anvil on my shoulders.

"This is the dock where Holden and I swam every summer growing up," I tell Ella, trying to keep her distracted. "We always liked it better than the ocean for some reason. Felt like our own private swimming hole."

"I can totally see that," Ella says as we walk along the wooden planks decorated with white twinkle lights. The party has expanded closer to the water, and we have to step around people. "It's charming here. Quaint. Did you guys spend a lot of time here as kids?" There's something in her voice that I can't place, something unsure.

I nod, hoping my enthusiasm will dispel her doubts. "Kinda, yeah. Holden's mom was always on some excursion or other, and my parents basically work nonstop."

"But now you live near me," Ella continues, like she's trying to understand. "What street was it again?"

"Uh, Spring Street," I say, feeling distinctly uneasy about this line of questioning.

"Funny," she says. "I have a friend who lives on that street. Which house is it?"

While I always prepare for questions like this before every case, her timing is making me feel sick. "Blue one with the white trim. You're welcome anytime," I say, replying with confidence I don't feel.

But she doesn't respond. She just chews her cheek and stares at the water.

"So, who should I introduce you to first?" I say.

She looks at me and her forehead scrunches. "Valentine," she says, and all the blood drains from my face. "I'd love to meet Valentine."

"Valentine?" I repeat, my real name sticking in my throat.

"Prem and Piper. They have a daughter named Valentine," she says, and my stomach seizes. "I remember reading it in a gossip blog."

I swallow. There was *one* article last year that mentioned me, and while I was delighted, my parents weren't. They had my name retracted. It was up for less than forty-eight hours. "How do you remember that?" I ask, shocked.

"I told you; my friends and I were obsessed with coming to this party," she says, and everything in me sinks. They probably saw me as their in—if they could find me and befriend me, that is.

"Ella—" I start, but she cuts me off.

"You look a lot like Piper," she says.

"That's kinda true of all our family," I say in a Hail Mary effort at keeping up our story. "Well, except Holden. No one knows where he gets—"

"You mean *Jonah*," she says, and I freeze.

54
AUGUST

"If we had been made aware of Valentine's last name, we'd never have come. But you both insisted on first names only," Ella's dad seethes, and while he still hasn't mentioned the kiss, the way he stares at me with disgust makes me feel like he announced it on loudspeaker.

"I apologize, sir," I say, because honestly, I couldn't be more annoyed at us, either.

"It's not your fault," Ella's mom chimes in. "We weren't on the guest list. It was a last-minute add-on type of thing."

But Ella's dad isn't having it. "It most certainly is their—"

Ella's mom touches her husband's arm, and he grumbles but stops midaccusation.

I glance toward the water. "I'll tell Ella you're looking for her," I say, cutting the conversation off, anxious to get back to Ella and Tiny.

"Please do," Ella's mom says. "I'll gather our things."

The instant she finishes speaking, I speed walk toward the dock, feeling like we might actually slip out of this mess. But as I approach Tiny and Ella, I know something's off. Their body language is stiff and Tiny's expression is strained.

"When you said Prem and Piper had no kids, the error didn't occur to me right away. But then I saw you all together—it was hard not to notice your resemblance to your mom," Ella says, and I stumble over my own foot. "So what I want to know is, why are you and Jonah both lying about who you are?"

Jonah. The realization hits me hard, like a wave that tumbles you in the ocean, scraping your back and legs against the sand before releasing you, gasping for breath.

Ella shifts her eyes to me, full of disappointment.

And suddenly all our mistakes come into crisp focus. If we hadn't gone to that art store. If Daisy hadn't been there. If we had spoken to Ella's parents more. If they hadn't snagged a last-minute invite. If. If. If.

"The thing is—" Tiny starts on what I imagine is an attempt to twist the narrative.

"August," I say, cutting her off, knowing our hand is played and we lost. "My name is August."

Tiny gulps.

"*August?*" Ella's upset kicks up a notch. "So you lied about your name not once *but twice*? And about living in my town, about . . . my god, is everything you said *a lie?*"

I stare at her, trying to find a way to tell it to her straight. But everything sounds like crap: "*We're kinda what you'd call relationship detectives.*" "*And it's actually a good thing your parents hired us.*" "*You see, your boyfriend is cheating on you.*"

Tiny looks at me like, *You need to say something. Now.*

I open my mouth, but I get cut off.

"Ella, honey, I'm sorry, but we're going to have to leave," Ella's mom says, as she and Ella's dad approach us.

"We just got here," Ella objects, her annoyance seeping into her tone.

"I have a work situation that's time sensitive," her father explains.

"You guys go," Ella says, keeping her eyes on me. "I'll call a car."

"No," Ella's mom replies.

Now Ella looks at her parents, frowning. "Please, I just need a minute." The upset in her voice stakes me through the heart, and her parents shift their focus to me, as though I might explain what's going on.

Ella notices. "Hang on a second. What am I missing here? Why are you looking at Hold—August that way?"

"We aren't looking at August in any way," Ella's mom compensates, and I cringe.

Ella holds out her hands. "Wait, everybody stop," she says like she's trying to make sense of us. "Why didn't you react when I said his real name?"

But it isn't Ella's parents who answer—it's me again. "They hired us."

No one moves, the bomb of my words going off and all of us frozen in place.

Ella's voice is disbelieving. "What do you mean, they—"

"To break up your relationship with Justin," Tiny continues, and I'm grateful. It would sound much worse coming from me. Tiny's tone is measured and her chin high, like she's come to terms with what she has to do even though she doesn't like it.

"*What?!?*" Ella says, this time with force. "What are you even . . . That's not possible. Mom?" Her eyes are pleading.

Ella's mom blanches. Ella's dad reddens.

"Justin's cheating on you," Tiny continues, taking control. And now the whole Becker family looks at her with matching expressions of shock. I know Tiny has to say it, that if she doesn't, this massive screwup could effectively push Ella further into Justin's arms. "I'm sorry. You weren't supposed to find out like this."

"*Find out like this?* Find out like—" Ella stammers, gesturing at all of us. "How *dare you*. I cannot *believe* . . ." She shakes her head, her tone lodged firmly between fury and tears. "Screw all of you!" She pushes past me and storms away.

I follow. "Ella, wait," I say, but she doesn't slow down. "Ella, please. Let me—"

"Get away from me!" she spits.

"Please let me explain—"

"Explain?" she yells, turning to face me in the middle of the dance floor. "What are you going to explain, *August?*" She makes my name sound like a curse. "That everything you've ever said to me is *a big fat lie?* That you're a manipulative asshole who I never should have trusted?"

"It's more complicated—"

But she's not done. "Complicated like you and Valentine pretend-ing to be my friends? Complicated like making me trust you when you were lying through your teeth? I told you about my grandmother . . . I . . . No, just no. Whatever you have to say, I *do not* want to hear it!" She forcefully brushes her cheek, where a tear has overflowed.

The crowd around us stares.

"I know you feel betrayed," I say, desperately trying to find a foot-hold in this quicksand-ish conversation. "I swear I never meant to hurt you. I was trying to help—"

She laughs angrily. "*Help?* Whatever you say Justin did, you've done *so much worse*. And don't even get me started on our conversation today. I can't believe I was going to—" She shakes her head. "I never ever want to see you again."

There it is. The irreparable hurt in her eyes. The finality of her words. The painful out-of-breath feeling of watching her walk away. The wall I built around my feelings years ago presses firmly against my ribs, crack-ing and threatening to drown me like a bursting dam.

There's no air. None.

I don't remember walking away.

I don't remember if Ella's parents said anything.

I don't remember Tiny.

I don't remember my mom following me to the steps or calling after me as I went up them. She's mad. Or upset maybe. Again, I don't know.

All I know is that I'm in my room, locking the door. Locking the window. Locking the world out.

55
VALENTINE

"You're certain he's cheating?" Mr. Becker asks me, his expression stone-cold angry.

"Positive," I say, the weight of the situation hanging heavily in my tone. "I have a recording."

Mr. Becker releases a long audible breath. "Good. When can I expect it?"

But it's not good. We were never supposed to betray Ella and strong-arm her into a breakup with a recording of her boyfriend and her best friend, much less give that evidence to her parents. This was supposed to be gentle; it was supposed to leave her feeling up-lifted and better about herself, ready to go to London and conquer journalism.

"I'm certain Ella and Justin will break up without it," I reply.

Ella's dad looks like he's going to explode. "Is that your way of telling me you're not giving it to me?" And when I don't immediately respond, he follows up with, "Then I guess you don't expect to be paid for this."

"Honey," Ella's mom interjects, trying to calm her husband.

While the last thing I'm thinking about in this turd of a moment is money, his comment pisses me off. He offered us three times our rate, and now he's threatening me with it. And while I'd love to just say *Fine*, *don't pay us,* I can't do that to August. So instead, I say, "If they break up, then we've completed our end of the job."

"No, you have not," he fires back. "You promised my daughter would be both happy and none the wiser. And you assured me there would be *no kissing.*"

For a second, I'm totally confused. "Kissing?"

"As in your colleague groping my daughter yesterday in his car!"

"Jim." Ella's mom's tone is stern. "I told you to *leave this one alone.*"

"Well, it needed to be said," he replies and angrily shifts his attention to what everyone is looking at—Ella and August arguing. I don't try to mediate, I don't even say goodbye when Ella's parents walk off, because all I can think is that August kissed Ella after he promised he wouldn't, and worse, he didn't tell me.

I stare after them, dumbstruck and angry. Bentley says my name, but I don't respond. I can't even think. All I can do is watch as Ella yells, as August walks away, as everything falls apart. And to make matters so much worse, my mom is headed toward me with a fiery glare.

"Valentine Sharma. Upstairs, *now,*" Mom says in a tone I haven't heard since I accidentally lost her grandmother's necklace when I was eleven. "Bentley, you'll have to excuse us—my daughter is done for the night and for a lot longer than that."

I follow my mom and her sequined dress, the one she spent a whole week picking out in order to look perfect tonight. Her steps are tense as she leads me through the crowd and into our house—even her French twist looks angry. But it's nothing in comparison to the cold calm of her expression when she shuts my bedroom door behind us. She doesn't say anything for a long moment; she just stares.

"You can imagine my shock when Mrs. Becker begs my pardon for leaving so abruptly because she didn't know that Valentine was our daughter, the same Valentine she hired to break up her daughter's relationship?" She pauses, eyeing me. "Now normally, I'd have set the woman straight, told her that she's obviously mistaken because *my* Valentine is a caterer. I should know. I see her leave the house most days carrying her work uniform. And more importantly, *my* daughter isn't a liar. But she was gone too fast for me to get a word in, chasing you around the lawn while people screamed and caused scenes at your father's *most important work event of the year*."

I swallow, feeling worse than I did ten minutes ago, which I honestly didn't think was possible. "There's a reasonable explanation for this, I swear," I start, which is apparently not a good move judging by the way her eyebrows shoot up her forehead.

"An explanation for why you have been lying to us for . . ." She gestures at me to fill in the blank.

It's hard to get the words out. "Two years."

"Two ye—" She presses her hand into her chest like I physically wounded her.

"Mom," I start, but she shakes her head.

"I don't think I've ever been more disappointed in you."

Death blow.

"You're definitely going to explain this. But it's not going to be now," she says. "I'm too angry. And your father . . . Well, if I were you, I'd spend your time thinking up the most impactful apology of your life."

56

AUGUST

Swee pushes his flat head into my hand, and I oblige him with a scratch. The pale morning light peeks under the bottom of my curtains, and I turn away from it, taking up a spooning position with my cat and tucking him under the blankets with me. I've been staring into the dark all night, and I'm not prepared for morning. I close my eyes.

After what might be a couple hours, my mom knocks on the door. "August, talk to me," she says, and I can hear her lean against the wood.

But I don't respond.

"I'm leaving you food, okay? I have to get to work."

She lingers a minute, and then her footsteps fade in the hall. I put my head under my pillow.

The morning passes painfully slow. I half read at my desk, half stare at nothing. I eventually eat the food Mom left, but I barely taste it. Everything seems dull and lifeless.

I turn in my desk chair and frown at my pants on the floor, where I discarded them last night with my phone still in the pocket. I haven't been able to bring myself to look at it—a thousand texts from Tiny and no texts from Ella.

Just thinking her name makes my chest ache.

As if my phone knows I'm thinking about it, it vibrates against the rug. And for a split second, I wonder—what if it's Ella, what if she did text?

I grab my pants and stick my hand in the pocket, but to my surprise, I pull out not one but two black phones. I frown, trying to sort it out. The first is definitely mine, only when I touch the screen, it doesn't notify me that I have endless texts from Tiny; in fact, I have none at all. Maybe she's as lost for words as I am? The other is the same model with a similar black case, but worn at the edges, and this one does have texts from Tiny—only her name is listed as Valentine. And the realization hits me. How in the heck did I wind up with Bentley's phone?

I think back to the party, to grabbing my phone off the table. I only grabbed one; I'm sure of it. But then I remember fervently trying to text Tiny in my pocket and failing.

I stare at Bentley's phone, Valentine's name at the top of his lock screen with the most recent message asking him if he's getting her texts. Just below is a text from Charlie asking if Bentley got laid by a hot musician. I consider tossing it out the window and being done with it. But for some reason I keep scrolling. It's not like I'm going through his conversations; it's just the front screen—anyone would do that to figure out who the phone belonged to.

Just as I'm about to switch it off and send a message to Tiny that I have it, I spot a notification from Cassie, Bentley's ex. She's asking him if they're still meeting up later, followed by heart eyes and a kiss emoji.

My grip tightens.

Of course he's meeting up with his ex. Like I said—dick. And so I take a picture of the front of his phone. I feel a little conflicted about it; it's not something I'd normally do, invade Tiny's relationship, but now that I've seen it, I can't ignore it, either.

I'll just give her the phone, and if she doesn't see the message herself or if their dating doesn't peter out in the next few days naturally, I'll show her the picture. My guess is that she's in deep with her parents for the foreseeable future and that probably includes not going to parties or the beach. I can't imagine Bentley waiting that out. I'd bet anything that after one week he's making out with some girl in a bikini and post-ing it on his social. No need to upset Tiny if I don't have to.

But as soon as I think it, I feel annoyed that my best friend is in this situation at all. Damn Bentley. I toss his phone onto my desk and unlock mine.

Me

Have Bentley's phone. Picked it up by mistake last night. Gonna drop it on your porch.

But before I can even stand up, I have a response.

Tiny

Oh?

She types something but erases it and starts again.

Tiny

You okay?

Which is a pretty restrained communication for her, confirming my suspicion that she doesn't know how to handle this blowup any better than I do.

Me

I don't know. You?

Tiny

IN THE DOG HOUSE.

Me

Sorry T.

There's a pause.

Tiny
Can you give the phone to Bentley?

I frown, realizing that if I do, she won't see the Cassie text.

Me
I'd rather give it to you.

Tiny
I'm home today. Have to talk to my parents.
So I'm not seeing Bentley.

There is no *pretty please, August of the house of good hair* or any of the flowery language she usually uses. Is Tiny mad?

Me
Okay.

I text her briefly that before the blowup at the party, Ella told me she was going to break up with Justin, but I have no idea if she followed through. I see her message bubble pop up and disappear, but in the end she doesn't respond. I don't text her again, knowing we're both in off moods and there's nothing to say anyway.

I stand up, ready to be done with the whole thing and Bentley in general. I reach for my jeans, but as I do, I reconsider and grab my swim trunks instead, hoping the water will distract me from my spiraling thoughts.

57
VALENTINE

My mind loops the many disasters from last night, all of which are impossible to mediate from my current hiding spot in bed. I kick my legs out of the fluffy comforter and grab my robe, scrolling through my text conversation from yesterday with Mr. Becker, rereading it for the hundredth time, trying to figure out how to handle it.

Mr. Becker

Once again, I must request the recording verifying that Justin is cheating.

Me

I'm sorry, but I cannot give that to you. Please trust me that a breakup is coming without it.

Mr. Becker

Do not forget that I've hired you for a service, one you are currently not providing.

I tried to call him earlier this morning, twice, but he didn't answer. So I sent this:

Me

I am here to discuss this if you'd like.
Please feel free to call me back.

But it's been crickets ever since. I haven't told August yet because honestly, I'm too annoyed to talk to him right now.

Once Bentley got his phone back, he asked if I wanted to chat, but I've yet to take him up on it. We never fully resolved our tiff from last night, but we both seem to have silently agreed that there are bigger problems afoot than Bentley's locker-room bragging, which honestly has nothing to do with me or our relationship. He assured me he never spoke about me that way, and I recognize that while it sounds bad, it's no worse than the way I've critiqued some of my dates' kissing styles with August. My pride was stung, and I was trying so hard to micromanage the interaction between Bentley and August that I got my back up. But once I took a breath, I could see the sense in the fact that everyone talks to their friends about relationships and hookups and that those conversations don't always sound admirable when repeated out of context.

I make my way to the top of the stairs, listening for my parents and debating going down at all. I know I can't live in my room forever, but I also don't think I can handle their disappointment.

When the smell of freshly baked cinnamon rolls wafts up to me, my stomach rumbles and I give in, grabbing the railing.

"Mom? Dad?" I say when I reach the first floor.

"Valentine," Mom replies from the living room, where she holds a cup of steaming tea on the couch next to my dad.

I drag my sorry self into the room, plop down in the armchair, and pull my knees up under my chin.

Dad puts down his book.

Mom blows on her tea. "I think it's time we had a talk. I'd like to hear that explanation now."

I nod against my knees, considering where to begin and concluding the only way for them to understand is to start at the beginning.

"I didn't know what to do after Des passed," I start, telling them all about August shutting down and not being able to reach him, about my plan for Summer Love and what I thought it might do for him. How relieved I was when it worked and how dedicated I've been ever since.

"And you believe this business you started has been cathartic for him?" Mom asks, not dropping the parental tone that clearly distinguishes her as alpha.

"I really do," I say. "And so many other people. We've helped a lot of families and friend groups. Until last night, that is . . . and well, you saw what happened."

"Yes, we did. And so did all my colleagues," Dad says.

"I'm really sorry, Dad," I say a little pathetically. "I know I screwed up. I know how important last night was to you both."

"There's also the matter of the press," he adds.

I hug my knees a little tighter. In the wake of everything that happened, I'd actually forgotten about the reporters who were there.

"I imagine we'll be seeing coverage in the next couple hours, and after the scene you caused, I'd be shocked if your name wasn't present," he continues.

I wince. "But you'll—"

"No," he says. "You're eighteen. I cannot retract your name."

I yank my phone off the coffee table, about to do a panicked search, but Mom gives me a look that has me drop it again. Even if the press got pictures, there's no way they could surmise anything about Summer Love. Right? Right. All they'd have seen is a fight and some drama— maybe one or two sentences on young love gone awry?

"And then there's the lying," Mom continues, and her words snap me back to the conversation.

"That's not who we raised you to be," Dad says.

This stings. Maybe because I don't think of myself as a liar or because I convinced myself that my reasons outweighed my wrongdoing. "I know," is all I say.

"Two years . . ." Mom says.

"How are we supposed to trust you going forward?" Dad asks.

And while maybe this is a legitimate question, it also upsets me. I said I was sorry. I feel terrible. But I'm still Valentine, their daughter; they know me. Before I can stop myself, I say, "The same way I trust you two even though you've clearly been keeping something from me."

They momentarily glance at each other. The surprised look on their faces tells me I'm right, but the quiet that follows is way more uncomfortable than I'd have imagined.

Mom takes another sip of tea. But all she says is, "Okay."

"Okay?" I repeat, looking from my mom to my dad, but he's clearly deferring to her on this one.

"Your father and I will discuss your punishment," Mom continues. "We'll let you know what we think is appropriate."

"That's it?"

"That's it," Mom confirms.

"But what about—"

Dad cuts me off. "That's not a discussion for today."

I drop my knees from my chest, my bare feet hitting the soft carpet, feeling frustrated about my unknowable punishment, their nonanswer, and the five thousand messes in my life right now. "So I have to be honest, but you don't?"

"Valentine," Dad says, his tone a warning.

Mom shakes her head. "You don't know what you're asking."

Which is an anxiety-inducing answer and now makes leaving it alone impossible. "No, I don't. What I do know is that you two have been weird for weeks."

They're both silent.

"Great. Silence. Not hypocritical at all."

"Valentine Sharma," Dad snaps, and I know I've pushed it too far. "You've just lost the privileges to your phone."

I can feel myself spiraling, anger and upset mixing in such a way that I'm not fully in control. I look at Mom. Bentley's comment about couples therapy and an affair blares in my thoughts. "Punish me however you want, but I'm right. Be upset about my lying, but also be upset about the example you set."

Both their eyes widen in matching expressions of shock. And the quiet that follows is so tense that it's hard to breathe. We sit there for so long that I'm certain my punishment will last until the end of summer.

I shift in the armchair.

"I'm pregnant," Mom says, and I freeze.

Then all at once I'm moving, walking toward her even though I don't remember getting up. "*What?!?* But you're . . . *That's not possible.*" I press my hands into my temples, physically incapable of computing. I'm eighteen. She's forty-six, and besides which, her fertility issues were so severe in her twenties that after she had me, the doctor said she'd never get pregnant again. They went to specialists in Boston, invested three years and most of their savings in treatments, all for nothing.

Mom opens her mouth, but I cut her off, flying onto the couch next to her. "This is a miracle—"

"Valentine, wait," she says, and her tone stops my hand on its way to her belly. "We don't know yet if everything is . . . We didn't want to tell you until we were sure."

My heart punches my ribs. "Sure of what?"

It's Dad who answers. "The doctors aren't convinced there won't be complications," he explains, and I can tell he's choosing his words carefully. "We've had some testing done, and we're waiting on results."

I pull back, looking at them and recognizing the fear of loss. "I don't understand." But I do understand. After Des passed, I asked Mom why she never had another child. That's when she told me about the endless hormones and the two miscarriages.

Mom presses her lips together. "We'll know more next week."

And while that's not really an answer, I recognize that she can't bring herself to say more. That the weirdness between my parents wasn't an impending divorce but fear of being too hopeful—a pregnancy she didn't expect, one she doesn't know if her body will allow.

"Now," Dad says, taking a breath and confiscating my phone from the coffee table, "breakfast?"

While I have a million questions, I know he's changing the subject for her. That she literally can't talk about this anymore.

"Yeah, okay," I say, my voice small.

Dad goes to the kitchen, and Mom heads upstairs with her tea. But I sit there on the couch, dumbfounded and unsure, feeling guilty I went on the offensive and hurt they didn't tell me sooner. I fall back into the cushions, pressing my palms over my eyes.

Please, please let my mom and the baby be okay.

58
AUGUST

Two days since my blowup with Ella. I stare at my phone, opening and closing my messages. There's nothing to say that she'd listen to. Still, I open my texts and consider another apology. I even type it out and hover over the send button. But before I make a decision, a message from Daisy flashes across my screen.

I'm about to swipe it away when I see the preview that reads: *Ummm . . . so your name is AUGUST?!?* with a link. I sit up so fast that Swee meows. I can't press the link quickly enough. And when the page loads, the title of the magazine article shoots so much adrenaline through me that my vision blurs.

THE BREAKUP ARTISTS:
PLAYING GAMES WITH THE RICH AND FAMOUS

The surprise of Prem Sharma's infamous Bright Records Summer Bash this year wasn't the guest list or even the drunk list but his own daughter, Valentine Sharma, and her friend August Mariani, who have the most gossip-worthy business we've ever heard of—Summer Love Inc.—an anonymous site where concerned

friends and parents fill out a questionnaire about their loved one's
problematic relationship in hopes of hiring these two to facilitate a
breakup. Yes, you heard that right—they're relationship assassins.
And to make things even more exciting, they currently have their
sights set on the daughter of James Becker, the owner of Boston's
largest hedge fund, or they did before they were publicly outed.
We've caught the resulting blowup on film.

I send a panicked text to Tiny before I remember her one-line email that said her dad took her phone. So I switch to email, forwarding the article.

I drop my phone, dragging my hands down my face. *Disaster. Absolute effing nightmare.* But then I pick it back up because it's impossible to look away. I skim the rest of the article, detailing our website and our claims of success. And that's when I see it, a quote from Ella's dad.

"Even though events didn't unfold the way we expected, Summer Love Inc. did obtain a recording verifying that our daughter's boyfriend was cheating."

"God damn it!" I stand up, throwing my phone onto my bed. I'm so mad I can barely think. Ella's dad gave a *quote*? But then all at once the realization hits me so hard I feel ill.

Tiny wouldn't give him the recording. He wanted to ensure Ella's breakup, and he didn't trust us. So he publicly accused Justin, knowing Ella couldn't ignore it. Of all the shitty things to do to his own daughter. I'm so angry my skin feels like it's on fire.

I pick up my phone, pressing the call button on Ella's number. But she doesn't answer. And when I get her voicemail, it tells me her inbox is full. I grab clothes, pulling a T-shirt over my head and running my hands through my messy hair. I head downstairs, but then I remember Mom's at work and Tiny's housebound. I have no car.

I call a car, pacing in front of my house for the full seven minutes it takes to show up. When the bright-blue Nissan does appear, I jump in the back seat, tapping my fingers on the armrest for the entire thirty-three-minute drive to Ella's house. And when it drops me at the entrance of her long driveway, I jog down it, pounding on her front door.

After five excruciating seconds, the door cracks, the maid's face filling the gap.

"Hi!" I exclaim, and by the way she frowns, I'm sure I look wild. "Is Ella here?"

"I'm sorry," she says, "but Mr. and Mrs. Becker aren't home."

"If I could just talk to Ella for one—"

"Sorry," she says again and closes the door.

I turn around, walking two steps down the driveway and pulling out my phone to text Ella, when I suddenly remember her story about the balcony. If I could find which window is hers, maybe I could yell to her? I look up at her house, but there are no balconies in the front. So I head for the wooden gate that leads to the backyard, pulling it open before I can think about the million reasons this is a bad idea.

After all of the crap luck I've had recently, I get a reversal. She's already outside, sitting on a small balcony adjacent a third-story window.

"Ella?" I say, jogging to the grass below her.

She wipes the backs of her hands over her eyes, but it's impossible to cover the fact that she's been crying. Her eyes widen as she registers me.

"Ella, I'm sorry," I call up to her. I glance at the latticework on the side of her house, which I could potentially climb to get to her. "I'm so . . . God, I'm an idiot. Worse than an idiot. I should have told you the truth. You have every right to hate me. But I need you to know—" I hesitate, my emotions sticking in my throat.

But she doesn't respond. She just climbs back into her room, closes the window, and draws her curtain.

I'm left on her lawn, my chest tight, staring up at her empty balcony.

59
VALENTINE

Sunday—day seven of a punishment that isn't grounding in name but feels like its identical twin. My phone was gone until last night. My Jeep privileges are trashed, and I'm not allowed to hang out with friends. My parents are calling it a period of self-reflection. I'm calling it an eternity of horrifying silence. And to make today even more crapola, it's our would-be deadline for finishing Ella's case. My dad gave me back my phone last night, but I haven't had the guts to turn it on. Not after that article that blew up Summer Love.

I sit at the kitchen table, slumped over my tea and picking at the edge of a pastry.

Within twenty-four hours my email filled up with friends and parents from past cases, and requests from the press for comment, which Dad informed me was out of the question. He said that if I gave any response at all I'd lose my laptop, too. But it doesn't matter because the damage is done. Our business is irrevocably smashed. People are pissed. And everyone in town will not shut up about it, or so Mom says.

Then there's Mom. My pregnant mother, who I can't even think about without getting teary. She's trying to act normal, not to snip or sigh, but last night I heard her crying in the bathroom when she thought no one was around. All Dad keeps saying is just wait for the results from the specialist. But it feels like that's not good enough, like we're failing her in some major way.

To top it off, there's my silence with August. I wrote him an email a couple of days ago checking in, and all I got in reply was a one-line response that he's fine and how am I. But since I didn't want to answer that, I haven't written back. And since he also didn't write again, I know with certainty that we both suck.

I glance out the window at him, where he sits in our "office" with his Snoopy coffee mug beside him on the dock. I can tell by his drooping shoulders that he's stewing.

"Same," I say under my breath and glance at Bentley's house, who's the only person I seem to be talking to normally right now. He hasn't put any pressure on me to explain. He hasn't asked me about the gossip. He's just been reassuring and patient and the perfect escape from all the crap in my head.

As if Bentley knew I was thinking about him, he opens his screen door, heading toward his weights. Only halfway there, he stops and glances at August.

"Don't," I warn him. "August will eat you alive right now."

Bentley apparently agrees with my assessment even though he can't hear me, because he looks away from the dock and throws his towel over his shoulder. But before I fully unclench, he looks at August again, and this time he starts walking toward him.

I jump up from the breakfast table, sending my chair screeching back. And now I do turn on my phone, running to the window and rolling it open as fast as I can.

I click past my million notifications and type out a warning text for Bentley to abort because August is in a foul mood. But he gives no indication that he has his phone on him.

I press my hands and forehead against the window screen. If I go out there, my punishment will likely get extended. If I don't go out there, they'll probably bite each other's heads off like hostile gerbils.

"Hey, man," I hear Bentley say. "Thanks for returning my phone."

August sips his coffee, still staring at the water. "Sure."

Can't you see he's brushing you off? Walk away, Bentley. Just slide on out of the danger zone and back to flexing your man muscles.

But Bentley tries again. "Crazy what happened at that party. Sorry about that girl, man."

August turns, and even in profile I can tell it's not going to be good. "Cut the shit. If there's something you came here to ask, just ask," he says, sounding exhausted.

Bentley momentarily tenses, but he lets it go. "Nah, I get it. Must sting. Valentine says you really like that girl." I can tell he's trying to be understanding about August's bad mood, but it definitely isn't landing.

August's eyes shoot to my house, and when he finds me pressed up against my kitchen window like a smushed bug, I know he's pissed. And I also know why—he thinks I told Bentley his personal business, which I guess I did.

"We done here?" August says, getting up.

"Uh, yeah. I'll leave you to it, man," Bentley says, gesturing at the water.

"Good," August says. "Then move."

Whatever patience Bentley was utilizing just ran out. "Way to be a dick, dude."

August's eyes darken. "Right," he says. "You're blowing smoke up my ass, and I'm the dick. Don't pretend you came here to check on me. Ask what you actually want to ask: *Did I see the text?* Yes, I did."

My heart jumps into my throat. What text?

Bentley looks confused. But a second later his expression clears as he obviously catches on to whatever August is talking about. "Wait . . . *you hacked my phone?*"

"Don't flatter yourself. I looked at your front screen, and it took me about two seconds to confirm that you're exactly who I thought you were."

Oh no.

I register August's expression and know that if I don't get out there, things are going to spiral. I run to the porch door, and for a split second I hesitate.

"Sorry, Dad! Emergency!" I yell to him in the living room and rush outside without bothering to grab my flip-flops.

My bare feet pad onto the wooden dock just as August growls, "Like I said, *move*."

Bentley follows it up with an equally Neanderthal, "Make me."

"Both of you knock it the hell off!" I say with feeling, and two surprised faces turn in my direction.

"I thought you were still housebound—" Bentley starts.

And under his breath August says, "Good thing Cassie was free."

Which only sets Bentley off again. "What the hell are you implying?"

August gives him a withering look.

I frown. "Cassie?" I say, confused, looking at Bentley for explanation.

But Bentley's not looking at me. "Just because you can't get a girl unless you pretend to be someone else doesn't mean you can take your frustration out on Valentine. No wonder Ella wants nothing to do with you. Who would?"

I physically wince. "Bentley, no," I say, my tone a warning. I don't care who's right and wrong here, or that I'm currently annoyed with August—he can't take a blow like that right now. "That's so out of line."

Bentley looks from August to me and shakes his head. "I can't believe I came over here to ask him if he was okay. I can't win with you two."

And for a second, I feel bad.

August scoffs. "Why don't you tell Tiny the truth, Bentley: you came over here to find out if I'd seen Cassie's text and if I was going to out you."

"Can someone please tell me what this Cassie thing is about?" I ask, annoyed in every way possible. Bentley isn't the only one who feels like he can't win here.

"It's nothing," Bentley says, which only makes me more uneasy.

"August?" I ask, which earns me a disappointed look from Bentley, but I don't have time for a long gentle discussion. I'm surprised Dad hasn't come out here already.

August pinches the bridge of his nose. "There was a text on his lock screen from Cassie asking if they were still meeting up. Followed by a heart and a kissy face."

I pull my shoulders up and in, trying to keep the storm of worry at bay. I turn to Bentley for an explanation, but he doesn't offer one.

"Did you . . . meet up with her?" I ask, unsure.

He hesitates, his jaw tight. "Yes."

His answer is like a beesting, fast and sharp and sure to hurt more later.

We all stand there, suspended in this long awful second.

Bentley turns on August, blame etched in his eyebrows. "This is when you walk away and let me clean up your mess."

"My mess?" August snaps. "Try again. You don't deserve Tiny, never will. Better to just bow out now."

"Coming from a guy who gets paid to mess with people's love lives?" Bentley fires back. "I mean, I might sometimes be an ass, but the one thing I never am is for sale."

"Right," August says. "You screw people over for free."

I hear their words, but my reaction is muddled and slow.

Bentley clenches his hands. "That's it—" he starts, but he's cut off. By my dad.

"Enough," Dad says from the porch, not even loudly, but in that dad tone that makes everyone freeze. "Bentley—your yard. August—yours. Valentine—inside *now*."

60
AUGUST

I slam my back door shut, hoping Tiny finally tells Bentley to eff off. But I stop the instant I step inside. Because there, sitting at the kitchen table, is my father and I'm . . .

Blindsided.

My throat goes dry and my vision wavers. I consider walking right back out.

"Thanks, Ruth," my dad says as Mom hands him a cup of coffee. "It's good to see you, August."

Good to see me, he says?

Whatever anger I felt toward Bentley amplifies by a thousand. But it's that low-burning anger, the kind that you can't let out because if you do, you'll destroy everyone and everything in the radius around you.

"Mom?" I say, looking for an explanation.

She leans back against the kitchen counter, her hair neatly wound on top of her head, her favorite floor-length denim shirtdress pressed with a popped collar, and lipstick—she never wears makeup. While I understand the desire to look good in this particular scenario, whatever that is, it only agitates me more.

"I asked him to come," she says, and now I'm even more confused.

"What? Why?" I say, still not acknowledging my father.

"Because . . ." She glances at him. "You need someone to talk to, and you won't talk to me."

All I can think is *WHAT? What???* "You thought I was going to talk to *him?*" My tone is still controlled, but my upset is seeping out around the edges.

Mom takes a deep breath. "I was hoping you would, yes."

Dad does his understanding nod, the one I used to think made him so adult. "How about we chat a little?" he offers like that's a thing we do. "Maybe I can help make sense of whatever's going on. Your mother tells me you got in a fight?"

But I don't hear anything beyond the obviously false offer of help, and it obliterates my train of thought. "No," I say, my voice tight.

He sighs. "Look, I know I haven't been around much these past few years. I know things have been, well, they haven't been ideal."

I blink at him; he can't possibly be serious. "I haven't seen you since Des died."

"I know," he says. "I'm sorry about that."

"I'm not," I snap.

"I know you're angry," he starts, but I cut him off, because he doesn't know.

"Damn right I am."

"August, language," Mom says, which might be the most ridiculous statement of this whole conversation.

"It's okay to be angry," he says, and that's the final straw. Who does he think he is, giving me permission to have an emotion?

"Let's just clear this all up right now so you can disappear back to Connecticut. I'm not sitting at the kitchen table pretending that you give a sh—crap." Even now, I can't help but appease my mom. "About either of us. I'm definitely not having a heart-to-heart with you. In fact, if I never speak to you again, that's fine by me." I cross the kitchen, stride through the living room, and exit the front door.

But there, parked in our driveway, is his car—a brand-new convertible—and it makes my blood boil.

"August, wait a second," my dad says, jogging after me.

I whip around. "Like you waited the day you left?" I say before I consider it, and I instantly regret my choice of words. My tone is hurt and childlike, neither of which I intend.

His face falls like I slapped him. "My leaving was never about you."

I glance up at the sky, trying to get my breathing under control. "Like I said, I don't want to have this conversation."

My mother lingers in the doorway, her forehead wrinkled with worry.

"I know," he says, quieter now. "You've always been like me that way. Guarded with your feelings." He pauses, and I clench my jaw. "Des was the opposite, though, wasn't she? Always communicating. I always thought that's why you two fit so well—"

"Stop, just stop!" I yell, and the volume surprises even me. "Do *not* talk about her."

His eyebrows push together. Again that godforsaken understanding nod. "I know your sister was—"

Something inside me cracks, and the emotion I was so carefully containing breaks free from my grasp. "Stop trying to relate to me! Stop pretending you care! You weren't there when it mattered. Mom fell apart. You didn't help. Des *died*. You didn't help. You never ask about the mountain of bills that piles up or wonder how we're staying afloat. Did you know that I've spent my entire college savings trying to keep the house from being repossessed? No, you don't. You don't know *anything* about our lives, and frankly if you do, then I really do hate you because once again, you did nothing. So get in your goddamn new car and go. Do what you always do and pretend we don't exist. Because more than anything I wish you didn't."

And just as I feared, everything in the radius around me is destroyed. I close my mouth, deflated and worn out, my arms hanging by my sides. I turn around. Mom calls my name, but I don't respond. I just walk onto the sidewalk and away, disappearing behind the trees.

61
VALENTINE

I fall face first onto my bed. All I can think is that August was right, that I'm one in a long line of idiots who fell for Bentley Cavendish's charm. That here I am stupidly spouting his praises and asking August to give him a chance, and meanwhile he's hanging out with his ex the second I get reflective-silence-not-grounded and can't see him. But my chain of thought gets cut short by my phone buzzing. I pull my face out of my comforter, and there on my screen is Bentley video-calling me.

"Yes?" I say after pressing accept, knowing I should probably wait, that I'm too revved up to think clearly, but also not possessing that type of herculean restraint.

He, too, sits on his bed. "Can I explain?"

"Depends." Anger tightens my chest. We messaged each other five thousand times this past week. I know which day he did his freaking laundry and that he lost his favorite sock, but somehow he forgot to tell me that he hung out with his ex-girlfriend? "Did you hook up with Cassie?"

"No," he says, but it's not an easy word. Bentley hesitates. And that hesitation speaks volumes.

Whatever slim hope I had of this being reparable disappears.

Something happened; I can feel it in my bones. And honestly, I don't think I want to know what it was, unable to handle one more disappointment. August was right, I know better than to get involved with someone like Bentley. And what pisses me off the most is that Bentley totally had me going on the idea that we had something special, that he was just waiting for me to have a real relationship. Even thinking it makes me embarrassed.

And so I do something I never do. I hang up. And when he calls back two more times, I block him. Then I cry into my pillow, a good long cry that feels like it might never stop.

62

AUGUST

My arms are exhausted and my shoulders burn, and when I pull myself out of the salty ocean, I collapse on the sand, taking big, labored breaths that catch in my throat. My skin tingles from the cold water, and the hot afternoon sun sets to drying it. But as my heart rate slows, my upsets come rushing back, oppressive and sharp. So I stand, running back into the ocean and diving under a wave, the hum of the water steadying me.

But even caught in the pull of the ocean, I can't fully erase my conversation with my dad. And with the thought of him comes the familiar formation of lines and shapes, which makes me so angry that I dive deeper, swim harder.

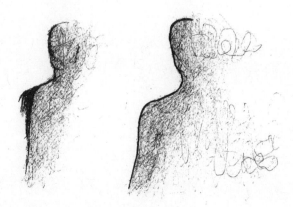

I stand up, gasping for breath.

"Stop!" I yell into the salty air, punching the water in front of me, but it's no use.

Ella was wrong. These sketches aren't a way to reconnect with Des; they're a curse. A reminder that I'll never again give her one. That she'll never yell in excitement. We won't laugh. And things won't be okay.

63
VALENTINE

Two days since the blowup on the dock. It's bad enough that Bentley's bedroom window is visible from mine, but now he's in clear view of the picture window, lifting weights in his yard while I'm eating dinner with my family.

"Do you want to talk about it?" Mom asks as I push my food around my plate. The last thing she needs to worry about right now is my failed relationship with Bentley.

"Nope," I respond. "Can I eat in my room?"

"I thought you hated your room, or so you told us a few days ago," Dad says, trying to lighten the mood. Between me and Mom, he's had one heck of a week trying to be cheery.

I shrug. "Changed my mind."

My parents look at each other.

"Okay," Mom says as I stand. "What if we told you that you've completed the self-reflection period; would you still want to go to your room?"

I know I should be happy to hear it, but it doesn't feel like good news, just pressure to handle five thousand disasters.

"Yup," I say and turn around, heading for the stairs.

I abandon my plate on the nightstand and fall onto my bed. I'll just stay here for the rest of the night, watch a movie, and pass out—deal with it all in the morning.

But after fourteen minutes of ceiling staring, I stand up, my cyclical thoughts getting the better of me, and I resign myself to talking to August.

"Whatever," I say to no one, not confident I'm making the right decision, but if I spend one more minute in my bedroom, I might torch it.

I change out of my pajamas and into a pair of cutoffs and a tank top. And I head back down the stairs. But as I near the kitchen, I hear my parents fighting.

"And how are we supposed to explain that to Valentine?" Dad objects.

"We don't," Mom replies in a tight voice.

"And what if your doctor's right that there could be life-threatening complications? What if you die?" Dad says, and my heart stops. "How do you think she'll feel, knowing we didn't tell her?"

"Prem," Mom says in a hard tone. "I'm not discussing this right now. Not until we know for sure."

Fear and nausea churn my stomach in awful ways. I'm going in there—I'm going to yell and plead with her to take care of herself. But she starts to sob, and it's so awful that I turn away before I reach the kitchen, my own eyes welling. Instead, I make my way to the door and quietly close it behind me.

I take a gasping breath on the porch, willing myself not to fall apart, and head toward August's house. I climb the ladder and slide through his window, my feet landing on his floor with a thunk.

He's in bed, book in hand.

"Hello?" I say, only it comes out sounding like a rude question.

He doesn't look at me. "I'm not in the mood to fight."

"Excuse me?" I say, my tone questionable. "I didn't come here to fight."

"Yes, you did," he says, finally looking away from his page but not closing it. "And I'm telling you that I don't want to."

He starts reading again, and for some reason it makes my blood boil. I came here to vent, but obviously he's too stuck in his own damn head to notice. I'm about to turn away and climb back out the window when I stop.

Frustration pulses through me. "You're not the only one who has bad things happen, you know. Have you even considered that maybe my life isn't going well, either? No, you haven't."

His eyes tense, but he remains fixated on his book. Part of me knows I should stop, but the other part of me doesn't care.

"This is exactly what I mean. Not one word asking me if I'm okay, what's going on with me, or why I've been so damn quiet. Meanwhile I've been bending over backward to help you for *years*. Every fight, every disappointment, and there I am. Faithful Valentine."

Still nothing but silence.

Anger rises in my chest, hot and unruly. "But you know what? Not anymore. 'Cause guess what, August? *I don't want to go to Berkeley.* And you know what's messed up? For a second there, I was going to go for *you.* Well, not anymore. Go to California by yourself!"

Now he does put his book down. But all he says is a quiet, "If that's how you feel."

"It is!" I say and storm out his bedroom door, not trusting myself on the ladder right now.

64

AUGUST

It's 12:30 a.m. and the dock is quiet. All the lights are off in the neighboring houses, including the one in Tiny's bedroom. Still, I stand on her porch, staring at her back door and contemplating going in, her words circling unresolved in my head.

I could text her to come out if she's awake. But it feels like our fight is too big for that. So instead I grab the doorknob, and it twists in my hand. Truth be told, I haven't snuck into her room in years. And the thought nags at me, reinforces what she said about our relationship being one sided.

I head in, stepping lightly along the floorboards and up the stairs. But it's mostly unnecessary because her house is new and doesn't creak the way mine does. Plus the central air provides a hum that covers small sounds. I pause when I get to her room, doubting whether this is a good idea. But it feels like if I don't do this, then I risk losing her. And that's unthinkable.

I tap lightly on her door in a rhythm we used when we were kids and push it open.

She sits up on her bed as I close it behind me. "August?" she says, her voice hoarse, and I wonder if I woke her or if she's been crying.

I sit at the end of her bed, studying my hands in the dark. "You're right," I say. "I haven't been there for you the way you've been there for me."

"I didn't mean—" she starts.

"Yeah, you did. And you should," I say. "I didn't even think to ask why you'd been so quiet. I've been going over it, trying to figure out how I could have missed that you were upset. And all I came up with is the lame excuse that you have a perfect life."

She snorts. "Yeah, well, I don't."

"I'm sorry I screwed up not being there for you. I'm a selfish dick."

She hesitates, looking at the lamp on her bedside table and deciding not to turn it on. "Mom's pregnant, and Dad thinks she's going to die from complications."

My head whips up. "*What?* Shit, Tiny. Is she okay?"

"I don't know," she says, lifting her hands and dropping them back onto her comforter. "We're waiting on tests? But something happened, something that made them worry. They haven't told me what, and I'm too afraid to ask." Her voice wobbles.

Without hesitation, I move toward her, pulling her into a hug. "Hey . . ." I say, as her chest heaves with emotion.

"And you're not selfish, by the way," she says through hitched breath. "You're just really obtuse."

"That, too," I agree. When her breathing slows, I add, "Tell me about your mom."

And she does. She tells me how worried she is and about the arguments she's overheard this past week, how her house doesn't feel like her house and her parents don't feel like her parents. I listen, giving her what advice I can and reassuring her that I'll be here for it, good or bad.

Then she asks me why I've been so distant. In turn I tell her about my failed attempt to talk to Ella and about my dad's surprise visit.

"My god, August. I had no idea."

I shake my head. "It is what it is."

"Do you think he'll come back?"

"My dad? Nah," I say. "He's not coming back."

"You mean ever?"

"Not if he has a choice," I say, and Tiny frowns.

She opens her mouth to ask another question but hesitates.

We're both quiet for a long moment, and then she shakes her head, like she's decided not to pursue that conversation. "So you kissed Ella."

Hearing it out loud makes my heart sink and my chest ache. "No. But I wanted to."

She waits.

"I just . . ." I start, but the words don't come.

"Have feelings for her?" she suggests.

I look away, surprised by how much it stings. "I should have told you about the almost kiss."

"Yeah, you should have," she says. "You let me get blindsided by Mr. Becker."

I sigh, feeling even guiltier.

Before I figure out what to say, though, she sighs, too. "But I guess where you undershared, I overshared. I shouldn't have told Bentley about you liking Ella. And I'm sorry he used it against you like that."

My eyes meet hers, and I'm grateful for the out. "Thanks," is all I say, and she seems to understand me. I change the subject. "Have you seen all the Summer Love emails?"

She tucks her hair behind her ears. "Giant mess."

We share a look, and even in the dim light, it's obvious we both know that it's over. That Summer Love is irrevocably broken, but neither of us says it.

After another few seconds of heavy silence, she shakes her hands out like she's tossing off the melancholy. "You know what we need? We need milkshakes and french fries from Bob's."

I glance at the clock on her nightstand. "It's one in the morning."

"And they're open until two, so it all works out." She slides off her bed, grabbing a sweatshirt and throwing it over her pajamas.

I open my mouth to argue but change my mind. "Yeah, okay. Let's do it."

She laughs. "I think I like conciliatory August. Can you be wrong more often?"

"Yeah, no."

She wags her eyebrows at me. "What would you say if I suggested matching outfits?"

"I'd say get a dog."

"Or maybe . . ." she says, going on to list ridiculous things that are never going to happen.

But I can't help but smile; she's pretty funny.

We exit Bob's Diner, stuffed on ice cream and greasy food, yet somehow lighter than either of us has felt in a good long while.

"I'll drive," Tiny says and puts her hand out for the keys.

"You never want to drive."

"Yeah, but it's a beautiful night, and I feel . . . different. So I figure, why not shake things up?" she says.

"If you say so."

While we talked a little more at the diner about all the crap that's been happening, we were careful to avoid the subject of Berkeley, not wanting to chance another fight. I'm just not sure if the nonmention is because she didn't mean it or because she did.

We climb in her Jeep, and she kicks off her left flip-flop, putting her foot awkwardly up by the vent, a driving position literally no one else employs.

"I'm proud of you, you know," she says as she starts her engine and turns down the music. "For what you did with Ella. Opening up like that."

"Didn't make a difference."

She heads out of the parking lot. "Still, it was brave. And romantic. And thoroughly un-August-like."

I shrug, looking out the window.

"I could help you think of a—"

"Tiny, she hates me."

She's quiet a second, glancing at me in that Tiny way that tells me

she's not giving up. We're about to pass the street where Des had the accident, and I study my hands, avoiding looking out my window.

Tiny notices, only instead of sighing or pretending she didn't see,
she slams on the break.

I look up. She grips the wheel tighter than necessary, like she's nervous, and instead of staying straight, she turns.

Then suddenly I realize what she's doing. I stare at her in shock.

But she doesn't look at me. She just drives down the dead-end street
with the soccer field on one side and the woods on the other and pulls
to a stop in front of *the* tree with the dent in it from Kyle's car.

My heartbeat rapid fires in my temples, and even though the windows are down, I can't get a single breath of air. "This isn't funny," I snap.

"No, it's not," she says so quietly I almost don't hear her. "But we
can't pretend it away."

I stare at her, stunned. "You think I don't know that *my sister died?*
You think I go one day, one hour, without thinking about it?"

"No, I don't. But even though we talked about deep personal things
tonight, we didn't say one word about Des. And at first, I thought that
was okay. I was just happy we made up. Touting myself as this perfect
friend who's always so supportive. And then it occurred to me that I'm
not. That I never talk about the one thing that hurts you the most."

"Which is fine," I say in my most controlled voice, "because *I* don't
want to talk about it."

"Des," she corrects me, like it makes her sad. "You can't even say
her name. And I think it's because you've convinced yourself that if you
don't talk about her, the past will cease to exist. It won't."

"I'm not . . ." My thoughts spin so fast they make me dizzy. But I
can't finish that sentence because it's not true.

"You didn't cry, August. You didn't cry the night it happened. You
didn't cry at her funeral. In fact, I've never seen you cry about it, not
once since that night."

"So damn what?"

"So I love you is what," she says, and her response only frustrates
me more. "And Des loved you. More than anything. She'd hate to see

you doing this to yourself. In fact, she'd probably do anything to make you stop. And since she's not here and I am, it's up to me to do this in her place."

"I'm done," I say, grabbing the door handle and stepping into the warm night air. But two seconds later Tiny's standing on the quiet road in front of me.

"Do you remember after your dad left and your mom locked herself in her room?" she says, her voice strained with emotion, her chin unsteady. "How Des let you sleep in her bed every night for months? Sat for your paintings and made your school lunches? She was always there when you needed her, when I needed her. Always. Always."

I press my lips together, shaking my head, not because I don't remember—I'll never forget—but because this conversation is bullshit.

"Des was the best older sister in the whole damn world. She loved you more than a brother; she took care of you like a mom and a dad. And I know that losing her was life shattering, that there will always be a Des-shaped hole in your heart. But this thing we do where we never talk about her? I'm not doing that anymore. And this thing where I let you hide? Never again. Because like I said, I love you, and what I've been doing isn't love."

"*Tiny*," I say like a warning, but it comes out more like a whisper.

Only this time she holds out her arms and tilts her head up to the sky. "I love you, Des!" she shouts at the stars. "I love you and it hurts. It hurts that you're not here when we get home from school, that I can't ask you for relationship advice, that you can't see the awesome company August and I built. Did you know we built it for you?"

I stand there frozen, unable to think, process, breathe.

"You've suffered an unimaginable loss, August, an unbearable one. And what I'm trying to tell you is . . . *stop bearing it*. For once in your life," she says, but her voice cracks, "lean on me. *Please*. Let me shoulder this with you."

"You can't," I say, and where her voice is clear, mine is barely audible.

"Let me cry with you. Tell stories about Des and laugh with you. Anything but what we're doing now. You think if you just hold it tight enough, bury it carefully behind your Wall, that your grief can be contained. It can't. The pain needs a way out, and if you keep holding it in like this, it will *destroy you.*"

I'm shaking, but it's not cold. I stare at Tiny, the ground under my feet no longer solid. "And so what?" I say, the words sticking in my throat. "I deserve it."

For a second, she pauses, shocked. "What? You *do not* deserve this. Don't ever say that—"

"It's my fault," I snap.

"It's not—"

"That night?" I half yell, half swallow. "That night I went to her door to say good night, and I *heard them.* Kyle was begging her to go out. I *knew* they were drinking. I *knew* Des had gotten into a blowout fight with Mom earlier and was having a rough day. And I knew that if I knocked, Des would tell Kyle no; she would stay home. But I didn't. *I walked away.*"

She stares at me. "Why?" she demands, matching my intensity. "Why did you walk away?"

"Because," I say, frustrated, "I didn't want to get in her way. Didn't want Kyle to be right, that I was a needy younger brother—"

"Because you *love* your sister," she says, cutting me off. "How dare you blame yourself for this, August Mariani. This is *not* your fault. You were a kid who wanted to say good night to his older sister and turned around because he didn't want to interrupt her fun with her boyfriend after a long day. You did *nothing* wrong."

I shake my head. I don't agree.

"Look at me," she says. "If this were reversed, if this were my mom who died, would you blame me?"

"Not the same."

"Yes the same. Would you blame me or not?" she says forcefully.

I rub my hands over my face. "This is stupid, Tiny. I'm going home."

But she pushes me with both hands. "*Would you or would you not* blame me if the situation were reversed?"

"No," I yell at her. "Okay? Are you happy? No!"

"Exactly!" she says. "Yell."

I clench my jaw.

"Yell, August," she repeats. "Look at that tree and yell!"

"I'm not—"

"Unless you want me to have this conversation with you on repeat until the end of time, you will yell at that tree. You will yell to your sister. And you will *stop* blaming yourself."

I press the heels of my hands into my eyebrows, desperate to be anywhere but here. But she just grabs my wrist and pulls me to the tree, placing my palm over the scar Kyle's car left in its trunk.

My mind screams at me to pull away, to take my hand back and leave, but I don't. I just stand there, frozen, with my hand pressed into the cool bark, bent and twisted from the fender. And something inside me uncoils—the crack that formed while arguing with my dad suddenly expands, fissuring my self-control, *my Wall*, as Tiny called it. And I do scream. I scream Des's name, loud and long and broken. I scream until my throat burns and my eyes pour onto my cheeks. I scream until I have nothing left.

65
VALENTINE

August and I spend the rest of the night screaming at the tree, shouting to Des. When we're too exhausted to stand, we collapse in the grass, chests rising and falling with the effort. And then slowly, quietly, we begin to speak—voices nearly gone—and tell stories. Stories about Des, our childhood, and what it was like after she left.

To say we loved her is as inadequate a description as saying the sun is yellow. We worshipped her, followed her everywhere. And she was the type of older sister who let us, who didn't make us feel small and stupid but would wrap an arm around our shoulders and say things like "Two goddamn creative geniuses. I swear. If I grow up to be half as interesting or funny as you two, I'll have achieved all my personality goals." And the admiration was mutual, because Des was larger than life, a bright spark in a dark night. She made you feel good about yourself with a smile or feel seen with a gesture. People used to joke she was town mayor, but in a way it was true.

As the sun starts to rise and a brilliant red line forms over the trees, we sink into silence once more, lying back in the cool morning grass.

"Thanks," August says, quietly looking up at the glowing sky.

And I slip my hand into his like I used to when we were little. He squeezes it. Once again we're August and Tiny, best friends extraordinaire who face the world together. No Wall, no silence. Just us.

66
VALENTINE

Something shakes my arm and I groan.

"Valentine," my mom says.

"I'm not human," I croak. "I need like four more hours." I sent them a text last night, several actually, telling them where I was and apologizing for being out so late. I'm not stupid—I literally just got un-reflective-period-ed or whatever.

"Valentine, we've come from the doctor's," Mom says.

I sit up so fast that my room sways. "What? Now? What did she say?"

Mom takes a seat on my bed, and Dad stands on my white carpet.

"Please tell me you're okay," I sputter before she can get a word out.

Mom pushes stray hair out of my eyes. "While there are no guarantees that this won't be a challenging pregnancy in all the normal ways, the doctor says that the tests look good. That the baby and I both look healthy."

"Best news I've ever gotten," Dad adds.

For a second, I just stare at them, trying to make sense of their words. *My mom's okay*, I repeat in my head. And the moment the idea takes root, my throat tightens. I try to swallow, but there's no stopping it; I start sobbing.

"Oh, honey," Mom says, pulling me into her and wrapping her arms around my back. "I know it's all overwhelming—"

"It's not that," I cry into her shoulder. "I thought you were going to die. I thought something happened—" But I can't go on because it's too awful to say.

"Where on earth did you get an idea like that?" Mom holds me tight, but I can feel her head turn to look at my dad.

"I heard you guys arguing about it," I say between stuttered breaths.

She's quiet for a beat, probably trying to sort out what I might have overheard. "Listen," she says, gently pulling back and looking me in the eye. "That was our mistake. Those were our fears, and not even things that had come to pass, just the projection of future obstacles that might be. The things we said to each other were not for you to take on. First and foremost, we're your parents. Best job of our lives and one that we take very seriously. I'm not going anywhere."

And while I get that it's all a moot point now anyway, I needed to hear her say it.

I wipe at my wet cheeks and then bury my face back in her shoulder. She holds me tight and I listen to her heartbeat, something I used to do as a little girl.

"Now," Dad says after a few minutes. "Since I've taken the day off, how about I make us all some celebratory blueberry-and-chocolate-chip pancakes?" he asks, and my mom and I both give enthusiastic approval.

"I'm just going to jump in the shower," I tell them, energized by relief. "Be down in ten minutes." I pull my phone off my nightstand as my parents exit and type a slew of excited texts to August about Baby Sharma.

But as I pass my vanity on the way to the bathroom, I catch sight of the spot where my Berkeley sticker used to be, and my pep fizzles. Now more than ever, it feels like there's no way I can go to California. And as much as I don't want to have that conversation, I know I can't avoid it.

When our celebratory breakfast is over, I put my dishes neatly in the dishwasher and know that if I don't do this now, I'll lose my nerve. "August," I say, like somehow the act of declaring his name will inspire bravery. Even so, I delay and make him a coffee peace offering.

When I finally do walk out onto my porch, I pause. August didn't bring Berkeley up last night, and the only reason I can figure he didn't is because he must have thought it was an empty threat, that I'd never in a million years abandon our plan.

While I deliberate, Bentley's screen door opens. And as it turns out, that's all the motivation I need. I bolt off my porch and into August's yard.

I climb into August's room and find him propped up on his elbows in bed, squinting at the early-afternoon light. "You're awake. Saves me the trouble of dragging you out of bed by your feet." I try to make my tone light, but I'm buzzing with nervous energy, and I miss the humor mark.

He rubs his hands over his face and thanks me for the coffee I shove at him.

August studies me for a second with that annoying best-friend expression that suggests he can hear my thoughts. "You cool?"

"Yes. I mean, no. Honestly, I'm confused." I pace on his rug, but the information doesn't flow out of me in a thoughtful explanation as I imagined. It doesn't even trickle; I say nothing at all.

"Tiny?"

I push my hair over my shoulder, taking a deep breath. "Man, I just . . . I do not know how to say this. I'm trying. You see that, right?" I open and close my mouth, attempting to figure out how not to ruin the bonding we did last night.

"So this is about Berkeley," he says in a knowing tone. There's something in his voice, a tightness that makes my mouth go dry and my stomach clench.

I can't bear to look at him. "Yeah."

August doesn't respond, and when I'm brave enough to sneak a peek, he's staring down at his coffee.

"Berkeley's great, but . . . it's a goal we created in fifth grade when we thought it'd be cool to be in summer weather forever. And now . . ." I trail off, picking at my nails, which I just painted.

Silence.

My stomach flips in a bad way. "I'm just not convinced California is for me. And my mom's having this baby, so."

"Tiny," he says, and even though his voice is quiet, it stops me. "You decided this before the baby. You took the Berkeley sticker off your mirror weeks ago."

"Yeah, but I guess the baby solidified it?"

He shakes his head, not accepting my answer. "Say you don't want to go, but don't blame it on an outdated goal. You researched every top-ten business school last year and came to the same conclusion over and over—that Berkeley was the best. Not the best in the country—that always changes—but the best for you."

I press my lips together to stave off a whimper at how right he is and how well he knows me.

"Last winter you literally spent three days making a schedule of all the non–New England things we could do in California. Not to mention the fact that the day we found out we were accepted, you canceled movie night so you could pick out classes."

I frown. "Fine. You're right. I just don't want to go."

"If I thought that were true, I wouldn't argue. But you're acting like one of the people from our cases, letting your fear stop you from doing something you care about."

My eyes whip to his. "That's a shit thing to say."

"Okay, then tell me one reason you don't want to, and not because you suddenly changed your mind, something substantial."

I open my mouth, ready to regale him with my best logic, but I only sputter. "It feels too far."

"Okay, why?"

"Because, August. I love this place, and I'm secretly a lame townie. Are you happy now?"

"I get that you love it," he says. "But—"

"No, you don't. You've been trying to get away since forever. You don't like being in your house. You're always frustrated with your mom. You barely talk to anyone besides me. You gave up on this place when Des died." I stop abruptly, wishing I could pull it back. We only just started talking about her, and now I'm on a path to muck it up. I break eye contact. "Sorry. I shouldn't have said that."

For a moment he just sits there, looking out the window and concentrating on something far away. And when he does finally speak, he says the one thing I never thought he would. "Everything you said is true. But if you think I don't understand why you love it here, you're wrong." He pauses. "And it's still not a reason."

I bristle. "You of everyone should know that you don't get to decide other people's lives for them. You say I'm acting like someone from our cases. Well, so are you—the crappy boyfriend."

"Valentine," he says, and the shock of him using my full name makes me freeze. He takes a breath, in what I can only assume is an effort to not snap back. "Last night you did something for me. You got me to confront a part of myself that I'd hidden away. And when I came home and laid down, it was the first time in forever that I didn't feel anxious in the quiet, that I wasn't sketching my fears onto the ceiling—"

"Sketching?" I say and glance at his ceiling.

"Imaginary sketching," he clarifies. "For months now, sketches have been appearing in my thoughts. These past few weeks they've gotten more insistent. I haven't been able to get away from them, like the parts of my personality I'd locked away were messing with me."

"Why didn't you tell me?" I say, my voice more subdued.

"Because I didn't want it to be real. It made me feel like a failure, like I couldn't even do one simple thing—give up art for my sister."

My eyes widen. "Des would *never* want you to give up art for her."

"I know," he says, thoughtful. "But it felt like I had to. And now I look at you, the best person I know, and I don't want you to make the same mistakes I did. If you don't want to go to Berkeley, if you've actually changed your mind, then I'll support you. You know that. But if you're doing it because you're scared, then I'll fight for you the same way you fought for me."

I let out a long exhale and drop into his desk chair, eyeing him suspiciously. Who is this open, expressive August? "It's not that I'm scared," I say. "It's that I'm worried."

He considers it. "Well, I'm scared," he says so genuinely that I think I misheard him.

"No. You're not."

"I am. I'm scared that I'll never paint again. I'm scared that I will. That I won't be able to afford Berkeley, that Mom won't be okay without me. I'm scared all the time, Tiny."

I press my lips together, straightening the neon bracelets on my wrist.

He waits, watching me as I try to untangle my thoughts. "Tell me what you're worried about."

I exhale. "I don't . . ." I stop, slowing down and really thinking about it. "It just feels like leaving is permanent, ya know?"

"Like you can't come back?"

"Exactly," I say. "I mean, I know I can come back physically. No one's stopping me. But I just worry I'll be different, that you'll be different, that everything will change."

"We will," he says, and my stomach drops. "But that's okay."

"But what if it's not?"

"Do you remember that time you decided to cut your own bangs?" he asks.

"Way to kick me when I'm down."

He smirks. "You freaked out, begging your parents to let you get hair extensions."

"And they refused like the heartless beasts that they are."

"Because you can't go backward, your mom said, that the only way through things, especially hard things, is forward," he says. "Even if you stay here, you'll change. Nothing stays the same, no matter how much you cling to it."

I chew on my bottom lip, studying my knees. "I just wish we could restart this summer, get a do-over on Summer Love, have a little more time."

"I don't," he says, which weirdly is the most surprising statement of this whole conversation. "Because if things didn't play out exactly the way they did, I'd never have had that conversation with you last night. And even if I got Ella to date me, it wouldn't work because I'd still be closed off."

I consider his words and the possibility that I'm holding on to some romanticized version of our lives, trying to trap myself in the amber of it. The problem is that even if I can rationalize it, it still feels like by moving away I'm losing something big and important.

"Besides," he says, "you love creating businesses. And you love Berkeley, almost too much. Do you really think you won't regret not giving it a chance?"

I frown at him, annoyed that he has a point, several actually. "Maybe," I admit.

"Does that mean you'll at least think about what I said?"

"I'll think about it," I concede, and even though I'm still unsure, I'm also grateful he's giving me space to decide—something I'm not sure I'd do if the situation were reversed.

My phone dings and I grab it. But when August's phone dings, too, I know what it is without looking—an email to our work account.

We glance at each other, an unspoken agreement to change the subject passing between us.

"Have you spoken to any of our clients?" he asks.

"No, have you?"

He shakes his head. "I think we should."

I sigh. It seems today is all about mess maintenance. And truthfully, I'm here for it. Things have felt like they were spinning out of control for too long. "Okay, well, first we need a good email explaining everything and letting them know we're here to talk."

"And we should call some of them, the ones who saw the article, anyway."

"Totally. We need a list," I say, swiveling in his chair to grab a notepad. Only as I turn, my foot gets caught on a bag under his desk. I reach down, pulling the handle off my sandal strap and spotting the art store logo on the bag. Unable to resist, I peek inside.

"Something interesting?" he says, walking up behind me, and I sit up so fast that I clip the edge of his desk with my head and start cursing.

He smirks.

"That's not funny," I protest, rubbing the sore spot.

"You're right, karma's never funny."

"Was that—"

"Yes, that's the stuff from my day with Ella. And no, I didn't throw it out for sentimental reasons," he says.

"Okay, that's it. Who are you and what did you do with my grumpy, secretive best friend?"

"I guess I yelled him out," he says with no hint of sarcasm, and I realize I'm glimpsing the old August, the one before Des passed.

I push, just to see if he's real. "You miss Ella, don't you?"

He sighs. "More than I care to admit."

My god, it's him. It's old August. It's painting August and snuggling-with-Des August and *talking* August. "What can I do?" I ask.

⸻

The rest of the day passes quickly as August and I manage the fall-out of our previous cases. The good news is that most cases are old and have moved on to better things. Daisy even tells us that she's glad her best friends hired us. Of course, we also get some frustration, but that's to be expected. Overall, though, I'd say people are understanding, which only makes me mourn the loss of Summer Love a little more. When we've put out all the major fires (except Ella of course), we decide to head into town for some dinner at our favorite restaurant, the one with the brick-oven pizzas with bubbly crust and good cheese.

"Menu?" the waitress offers as we sit down at a window table.

"We know what we want," we say in unison.

"Well, all right then."

August gestures to me and I rattle off our order. But when I stop speaking, he's staring out the window, his expression serious.

"Ella?" I ask, because I know he's been thinking about her all day.

He shakes his head.

"Your dad?" I try again.

"Berkeley," he says, and I hesitate.

I know we didn't leave that conversation on a resolution, but I also thought he'd give me more than a handful of hours before bringing it back up.

"I said I'd think about it," I remind him.

"It's not that." He takes a long pause. "There's something I didn't tell you."

I gesture at him to spit it out. "You know I suck at suspense."

"The thing is . . ." He uses his straw to dunk the ice cubes in his water glass. "I can't afford the tuition."

For a second, I don't compute. "But your savings—"

"Spent it all on bills this past year to bail my mom out."

"*All?*" I choke, and he nods.

Everything we've worked for, eviscerated? And now our business is boarded up, with our last and biggest case refusing to pay us. "I'll lend you—"

"No," he cuts me off in a tone that tells me that subject is nonnegotiable.

"Scholarships," I say. "I'm certain you could get one."

"I did. It only covers five K."

"What about a loan?" I say, and a sick feeling ripples through me. Even if he gets one, he'll be in forever debt. And it just seems so unfair after how hard he's worked. "We can start a new business and—"

"We can't get a business up and running fast enough and you know it. But yeah, I'm looking into a loan. I just thought you should know."

"Even if we can't get a business up in time to help with the first year's tuition, it'll definitely help with the other three years," I say, determined to find a solution.

Some of the worry leaves his face, and I instantly realize my mistake.

"Does that mean you've decided to go?" The hope in his voice makes me squirm.

"Uh, well . . ." I say, breaking eye contact, feeling like a major idiot.

"Sorry, I wasn't trying to—" he starts.

I cut him off because I'm not sure I can handle the level of guilt associated with him being this understanding. "I didn't think you were."

He nods and I stare at my water glass, feeling terrible.

Our waitress brings sodas and warm garlic knots, but I barely notice. The only thing that makes me look up is August asking me if maybe I want our food to go.

I give him the side-eye. "Why would you—" But then I follow his gaze out the window.

Bentley is on the sidewalk, and worse than that, he's not passing by; he's headed for the restaurant's front door.

My face reddens, and my mood goes from bad to worse. "You've got to be kidding me."

August looks at me doubtfully. "You want me to talk to him?"

"No, I'm going to ignore him. And that's that."

Which is fine, except now Bentley is at the hostess stand and she's leading him to a table. The only one that's empty, which happens to be two away from ours. He sits with his back to us; I'm not even sure he knows we're here. It's a table for two. And all I can think is that he's on a date. That a girl is going to walk into the restaurant, maybe even Cassie, and my head is going to shoot off my body like an eff-you rocket.

After what feels like four hours but is probably four minutes, I lose my patience. I stand, throwing my napkin at my seat. "I'm going to kill him, August," I angry-whisper. "And you're going to bail me out of jail when I do. You hear me?"

Then I march over there like the Hulk.

I point at him. "This is my favorite restaurant and you know it," I say, all fire and determination. I can't so much as breathe or walk out my door without glimpsing Bentley with his siblings or lifting weights or jumping off the dock, and as much as I want to just bounce back and brush it off, I can't. He meant something. More than something. And I'm angry he broke it.

"Valentine," he says like he's relieved, and it's such an unexpected reaction that I pause.

I glance at the empty seat at the table, and I feel the pain of it deep in my chest. "I can't believe—"

His eyes widen. "I'm not on a—I mean, no one's sitting there. I'm here by myself," he stumbles like he can hear my thoughts.

"Why would you come here by—" I start and stop. "My god, you *followed* me here?"

He raises his hands in surrender. "No, definitely not," he says quickly. "I wasn't following you. I was actually on my way to the hardware store when I . . ." His voice trails off, and he looks down at his hands. When his gaze meets mine, he seems thoroughly embarrassed. "I was walking by when I saw you and August in the window. You were making that expression you make when you're really upset. And well, I just wanted to make sure you were okay. I was only going to stay a minute, just to see . . ." Bentley trails off again and his laugh is sad. "Now that I'm saying this out loud, it sounds ridiculous. It was a split-second decision. I didn't think it out that well." He pushes his chair back and gets up from the table, looking thoroughly sheepish. "I do want to talk to you. A lot. But I never meant to put you on the spot. I was trying to respect your space. I just . . . Anyway, sorry. Again."

He walks away, head hanging. I glance back at August, who is diligently studying his straw, meaning he heard the whole thing. Bentley opens the door to leave, and yet I stand at his table, frozen by indecision.

He was worried I was sad, I think, some part of me reflexively softening. Ugh. No. I *am* sad. And he should feel bad about it. I press my lips together, telling myself to go back to August, but still I stand there. When Bentley disappears from view, my chest tightens, like the invisible tether that once bound us together is pulling on me to follow. And like a fool, I head for the door, yanking it open and stepping onto the sidewalk.

The humid air is scented with sugary cinnamon from the donut shop next door, and the cheeriness feels like a personal affront. A second passes before I spot Bentley, who's turning the corner, not toward the hardware store like he said, but away from town.

I jog up to him, and he looks so genuinely happy about it that I scowl.

"You followed me," he says gently, like he's afraid he might spook me if he speaks full volume. I feel his yearning so viscerally that it tugs at me.

I look up at the canopy of leafy green over our heads as though there might be an answer in the tree branches. I shouldn't have run after him. Why on earth did I think this was the right move?

"You never gave me a chance to explain," he says quietly when I don't speak. "You hung up on me."

His words needle me, and I find my voice. "Because you lied to me."

He exhales. "You're right. I did."

My heart breaks all over again. "Look, I don't want some lame excuse or an admission that you can be better. The one thing that made me trust you—the honesty pact—is broken and irreparable."

"I deserve that," he says, which only frustrates me more.

"Yes, you do," I agree. And for a second, I stand there awkwardly. How do you argue with someone who isn't arguing with you?

"But you don't know why you're mad," he says.

"I know enough."

"Do you?" he asks.

For a brief second, I doubt myself. "Did you or did you not hook up with Cassie?"

"I didn't," he says.

"You hesitated on the phone. I know—"

But this time he cuts me off. "She asked me to come over. I said no. Then the next day she called me, hysterically crying."

I eye him suspiciously.

"Something to do with her parents—without going into detail, they suck. And she needed a friend. So that's what I was—her friend, *just* her friend."

My stomach sinks. Cassie was the girl with the messed-up parents and the affair he told me about? "And so?"

"And she tried to kiss me."

There it is. "Did she succeed?"

He shakes his head. "I swear. I stopped it immediately. I left, and I haven't talked to her since."

I open my mouth and pause. "If that's true, then why didn't you tell me when it happened? You told me every detail of that day, including what you fed the twins for lunch, and yet somehow omitted Cassie's tongue."

He shakes his head like he's asked himself the same question a hundred times. "Because I'm an idiot," he says. "And because I like you—like, really like you."

"Don't even. This has nothing to do with you liking me and everything to do with you lying."

"You're right. What you said about me being in a bunch of short relationships is true. I got that in my head and was trying so hard not to screw it up that I screwed it up. It's new to me . . . caring like this. And honestly, it scares the crap out of me." He smiles sadly. "I haven't slept in days. I haven't gone surfing. Nothing. I'm a wreck. All I can think about is you."

I purse my lips, not sure how to react. I've been furious because I thought he cheated on me, and finding out that isn't true is disorienting.

"Look," he says, sighing. "I totally get that I broke your trust."

"You did."

"But if you'll let me, I want to earn it back," he says.

I eye him. "You sound confident."

"I am. I have to be. My sleep depends on it." He pauses. "The thing is, I need you in my life, Valentine. And whether or not you want to hear it, you *do* make me better. I actually like who I am when I'm with you."

"'Need' is a strong word."

"I know," he says.

We look at each other for a long moment, and the way he stares at me is so hopeful that I can feel myself reacting to it, reflexively softening to the plea I see in his eyes.

"I thought about standing outside your window with a homemade sign," he admits. "I even had the twins help me make it."

"You did not," I say, some of the ice gone from my voice.

"I really did. It said *VALENTINE SHARMA, PLEASE LET ME EXPLAIN* all in caps with a picture of a sad puppy underneath."

I laugh before I can stop myself. "You know that's the most ridiculous thing ever, right?"

"Desperate times . . ." he says with a smile that cuts right to my core.

I shake my head at him, trying to look fierce but failing. "Don't look at me like that."

His grin only widens, and I swear I move a step closer without meaning to. "Like what?"

I wave my hand at him, practically grazing my fingertips on his chest, his very beautiful chest. "You know exactly what."

"I can't help it; you're smiling," he says like this is the moment he's waited for his whole life.

But try as I might to grasp at it, I feel my remaining frustration evaporating in the warmth of the summer air.

I lift my hands and drop them again. "Fine."

"Fine?" he asks, and the hopefulness of his tone pushes me right over the edge.

"*Maybe* we can hang out tomorrow."

He reaches out like he's going to grab me and twirl me in the air but remembers himself at the last moment and drops his arms. "Really?"

"Yes, really."

"Woo-hoo!" Bentley yells, raising his fist to the sky.

"Now go," I say, trying to resist the urge to grin at him. The truth is I missed him. A lot. And any other week I'd have tried to talk things out with him, to understand fully before I wrote him off. But this week was too much. It strained me in every way possible, compounding and confusing all my problems until I couldn't tease them apart and I just wanted to torch everything.

"Going," he confirms, backstepping for a few seconds to get one last look at me.

I head toward the restaurant, making eye contact with August through the window. He shakes his head in a way that says, *Oh great, this again.* But for some reason I don't worry about it the way I once did. Things are different with August. Good different.

67

AUGUST

The early-morning sun streams through my open window, and an ocean-scented breeze billows my curtains. My room doesn't feel like the confining trap it did a few days ago, but lighter and more breathable. And I feel lighter, too, like a version of myself I forgot existed. I even have more energy, as though all the time I spent repressing parts of myself took something out of me I was unaware of. Even though it's early, I don't try to fall back asleep. I take a deep breath, enjoying this new August in his new room with his new perspective.

The conversations Tiny and I had with old cases yesterday play in my head. It was strangely nice to check in with them and hear how everyone's lives have changed for the better, and even more so to do it as August. Of course, there's one person we haven't talked to yet—Ella.

The moment I think her name, I audibly exhale. Ella's dad has yet to return our calls, and calling her won't work. Even if it would, I don't want to talk to her about this over the phone.

My eyes flit to the bag of craft supplies under my desk, and while I know that completing our art challenge isn't an answer by a long shot, it might be a starting place. So I swipe the bag, open it, and stare down at the contents. Only there's something in the bag I wasn't expecting, peeking out from under the fabric. My heart thumps and my breath quickens—*Ella bought me drawing pencils?*

The realization hits me hard. Maybe because she unknowingly got my favorite kind. Or maybe because it reminds me of something Des would have done. And even though everything with her is uncertain, there's one thing I know—if Bentley can make a sad-puppy sign, I can do one better. I dump the bag of supplies onto my desk and get to work.

The act of making something is calming, meditative almost. It does what I'd hoped—it lets me think. But the conclusion I come to, or rather the idea I come up with, is nuts.

"Thoughts, Swee?" I ask.

He grooms his paw in response as if to say, *I cannot answer that because I don't participate in activities that take place off this bed.*

After a half hour of pacing and an inability to come up with anything better, I give in and get dressed. I text Tiny that I'm coming over and head downstairs.

I pull a mug from the cupboard, and when I'm halfway through pouring my coffee, Mom walks in.

"August?" she says, like she's not sure if I'm real. To be fair, I've barely left my room for the past week.

"Aren't you supposed to be at work?" I ask, also unsure.

"It's Saturday," she replies. "I was just going through my artwork."

"Oh," is all I say.

"The director from the gallery called. She's starting a new exhibit, and she wants to showcase some of my pieces." There isn't the twirling and declaring that we'll be millionaires by the end of the summer that I'd expect. She's almost quiet.

"That's great," I say and mean it. It's been more than ten years since Mom had a show. And the gallery in town does good, consistent business with the tourists. While it isn't a surefire solution to our problems, it will definitely help.

"Yeah, it is," she says. Again, no giddy twirling. "Can we talk?"

I hesitate. "Um."

"It wasn't really a request," she says and gestures at the round kitchen table.

I reluctantly take a seat.

She pulls out a chair and joins me, thinking for a long time before she speaks. "I know we haven't had the easiest time of it these past few years—"

"It's not—" I reflexively start to downplay it.

"Let me finish," she says, and I close my mouth. "I know that a lot of stress, financial and otherwise, has fallen on you, and I know that's my fault. But what I want you to know is that things are going to change around here. They already are." Her voice is level and calm.

"Okay," is all I say, not really sure what that means.

"Your dad—"

"Mom, I really don't want to talk about him."

She shakes her head. "I didn't ask him to come speak with you. I don't know why I said that. I mean, I hoped he'd want to. But that's not why I called him."

I glance at the door, wishing I'd climbed out the window and avoided this entirely.

"I called him to tell him that either he pays what he owes in back child support, including taking responsibility for his share of Des's funeral expenses, or I'll take him to court."

I stare at my mom. Des tried to convince her to insist on child support over and over, and she wouldn't even discuss it. "And he agreed?"

"Well, he did when I told him that I wouldn't hesitate to enlighten his new fiancé on a few . . . personal matters."

I don't ask her what she means by that, and she doesn't explain. "You threatened him?" And for the first time during this conversation, lightness sneaks into my tone.

"'Threatened' is a strong word. I like to think of it as persuasion to do the right thing." She gets up and moves to the counter, grabbing something from the stack of bills.

She holds out her hand, and there, sitting in her palm, is a check.

But when I see the recipient, I nearly fall out of my chair. "Wait . . . hang on," I say, standing. "This check is made out to *me*?"

She smiles. "It doesn't come close to what you deserve, but it's a start."

I stare at her in disbelief. "But the—" My eyes move to the bills once more.

"Between the Kellermans and the gallery, I'll be able to handle things around here for a while."

"I honestly don't know what to say," I reply. And after reading the check two more times just to make sure it's real, I do something I never do—I hug her.

And she's delighted. She pulls me close and wraps her arms around my back. She smells familiar—like canvas and lavender, reminding me of all the times I used to sit on her lap and watch her paint as a child. For a moment I consider pulling away, but something in me doesn't want to—the part of me that unlocked when I yelled at that tree. So instead, I relax, pressing my cheek into her hair. As I do, I catch sight of the paint splatters on the floor, the ones Mom swore would come up and never did.

"Throw it! Throw the paint at the canvas!" she exclaimed.

"But what if I miss?" I asked, looking at the clean kitchen and wondering what Dad might do if he found us slinging paint in it.

"Then you miss. Mess is part of life, August; you can't avoid it."

"What about Dad?" I asked. "He's never messy."

She studied me. "Your dad is one of those people who thinks that if he seeks order, he can stop mess from existing at all. Like people who think that if they chase happiness correctly, they'll find the magic solution to avoid suffering. But it doesn't work like that. Mess defines order. Suffering defines happiness. You cannot have one without the other. Me? I embrace mess. I invite it in, because once in a while it's absolutely glorious."

She scooped up a blob of paint with her finger and winked at me. So I did the same. And we attacked the canvas. We wiped our hands on it. We threw paint at it. We laughed until we couldn't breathe.

"Thanks, Mom," I say as she releases me from the hug. "Really."

"And August?" She tucks a stray curl into her loose bun. "I don't want you to feel like this means you need to talk to your dad. That's still entirely your choice."

"I appreciate that." And it feels intrinsically good to not be pressured.

I grab my coffee and head for the door but turn back and say, "I think you're going to do great at that gallery. I'm really proud of you." And when I close the door behind me, she's beaming.

Relief washes over me. My mom—she went to bat for me. It gives me a strange feeling, one I haven't had in so long that I'm not even sure what it is—reassurance maybe? A word I've used to describe Tiny's life, but never my own.

It's not because Tiny has money or a nice house. She has the type of security that tells her every morning when she wakes up and every night when she goes to sleep that she's safe. That her mom isn't going to forget to pay the electricity bill or leave foreclosure warnings taped to the door. That her parents won't go to bed without knowing she ate dinner. That people are watching, caring. And because of this she owns a type of confidence I've never known.

I walk across my lawn toward Tiny's porch, where she lounges on a love seat, goofy-grinning at her phone.

"Bentley?" I ask, even though I already know.

She puts her phone on the cushion next to her. "Well, look who's up early."

I step onto her porch, a cool breeze blowing my hair into my eyes. I push it back. "I had an idea—" I start, but Bentley's screen door opens.

"Dudes!" he calls across the lawn. He wears plaid pajama pants and no shirt (I swear he doesn't own any). "Big news. Dinner at my house tonight."

"I feel like I'm having déjà vu—the bad kind," I say to Tiny.

"Didn't hear what you said, August," Bentley continues. "But the answer is yes, there will be blow-up narwhals for swimming later."

Tiny laughs and then looks at me. "Might be fun," she says at a volume Bentley can't hear, and while I have every intention of keeping my eye on him, I realize this is an olive branch.

"Sure," I say, and her face lights up.

"We'll be there!" she calls across the lawn.

Bentley pumps his fist in the air before his siblings call his name and he goes back inside. While I'm certain he'll annoy me till the end of time, I also get that he matters to Tiny. And well, that's important.

Tiny stares at me as I sit down in the cushioned armchair.

"What?"

"Nothing . . ." she replies, then changes her mind. "Actually, I was just thinking that in a weird way, Summer Love changed us."

I nod because I feel it, too. Everything's different. The tightly wound part of me that made me push her away, that made me snap for no reason or punch Kyle in the street, has unwound. And while I still think he sucks, I'm not consumed with blame anymore, a blame that made me hate him and myself.

She sits up, gripping the cushion on either side of her knees. "Okay, new happy August, how about we go grab some food?"

I hesitate.

"Before you object, consider the fact that hash browns are everything and that we don't have any in my house."

"It's not that. It's just . . ." I scratch the back of my neck. "I kinda have a plan to talk to Ella."

"Really?" Tiny says, bouncing.

"Yeah, one that requires your help."

She leans forward, conspiratorial. "Um, yes, obviously. Tell me everything."

ୢୣୣୣ

For the first time since I can remember, I don't look away as we pass the street with the dented tree. Tiny doesn't pretend not to notice. And an awkward silence doesn't descend.

Instead, Tiny sings to music, arm hanging out the window, riding air waves as we head down the coastal street toward Ella's town. I review my plan as we go, but the drive feels like it disappears in two seconds.

Tiny intermittently looks at me and bursts out laughing.

I give her a warning glare.

"I'm sorry. I just can't believe this is happening." She gestures at my outfit, which is a close approximation of Leonardo DiCaprio's nineties chain mail knight getup in *Romeo and Juliet*, cobbled together from our past Halloween costumes and the local vintage store. We even managed shoulder armor and a fake sword. She snaps a picture on her phone. "Seriously, though. The most epic of epic ideas! You, my friend, are a genius. The student is the master. The August caterpillar is a butterfly. The—"

"You know Ella's probably going to shoot me down, right?"

"If she does, she officially has no heart."

The Jeep slows as I pull into Ella's driveway and park, my insides so knotted that I touch my stomach.

"Here goes nothing," Tiny says.

"Or at the very least, here goes my pride."

Tiny jumps out of the Jeep and winks. "I'll text you when it's safe. And good luck."

She walks toward Ella's house, and I lean back in my seat, trying to breathe.

While the drive felt short, the time waiting for Tiny to give me the okay feels like forever.

Tiny

Talking to parents. Ella's upstairs. GO GET HER, ROMEO!

I jump out, careful to loop around the house toward the back gate. I lift the latch and creep up to the patio, where the picture windows in the living room look out over the pool. Tiny and Ella's parents sit on oversized couches inside, and while they aren't facing the windows, I'm still in their peripheral vision and they would likely notice if a weird, armored guy sprinted across their deck.

Me

In backyard. Need distraction.

Tiny glances at her phone, but she doesn't look out the window or give any cause for suspicion. She says something to Ella's parents, and while I don't know what it is, it's obviously incendiary given the way their heads whip toward her. Which is my cue to run, as fast as I can in this getup, to the other side of the deck.

I stop under Ella's balcony, pulling out a small pouch and gauging my aim. I toss it at her window, and while it's lightweight, it still hits with a sizable clunk. And I wait.

As the seconds tick by, I wonder if Tiny was wrong about Ella being in her room.

But then her window slides open and Ella's confused face pops out. Her hair is in a messy bun, and she's wearing pajama shorts and a tank top. She spots the pouch and steps onto her balcony, picking it up. But when she catches sight of me in the grass below, all the color drains from her face. Anger narrows her eyes, and I know I have less than a second before she tells me to eff off. In fact, she's already turning.

So I start reciting Shakespeare.

I throw my hand in the air dramatically. "But soft! What light through yonder window breaks? It is the east, and Juliet is the sun."

"What the hell?" she breathes, confusion replacing her anger as she clocks my outfit.

I skip forward a couple of lines, placing one hand over my heart, admitting what I couldn't the last time I saw her. "It is my lady; O, it is my love! O that she knew she were!"

She opens her mouth, glaring at me like I've lost my mind.

I think about Mom and the messy canvas, about yelling at the tree, about what Des would do if she were here, and so I get louder, more passionate. "She speaks, yet she says nothing. What of that? Her eye discourses; I will answer it."

I head for the latticework beside her balcony, grabbing on and hoping like hell that it doesn't rip off the side of her house.

"What do you think you're doing? Get off there at once," an angry Mr. Becker exclaims behind me. But I don't stop. I can't. I need Ella to know this matters, that *she* matters. I recite as I climb, pouring myself into the words. "As daylight doth a lamp; her eyes in heaven would through the airy region stream so bright that birds would sing and think it were not night." I grab ahold of her balcony railing and pull myself over it.

Ella stares at me like she's not sure if she's impressed or horrified—probably both. Her parents argue below us, but I don't care, because all I'm focused on is Ella.

"Ella, I'm sorry. Really and truly sorry I hurt you," I say before she can recover from the shock and remember she hates me. "I know that doesn't fix what I did by a long shot. But please, let me explain why I did it in the first place."

She chews on the inside of her cheek, considering my words, and glancing down at her parents and Tiny.

After a couple of excruciating seconds, Ella huffs. "Fine," she says. "But if I decide I never want to speak to you again, you have to accept it and leave me alone. No questions asked."

"Agreed," I say to her high-stakes deal.

"Let me handle this," she yells down to her parents. Her dad looks pissed, but her mom says something, and he reluctantly follows her inside.

I turn back to Ella, suddenly aware of how small this balcony is and how close I am to her. I can smell her vanilla shampoo. "There were things I told you that were untrue."

"Everything," she interjects, and her tone is barbed.

"Not everything. My name, my mom owning a yacht, and the fact that I like boat shoes . . . those things were definitely lies. But everything else was true—the stuff about my sister and about my painting, for instance," I say, and she crosses her arms like I'm going to have to do a lot better than that. "Here's what I didn't tell you. My mom's a painter, a good one, and an often out-of-work one. She's not fancy. We don't travel the world or own a mansion. In fact, we barely own a beat-up station wagon. And when my dad left us, my mom kinda fell apart. Stopped paying our bills, stopped cooking dinner, just stopped. And well, my sister, Des, stepped in. She made my school lunches, she made jokes when things got heavy, and when I'd have panic dreams in the middle of the night, she'd lay in my bed until I fell back asleep." I pause. "She was my rock."

While Ella doesn't yet look convinced, she isn't pushing me off the balcony.

I glance at my hands and back up. "And then Des started dating this guy Kyle. He was charismatic. He was selfish. He was actually a lot like Justin."

She gives me an evaluating look, like she's not sure if she should be annoyed.

"Everyone admired him. Even me . . . until he started pushing her to change, to 'relax,' to do things she never did before—drinking, lying, sneaking out." While I'm certain she gets that I'm drawing a parallel, she doesn't acknowledge it. "Anyway, he had this sports car that he used to race on a dead-end street near my house."

Worry pushes her eyebrows together.

"Then one night we got a call that there was an accident. When we got there, the sports car was wrapped around an old oak tree. Kyle said a deer ran into the road and they swerved, losing control. I don't know," I say, and as I do, I realize that this is the first time I've ever told this story to another person. "All I know is that my sister, the person I loved most in the whole world, was gone. And I was lost."

She takes a fast breath, and maybe I'm imagining it, but her eyes soften.

"Tiny is the only reason I'm—she saved me. With an idea. That maybe we could help other people, people stuck in relationships who were making choices that could hurt them long term. An idea for a company. And while I understand that you're probably angry that company exists, much less that you were an unwilling participant in it, I'm not. I don't regret the jobs we've taken, not even yours. I couldn't save my sister, I didn't know how, but I'll be damned if I won't try to help others. Even when I accidentally fall for the girl I'm attempting to help. Even when she decides she hates me."

"I don't need you to save me," she says.

"I used to agree. But I'm not so sure anymore. I'm not convinced that we don't all need someone to show up for us in critical moments, take some of the weight off. Sometimes things are too big to conquer on our own, and that's okay." I take a breath. "I'll be the first to admit that I need Tiny. That she's saved me over and over, that she does it every day when she climbs in my window with an absurd idea and a thoughtful cup of coffee. And if I'm being honest, you saved me, too."

"Me?" she says, disbelieving.

"I talked to you about things I planned on never talking about again. You made me excited to go to the art store I swore I'd never return to. And more than that, you made me feel something I didn't know I could."

"What?" she asks like she doesn't want to but can't help herself.

"You made me feel like myself, or rather a version of me that was no longer terrified to care about someone else, a version that cares about you."

She exhales, annoyed. "Damn it, August."

My chest swells as I hear my real name on her lips—it sounds better when she says it.

She rubs her hands down her face. "I want to hate you. Like, really hate you. So knock it off."

I give her a questioning look.

She gestures at me. "That explanation . . . the, I don't know, the sincerity."

"You want me to stop being sincere?"

"Yes, I want you to be exactly the jerk I imagined in my mind so I can make dartboards of your face and write thinly veiled insults about you on my blog," she says in one breath, because as much as she's trying to be mad, the edge is gone from her tone.

"If you want, I can help you come up with them. I'm the first to agree that I totally deserve those insults."

"Shut up, you," she says, in an attempt to maintain her frustration. "Tell me something—did you or did you not dump that coffee on me on purpose?"

I scratch my eyebrow, wearing a guilty expression.

"Oh my god," she says with feeling. "I can't believe I liked someone who spilled coffee on me *on purpose*."

"Liked?" I repeat, my stomach doing a flip.

Her cheeks flush. "Yes. Past tense. *L-I-K-E-D*."

I can't help it; I smile. "Time is a construct—past and future are the same thing."

"Which is why you're dressed like you're medieval?"

"Your favorite play is *Romeo and Juliet*—"

"I haven't forgotten," she says, once again not giving an inch.

"Here's the thing: before I met you, I'd have argued that Romeo was a ridiculous sentimental idiot."

She raises a questioning eyebrow. "And you've suddenly changed your mind?"

I hold her gaze. "He fights against all odds for the person he loves."

For a second, she's perfectly still. "What are you saying?"

"I'm saying that almost kissing you was hands down one of the best things that's ever happened to me."

She presses her lips together, like she's unsure. "I'm going to school in London to study journalism," she says, almost quietly. "I got in my acceptance before the deadline."

I can't help it; I beam. "That's amazing."

She gives me a questioning look, one she employs when she uses her journalism interview tactics on me. "How can you think that's amazing if almost kissing me meant that much to you? Shouldn't you be arguing for me to stay?"

"Never," I say. "In fact, if I ever suggest you put my wants before your dreams, I give you full permission to throw me off this balcony."

Ella stares at me like she's arguing with herself over something. Then after a couple of long seconds, she nods like she's made a decision. She holds up the pouch. "What is this anyway?"

"Open it."

She pulls the strings and slides out a patch of fabric with an embroidered Leo lion head on it and a Scorpio symbol in the background. There are four safety pins at the edges and junk jewelry in the lion's mane in honor of Des. She rubs her fingers over my mediocre embroidery work and looks up at me, her expression softer somehow.

"You made this?" she says, surprised.

I rub my neck, a little self-conscious, and repeat another line of Shakespeare, quietly this time. "Did my heart love till now? Forswear it, sight. For I ne'er saw true beauty till this night." Then in plain August speak, I add, "I'm falling for you, Scorpio."

Her cheeks flush, and my eyes involuntarily flit to her lips.

"I see you," she says, referring to my gaze, only she doesn't make it sound like a bad thing. "And all I'm saying is . . . maybe."

My heart immediately starts pounding, and I swallow. "Maybe?"

"It's your favorite word," she replies. "You figure it out."

And now I'm grinning so hard that I worry for my cheeks. I lift my hand, lightly grazing the star constellation on her cheekbone and tipping her delicate chin upward. And when her lips turn up at the corners, I kiss them slowly, teasing them apart and drinking in the warmth of her breath. My hand trails a silky path from her neck to the small of her back, memorizing the taste of her peach lip gloss and the feeling of her mouth moving in rhythm with mine. She tangles her hands in my hair, standing on her tippy-toes, and where our stomachs touch, heat pulses. I can feel her smile, turning my gentle kisses into hungry ones. The feeling of her vibrates sensation to my very core, and I lift her up, her legs wrapping around my waist. And I wonder if there could ever be anything better than this.

Maybe Tiny was right all this time—maybe this whole love thing is pretty great after all.

68

VALENTINE

I pack up a container with cream-cheese-stuffed French toast to share with August. Mom has been having all kinds of amazing cravings, and I'm shamelessly reaping the benefits.

For the past hour, I've been telling my parents how August made an epic play for Ella and how I had an equally epic sparring match with her parents, where they not only apologized for revealing our website to the press but agreed that maybe it was okay for August and Ella to see each other. I even tell them how her parents admitted it was wrong that they lorded money over us, and that I in turn said we didn't want to be paid.

"I know August wouldn't accept it," I say. "And I totally get why. But they *may* have agreed to anonymously contribute to his college tuition after I laid out the fact that we got Ella back on track to follow her dreams while they not so nicely ruined our business, inhibiting our ability to pay for ours."

"You know we'll help, right?" Mom says, sipping her lemon tea. "Even if they don't do the right thing. August is family."

I smile. "While I don't think he'd easily accept, I *do* think he'd buckle if it was for an off-campus apartment where he could bring Swee," I say, and I can already see the wheels turning in Mom's head to make this happen. "Who knows, though, maybe Ella will soften him? You should have seen him in that Romeo costume. I wanted to videotape it so bad." It feels good talking to my parents openly about Summer Love. I shove the food in my shoulder bag and swipe my finger through a glob of whipped cream, licking it clean. "Okay, I'm going to get these over to August before they lose their warm gooeyness."

I head out the back door and skip down my porch. Bentley is already outside working out, sans shirt, and I waver, promising myself it'll be a quick detour.

"Don't mind me, I'm just here to engage in pointless small talk while I secretly stare at your six-pack," I say, repeating back his joke from a month ago.

"Finally!" he laughs, like I've come to my senses. "What do you say to a beach day, Valentine? You and me, waves, sand, me pretending I tripped so I can rub shoulders with you?"

"Wellll, I was going to make you stew in your doghouse a little longer."

"Believe me," he says. "The stewing has been real. Go ask the twins."

"But then there's always the argument that summer is short," I say. "And that I'm going to California soon, so we should probably take advantage of this."

"Exactly," he says and reaches for me with a look that asks if it's okay. And when I smile in answer, he places his hands on my hips, pulling me forward. "No time like the present."

I laugh, giving him a coy look and lightly resting my fingers on his chest. Our mouths are only inches apart.

"You're awfully close," I tease.

He grins. "I'm just a close-talker. This is how I talk to everyone."

I raise an eyebrow. "Really?"

"Yup."

"Your teachers and Old Man Hairy-Nose at the supermarket?"

"Especially them."

I laugh, and he smiles down at me, his eyes so focused on mine that

I feel tipsy. "And about California," he says quietly. "I hear they have some good waves. Might have to check out setting up a surf camp there."

My chest flutters, and on impulse I run my fingertip across his lower lip. He inhales a fast breath, and the hungry look in his eyes tips me right over the edge. I kiss him, hot and fast and greedy.

"Okay," I say, pushing my hand against his chest, trying to regain my composure. "I have to go." I take a step. "But I'll come find you in a few hours."

He falls backward into the grass, gripping his heart like I've slain him.

I force myself to turn away, a grin lighting up my face all the way to August's.

I climb the ladder and slide through the window. "Rise and shine, Romeo—" I say, but the only one in August's rumpled bed is Swee, who's belly up and snoring.

I walk into the hallway, heading for the stairs, when I hear something clunk in Des's bedroom. For a second, I think I imagined it.

"August?" I say, stopping in my tracks.

"In here," he calls, his muffled voice giving me a start.

I gently push Des's door open, my heart rapid firing. But I'm not greeted with the musty smell of stagnant air. Des's windows are open, blowing in a fresh breeze, and her summer-rain candle is lit on her nightstand, a scent so familiar that I half expect to find her lounging in bed, doing her nails and reading poetry.

August sits on the floor surrounded by photo albums.

"Sorry," I say, feeling like I intruded on something private. "I didn't mean to interrupt. Mom just ordered you some food and . . ."

"You're not interrupting," he says and looks up at me. "I just thought I might go through some of this stuff. Maybe reclaim my paints?"

"Yeah?" I say, my throat suddenly tight. "I mean, great. Yes, you should totally do that."

"If you want, you could—"

"Yes!" I exclaim, before he can finish. "I want to."

He smiles as I sit across from him on the rug, a familiar spot we occupied as kids. Des wasn't ever annoyed by us following her around; in fact she encouraged it—said it made her feel like the captain of some awesome team. Childhood memories swirl around me, projected translucently in the air like an old-time movie reel. I reach out to where a ten-year-old version of myself once rolled on her back, choking on laughter, creating yet another business with her best friend, building a future out of fanciful ideas and dreams.

And then I find myself staring at August, the emotionality of the memory resting high in my throat. "When you said you wouldn't come home for summers, did you mean that?" I don't know why, but this feels like the most important thing I've ever asked, like somehow those happy childhood versions of us hang in the balance.

He lifts his head, thinking for a few seconds. "No," he says, and his eyes dip downward, vulnerability flushing his cheeks. "I'd miss it here."

This simple admission hits me hard. Knowing he feels it, too—that inexplicable connection to home—is comforting, like a hug I didn't know I needed. I find myself fast-nodding, pushing my chin upward to keep it from wobbling. Once again I see us, not ten anymore but college students, wearing matching Berkeley hoodies like dorks, still laughing, still creating. Only it doesn't feel separate from this place, the way I once thought. Our office on the dock and the ladder to August's window aren't forgotten but right there, woven into the fabric of our beings.

He lifts his eyes, and when he sees my expression, he pauses, a question lingering on his parted mouth. But all he says is, "Tiny?"

"Well, I hope you don't think I'm going to let you enjoy a life of endless summer and epic business classes without me. Because I'm not." I mean it to sound lighthearted, but instead my words are weighted—an admission that while I'm going to miss being home, I'd miss something bigger if I didn't go.

He nods. No gloating. No grumbling about how long it took me to decide. Just a smile that's so uninhibited that I have to look away so I don't get blubbery. August and Tiny. Tiny and August. Off on an adventure once more.

"I'm hanging out with Bentley later," I tell him, changing the subject and for the first time not feeling uncomfortable about bringing it up. "What about you? Are you seeing Ella?"

He smiles. "She's coming over."

"Here?" I say, totally taken aback. August hasn't invited anyone to his house in I-don't-know-how-many years. He doesn't even invite me. I just show up.

"We're going to the gallery in town so I can show her Mom's art and then, I don't know, maybe Bob's Diner and the beach?" he says, and my mouth opens so wide that it practically ricochets off the floor.

"You and Bentley can come if you want," he offers, and now my mind explodes.

"Did I faint? Am I conscious?" I ask him because I'm really not sure.

He laughs and I laugh, too. I tell him I wouldn't miss his long-anticipated town debut as August Hottie Hair for all the world, and ask if he wants to wear matching outfits on our double date. To which he does not respond. Yet I'm smiling. Bigly. I don't know if Bentley will wind up coming to California, or if August and Ella will make it long distance, but none of that really matters right now because it's summer, and like our business name implies, summer is most definitely for love.

He returns to his photo album, and I peek inside one of the boxes August pulled out. Under the flap is a stack of watercolor paintings. The top is a portrait of Des on the dock, with wild hair and kind eyes. Then another of Des lying in the grass with her arm over her eyes. And one of her sitting at her desk, looking out the window. On and on. Dozens of paintings, all capturing the familiarity of her so well that it makes my chest constrict. Is this what he was doing in the silence after she passed? Pouring his memories onto paper? No wonder he gave up art.

I press my lips together, trying to will myself not to get misty and make him regret inviting me.

When I dare to look at August, he pulls something off the bedside table—Des's journal, which he told me in no uncertain terms that we'd never read. My heart skips a beat and I'm afraid to move, like in doing so I might shatter the moment.

69

AUGUST

I take a sip of coffee, and as I place my mug on Des's nightstand, I graze her journal. Only I don't pull away; I pause, my hand resting on the embossed cover, and pick it up. It's weighty in my grasp, stuffed with Polaroids and ticket stubs from concerts. Almost instantly my mind begins sketching, not one image but many, a portrait of Des— the way she looked the last time I saw her write in it, bent over on the floor of her room much like I am now. I sketch the scent of her chocolate-chip pancakes, the sound of her laugh. And as the drawings evolve, I smile at them, promising for the first time that they won't just live in my thoughts. Ella was right; in a way my art has always been a conversation with Des, with the world, a way to communicate when I didn't know how.

I run my finger down the journal cover and open it to a ribbon marker. I always thought that opening this was a violation of her privacy. And maybe it is. But damn, I miss my sister, and the pull of reading something she wrote outweighs the rest.

I clear my throat, reading aloud.

It's the last Friday before school starts, but I don't mind. I'll miss summer, but I also long for autumn sweaters, pumpkin spice hot chocolate, and taking August and Tiny on a very important homemade ice cream / leaf peeping trip to New Hampshire. I can actually hear them in August's room laughing right now. Or snorting might be a better way to describe it? I'm so glad he has her. I know I write that a lot, but these past few years with Mom have been hard. And more than that, I'm so glad I have them. *They don't know it, but they ground me with their joy.*

I look up at Tiny, whose eyes are brimming. And I smile, grateful for the time I got with my sister and for every day I have with her.

Maybe Tiny was right years ago when she wondered if there might be lots of us out there, lots of Tinys and Augusts best-friending it up. And now I secretly hope there are. She never gave up on me, never deemed me too difficult or too broken. And while the weight of losing Des almost crushed me, I realize that I still have someone I can count on, that I'm not alone. Everyone deserves a best friend like Tiny.

ACkNOWLeDGMeNTS

Books are magical things. They start as a wisp of an idea, a tendril of smoke with no real substance or staying power. But if you build upon them, they become a roaring hearth fire, something beautiful meant for all to share. Of course, this only happens with the care and hard work of many. For me it starts at home—with the love of Wolf, Pirate, Sasi, Nonno, and Kit—family who cheer me on and bolster my spirit, creating kind spaces from which to create. I don't know how I got so lucky.

Then there is my dearest agent, Ro, who is my work family. She's unfailingly supportive and kind, and knowing she's there makes the world a little brighter.

I'm so happy to have the wonderful crew at Blackstone who have lent their creativity and love to this book—Dan Ehrenhaft, Lydia Rogue, Josie Woodbridge, Sarah Riedlinger, Rebecca Malzahn, Tatiana Radujkovic, Francie Crawford, Nikki Carrero, Brianna Jones, Katrina Tan, David Baker, Amy Craig, and Riam Griswold.

Thug je che na, Geshe Dorji Dumdal-la, for translating the quote from Shantideva's text *Bodhisattvacharyavatara*. He has been endlessly patient and kind throughout the many years I've known him, answering all of my philosophical questions and challenging me to view the world from new perspectives. It's a blessing to know him.

My wonderful critique partners—Kerry Kletter, Jennifer Niven, Lana Harper, Jilly Gagnon, Chelsea Sedoti, Jeff Zentner—they are on the front lines before anyone else sees my books, and there cheering when they come out. You guys are the best!

Also a big thank-you to my doctor, Effi Hochberg, for saving my life and giving me a second chance that makes every day special and turned living into the best adventure!

Last, but never least, to my lovely readers and FAMB members. You are seen. You matter more than you know. And I love you.